TITAN'S FLAME

A Novel

C.S. WOOD

ISBN: 979-8-9889473-0-1 (Ebook)
ISBN: 979-8-9889473-2-5 (Paperback)

"Two possibilities exist;
either we are alone
in the universe
or we are not.
Both are equally terrifying."

– Arthur C. Clark

Prologue: Olen

Death stalked the stubborn old woman. For nearly a decade, Olen had endured the blistering heat of the planet's three suns that tried their best to kill her, and the day had come when she finally decided to let them. She had been the planet's sole inhabitant.

Zaspel, an ivory and rust colored ghost world most star charts didn't bother to map, had been left irradiated and abandoned centuries ago; its arid surface was a sweltering wasteland scarce in water and reliable food protein, marked by the Protectorate as undesirable for colonization. The old woman disagreed. Zaspel had no standing buildings. No fences. No metal bars or containment cells, but it was her prison. Its chilly blue suns were the same cobalt blue as her triple-lidded eyes. After nearly ten years of confinement, she'd finally had enough. At least death would be cooler.

Death hadn't taken her sooner because of her biology. She was an Asabi. They were a species with a remarkable cellular resiliency, but at the cost of a shorter lifespan. Fifty-two years, on average. Olen was a decade short of that, but the sun's harsh rays had aged her. Olen's skin became dry as tree bark and her bones were brittle as glass. Two arms, two legs, four hearts. The hellish environment had made them all deficient, eroding away her youth, and worst of all, her hope. She would never forgive herself for that.

Asabis were generally short, their epidermis spotted with a copper hue, their skin stripes of black and beige in a vaguely camouflage pattern. Olen wore her mess of cracked calluses like a full body scar. Her hair, once ebony black and healthy, was now a sheet of stark white. She'd shed too much water weight. A tattered sari covered her sickly thin frame, a frayed head scarf battered by time shielded her face from the burning suns; the three shadows they cast haunted her like phantoms.

Loneliness was its own unique kind of killer. Slow and ever present, it stalked just outside of her peripheral. It competed with Olen's sense of failure, having eaten away at her mental state like a slow drip of acid during the years of her imprisonment. The suns would set and darkness choked the landscape. The technology she'd brought with her hadn't survived. The only light she had came from the stars and the orbiting gas giant that loomed in the night's sky like a glowing ball of churning magnesium.

The sands crawled with an assortment of desert critters and insects, all poisonous. Olen's Asabi stomach enzymes were acidic enough to digest the most venomous creatures, breaking down their bones and thick scaly skin. They all tasted like wet grass clippings. Only the birds were filling, but they were harder to catch. Red ravens were quick and contained the most meat.

Olen would reach out with her mind and pull flocks of ravens out of the sky, one or two at a time. It was called tuning; an uncommon ability she'd been given before her exile. Using her powers always came with a cost. It strained her deteriorating nervous system and weakened her muscles, a price her mind and body could no longer afford to pay. Tuning hurt.

Everything hurt.

Her arthritic fingers and bone-thin legs would occasionally prickle with pain. Her entire life had become pain. This was her punishment, her penance for the lives she'd failed to protect. She accepted it, but the planet wasn't satisfied. It wanted her life and worked every second of every day to claim it. Three of her four lungs weren't pumping enough oxygen into her blood. It made her delirious.

Olen had always been a small woman, even for an Asabi. The planet's gravity weighed heavier than the gravity she'd grown up under. Ten seasons of the well's gravity compressed her spine, making her even shorter. She'd gotten used to the agony. It became white noise. There, but ignorable. Until it wasn't, and she just wanted to die.

In the evenings, charged particles from Zaspel's gas giant would collide with the atmosphere and create an aurora borealis of iridescent streams of greens and blues and violet light. This meant two hours of daylight left.

Olen was on her way back to her hovel when an electric pain shot up her back and her balance got away from her. A brief moment of free-fall and she spilled onto the burning sands. She rolled down an incline, a plume of dust clouding the air around her. Olen tried to pull herself back up. The pain denied her. It left her helpless, yet content. Direct exposure to the three glittering suns would cook her to death in hours, if she let them.

She decided to.

The night creatures would come and consume her corpse and she would join the bodies she'd buried beneath the sands all those years ago. Olen's last hours were upon her. She welcomed the coming darkness. The suns blinded her as she stared into the blazing sky. Her inner eyelids hadn't gotten the memo; they tinted to protect her retinas. The sky appeared to darken for her as she lay atop the warming sands waiting for the end. It felt like a lifetime.

High in the sky, a comet appeared.

It streaked down in a straight line, a ball of fire at its head and thick white smoke trailing in its wake. Then it moved, laterally, changing course.

A ship.

Olen's flesh felt sick; dehydrated and suffering from heat stroke. A hallucination. It had to be. The alternative being too painful for her to consider. A sonic boom from the ship's braking thrusters shockwaved through the air and it slowed, hovering.

This was real.

Olen's hearts beat so hard against her ribs she feared they would burst. The old woman concentrated as hard as she could and used her powers to pull her body up to her feet, as if she'd been lifted up by invisible hands. The act made her head ache something terrible. Using her powers had drained much of her dwindling strength. She'd begged for death like a hungry animal begging for the last scrap of food. Now it terrified her. Her timing couldn't have been worse.

She shielded her eyes, tracking the object in the sky; her vision spotted with little white floating halos. It wasn't a large ship. All black and angular, like a seven-story tall hair trimmer with three drive engines bolted to its bottom. The ship's engines slowed its descent for landing, then cut off as the vessel tipped over onto its belly, its RCS thrusters further softening its descent.

The ship aimed to touch down near the old burned down settlement. Olen's hearts dropped. It was too far. She was more than an hour's walk away.

No. That wasn't true. She would've been too far away, if she hadn't collapsed. If she hadn't given up. If she hadn't lost hope. The settlement's ruins were twenty minutes away. Less if she ran, which she couldn't.

Olen forced her old bones to move. She ignored the ache in her withering muscles, risking a series of debilitating cramps. A single-minded focus overcame her. She couldn't see anything else. Olen stepped on a rock and her ankle bent. She almost stumbled again. Fear gripped her. If she let herself fall again, she knew she wouldn't get back up. She didn't fall.

The settlement had been Olen's first home upon settling the planet. It contained living habitats, hydroponics cubes, medical pods, even a school for her people's future children. Olen imagined it as it had been, before sheets of dancing flames blanketed the area. The stink of smoke and burning flesh still carried on the wind.

In the here and now, it wasn't fire she saw, but dust. The mystery ship's landing thrusters had kicked up a small tornado of sand and regolith into the air that covered the site in a thick curtain of white mist, back-lit by the sun that rose in the northwest. As Olen approached, a gust of wind split the air and cleared the fog just enough for her to make out the silhouette of a person. It was taller than her. Wide at the shoulders and slender at the hips, common physical attributes of a male across most species.

Standing in profile, he stared at the graveyard. Or rather, the mounds of dirt and rock she'd called a graveyard; three rows with twelve to a row. She could only visit it once a season. Any more than that hurt her too much.

Olen shuffled forward, her ragged sandals scuffing the sand. The male turned and saw her and he froze. Her vision wasn't as clear as it used to be. The man was human, dressed in black with a shaved head and tribal tattoos covering his exposed arms.

She had never met this man before, but she recognized him.

"Hiroshi Martel," she called out to the young human in her deep raspy voice. "What took you so long?" A moment ticked by before he spoke, but she couldn't hear him. Her ears rang and her sense of up and down had gotten away from her again. The young man appeared next to her, like her mind had skipped a few frames. His grip around her waist was the only thing keeping her from falling.

"Hold on," he said, a tinge of panic in his voice as he lifted her up into his arms. She was so small and thin she weighed almost nothing. He carried her to his ship. Up close she could make out the fine intricate details of the black ship's embossed skin, the vessel resembling a narrow building lying on its side. There were no windows, a standard design for interstellar starships.

The light from the three suns faded abruptly and she was inside. The coldness shocked her, too cold for someone used to the warmth of trinary suns. That familiar dull stink of recycled air burned her nose, a sensation she never imagined she'd ever miss. The infirmary was a metal box covered in anti-spalling material and the room held half a dozen bio-beds, but only one primary operating table. He laid her down on the icy table and a series of medical scanners penetrated her skin.

Blue light from the medical readout display splashed the young human's face; he looked as if he were under water. The longer he read the medical report the more his face darkened. "You've been irradiated," he said, the words stabbing his tongue. "You're suffering from severe heatstroke. Two of your lungs have collapsed. Your liver's atrophied and you need new hearts. The med doc is advising you be put in hospice."

"Oh. What's the bad news?" She'd hoped for a laugh. She didn't get one. "I know I'm dying," she continued. There wasn't any fear in it. "I held on long enough so that I could give you the gift of my knowledge."

"I just found you," he said, his voice raised in grief. "I'm not about to lose you. I can override the med doc and put you in stasis until I can get you to a surgeon."

"And if I die before that happens? Or during the surgeries? I could fall into a coma and I will have suffered for nothing." Her thin frail arms reached out for the young man. He held her crippled hands in his. It'd been so long since she'd touched the skin of another. It was a unique kind of warmth she hungered for. It intoxicated her. She wished he'd held her but knew that would be asking too much. "I can't risk everything I know, everything I am, dying with me. Let me do this," she said before being cut off by the colossal weight blooming in her chest.

The med doc shrieked alarms. Her hearts. Her throat closed up and the edges of her vision blurred and darkened. The end was coming.

The young human stabbed his fingers at the display console and a pair of medical arms folded out of the wall above her head. Four syringes extended out of the left arm's primary finger and shot into her torso. They pierced her hearts hot as ice, the medicine working their way through her veins like a spreading fire. She inhaled long and deep, followed by a grotesque coughing fit that transitioned into vomiting.

Hiroshi Martel ignored the stinking mess she'd made and held her. She looked up at him and the room's overly bright ceiling lights glowed around his bald head, giving him a halo. She didn't know if he'd been considered to be handsome among other humans, but to her, he was beautiful.

Ignoring the pain, she uncurled her stiff fingers and placed them on the young man's scalp. She pulled him in close until their foreheads touched, so that she could link her mind with his.

He stopped her. "No. I've stabilized you but you're still too weak. The attempt could kill you."

She managed a painful smile. "I have faith."

Chapter One: Jaxon

The story of humanity's first contact with an alien species was a tale every human child grew up knowing, like the story of Jesus or the myth of Santa Clause. What the history books didn't tell them was how the entirety of the human race had collectively shit itself. Fear and rumor spread fast among the humans. Many believed the alien had come to enslave them, or to blow up their national monuments, or to steal their natural resources. It took months of diplomatic communication before the humanoid alien being could convince the humans that he just wanted to sell them things.

The alien, Sil Dasmis, was an Iskaran; a bipedal species with thick leathery banded snake-like skin that came in several distinct shades. His people were tall, well over two meters on average, with their females being dimorphically taller. Dasmis had been smuggled off of his oppressive home world as a child and became an explorer and a entrepreneur. He'd purchased an old rundown cargo vessel and set out for the uncharted areas in the hopes of finding his fortune. A navigational error had dumped him on humanity's doorstep undetected. After weeks of monitoring the planet's communications his technology had learned their languages and he decided to make contact.

As fate would have it, humanity was sitting on a goldmine. They controlled an expensive and rare medicine that would save billions of alien lives; a stimulant colloquially known to humans as cocaine. A deal was made: ten metric tons of the miracle white powder, in exchange for the stars.

The Gravity Drive made interstellar travel possible, and humans had just bought the blueprints to build their own. Human technology leapfrogged by decades and within a few years the other known worlds took notice of the small blue planet with its life saving cocaine. Earth was approached to join The Protectorate of Allied Worlds, a coalition of twenty-seven allied worlds in as many star systems spread across the known galaxy.

One hundred and twenty-four years after first contact, almost twenty percent of Earth's fifteen billion souls were non-humans. Tourists, business entities, transplants, and refugees from all over the Protectorate worlds as well as the independent planets were drawn to the tiny blue rock which had become a major exporter of medicine, goods, and entertainment.

This was why the Kaijen needed to establish a chapter here.

Jaxon Troy was a heavyset human boy of seventeen when he first heard of the warrior religion and abandoned his mechanical engineering apprenticeship to join them. He hoped to become one of only three humans granted the knowledge, memories, and telepathic abilities that all Kaijen warriors possessed, but the powers didn't come without a cost.

Taking the Kaijen oath meant renouncing all material possessions, ending all personal relationships, and vowing never to have sexual contact with another living being ever again. That last rule had kept new admissions low. Jaxon had lived within the same eight blocks of Philadelphia in Atlantic America for most of his life. He chose to take the oath at such an early age because he was young and stupid and didn't know any better. He hadn't been born with wealth or good looks. He had inherited no unique talent or skills. He was nothing. He had nothing. So he risked nothing.

Except for the possibility of sudden brain death, which had killed a large number of Kaijen initiates. Having your mind altered through telekinesis tended to have that kind of effect.

Jaxon arrived at the Kaijen's Earth monastery, which resembled a massive stone castle from the Middle Ages positioned near the coast of Auckland, New Zealand. It stood on the great barrier island, surrounded by tall trees. Kaijen warriors led Jaxon into the main hall. The dry air inside chapped his full lips and the high vaulted ceilings echoed with noise. A Kaijen priestess of nobility headed each monastery.

Priestess Nisame was a Nezu, a species of thin furry bipeds with large fox ears and tricolor eyes that were twice as large as a human's. Where her nose would have been sat a small bump the size and shape of an almond. She breathed through the scent glands that slitted the sides of her cheeks and resembled stretched out nostrils. A bicolor of pecan brown coated her fur; a dotting of rosettes and maroon highlights contrasted against paper white similar to a tuxedo cat. Like all priestesses, she wore an ornate Kaijen sari with vibrant colors and hand stitched embroidery that punctuated her status as headmaster. It appeared far more extravagant than it was when compared to her student's meager light blue robes and dirty gold and blue tunics that were just above the quality of a potato sack.

Jaxon was stripped of his street clothes and dressed in a light blue initiate robe, then brought to the monastery's main hall for his induction. The ceremony could be seen as a wedding or a funeral, depending on the outcome. Two human initiates had died days earlier from massive brain aneurysms, both males. Men rarely survived the process. Fear and anxiety of his impending death dissolved in Jaxon's blood. He wanted to vomit but feared embarrassment more than dying.

"There is still time to turn back," Priestess Nisame's calm voice spoke, reading his dread like subtitles.

He shook his head. He was committed.

They stood in the hall's center, surrounded by the other novice Kaijen who trained at this monastery. They gathered around him and the priestess and sat in a semi-circle.

"Prepare yourself to receive the gift of knowledge," Nisame said with an air of confidence and wisdom that came with the penalty of age.

Jaxon knelt before her with his head bowed. "I am prepared," he said, his voice tight and nervous. Now he had to pee. Badly. Jaxon closed his eyes, blood rushing to his cheeks as the older woman placed her cold hairless palms on the crown of his head. She pressed her forehead to his. This was how she initiated the link; the one-way telepathic transfer of a Kaijen's knowledge and power from one person to another.

At first, Jaxon felt nothing. Did something go wrong? Had the priestess stopped? Seconds stretched. Soon he felt the unnerving itch of insects crawling up his spine, then writhing around inside his skull. His body tensed and the itching sensation graduated into a burning. Sudden intense pain shot through Jaxon's brain, like nails coated with acid. They sliced their way through each of his neurons. The agony shockwaved through his nervous system in arcs of lightning that caused his muscles to spasm and his mind to seize, the first signs of a fatal aneurysm.

The world fell away and Jaxon was swallowed by darkness.

This wouldn't be the last time that he would die.

***

The loudness of the buzzing was unimaginable. Like a fly the size of a house, darting past his ear. It stirred Jaxon into consciousness. The sun's heat warmed his espresso brown skin, but as much as he tried, his eyes wouldn't blink open. He forced them to, and a thin ribbon of light parted the black. His mouth was dry as a camel's ass and his head ached. Everything ached, as if he'd been beaten.

Jaxon lay on his back and his stomach was hollow. His body was different. He'd lost an alarming amount of weight in a short period of time. He hadn't just awoken from a nap. He had to have been unconscious for a long, long time. The room was small and made of stone with a square window that let the light in. The bed was hard as slate and Jaxon's back creaked when he sat up. He tried to talk, but his words refused. He heard footsteps and the door opened.

A young human woman with bright red hair backed into the room, dressed in her gold and blue Kaijen tunic. In her hands were a tray holding a bowl of water and towels. She turned and her light green eyes ballooned when she saw Jaxon staring back at her, nearly dropping her tray in shock.

"Holy shit," the woman said. She was thinner and shorter than Jaxon. Her alabaster skin clashed with her vibrant fire engine red hair tied in a French braid style ponytail that went midway down her back. Jaxon failed to speak again and pointed to his throat. "Oh," she said, then rushed to his side with the bowl of cold water. Jaxon had never tasted anything better.

"That's good," Jaxon coughed. He choked down the rest of the cold liquid while the woman stuck her head out into the hallway.

"He's awake!" she announced in a way that Jaxon heard as *He's alive!*

"How long?" Jaxon asked.

The woman's eyes shot up and to the left, then squinted. "About… six weeks? You slipped into a coma. You had almost no brain activity the entire time. We didn't think you were ever going to wake up. The priestess was just about ready to have you buried." She laughed, then regretted it. She cleared her throat, her hand cupped around her left wrist. The two stared at each other for an uncomfortable moment. "I'm Akeema. I'm glad you made it. It'll be nice to have another guy around here."

Jaxon's face twisted into a question. "Another?" The door swung open and a human male with shiny dark hair entered. He was olive-skinned and a full head taller than Akeema with a lean build, his Kaijen tunic soiled with dirt. He approached Jaxon with hesitation, as if his steps might damage the young man. "You must be starving," he said, his voice deep and concerned.

"I could eat a whole chicken," Jaxon said.

"You're a Kaijen now. We don't eat animals," the man said.

"This is Castor," Akeema cut in, a tinge of annoyance in her tone. "He usually has better manners than this."

"You're one to talk," Castor said, and she replied with a skeptical look. Then they both smiled. Not an intimate one. More like comrades. Siblings, though they clearly weren't. Castor reached Jaxon's bedside. "Can you stand?"

Jaxon struggled to swing his legs over the side of the bed and he realized he was wearing a diaper. It made sense. A ripple of embarrassment staggered him. The image of someone seeing him naked and changing his underwear unsettled him. He shelved that thought and stood. Two steps forward and the room spun around him. Akeema and Castor caught his arms and sat him down on the bed.

"Easy," Castor warned. "Disorientation and vertigo are common post-link symptoms. Your mind and body haven't had enough time to acclimate. We need to get some calories in you." He let Jaxon go while Akeema laid him down. Jaxon noticed the tattoo on Akeema's right forearm, a zero and a one inside of a triangle. She juxtaposed it next to Jaxon's own forearm tattoo of a triangle with a sprocket at its center.

Akeema smiled. "Hey. Looks like we both ditched our tech apprenticeships to become warrior monks with superpowers."

Castor frowned. "We're not supposed to talk about our past lives. You know that. You know the rules." Akeema rolled her eyes at the mention of rules. She was about to say something when Priestess Nisame appeared in the doorway. Jaxon had grown up in a species diverse city where humans and outworlders had lived and worked side-by-side for decades before he'd even been born, but there was still a strangeness to seeing non-humans.

Sunlight lit up Nisame's sari. It made her look ethereal. Her large dark eyes stared deep into his and her fox ears were positioned straight up and forward. "Jaxon Troy," she said in a motherly way. "You've come back to us. Your recovery is nothing short of miraculous. Rise."

Jaxon shot Akeema and Castor a look and they stood back, giving him room to rise on his own. He stood again. The nausea wasn't quite as bad this time. He stepped towards his priestess, his legs shaking and his knees threatening to buckle. He didn't let them.

Priestess Nisame cupped his face in her soft hands. Her smile didn't quite reach her large eyes. "Come my child, your new life is just beginning."

***

Days passed before Jaxon recovered fully.

In that time, the young man was shown around the monastery and the grounds surrounding it. He met each of his fellow Kaijen students, a collage of almost a dozen female aliens from as many different species. These were his new sisters. The Kaijen didn't rely on any of the automated technologies that had made living in a modern society easier. Everything they did was done by hand, which included growing their own food. The extra pounds continued to melt off of Jaxon as his diet mainly consisted of rice, cold noodles, corn and protein harvested from crickets. They also desalinated their own water from the ocean. Jaxon gained a bit of lean muscle from carrying buckets back and forth from the ocean to the monastery.

When they weren't busy farming, Jaxon and his fellow students were being trained in the ways of Kaijen fighting techniques. This included practicing with a crossglaive, a collapsible energy sword, the signature weapon of a Kaijen.

Accessing the memories and knowledge they'd been given wasn't an easy matter, and moving objects with the power of the mind, tuning, was a much harder skill to master. All of the students were capable of some small measure of telekinetic ability they had inherited from their telepathic link with Priestess Nisame.

All except for Jaxon.

He'd spent the next two years practicing hours a day attempting to awaken his ability to tune. He developed no special powers over that time. Nothing. He remained more or less the same as he had before the link. A failure.

Even initiates that had come to the monastery after Jaxon were capable of tuning small light weight objects to their hand or levitating them in the air like a magic trick, if only for a few seconds at a time. Tuning was extremely difficult to maintain and taxing on the mind; overexertion was common, and in rare cases, fatal.

Whenever Jaxon attempted to tune, it was like trying to move a bolder with his pinky finger. He could sense Priestess Nisame's growing disdain for him with each failure. She was his mentor, his surrogate mother. She was the one person he'd come to idolize and respect over all others. He craved her approval. Seeing her disappointment ate away at what little confidence he still had.

Jaxon only felt safe confiding in Akeema. She had agreed to help him even though tuning without the priestess's supervision was against the rules. Twice a week they'd sneak away to a secluded area in the surrounding forest to practice. Akeema's swordplay skills were far better than his, but the beauty of a crossglaive was that you didn't necessarily need to be a good swordsman. You just had to swing. An energy cell in the sword's hilt made the thin metal blade hot enough to cut through cargonite steel, let alone flesh.

And Akeema could tune.

Castor had her beat in experience and longevity, but she could pull a small pebble-sized object with her mind almost a full meter before she tired out. Jaxon's attempts to mimic her always ended with the same result: failure.

"Try again," Akeema panted, still fatigued from her last tuning attempt. Locks of her deep red hair had broken free of her braid and hung loose in her blushing face. "You just have to focus on your target. This is quite literally mind over matter. If I can do it you can do it. Hold your breath and concentrate."

Jaxon targeted a small rock on the ground and focused on it. Tuning turned his brain into a pressure cooker. The rock vibrated just enough to be noticeable, but the stone was defiant. It refused to move. The longer Jaxon tried the more intense his headache became. Overwhelmed, he crumpled to the ground in exhaustion.

Akeema sat down next to him as he sucked in air. "That was... not nothing," she said, doing a terrible job at comforting him.

"I'm thinking of leaving the Kaijen," Jaxon said between breaths. He couldn't look her in the eye, but he felt her gaze.

"Don't be ridiculous," Akeema said, but with a sliver of worry. "You're not a quitter. So what if you can't tune that well? Who cares? You make up for it by being a wonderful house mate. No one cleans dishes or mops floors or services toilets or scrubs bed sheets better than you do." Her tone was light hearted and playful, but she wasn't wrong. He'd made up for his lack of telekinetic abilities by cleaning up after the others. It never once occurred to him that he'd risked his life and given up his freedom to become a maid. "Besides," Akeema continued, "if you leave that means we can't be friends anymore. Castor would miss you so much he'd probably cry. And who else besides you can stop Saveon from running her mouth all the time?" Jaxon laughed, but there was no mirth in it. She hugged him. "There is nothing for you out there. Everyone that cares about you is right here. I would never give up on you, so don't you go giving up on me. Alright?"

Seconds ticked by as the sun hung against the horizon. Jaxon nodded. His focus remained on the stone as it sat still on the ground in front of him. Mocking him.

***

Jaxon was on his knees pulling fresh vegetables from the community garden in preparation for the night's dinner when he heard approaching footsteps. He looked up and saw Priestess Nisame, her long furry fingers laced in front of her; her expression blank, though vaguely annoyed. Jaxon stopped everything and stood at attention, his tunic smeared with fresh soil.

"Jaxon," Priestess Nisame said in her soft nurturing tone. "I have a special task for you. What do you know of the planet Giannis?"

Jaxon hesitated. Was this a test? Had she told him about this planet before and he'd forgotten about it? His desire to win her validation was great enough that he considered lying. He cautioned against it. "No priestess," he said with a nervous tremble.

"It's an independent world full of heathens and degenerates," Priestess Nisame sneered. "The Quorum of Elders wish to establish a Kaijen monastery there. I've been instructed to send an envoy to observe their culture and report back. I have chosen you."

Jaxon's gut tightened. He'd never gone off-world before. Space travel was terrifying. One mistake and he'd be left to float among the stars forever. The thought scared the hell out of him. "Why me?" Jaxon asked, unable to hide his fear. "With respect, I don't think I'm the best person to represent the Kaijen."

"You question my decision?"

"No, priestess. I would never. I just... I'm more useful here at the monastery. If I could nominate someone else? Akeema. She would be a much better choice. She's smart and capable and—"

"My choice has been made," she asserted, her warmth having chilled. "Your transport leaves in two hours. Your taxi will be here in five minutes. Prepare yourself." She turned on her heel and moved away, ending the conversation.

As a Kaijen, Jaxon was forbidden from owning any material possessions, so it didn't take him long to pack. He had the clothes on his back, his handheld, his crossglaive hilt and what little dignity he still retained. Five minutes wasn't enough time to say goodbye to everyone, so he didn't try. He walked straight to the courtyard and waited for his taxi to arrive. Jaxon flipped open his handheld, a rectangular piece of thin laser cut metal with a scratch resistant screen covered in scratches. He started to type out a message to Castor and Akeema when his taxi dropped out of the sky and landed, its rear passenger scissor door sliding open. Jaxon canceled the messages. He flipped his handheld closed and entered the taxi, the door folding shut and locking behind him. The vehicle's bubble-shaped VTOL engines spit cold flame, lifting it up into the sky.

Through the window, Jaxon looked down at the Gothic monastery. He saw two figures running into the courtyard who could only be Castor and Akeema. He waved them goodbye even though they were too far away to see him.

***

The flight to Giannis took thirty-four punishing hours on the 400 passenger starliner. Jaxon vomited at least twice. He experienced peeing in low gravity for the first time. Inside the small metal cubical that was the restroom, he inserted the head of his penis into a suction apparatus that caught his dribbling urine. A sign warned passengers not to use the device to masturbate. He laughed. They wouldn't have bothered to make a sign if it hadn't been a common enough occurrence. He obeyed the sign.

Jaxon imagined space travel was something people only wished on their worst enemies. And their children. And their pets.

He'd learned about the Gravity Drive in primary school. It produces and fires a concentrated beam of gravitons that resembles a beam of light that pierces space-time, contracting the space in front of a ship while expanding the space behind it, allowing the ship to slip into the space between space; a wormhole commonly known as slipstream. A ship dropping out of slipstream is preceded by a triple staccato burst of light that cushions a ship's reentry back into normal space. When the starliner did this, Jaxon's stomach protested. The ship flipped and started its deceleration burn which lasted another two hours. Passengers could view the approaching planet on a monitor.

From orbit, Giannis resembled a black billiard ball peppered with swaths of colorful light. Giannis was the satellite of a much larger uninhabitable planet and remained hidden in its shadow for eighteen of its twenty-two-hour long daily rotation.

The starliner docked with an orbital transit station. Jaxon and the other departing passengers were placed on a drop shuttle. The descent through the planet's atmosphere was grueling. The roar of flames rapped on the shuttle's skin like a violent hurricane while turbulence vibrated through Jaxon's body so hard his teeth hurt. Soon it stopped and gravity began. Braking thrusters pushed Jaxon's guts up into his throat, threatening a vomit encore, but the shuttle evened out and set down on a landing dock before his stomach could purge.

Jaxon stood. He felt heavier, like his shoulders were packed with lead. The planet's gravity was fifteen percent more intense than that of Earth's. He retrieved his crossglaive hilt from passenger storage and tucked it into his hip-holster. A rail train heavily tagged with graffiti carried him into the city. When he reached his destination, Jaxon exited the train car and stepped into a universe of garish neon lights and bizarre fashion choices.

Almost every single person Jaxon saw had some kind of piercing, tattoo, or cybernetic body modification that were so extensive they could almost pass for a mecha. The rain never stopped. It washed away his fear of being so far away from home.

The perpetual stink of halogen and mildew was constant. He saw no other humans. Walking along the neon lit streets dressed in his soaked Kaijen rags, Jaxon stood out like a nun at a heavy metal concert. No one noticed him. No one cared. Everyone else was too busy going about their own lives or talking into their handhelds. Jaxon heard so many different languages his subdermal translators inside his ears couldn't keep up. The languages the implants couldn't decipher were just background noise.

He ducked under a huge neon sign like a lost child to hide from the rain. He flipped open his handheld and connected to the local wireless network. Jaxon brought up a satellite view of the city and the distance to the hotel he'd been preregistered at. It was several kilometers away, on the other side of the city. So, not good.

There were only a handful of mobile vehicles on the roads. No buses, trains, or other forms of public transportation. On his handheld, Jaxon searched for a local jitney service and found none. He looked upward and noticed someone staring at him. A fit handsome lemonade skinned male with slick dishwater blonde hair and tight wet clothes that left little to the imagination. Jaxon didn't recognize the man's species.

"You looking for some company?" the golden alien asked.

"What? Oh. No," Jaxon said, his dark skin hiding his blush. "I mean, you're very handsome but you're not exactly my type."

The golden alien smiled as his chiseled jaw began to shorten and narrow. His hips widened and his stomach flattened. As his lips filled out, his pecks turned into full breasts and his hair lengthened, extending down his back. In the span of three breaths, the alien man was now a wasp-waisted she.

"How about now?" the alien woman asked in a husky feminine voice, a cute smile on her lips.

"Wow," Jaxon stammered. He was trying to keep the rain out of his dark eyes. "You're gorgeous. But I can't. Sorry. It's against my religion."

The golden woman tilted her head, skeptical. She never lost her smile. "I won't tell if you won't." The neon light reflected bright gelatin colors off of her wet skin like oil.

Jaxon said, "I was wondering if you could tell me where to find a taxi?"

"I don't do anything for free," the golden woman said in a sheepish sort of way.

Jaxon prepared a money transfer on his handheld. "Twenty cubits? That's all I can spare. I'm on a tight budget. Please?" Jaxon wore a friendly grin. The golden woman gave him an appraising stare, her hands on her hips and her wet clothes hugging her body like a second skin.

"You're very polite," she said. "People like me don't see much of that around this city often."

"I'm new here."

"Very new by the looks of you. The transportation union has been on strike for weeks. If you don't have a ride you're going to have to foot it."

"Thanks," Jaxon said and transferred the money with the flick of his finger. The golden woman pulled her handheld from the butt pocket of her shorts and declined the transaction.

"Keep it," she said. "For later, when you change your mind."

"I'd have to know your name."

"Sherae."

"Jaxon."

"Be careful, Jaxon. These streets are dangerous to nice young naive visitors like you."

Jaxon thanked Sherae with an amiable smile. She slinked away to find new customers, looking back over her shoulder to smile at him one last time.

Rain soaked Jaxon's feet and dribbled off of his eyebrows and short woolly black hair. Walking to the hotel would take hours. Jaxon was sure he'd melt before he made it a quarter of the way.

A noise in the air drew his attention. A rocket.

In the starry sky above, some crazy bastard was flying around in a pair of rocket boots. Jaxon had heard about how many people had died in horrible accidents using them. He imagined himself up there, flying. At least it would be a fun death.

***

The downpour slowed to a mild drizzle.

Jaxon walked the wet neon streets for the better part of ten minutes en-route to the hotel. He followed the path suggested by his handheld. It told him there was a shortcut through a maze of narrow back alleys, so that's where he went.

That was where they cornered him.

Two giant, hairy hulks with large eyes the color of egg yolks, a wolf's snout and finger claws. Both aliens had mouths full of shark teeth and bad mullets. They reminded Jaxon of werewolves. Neither of them had any visible cybernetic mods. They weren't locals.

Before he realized it had happened, a searing pain shrieked through Jaxon's abdomen. Confused, he looked down and saw his blood and little chunks of his flesh dripping from the claws of the bigger monster, the bruiser who was thick with muscle. Jaxon was sure he was screaming, but he couldn't hear it over the agony.

The smaller monster, the one Jaxon nicknamed Skinny, was behind him; his razor claws slashed at Jaxon's back. It stung like a bite. This time he heard himself cry out, loud and clear.

Jaxon's mind swam in chaos. How or why this was happening he didn't have time for. The werewolves were going to kill him. Or, so they thought.

It must have surprised them when Jaxon drew his crossglaive, the programmable metal inside extending into a straight single-edged energy blade that glowed white; a super-heated instrument of death. Jaxon was never good with his crossglaive. Clumsy, his priestess had called him. But when you had a weapon that could cut through tungsten like paper, you didn't have to be good. You just had to swing.

The bruiser's arm fell away from his body and splashed into a puddle, its light red blood gushing out of its stump like a garden hose. The monster threw its head back and let out a painful howl at the night's sky.

How were these not werewolves?

Jaxon turned around to focus on Skinny; the hairy hulk backed off, either out of caution or fear. Jaxon was leaking too much blood. His vision blurred. Loss of consciousness was soon to follow, but he wanted to ask them questions. He wanted to know why they'd done this. Why him?

The gun in Skinny's hand changed his mind. Jaxon turned and ran. He was halfway out of the alley when the bullets struck near him and he stumbled. They were high impact rounds that could put a baseball-sized hole in concrete, or soft flesh. The shots missed him, and found the bruiser. He turned back and saw the fist sized hole that gaped the monster's forehead.

Jaxon cleared the alley, stumbling like a drunk and colliding with pedestrians on the street. They shoved him away. Skinny attempted to follow him, but he was too far behind and lost sight of Jaxon in the crowd. Jaxon raced back the way he'd come from for what felt like hours but couldn't have been more than a few minutes. The four hour long smoky haze of dawn that passed for daytime would arrive soon and his hand was doing a terrible job at keeping his blood inside his body; the rain washed it down his clothes, leaving a diluted trail.

He caught sight of a familiar face and staggered towards it. "That didn't take long," Sherae said with a self-satisfied smile that quickly morphed into horror. Jaxon collapsed in her arms, his blood smearing her outfit, soaking through it.

"Help me," he muttered before the darkness took him.

Chapter Two: Akeema

"I heard you got stuck with window washing duty," Akeema said. "I have laundry duty. Trade?"

Akeema had cornered one of her Kaijen sisters, Bisu, in one of the monastery's drafty corridors. Bisu, being a Kaloidan, had brown wrinkled sandalwood skin streaked with mustard spots in the shape of tiny amoebas. She wore her silver hair tied back in a tight bun that made her look more intimidating that usual. The most distinctive Kaloidan trait was their eyes; Bisu's were long thin black slits that stretched up into the sides of her forehead in a way that made her look threatening. Even more so when she smiled. It made her facial expressions impossible to read.

Bisu's head tilted to one side. "What's in it for me?" Her voice carried an unnatural reverberation.

Akeema put on her brightest fake apple cheeked smile. "My respect and adoration." Bisu was quite a bit taller than Akeema and had to look down to see her. Akeema stood on her tiptoes to close the gap between them. Doing this reinforced her insecurity about her height, or lack thereof.

Bisu crossed her arms and inclined her chin. "Why don't you ask Qan?"

"Because I'm asking *you*. And because you're nicer than she is." Her fake smile widened.

Bisu drummed her long-pointed fingers on her arms for a moment, then in a hushed tone she said, "I want you to jailbreak my handheld."

Akeema's eyes fluttered. "I don't know what you're talking about," she lied, then motioned to an open door. Bisu followed her into a vacant room and closed the door behind them. "Who talked?"

"Saveon," Bisu said with a near invisible smirk. "She wouldn't shut up about it. Told me you did Tykka's too."

Akeema cursed under her breath. "I knew those bitches couldn't keep their mouths shut. If the priestess finds out she'll schedule me for a reeducation session or I'll be expelled."

"I can keep a secret."

Akeema frowned. "If that were true, we wouldn't be having this conversation, now would we?" She held out her open palm. Bisu placed her handheld in Akeema's hand. When they became Kaijen they'd all been issued special stripped-down handhelds that denied access to unapproved social forums and censored undesirable newsfeeds broadcast over the wireless network. Akeema hadn't planned to hack her own handheld. She just wanted to see if she could. If her Level 4 programming skills were good enough. Which they were. Then she'd made the mistake of leaving her handheld unattended near Tykka, who was a nosy snoop. Tykka was a true believer, the type who'd taken the collectivist teachings of the Kaijen code to heart, yet had no problem using blackmail to get Akeema to do what she wanted.

Akeema paired Bisu's handheld with her own and her fingers went to work. While her hacking program did its job, Akeema's thoughts fell on Jaxon. He'd been chosen to go off on an adventure with no supervision while she was stuck here in this boring place. Novice Kaijen like her weren't permitted to leave the island without Nisame's approval, which was rare. She imagined Jaxon off having the time of his life. She wasn't jealous. At least, she told herself she wasn't. Then she remembered their last conversation and her mood darkened.

"Have you ever thought about leaving?" Akeema said out loud before she had time to stop herself.

Bisu tilted her head in curiosity. "You mean the grounds?"

"No. I mean the Kaijen. The religion."

"Why would I?" Bisu said, the corners of her eyes curling like a Fibonacci spiral. "Here I have friends. Free food. Free clothes. A free place to stay. It's comfortable here. It's safe. If I left the Kaijen I'd have to go back home. I'd be expected to marry and join my tribe's military and fight in their regional war."

Akeema cocked her head. "But the Kaijen are a warrior religion. Eventually we're going to have to go to war with someone."

Bisu paused. The silence stretched longer than it should have before Bisu erupted with a haunting chuckle. "Look around you, Akeema. The galaxy is experiencing the longest duration of peace anyone has ever seen. The Kaijen have no more enemies. They're all dead."

***

The monastery was only a few decades old, but the exterior looked like someone who'd partied hard in their twenties and was now paying for it in their thirties. Being so close to the coastline's misty salt water didn't help, though it made for a great view.

Akeema got to work cleaning the ugly building's tall exterior windows with the aid of an old antiquated cherry picker. A task that would've taken a basic maintenance mecha twenty minutes to do was going to take her hours. The Kaijen religion didn't permit the use of mechas, because mechas were property, and the Kaijen were forbidden to own possessions. This somehow excluded the monastery, which the Kaijen legally owned. Akeema wasn't sure exactly how that worked. She carried a wooden bucket of water into the cherry picker's cab and directed the machine to hoist her up several meters. Its gears were old and rickety, grinding the entire way. The wind picked up and blew her ponytail off of her shoulder.

The only thing Akeema despised more than her lack of height was her hair. As far back as she could remember her hair had been cartoonishly red.

In her girlhood, Akeema's snotty classmates accused her of dyeing it or teased her for being the offspring of a circus clown. Then they got punched. Her decision to become a Kaijen hadn't come easy. She didn't own much. She had few friends. Her only family consisted of her father whom she'd grown estranged. As for giving up sex, well, she couldn't miss something she'd never had. There was no desire for her to marry or procreate. Her children might have inherited her flaming matchstick red hair, which was even more reason not to reproduce. Not every woman needed to be a mother, least of all her.

Akeema was nearly three meters off the ground when she looked down and saw Castor staring up at her. "Can I help you?" she called down with a thick layer of snark.

"I heard you swapped duties. Thought you could use a little help."

She wet her sponge and continued washing. "No thanks." His sigh was loud enough to hear even from this distance.

"How long do you think you're going to get away with it?" he said, and she knew what he meant.

"I'm not in the mood to be lectured."

"We can have this discussion yelling out loud or we can have it privately." Akeema groaned and lowered the cab down, the twisting gears grinding even louder than they had before. She tried to hide her scowl and failed. She was never good at hiding her anger despite having daily opportunities to practice.

Castor stood rigidly on his heels, arms crossed. "You told me you were going to stop hacking handhelds."

Talking over him she said, "Are you going to tell on me?"

His posture shifted to a tad less tight-assed. "First of all, fuck you," he said in a playful way that won a smirk from Akeema. "I'm not an asshole. No one has your back more than I do. But I can't speak for the others. They might talk. Then where will you be? You can't keep biting the hand that feeds us as if the rules don't apply to you."

She rolled her eyes and thumbed her ponytail back over her shoulder. "It's an unfair rule."

"Which you agreed to follow when you became a Kaijen," he said. "You can't just pick and choose which rules you don't want to follow whenever you feel like it."

Akeema's jaw tightened the way it did when she was trying to contain her anger. "That was before I knew what it was like to have someone else's memories beamed into my brain. Turns out dreaming about alien beings I've never met or faraway places I've never been to isn't as much fun as advertised."

Castor stroked his thin beard, his expression evolving from concern to surprise. "Sounds like you're saying you regret becoming a Kaijen."

"No," she said, lingering on it. "I just... I was sold a promise that I'd be transformed into a super skilled badass warrior who would go on epic adventures fighting the forces of evil and protecting the oppressed and the disenfranchised." She shrugged "At least that's how I imagined it in my head." She gestured to the monastery. "Instead, I'm a fucking window washer."

Castor tilted his head to one side and nodded. "Oh. Now I get it. This is about Jaxon. You're jealous he got to go off-world on an adventure and you didn't."

His words hit Akeema like a splash of cold water. "That's bullshit," she said, fairly certain it wasn't a lie. "I'm happy for him. He needed to get away from this place."

Castor's skepticism was apparent. "But?"

Akeema dodged his gaze. Jaw tight. "But... it would have been nice to have gone with him, is all."

Castor laughed at her. She laughed at herself. "He's probably gorging himself on pounds of cooked meat and getting drunk on Sidonian booze as we speak."

Castor laughed harder, then sighed. "I'm sure he'll tell us all about it when he gets back. But until then, no more hacking, okay?"

"No more hacking," she agreed.

"No more hacking," he repeated. There was an edge to his words.

"No more hacking," she reassured with a polite smile that he likely knew wasn't very polite.

Castor peered up at the monastery's windows. "You're never going to get all these cleaned in time for tuning practice."

"Not without some help," she added, then tossed him a squeegee. The cherry picker's cab was roomy enough for two. She worked the controls and it elevated them three meters high. A strong wind picked up and whistled like the sound of air being blown over the mouth of an empty bottle. A strange mechanical noise carried on the wind. It could've been the cherry picker's gears, but Castor heard it too, coming from the coast. Akeema shielded her eyes from the sun to see it.

A ship.

All black and tower shaped, like a thick soldering iron with round edges, peppered with dozens of odd angular protrusions in its skin. It shot through the air like a missile, then its braking thrusters slowed it down. At first it appeared to be heading for the monastery, then it veered off sharply towards the surrounding trees where she lost sight of the vessel.

"I wonder what they're doing all the way out here?" Castor said.

***

It was midday.

Akeema and her fellow students gathered in the monastery's main hall for training. Akeema saw it more as a glorified aerobics class. They divided into pairs. She chose to spar with Castor. He threw his punches and kicks at her slow enough that she could see them coming weeks in advance.

"Faster," Akeema demanded. She saw Castor's smile, followed by a streak of knuckles coming at her. She ducked, dodged, and countered the blows with a few of her own. None landed. She began to sweat and tire out when a blur of leg came into her periphery. Castor's foot caught her in the ribs and Akeema stumbled.

Castor stopped. "You okay?"

Her ribs ached. Akeema wiped sweat from her brow before it could reach her eye, breathing heavy from exertion. "I can take it. Especially when you keep holding back."

"Oh. So you *want* me to hurt you?"

Akeema squared up. "You wouldn't be the first man to put his hands on me."

"You and I have very different definitions of what that means," Castor said. He relaxed his shoulders. "I'm your friend. Your brother. If I accidentally hurt you, well, I'd feel really bad about it for a good... five, maybe six seconds?" Akeema laughed through her Greek nose. "Besides," Castor went on. "I'd hate to be the one responsible for damaging our new window washer." Akeema's mouth fell open. She threw a kick aimed at Castor's balls, but slow enough for him to deflect it. They laughed together.

They drew the ire of Priestess Nisame, her face hard as granite. It wiped the pleasure from Akeema and Castor's faces. They continued their exercise.

Priestess Nisame weaved her way through the groups of

partners, observing the technique of her students with a critical glare. She snapped her fingers and they lined up, standing an arm's length from each other, their hands clasped behind their backs.

The priestess paced between them, her eyes staring down each of her students, peering deep into their very souls. "A Kaijen's strength does not come from the individual," she began. "It comes from those around you. From our numbers. Our shared thoughts and experiences. Our diverse culture. The elimination of all distinctions. That is the true power of the Kaijen."

Akeema grimaced. It only lasted a second, but the priestess had caught her. Those large eyes of hers didn't miss anything.

"You wish to question, Akeema?" Priestess Nisame asked, not looking at her.

Akeema hesitated. Everyone was facing forward, but she could feel their eyes on her, amplifying her self-consciousness. "It... it doesn't make sense to me, priestess. When you linked with us, we all received your memories and skills, right? So why do we have to relearn lessons we should already know?"

Priestess Nisame turned on her heel to face Akeema, locking eyes with her. Then her gaze shifted to the group. "Which of you can answer her? Castor."

Castor stood at attention; his back straighter than a steel beam, his chin up with pride. "Our minds are a muscle," Castor recited with proud confidence. "If we don't exercise it, it atrophies."

"Correct," Priestess Nisame nodded. "Your minds contain the knowledge of the Kaijen I gave you, but that does not mean your mind and body are accustomed to accessing it. Akeema, I am going to attack you."

"What—" Akeema managed to utter before her feet were swept out from under her. A moment of weightlessness, followed by her back slamming into the stone floor. She groaned in pain, but more out of embarrassment.

"See?" Priestess Nisame said to the group. "I telegraphed my movements and Akeema was unable to stop me. She still requires much discipline. As do you all."

When Akeema hit the floor, her crossglaive hilt came loose from its holster and skittered across the stone floor. She reached out to recover it.

"Stop," Priestess Nisame snapped. "I want you to tune the crossglaive to your hand."

"I'm not advanced enough to—"

"And you never will be if you refuse to try."

Akeema's jaw tightened. She hated being put on the spot, her hand cupping her left wrist on impulse. The other students were just as amateur at tuning as she was, but Nisame had never forced them to make a fool of themselves in front of everyone as much as she did Akeema. The scarlet haired woman quieted her mind and focused on her crossglaive hilt on the cold floor. She extended her hand and imagined the hilt springing into it.

Tuning burns off a lot of energy.

All of Akeema's past attempts had been tantamount to swimming upstream with an anchor tied around her neck while breathing fire into her lungs. Akeema reached out to the crossglaive with her mind. The ache between her temples throbbed, like a pair of giant hands crushing her skull.

The hilt vibrated, twitched, then rolled... away from her. Exhaustion made her stop. She breathed hard and fast as if she'd just run ten kilometers straight.

"Disappointing," Priestess Nisame said, frown wrinkles stacking up on her tall wide forehead. She opened her palm and the hilt flew into it like a magnet. She held the weapon out to Akeema, forcing her sassy student to come get it. More humiliation. Akeema accepted the hilt, avoiding the judging eyes of the other students, two of which being the large green and blue fish-like irises of Saveon Xux.

Saveon was a Herekin, a bipedal aquatic species with gills that could breathe on land. She was hairless with blue-pink scaly skin and unique white spot patterns on her face, hands, feet, and chest. "Permission to speak, priestess," Saveon gurgled. She received a nod. "How is this fair? None of us are as advanced as you are. You ask too much. We will never be your equal."

"That's wrong think," Priestess Nisame said. "We are all equal. That is what it means to be a Kaijen. We all possess the same abilities. The same thoughts. We are all capable of the same feats with no distinctions. Do you think I began my tenure as a Kaijen this skilled? Only with time and practice can you master your ability to tune and reach your full potential just as I did."

Saveon found herself under attack.

She wasn't knocked flat on her ass as fast as Akeema had been. Saveon fended off the fox-eared woman's assault for a brief moment before a swift kick to the gut dropped her; Saveon fell to her knees and her chunky vomit sprayed the floor. Akeema hoped it wasn't her turn to mop the main hall.

All eyes were on Priestess Nisame; her frustration was palpable. "You should be better than this. Open your minds. Sense those around you. Anticipate. We can no longer think of ourselves as singular beings, but as a group. All connected. As one collective."

Priestess Nisame moved too fast to track and Castor was the next one being attacked.

Akeema loved Castor as a brother, though she'd always felt he was a bit too try-hard. He prided himself on being the first to class and the last to leave. He spent far more of his free time practicing than any of the others.

Here it paid off.

Castor, despite Akeema rooting against him, fended off Priestess Nisame's blows in an impressive display of skill. It exhausted him, almost to the point of collapse, but he remained on his feet until she stopped.

Nisame hadn't even broken a sweat. The corners of her mouth curved up for a change. "Well done, Castor. With more practice you could one day become the first male to reach the rank of priest, or even an elder."

"I didn't realize a male could become an elder," Castor said, holding back his shit-eating grin.

"There is a first time for everything. Your opportunity will come. I believe in you."

"You honor me, priestess."

Akeema sometimes forgot how much of a kiss-ass he could be. "When will we get to use our abilities in combat?" Akeema asked as she stood, ignoring the growing ache in her back. "The Protectorate has maintained the peace for over forty years. The Kaijen have no enemies to fight."

"Evil will always exist," Priestess Nisame said. "So we must always be prepared. The Kaijen exist to fight the oppressors of the galaxy whenever they reveal themselves. Because they will. The elders have predicted it."

"You mean the elders can see the future?" Bisu asked.

"Some can see glimpses. But that skill is reserved for only the most gifted of Kaijen. Heed my words, young ones. A war is coming. And when it does, we will not lose because I failed to properly train you. I promise you; we will win it."

A chime rang at the room's communications console; an incoming off-world transmission.

Space was enormous. Because of light delay, sending a connection request to any of the other distant worlds could take eons. To combat this, the Protectorate deployed superluminal communication arrays throughout the known galaxy, over six million units in total. They formed the comm net. Now the delay between transmissions could take as little as a few seconds on a good day. On a bad day, it could take hours.

The connection came from Giannis.

Priestess Nisame accepted it and Jaxon's distressed brown face appeared on the screen. The image distorted and jumped. It wasn't a perfect connection, the delay being six seconds. Jaxon wasn't wearing a shirt; a sash wrapped around his shoulder and waist. With the bad image quality, it took Akeema a moment to recognize they were bandages, with another one around his arm. He'd been hurt. Or someone had hurt him. That old familiar sense of spiked rage Akeema had held in her youth crept its way up her spine and into the base of her skull where it nestled.

Jaxon didn't look scared or angry. He looked relieved. *"Is everyone alright?"* Jaxon asked, talking too fast. *"Are you all safe?"*

"Certainly, Jaxon," Priestess Nisame said. She sounded odd. "I wasn't expecting your report so soon. You look injured. What has happened?"

Hearing Priestess Nisame's voice appeared to calm Jaxon. He breathed a heavy sigh out of his lungs. *"It was so real..."* Jaxon said, fatigued. *"I dreamt... I dreamt a tattooed man in black entered the monastery and killed all of you—"*

His image sputtered out and the connection was lost.

Without being asked, Akeema stepped to the computer terminal. Her hands worked the keys like a pianist, trying to get the connection back. "Something's wrong with our comms. They're jammed."

Priestess Nisame's eyes narrowed knowingly. "We are being attacked."

The monastery's heavy main doors swung open and the tattooed man walked in. He was muscular. His exposed arms were covered in intricate tribal tattoos that must have been painful. His scalp was shaved bald and he wore what appeared to be black leather.

Priestess Nisame recognized him. If she had the power to kill someone with her eyes, this man would be dead. "Hiroshi Martel," she said. "You are supposed to be long dead."

"It didn't take," Martel said. It sounded like an apology. The hall's acoustics amplified his voice.

Priestess Nisame stood between him and her students. Her body radiated ferocious excitement. "I'm glad. I feared I had been deprived the chance of ending you myself." Martel approached the priestess at a slow, deliberate pace. Each movement a provocation. Priestess Nisame's hand found her crossglaive hilt. "You move too slowly, Hiroshi. Come closer so that I may cut you down properly."

"If you surrender now," Martel said, "I swear I'll leave you the use of your legs." Nisame scoffed, her scent bladders engorging and deflating.

Akeema was taken aback by the man's audacity, by his complete lack of fear. Priestess Nisame was the most dangerous being she'd ever known, and here was this bald asshole disrespecting her. She sensed the coming fight. It was exhilarating. She longed to see her mentor use her abilities in action. Akeema had all but prayed for this. She'd just been gifted a front row seat to a first-class ass whooping and wanted to pull out her handheld to record it. She resisted the urge.

"Hey," Martel said to the students in a calm indifferent tone, like he was addressing dogs. "My problem isn't with you all, alright? Just Nisame. She tried to kill me. So, I'm just gonna kill her real quick and I'll be on my way—"

"You will be silent!" Nisame snapped. Akeema had never heard the woman raise her voice. "You betrayed us. The Kaijen took you in when you had nothing. It's fitting that you would return here to meet your end at the tip of my blade."

"Believe that, if it makes you feel good," Martel said. His flat indifferent tone remained unchanged; no hint of fear or anxiety. "Now, are you going to keep talking a big game? Or are you going to come over here and put me in my place?"

"Very well," Nisame said. The collapsible blade of her crossglaive sprang from her hilt and the energy cell hidden inside the grip ignited the metal; the blade's cutting edge glowed white with superheated energy. "Stand back everyone, and observe how I destroy evil."

Martel didn't respond. He didn't draw his own weapon or move to defend himself. He just stood there, patiently. Waiting.

Priestess Nisame's approach was slow at first. She sidestepped her opponent, her fox ears high on alert. Martel remained still. Then she moved fast, faster than Akeema had expected from the older woman. She'd closed the gap in a blink.

Martel activated his own crossglaive with such speed it looked as though the weapon had just appeared in his hand. He deflected her thrusts, catching her blade with his cross-guard which spit out sparks. Akeema wanted to savor the moment. She worried the match would be over too fast.

And it was.

The combatants danced around each other, their blades clashing and sparking another five or six times before Priestess Nisame shrieked and her hands fell away from her body; her crossglaive dropping along with them. She froze in utter shock. Next were her legs, which were cut out from under her at the knees. She screamed. Her torso crumpled to the floor, her four stumps spurting blood.

"Told you," Martel said with no remorse.

Shock gripped Akeema. It was like watching it happen through a screen. Her wide-open eyes darted from her mentor soaking in an expanding pool of her own blood to the woman's cold blooded attacker. "Murderer!" Akeema screamed. Her crossglaive roared to life. The other students hesitated, then copied her.

"Whoa whoa whoa," Martel began, the palm of his free hand out in front of him in defense. "Hey. This wasn't about you guys, okay? It was about *her*. Trust me, she had this coming. Just give me a second to finish up and I'll be out of here."

"You monster!" Saveon yelled, the hilt of her crossglaive clutched so tightly her wet palm squeaked against the metal. "I'll kill you where you stand!"

"Don't do it," Martel said with a pained expression. Saveon was already throwing herself at him.

Two moves. A flash of blazing hot light from his crossglaive. Saveon cried out, then she was gone. Her insides spilled out onto the floor like a broken fish tank. There looked to be more water than blood. Her mouth opened wide like she was screaming, but no sound came out. Then her mouth closed, and opened again. Closed, then opened. Closed, then opened, and stayed open. Martel's blade sizzled, burning away the internal fluids on its edge.

There was no time more mourning.

Akeema and the others swarmed Martel and his calm stoicism changed. Now he looked worried. For them. "I didn't come here to hurt you people," he said. "You're outmatched. Back down and no one else will die. You have my word on that. Challenge me and I will kill you all. You have my word on that, too."

No one listened. No one wanted to.

So another student fell dead. This time it was Bisu. Her face remained unreadable as Martel ran her through. She didn't make a sound as the alien woman's blood sizzling on his blade. The fear among the remaining students hung in the air thick as smoke.

Akeema didn't care. Her vision had tunneled, her blood hot and loud in her ears; a bomb could've gone off beside her and she wouldn't have noticed. None of them backed down. They swarmed the tattooed killer. Martel's crossglaive swung through the air and caught flesh. More screams echoed. Bodies hit the floor, staining the stone an even deeper red.

Four students remained.

"Motherfucker!" Castor called out.

Martel shook his head. "I warned you. I'm not the bad guy here. The Kaijen have your minds all twisted up. They're using you."

"Fuck you!" Akeema screamed loud enough to make her throat raw. She charged forward and he parried her attack. His eyes burrowed into hers.

"Akeema Barbeau," Martel said in a soft, almost friendly tone.

"How do you know my name?" Akeema said through clenched teeth.

"I know all of your names. I was a student here. Until I learned the truth. The Kaijen aren't noble. Or virtuous. They just pretend to be to get power and increase their numbers. *They are lying to you—*"

She attacked again, and again he parried. His foot shot into her back. Akeema stumbled, but caught herself from collapsing.

"I don't believe a fucking word out of your mouth!" she said.

"Yeah? Well, your technique sucks," Martel said. "You can't beat me. Keep coming at me and I will lay you out. Yield and maybe you'll live long enough to get better."

Over Martel's shoulder, Akeema saw Castor maneuvering behind him. This was their chance.

"If you want my weapon you'll have to come and take it," Akeema said, keeping his attention on her. "I'm not afraid of you."

"Yeah, you are." It wasn't a lie.

Akeema and Castor attacked him at the same time, their swords swinging and thrusting in unison. They only stabbed the air. Akeema saw an opening and swung, but too hard. She exposed her back to Martel and didn't feel the heat.

The tip of his crossglaive started at the base of her spine and cut upward in one smooth motion. Her throat seized. Akeema didn't feel the pain, only her own confusion. Black nothingness closed in around her like a drawn curtain.

She knew she'd just been killed.

Chapter Three: Martel

Hiroshi Martel had spent most of his teenage years working. Earth had a number of transport docks, the largest and busiest being located in southern Colombia. The region contained one of the largest coca fields and cocaine processing plants ever constructed, spanning the length of a small city. The coca plant was all but impossible to grow off-world without Earth soil, making the white powder it produced the lifeblood of the planet's intergalactic economy for over a century. There were similar processing plants located in Bolivia and Peru and they were always eager to hire new workers.

Dozens of cargo ships left the planet's surface daily, their cargo holds packed to the gills with medical grade cocaine as well as other major exports like beef, processed sugary foods, and tobacco. The use of mecha labor had been outlawed decades prior to ensure that human labor was always in demand. It was hard grueling work, but it kept Martel lean and his arms strong. Most important of all, it taught him discipline.

The problem was the pay. It was shit. No, shit was more valuable. The turnover rate for plant workers remained one of Earth's highest. Workers would use what few cubits they'd saved to go off-world, or apply for STEM internships. That was what Martel did, having been accepted into an engineering apprenticeship program in Australia.

When he wasn't learning about how to fix starship engines and air recyclers, he wrangled cattle on the side and earned what few extra cubits he could. He wore his sandy blonde hair tied into a top knot in the style of his grandfather's samurai ancestors for whom he'd been named; a loose strand of hair always found its way hanging over his left eye, hiding its blue shimmer.

He'd been out drinking a lot in those days. Too much. He was in a dive bar with friends in Melbourne when he first heard of the

Kaijen and the alien religion that granted their followers superpowers. Assuming one didn't succumb to a fatal brain aneurysm that mostly affected those with a y chromosome. The threat of death made it all the more alluring to join. The possibility of becoming a powerful warrior with telepathic abilities consumed his dreams.

The religion attracted the naive and the idealistic; talented, artistic, mostly privileged in upbringing, with a passion for justice who wanted to bring an end to all wars. They tended to despise the entrenched hierarchies of the old order and longed for a new society in which everyone had an equal chance. The Kaijen interpretation of freedom meant freedom from material want. Their version of justice meant a planned distribution of goods. The end of war for the Kaijen meant a new form of war against the wealthy and privileged who they believed created the wars.

Martel hadn't known any of this at the time.

Not that it would have changed his mind. There was too much to be gained by joining them, the pursuit of power having blinded him. Martel's admission was accepted. He'd been reminded of the ninety percent death rate among males that the Kaijen would not be liable for. He accepted the risk. If he died, then he died. If he didn't die, then that would be interesting.

Martel sat in the lotus position in the monastery's main hall dressed in his powder blue initiates tunic. Priestess Nisame placed her hands on his head, initiating the link and he fell into a deep coma, waking after eight days. Martel had become, as far as he knew, the first known male to survive the linking process in decades. He joined the ranks of the sacred Kaijen warriors with immense pride.

And then came the nightmares.

Martel would try to sleep. Behind his closed eyes were screams. First it was once a week. Then every other night. Then every night. It went on for months. He was experiencing memories that were not his own. This wasn't just his imagination. They were real memories of real people who had all been killed. The deaths took place on a desert planet he'd never been to, where he saw the faces of the dead non-humans he'd never met. Coils of thick white fog surrounded him, swallowing him. He choked on the stink of sulfur and cooked meat.

It was the smell of bodies, burning.

Months ticked by before he could fully see the faces of the alien beings in detail. In the nightmare, he watched them being murdered with a level of violence even black-market snuff movies wouldn't dare replicate. Watching these helpless people being slaughtered night after night after night traumatized him to the brink of insanity. He smelled their blood and felt heat from the fire that burned them. Smoke and scorched flesh filled his nostrils and it made him physically sick. It wasn't just a nightmare. It was purgatory.

And the screams. Oh, God, the screams. They went on for infinity, echoing in his mind like the beat of a drum that wouldn't end. His upbringing had taught him that boys who complain about their personal problems were, at best, ignored. And at worst, despised. His sense of masculine bravery had made him keep his suffering to himself until it was outweighed by his fear and anxiety. One night he worked up the nerve to confide in Priestess Nisame. She agreed to meet with him in her private quarters.

"They are just dreams," the priestess assured him. "They cannot hurt you. In time they will be forgotten." They'd been sitting at a small table. She placed a cup of steaming hot Iskaran tea in front of him. It had a strong smell Martel couldn't place. He'd been so high-strung from the nightmares that he hadn't even changed out of his clothes from the previous day; a pair of worn tattered trousers and his gold and blue Kaijen tunic.

"They're more than that," Martel said, his hands shaking, preventing him from bringing the cup to his mouth. His eyes were fixed on the tea, his mind lost in its amber color, as if it were a window he could peer into. "I saw her today. The pregnant woman? Just as you called me into the garden. I was in the kitchen and I turned around and there she was. Standing right in front of me. She was real." Nisame flinched. It was subtle, but he noticed. "But she looked different. Older. Weathered. She looked sick."

Nisame's scent bladders quivered. "Did this woman say anything to you?"

Martel looked up into her large oval eyes with tears in his. "She wants me to find her." He calmed himself by drinking half his tea in a single gulp. It was bitter with a chalky aftertaste. "She's in trouble.

She needs our help."

"You imagined it," Nisame asserted. "You haven't slept in days. You're hallucinating. She wasn't real."

"Please," he pleaded. "I would like your permission to leave the monastery so that I can find her."

"That's not possible," Nisame said dismissively. "It is against your pledge as a Kaijen. If you leave it would be for good. You could never come back." She bit the words.

Martel sat in silence, coming to terms with the decision he'd already made before the conversation even began. "I understand. But, with all due respect priestess, I have to go. That woman was real. I could feel her. She exists out there, somewhere. I'm going to find her. I have to. Then, maybe, the nightmares will finally stop. I renounce my station as a Kaijen warrior. Please, please understand. And thank you. For everything." Martel rose from his chair and almost made it to the door when his head began to spin, like leaning back in a chair too far. His center of gravity slipped away from him.

The violence came sudden and quick. He wasn't ready for it, or the surge of fear that followed. An invisible force gripped his body, squeezing him tight. Nisame was tuning. Martel's body slammed against the room's stone walls and he went dizzy.

What happened next was a blur, but one thing was clear: Priestess Nisame was trying to kill him. She spoke, but he couldn't hear her over the throbbing in his ears. Martel turned back to look at her, the acrid smell of ozone hitting his nose. It was her extended crossglaive. He didn't understand what was happening, but he'd been in enough scrapes to know when his ass was in danger. He'd left his crossglaive in his room, leaving him completely defenseless. He had to run. His legs felt like cooked noodles, but they got him through the door. Nisame reached out with her tuning power and sent him spilling into the corridor. It hurt.

Martel scrambled to his feet. He saw one of his Kaijen sisters standing guard at the mouth of the corridor. His clamoring drew her attention. "Ynara!" he cried to her. She was a waifish brown skinned Misakian woman. Her species had beady white eyes with matching white wavy stripe patterns that ran the length of her body and four gangly fingers on each hand. Her violet hair was short and spiky.

"Help me! Please!" he continued. "The priestess, she's—"

Ynara drew her crossglaive.

In a breath she was thrusting its tip at his chest. Martel dodged, feeling the blade's heat pass his skin, and pushed her away. She rallied and swung the blade around, aiming for his head. Its heat brushed his neck before ducking out of its path. "Stop!" he yelled, a tremor in his voice. She wasn't listening, her crossglaive raised above her head in a striking position, its glow reflected in Ynara's wild eyes. She stabbed down at him, the blazing hot blade warming the air. She missed and struck the floor, the blade having burned a dark smoking slit in the stone. She pulled the blade out and cinders spit up out of the hole like tiny fireflies.

Her leg cut through the air and sent Martel tumbling down the stairs. He spilled onto the landing with a groan. Ynara pursued.

There wasn't time to think. Nisame was seconds away. He couldn't hold off both of them. Ynara pressed her attack. He guessed the path of her blade, working hard to keep himself away from it. Martel was successful until he wasn't. The weapon's thin superheated tip caught his flesh and seared a long agonizing swath across his upper chest. The pain staggered him. Another thrust came, the tip aimed for his head. The blade's flat edge grazed his arm, burning it like a hot iron. His scream echoed. The stink of cooked flesh wafted the air, resembling barbecued pig.

He had to stop her or he was going to die.

Martel had spent his time at the monastery learning the Kaijen's sacred fighting techniques, attempting to master the inhuman powers they'd given him. By his own admission he hadn't been the best of his rank. Not even close. However, he'd excelled at non-violent defense. It didn't take much effort to turn defense into offense.

Ynara's crossglaive made another blind thrust for his center mass, intense heat radiating from the glowing blade. He ignored the pain spiking across his chest and positioned his foot behind himself, slightly off to the side. He turned on his heel, dodging the blazing crossglaive and seizing Ynara's wrist. With a twist of his hand, he'd stolen her crossglaive from her. Ynara's narrow alien eyes widened, her face awash with surprise. The sword bored into her, the blade piercing her chest and melting her insides. She didn't cry. She didn't scream. Her face twisted in a grimace of shock and betrayal that mirrored his own. Her body slumped to the dirty stone floor, the crossglaive blade sliding out of her. Ynara's blood fountained onto Martel's face and hands. It left the glowing blade smoking. Martel turned to run.

Then he paused. Not of his own will.

Nisame.

She'd been watching from atop of the stairs. Her tuning power lassoed his chest and stopped him, like hitting a brick wall made of air. The grip tightened, forcing air out of his lungs. He couldn't breathe or move. Before he could pass out the tension released; Nisame's excessive tuning had drained her. Martel crumpled to the floor, coughing in oxygen. Nisame approached, ready to deliver the killing blow. Her skills far outmatched his. Fighting her was a death sentence.

Get up! Get up! Get! Up!

Martel dug deep inside himself for whatever tuning energy he had buried in his mind. He leapt up into the air, higher than a normal human was capable of, and crashed through one of the monastery's stone glass windows. He fell, landing in the high brush surrounding the property.

He ignored his fresh wounds and forced himself to run, fleeing into the forest under cover of darkness until the soles of his old wooded sandals splintered and began to break apart. Twigs and pebbles poked through and pierced the thick skin of his feet. Shortness of breath crept up on him like a predator and for the second time that night he found himself on the verge of losing consciousness. His legs ached and the cut on his chest oozed blood. His lungs burned hot enough to start a fire. He wanted to stop.

Martel forced himself to keep running.

Then he ran some more. He reached the coast before his stamina ran dry and his body made the choice for him. He collapsed in a huff, his knees stabbing the sand. Martel looked down at his blood smeared Kaijen tunic; some of it his, most of it Ynara's. The deep crimson stains made his gut clench. He fought the urge to vomit. Glass from the window cut gashes into his arms and face. Dried blood glued thin slivers of glass to his skin in a way that bordered artistic flare. The shards glittered in the moonlight.

Hiding wasn't a long-term option. There were only so many places a murderer could hide from bio scanners. He had to escape the planet.

Hundreds of transports left Earth daily, but the Kaijen had eyes everywhere. Martel could be tracked through his handheld. He ditched it. He left footprints on the coast leading into the ocean along with his bloodied clothes, then doubled back in his own footsteps. He hoped to convince his pursuers that he'd walked into the water and drowned.

Martel trekked south of Aotea Island and swam 70 kilometers to Clifford Bay where he nearly did drown. He hitched a ride on an old fishing boat headed for Australia. Martel expected to see his face plastered all over the newsfeeds. There was nothing. No bolos. No all points. The newsfeeds hadn't reported a word. The Kaijen had spent so much effort selling the public on their wholesome persona that they wouldn't risk jeopardizing their reputation for him. Even if it meant letting him get away with killing one of their own.

Before Priestess Nisame linked with him, Martel had been a pretty good mechanic. After the link, he'd become an expert in basic starship maintenance overnight. He offered his services in exchange for passage on an old junker cargo ship out of Wallis Colony called the *Thessalia*. The captain and most of her crew were of the Wazny species, a race of chalky red skinned beings covered in black tribal tattoos that detailed their family's entire history. They had bizarre cat tongues that freaked Martel out. The *Thessalia*'s crew appreciated his hard work to the point where they honored him by inking full sleeve tattoos on both of his arms.

The crew hadn't been exclusively Wazny. There were a few humans.

Jenapher, a short slender woman with brown eyes and a flat face, worked as the ship's software technician. She was smart and quick-witted and worked harder than anyone he'd ever met. Martel shadowed her because he wanted to know as much as she did on how to repair a ship's core code.

Or how to hijack it.

Jenapher interpreted his desire to learn with flirting. He

pretended not to notice. Martel hadn't been interested in casual sex or short-term relationships. Instead, he fixed the ship's shitty water reclamators and its twitchy graviton emitters that threatened to turn the ship into a ball of superheated gas every time they slipstreamed. Burying himself in work kept him focused. Kept him on his purpose.

After three months of cargo runs to various backwater worlds the *Thessalia* docked at Kidwell Station, the largest orbital space station outside of Protectorate control. Martel said his goodbyes to the crew of the *Thessalia* and discharged himself.

Kidwell had been built for a capacity of one and a half million residents. Its current population was four million. He disappeared among them unnoticed. Kidwell's docking ring wrapped around the bloated station like a spiked collar. Thousands of ships. At least five percent of which were impounded or abandoned because the owner died or was imprisoned or couldn't pay the docking fees.

If Martel was going to find the woman from his vision, he needed a ship of his own.

He'd earned two thousand cubits working on the *Thessalia*, not nearly enough to buy a ship. He would have to steal one. Tricking the station's antiquated computer systems into thinking he was the owner of an abandoned ship wasn't hard. Martel tapped the slivers of Kaijen knowledge transferred into his brain; a linked memory bloomed in his mind and he saw the path to his goal.

He needed a security handheld from one of the station's attendants. Martel shadowed a station manager to a bar, a large Herekin man who needed liquor as much as he needed oxygen. When he spoke, Martel could hear the cholesterol in the man's gurgling voice. He'd been distracted while watching a game of Volley Run over the wireless, a game that reminded Martel of football but with knives. The thick man didn't feel his handheld being lifted from his pocket. Martel jail-broke the device, and after a little tinkering and a few rewritten commands, that part of his plan was done.

Tricking the station into releasing the docking clamps on his chosen ship would be harder, but not by much. He dug around the station's root code which had been written decades before he'd even been born. Martel found a subroutine in the command tree, an emergency purge protocol that would release all the station's docking clamps simultaneously in the event of catastrophic failure or if the fire suppression systems wouldn't respond.

The last step was choosing the ship. Most were outdated hunks of junk, but one was a small black and gold attack interceptor. Like most ships of the era, it was built vertically in an office tower configuration with gimbaled decks that could adjust for thrust gravity or when in atmosphere. This particular design reminded Martel of an oblong mortar round with three drive engines at its base arranged in an evenly spaced star-pattern.

He waited until after the *Thessalia* disembarked before initiating the cascade. No reason to stab the hand that had fed him. Martel spoofed the interceptor's security lockouts and boarded, then executed his plan. Thousands of ships floated away from the massive station like grains of sand being scattered by the wind. Only one of the tiny ships, the interceptor, came about. Its main drive spun up and a beam of light shot out of its nose, pulling the vessel into slipstream. It was registered as the *Teta Eillglen*. Martel reprogrammed its transponder and rechristened her the *Jezebel*, an offensive word for a fallen or abandoned woman. Martel wasn't a woman, but the metaphor felt appropriate.

His next task was finding the planet from his nightmare. Trying to access linked memories was a lot like lifting weights. Difficult, but easier with time and discipline. Martel had both in spades. He'd spent hours scrolling through endless lists of cataloged planets and moons, limiting his search to the uninhabited bodies and the disputed systems.

One spoke to him.

Zaspel, one of several dozen worlds ruined by war and left unsuitable for colonization. It didn't even appear on any of the more up to date navigational charts. Something about the system felt familiar to him. It took almost two weeks of slipstream travel to reach.

Even from orbit the planet looked dead; scarred and pockmarked from centuries of abuse. His scopes found the remnants of an old burned down settlement on the southernmost continent. He angled the ship for entry and the *Jezebel* dropped ass first into the planet's atmosphere, carving its way through the sultry sky. The ship's maneuvering thrusters kicked up a haze of dust as its landing struts dug into the ground. The air was thin and stale and stank of decay.

He'd arrived at a sandblasted ruin. It was the same settlement he'd seen too many times in his nightmares, where it burned. Martel tried to imagine what the settlement looked like when it was thriving, before it was torched. What he didn't expect to find were the graves. Someone had given the dead a proper burial. These were the people whose agonizing screams had pushed him to turn against everything in his world he'd come to cherish.

Martel knelt, paying his respects to the mounds of dirt, the whipping sand scratching at his unprotected skin. He'd taken radiation meds before landing. His time down the well had to be short. He didn't understand how anything could survive on this rock.

That's when he met her.

The frail Asabi woman approached him at a steady deliberate pace. She looked exhausted, barely able to maintain her balance. Her snowy white hair hung out of her old dirty gray sari, hiding her dry cracked copper face. She looked so different from his memory. Her eyes, though. Still defiant as ever.

"Hiroshi Martel," the old woman said in her deep raspy voice. "What took you so long?"

***

Akeema Barbeau's lifeless body hit the monastery's stone tiles with a dull thud, Martel's energy sword having left a bloody gash down the length of her back, destroying her spine. The stink of ozone and singed hair filled his nose, his blade having severed her red ponytail.

I am a monster, Martel thought. Anyone looking at his situation from the outside would think the same, but he had a mission to carry out. If the price was looking like a monster, then a monster he would become.

Only three of Nisame's students remained; two alien females and a human male, the proud Castor Zhecheva. In ways, he reminded

Martel of himself, back when he'd still been one of Nisame's useful idiots. None of the current students had been here when Martel was still a Kaijen. He assumed they'd all been relocated or sent to a reeducation center to minimize the chances of the truth getting out. He was thankful for that. Cutting down enemies he didn't personally know made his task easier.

"There's still time to leave," Martel announced to the three standing. "I don't want to do this. This isn't even about you." His words were meaningless. They couldn't compete with the blind hatred he saw in the young fool's eyes.

"We'll kill you if it's the last thing we do!" Castor said, spitting the words.

"Oh, it will be," Martel said. "Or you can back down and live. Your choice." Silence fell. Only the low sizzle of their energized crossglaives filled the large hall. A moment of stillness.

He read Castor. The man's eyes telegraphed his attack. When he moved, Martel's reaction speed was instant. Castor stopped short, flinching.

"Don't," Martel warned. Castor backed off, his eyes shifting between Martel and Akeema's lifeless body, a charred stripe running down her back.

The other two students attacked Martel at once. The first woman, a Sabrac with a horned nose and fluorescent alabaster skin named Tykka, he impaled through her broad chest. A puff of warm moist air burst from the wound as his blade punctured her lung like a popped balloon. Martel grabbed the woman's sword hand, making her spear her fellow comrade, Qan. She was a three-eyed Chibak with oily green skin and cranial ridges. He'd stabbed her straight through her third eye.

Only Castor remained. The sight of his beloved teacher and all of his comrades dead at his feet put tears in the man's eyes.

"They had a choice," Martel said, remorseful. "You still do. Learn from their mistake. Walk away. I won't harm you. You have my word."

His words only steeled Castor's resolve.

Their blades swung and clashed at dizzying speeds. Castor was fueled by pure anger; his flurry of sword strikes were fast and strategic. With more training he could have been formidable. Martel was simply the better fighter. He headbutted Castor, staggering him, then followed with a hard kick to the chest. It knocked Caster off his feet, the momentum sending him crashing into a wall. Every bit of wind Castor had in his lungs had evacuated. He coughed blood. Ribs were surely broken.

"Stay down," Martel urged, lingering on each word. *Please stay down. Don't make me kill you.*

Castor groaned to his feet, his faced twisted in pain.

"Alright. I get it. You're tough," Martel said. "You're trying to be a noble Kaijen. But the Kaijen aren't noble or virtuous. They just pretend to be, to manipulate idiots like us into thinking we're fighting for the right side. It's all one big lie and I can prove it. Let me show you."

"Fuck you!" Castor growled, then rushed at Martel like a wild animal; his swings were wide and sloppy, easily deflected.

"Stop!" Martel pleaded, but the man had made his decision. Martel felt it was his solemn duty to give Castor the warrior's death he so desired.

Two moves, and Castor's sword hand fell away from his body, just past the wrist. His body seized, clutching his leaking stump. Castor's face strained with agony and disbelief.

Martel moved to kill him. A quick thrust to the head or heart would have ended it. But he hesitated. Castor fell back, landing hard on his ass, in someone's blood. Someone's crossglaive hilt lay next to him.

Don't, Martel thought. If Castor reached for it, that would be the last thing he'd ever do. Martel could see the man thinking. Weighing his options. Playing it out in his mind. Castor wanted to do it. He was dying to die. Then some combination of pain or doubt stopped Castor from getting himself killed. He just lay there, shaking, cradling his bleeding stump and sheeted in sweat.

Martel stood over Priestess Nisame who, despite her fatal wounds, remained conscious. Blood abandoned her body like rats from a sinking ship.

"Damn you," Martel hissed. "This was *your* fault. Their blood is on *your* hands."

"Your fighting form," Nisame coughed, blood oozing from her lips. "I recognize it. But it can't be. She's dead."

"I didn't just come here to kill you," Martel said. "I want the album. Give it to me and I'll call a medic."

Nisame gurgled a sick, painful laugh. "Why? I've lost far too much blood. You've killed me. You have nothing left to offer or to threaten me with."

Martel nodded in agreement. "Yeah. I really didn't want to have to call that medic anyway."

Nisame's eyes widened. She saw the end coming. "Give Olen my regards," she said, blood on her teeth. One swift thrust with his crossglaive and she was dead.

Martel found the room's computer terminal and inserted a small data rod; it released a data collection package, searching the computer's core banks for the album. The search came up empty. Martel's fist pounded the terminal controls, keys flying off and peppering the floor. A knot formed in the pit of his stomach as his face stung with anger. "All this for nothing," he said to no one.

A sound drew his attention.

Castor had crawled over to Akeema's body and cradled her. Martel knew they were close. He wondered just how close. Martel stood over Castor, his crossglaive still blazing with energy.

"Go on," Castor pleaded. "Finish it. I have no fear of death."

"What would be the point?" Martel said, then collapsed his blade. "It didn't have to be like this. But you'd rather die than listen. Next time, back down sooner." He left the monastery, his feet tracking bloody footprints behind him, and sent out an anonymous medical alert from his handheld.

The *Jezebel* sat parked in a nearby clearing a short run from the monastery. Martel noticed the blood on his clothes and hands. It wouldn't rub off. It would never rub off.

He'd left the *Jezebel* in the hands of Selassie, a maintenance mecha he'd salvaged and reprogrammed to be his co-pilot and nurse. He talked to her through his handheld. "Sel, prep for dustoff."

"Yes yes," the mecha said, her stuttering electronic voice sounding flat on the handheld's speaker. Martel moved to board the *Jezebel* via its loading ramp when he stopped and turned.

Someone was standing in the clearing, watching him. Not a person.

A ghost.

No, it just looked like a ghost; out of focus and jittering like a bad video connection. Curious, Martel approached the strange blurry non-person stalking him. The closer he got, the clearer the image became. Clear enough to recognize its face.

"Jaxon Troy," Martel said.

The ghost vanished.

Chapter Four: Jaxon

The dream ended and a sharp sting jolted Jaxon awake, sweat sheeting his skin. Pain from his claw wounds snaked through his body and bit new places. He was stiff everywhere except where it counts. His head swam in a foggy haze of terror and confusion.

Jaxon looked around and had no idea where he was or how he'd gotten here. It had bio-beds and medical equipment and the air stank of feet and antiseptic. So, a hospital, or some kind of clinic, or a close enough approximation of one. The walls had an impressive amount of flecked paint and the floors were heavily stained with bodily secretions.

He was in a splicer lab, a place where the poor or unchipped came to get cheap medical care or body modifications or sex changes. Or where criminals could get a variety of illegal surgical procedures, or where parents could have a clone of their dead kid commissioned. He felt he was a breaking a law just breathing in the air.

Jaxon dragged his fingers across his bandaged wounds. They were tender. This place may have been a shithole but it had kept him alive, and for that he was grateful.

"*Shin okie lagra!*" a gruff male voice cursed. Jaxon's subdermal translators didn't recognize the phrase. "I just lost twenty cubits on you."

Jaxon turned, his eyes focusing on a flabby four-eyed humanoid alien with mottled skin and an elliptical skull. The alien man had a receding hairline and dozens of minor cybernetic mods were scattered across his oily body. The man held a lit cigarette between two of his thick nicotine-stained fingers. "I mean, sure I'm a great surgeon, the greatest, but I would have bet my third testicle that you were a lost cause. Sometimes I impress even myself." His loose skin jiggled when he talked.

Jaxon sat up with a groan and asked, "Where am I?"

"You could start with a simple thank you," the alien surgeon said through a haze of smoke.

Fair point.

"Thanks. For saving me. I think," Jaxon said.

"Actually, don't thank me. Sherae's the one who dragged you in here. Nearly pulled a blade on me when I kindly suggested carving you up for parts. We don't get many humans out this far. Makes you rare. Name's Murhaf."

"Jaxon." He attempted to stand. His inner ear disagreed.

"Hold on there, you have to take it slow," Murhaf said, catching Jaxon before he could tip over. The man's hands felt hard as tree bark. His cigarette bobbed between his thick lips as he talked. "You were mauled by a Thurlbii. They coat their claws with a paralytic. Makes it easier to subdue and disembowel their prey."

"Two. There were two of them."

Murhaf's eyes widened in amazement. "No shit? And you got away? That's a good story. They're barbarians, you know. Eating perfectly good organs I could sell." Murhaf took a drag from his cigarette, smoke venting out of gill-like slits in his neck.

"I need to report my attack to the authorities."

"Why?" Murhaf asked with a chuckle. "You weren't shot. Cops only care about gun violence. Go in there with these scratches and they'll laugh you out of the station."

Jaxon's face went ashen. "But... someone tried to kill me."

"And yet, here you stand. You walked away with your life. Don't waste it complaining."

Panic stung Jaxon as he worried what Priestess Nisame would say about his poor combat performance. The moment was overwritten when his memory came back to him like a slap. Akeema. Castor. Priestess Nisame. His dead Kaijen sisters. Their blood. Martel. He'd seen it all happen. *Was it just a dream?* he wondered. "I — I need to send an off-world connection request," he stammered.

"Sure, I'll add it to your tab," Murhaf said, chuckling. Jaxon flipped open his handheld.

A bill of two thousand cubits deducted from his account. "Shit," Jaxon muttered. With a groan he shoved himself off the bed, ripping its paper sheets. Jaxon hobbled over to the room's comms terminal and dialed the Earth monastery. Light delay and relay interference created a queue. He waited with growing anxiety for the connection to be accepted, every second feeling like hours. It turned into minutes. *They're dead. No one's answering because they're all dead.* Jaxon stared at the blank screen with dread, praying, hoping, he was wrong.

The connection was accepted and Priestess Nisame's image appeared. Over her shoulder was Castor, Akeema and the other students who he'd witnessed being killed. All alive. Jaxon exhaled the biggest sigh of his life. "I can't believe it. Is everyone alright? Are you all safe?"

"Certainly, Jaxon," Nisame said. "I... wasn't expecting your report so soon. You look injured. What has happened?"

"It was so real," Jaxon began. "I saw—" He stopped, terror splashing his face. *Deja vu.* This was part of his dream. He knew what came next. "Get out!" he yelled at the screen. "He's coming! You can't beat him! Get everyone out of there! He's going to kill you all—"

The connection died. Dread poured down Jaxon's spine like scolding water. "No," he muttered, and dialed the monastery again in a panic. It wouldn't connect. He knew why. It was impossible and didn't make any logical sense, but he knew.

Jaxon moved fast. He dressed in his dirty bloodstained tunic and robes, his healing wounds shouting at him. He went to slip on his worn sandals and only found one. He'd lost the other one somewhere between coming here and the attack. Murhaf offered him a used pair of shoes that fit. For a fee. Jaxon pocketed his handheld and placed his crossglaive hilt in his hip holster.

"Thanks. And tell Sherae I greatly appreciate her help," Jaxon said, then paused. "She's a she, right?"

Murhaf's smile was a spasm. "When she wants to be."

"Tell her I will pay her back as soon as I can."

"Sure thing kid," Murhaf said. "And if you ever want to sell any of your organs—" Jaxon rushed out of the clinic before Murhaf could finish.

***

The travel office was a small narrow shop wedged between two larger buildings with a vibe that screamed claustrophobic death trap. Jaxon ducked in out of the rain where he could barely see the travel agent through the thick cloud of her cigarette smoke. It amazed him how humanity had made one of its biggest marks on the galaxy by turning entire worlds full of aliens into nicotine addicts.

The agent was a zaftig blueberry skinned woman with no neck and short stubby arms from the Dawida species. Her scalp was hairless, replaced by bumpy cartilaginous scalp crests that made her appear as though she were wearing a seashell as a permanent hat. She dressed in a way that reminded Jaxon of a kindergartner on picture day, except she looked to be at least a thousand years old.

"What can I do for you, sweetheart?" the old travel lady said in a haggard voice that sounded like metastasized cancer.

"I need to book the next transport to Earth," Jaxon said, coughing the secondhand smoke out of his throat and swiping at the air.

"My pleasure," she said while her wide fingernails tapped keys on her terminal. "That'll be ten thousand cubits." Jaxon winced. He flipped open his handheld and checked his bank balance. He only had six thousand cubits and change. He turned and left the travel office.

The streets of Giannis had lost their appeal, the cacophony of flashing neon lights having become an epileptic nightmare. The rain just made his grief wet. On his handheld, Jaxon searched for freelance pilots in the city, sorting the listings by rating. All the top five-star pilots were too expensive. He scrolled past the four-star rated pilots for the same reason.

Only one three-star pilot charged a rate Jaxon could afford. He accessed the profile listing of one Yoko Tiro, a silver-skinned alien woman with dark hair and a joyless grin. Her customer reviews were... not kind. Apparently, she had an attitude problem and was a confrontational drunk, but she only charged three thousand cubits. It was either her or no one.

Jaxon sent a connection request that went straight to voice mail. He didn't imagine this was the kind of pilot who could afford to turn down work. When they were on the clock, freelance pilots tended to keep an open locator active in case they were busy or away from their handhelds. Jaxon pinged the pilot's location. She was in a casino on the opposite side of the city, a long distance to walk in the rain for a man recovering from a near-fatal assault. Jaxon looked up from his handheld. Across the street, a Herekin man with dark scaly skin made slick by the rain. He was walking with his small child whose scales were a noticeably lighter tone, the man was showing his kid the sights and sounds of the city. The kid seemed happy and excited to explore a place where werewolf-like creatures could jump out and maim him at any moment. Jaxon caught himself staring just a bit too long and the kid noticed. The dad followed his child's gaze and stopped, assessing a potential threat to his kin. The dad's hand reached for his hip where a weapon likely was.

Jaxon looked away from them and moved fast in the direction his handheld told him to go. He didn't look back.

On foot, it would take him the better part of three hours to reach the casino. The rain drowning his feet would turn them into mushy prunes by then. Jaxon walked in the rain for a short while before he passed by an electronics junkyard. It was a huge hangar, fenced off from the street, as if that would stop anyone determined enough from sneaking in. Jaxon paid the mecha attendant the ten-cubit admission fee plus an extra five cubits for a small toolkit and entered a sea of electronic parts; bionic body limbs and various mechanical devices stacked up into towers. Everything looked random and disorganized. Dozens of tarps strung together acted as a makeshift cover to shield most of the junk from the constant drizzle.

It took him almost half an hour to find what he'd come here for: a rocket boot. It took longer to find one his size that wasn't completely trashed, an older model for a left foot. Jaxon found two more lefts before he'd uncovered a matching right boot tucked under a skeletal mecha torso. The power cells in both boots were drained. He went back to the two left boots. Their power cells weren't quite dead, just enough for a short flight.

With the little toolkit, Jaxon cannibalized parts from the other junk boots and got his salvaged boots to turn on. He sifted through a different pile of junk tech and found a wrist-mounted controller he slaved the rocket boots to. Jaxon removed the shoes he'd purchased from Murhaf and slipped on the rocket boots; they automatically adjusted to fit tight on his feet. They were padded and comfortable to walk in compared to his sandals.

One tap on his wrist controller and the boots spit plumes of blue plasma from repulsor jets lining their soles. Jaxon levitated a meter off the ground in a jerky unbalanced way. The boot's thrust increased unexpectedly and threw Jaxon into a pile of parts before they sputtered out.

"Ow," he groaned. The impact got his wounds screaming at him again. Jaxon ignored the pain needling his back and crawled out of the pile. He stood up, his muscles screaming even more. Jaxon used his tools to adjust the boot's repulsors and tinkered with the default settings on his wrist controller, then tapped the ignition button. The boots lifted him up. This time he wasn't thrown.

On his way out of the junkyard he returned the toolkit and paid for the boots. In doing so, he had automatically broken his Kaijen vows: no ownership of personal possessions. His sense of pride and triumph at repairing the boots turned into ashes in his mouth. Days earlier he'd contemplated leaving the Kaijen. Now the possibility of expulsion terrified him. That would be the least of his problems if his vision had come true.

Two taps on his wrist controller and the boots sent him blasting off into the sky, drops of rain pelting him. He'd already decided to ditch the boots before he returned to the monastery, but he had to admit, flying through the air like a goddamn superhero made him feel cool as hell.

***

Jaxon landed outside of Decadence, the techno lair housing the casino, as well as a bar and night club. He felt heavier, like someone had turned up the planet's gravity on him. He approached the building, the familiar thump of loud electronic music radiating outward for several blocks, broadcasting its rhythm to the universe. Jaxon paid the fifty-cubit entry fee and left the rain behind.

The place was packed. Bodies from a dozen different species twisted and writhed in unison to the pounding music like one giant organism. Jaxon waded through the sea of gyrating beings, most of them sporting some form of visible cyberware; many artificial limbs, some mechanical attachments, and a ton of face mods. Most of the ocular implants looked like camera lenses. The music pulsed through the crowd strong enough to press lungs with lyrics Jaxon's translators couldn't make sense of. Jaxon squeezed his way through the crowd, making skin to skin contact with dozens of partiers. The stink of hot metal and oil-based lubricant bled through walls.

Jaxon found the gambling level. Here the atmosphere was the exact opposite of the night club; calm with the hum of conversation over the low distant music, the clank-clank-clank of stacked chips, and the brisk whir of shuffled cards. A haze of cigarette smoke misted the air. Jaxon wandered from table to table like a lost child looking for his parents until he caught sight of the silver pilot.

Seated at a private table protected by security guards was Yoko Tiro. She was a Kish, a race known for their unique gray monochrome skin and lips that were so blue they were almost black. Her matching jet-black hair was styled in a short bob with a gravity-defying curl that twisted forward in a spiral that perfectly framed her round impish face. She wore cargo pants with far too many pockets, black boots and a matching flight jacket that looked a little too big for her. And she was petite, more than a full head shorter than Jaxon.

He stood on the sidelines with a small crowd of spectators while Yoko played a high stakes card game. Jaxon didn't understand the game, he just knew the cards were round, the chips were hexagonal, and Yoko was losing. Badly. That didn't stop her from signaling the wait staff to refill her empty glass of brandy.

Seated across from Yoko and winning all of her chips was Uthay, a burly Tzipkan brute. His pale blue skin made him appear as if he were being suffocated. Weird horn-like protrusions lined his neck and eye sockets and his lantern jaw that held a spider-veined tongue. A horseshoe of balding topped his head. Everything about him, from his reserved calm demeanor to his expensive clothes and gaudy jewelry, said organized crime. However many chips Yoko had started with, Uthay had left her with an anemic stack. She splashed a third of what she had into the pot.

"Raise. Two thousand," Yoko announced with a thick guttural accent. She tried to sound cocky and upbeat. Her eyes betrayed her.

Uthay saw it too and chortled. "Someone must like what she has." His accent was heavy and politely menacing. "Tell you what. I have an awful hand, but I'm going to call and raise you whatever you have left because I am convinced you're just that unlucky."

Yoko's thick caterpillar eyebrows furrowed, her confidence having dissolved. She checked her cards and winced. Yoko's gaze shifted from the mess of chips piled in the center of the table, back to her cards, then to Uthay. She added the fistful of her remaining chips to the pot with a defeated sigh. "You just can't let me win, can you?" Yoko fumed.

"It's not about who wins, it's about who loses the least." The dim sparkle of hope in Yoko's eyes died when Uthay revealed his hand. His smug grin stabbed at her. Uthay had three black crows with seven red dragons, a high hand she couldn't beat.

"*Shin okie lagra*," Yoko growled. Jaxon deduced the phrase was some approximation of *son of a bitch*. "Eh... double or nothing?"

Uthay's laugh was all teeth. "Yoko, you already owe me double. I take not being paid very personally. Now you can either give me my six thousand cubits or I can take it from you."

Yoko reacted to his threat as if he hadn't made it. She defused the danger with a friendly smile that didn't reach her eyes. "C'mon, Uthay. If I had that kind of money you think I'd be in this rat hole losing it to you?"

"What about that pile of scrap you call a ship? If I sell it for parts that just might cover your debt."

"Hey, hey, hey," Yoko said, talking over him. "Insult me all you want, but never insult my ship."

Uthay puffed his chest, asserting his dominance. "You mean *my* ship. You know what? I think I will take it. As a down payment. Just because I know how much seeing it torn apart would damage you." He signaled to his escort of six multi-species goons decked out in cyberware mods. They moved to surround Yoko.

"Foosha," she cursed before flipping the card table, sending her drink spilling all over Uthay and staining his suit. Yoko bolted. The goons, who ranged between ugly and stupid ugly, grabbed for her. The silver woman was too small and too slippery. She slid underneath or jumped over everything in her path.

Uthay sneered at his stained suit, not so much angry as annoyed. "You're just making this harder for yourself," he said, not quite shouting over the commotion.

Jaxon tried to get Yoko's attention. "Hey," he said as she pushed her way past him. The goons shoved him to the side in pursuit. Jaxon followed them, ending up back in the club section, the shrill techno music returning. Yoko made a beeline for the exit, which was blocked. She changed course, cutting through the dance floor and pushing through an emergency exit leading to a back alley. The goons chased her and Jaxon chased them.

Outside, the rain came down hard and sounded louder than the music, the planet's increased gravity making the raindrops hit like hail.

Goons had blocked off the alley's mouth and were sprinting towards Yoko. She darted in the opposite direction and met a high fence. Jaxon watched from a distance as Yoko attempted to scale it. Bionic hands clamped down on her ankles and wrenched her hard into a puddle, ruining her hairdo. Uthay caught up, hustling past Jaxon with a heavy limp. The gangster lifted Yoko up by her collar, her feet dangling, and pressed her against the fence.

"I am more than willing to negotiate," Yoko said with a fake friendly smile. Jaxon could barely hear over the rain and muffled drone of the club music.

"Always the talking with you," Uthay mocked. "Why did you run? What would you have done if you had gotten away?"

Talking fast, she said, "Gotten you the money I owe you and came straight back here and paid you and not have left the planet immediately. I swear."

Uthay chuckled. "Yoko, darling, your lies hurt my feelings. It is only fair that I share that hurt with you." He buried his meaty blue fist into her stomach, but not at full force. He was a gentleman gangster, after all. Yoko ate the blow with almost no sound. Jaxon winced on her behalf.

Through clenched teeth Yoko said, "You're right. That's fair. I deserved that."

"You will get me my money, Yoko. On time and in full. But you must be taught a lesson. I can break your arms or I can break your legs, you choose."

"Neither. Can I choose neither?"

From his suit, Uthay pulled an expensive blade similar to the crossglaive with a superheated edge that glowed sun-hot; raindrops sizzled and evaporated on contact.

Yoko's breathing quickened, her thick caterpillar eyebrows hiked up her forehead with worry. "I can't get you your money with broken limbs."

"You Kish heal fast, don't you?" Uthay said. "Even grow back parts you've lost, right?"

"That will be time spent not getting you your money. It's counterproductive. You can hurt me or you can get paid faster, which sounds better?"

Uthay paused, tasting her words with a cocked eyebrow. He nodded. "That's... actually very sound logic."

Yoko flashed a relieved smirk. "Thank you."

"But you ruined my suit, so I'll settle for cutting your face."

"Wait, wait, wait, wait—"

Jaxon watched in horror as the blade slashed a black scorch mark on her silver cheek, her red blood cooking on the knife. Yoko held in her scream, but couldn't hold in her tears. The rain hid them.

"Excuse me," Jaxon said from behind the group. "Would you stop that, please?"

They all turned, took one look at Jaxon's dingy Kaijen robes, and promptly scoffed at his existence. "As a matter of fact, I will not," Uthay said with an annoyed glare. "Get fucked human."

"Yeah! Foosha hoo-mon!" Yoko said, equally annoyed. "I don't need your help. I have these *baizuo* right where I want them."

Uthay's eyes narrowed, surprised by her audacity. He rewarded her with a punch to her snub nose, breaking it. More crimson on her monochrome skin. The situation stank of familiarity to Jaxon; a cornered victim, outnumbered and being attacked in a neon-lit alleyway. Another case of deja vu all over again. The night seemed full of them.

Jaxon didn't realize what everyone was looking at until he followed their gazes to the extended crossglaive in his hand; the blade steaming from the rain. The demeanor of Uthay and his goons changed from not seeing Jaxon as a threat to *we're about to fuck this guy all the way up.*

"I don't need your help, stupid hoo-mon *baizuo!*" Yoko said over the rain, anxiety tinting her voice. "You're just making it worse."

Uthay signaled with his eyes and the goons moved on Jaxon. A lightning bolt of fear surged up Jaxon's spine. He'd never been a great fighter. Sub-par at best. Even less so with his current injuries. *But they didn't know that.* He doubted these thugs had any formal combat training. At most they were brawlers who relied on their mods more than teamwork or precision. Jaxon settled into a combat stance. His breathing quickened.

The goons flanked him. From their clothes they revealed a combination of daggers and hatchets, all with glowing blades similar to his but lacking the penetrative power of a crossglaive. No guns, thankfully. Bladed weapons meant no police. *At least these criminals were following the rules.*

Jaxon's blade swung at the goons. It felt heavier than usual. His practiced strikes came out as slowed lurches, the blade only hitting air. And worse, the goons weren't stupid. They surrounded him like hungry lions circling a wounded gazelle. Jaxon kept his body moving and his head on a swivel. When one of the goons got too close, he swung, but they retreated before his blade could catch them, smiling. They were playing with him. It was on the third or fourth swing that Jaxon swung too wide, creating an opening for the goon behind him. A boot slammed his hip and he stumbled forward.

A searing hot blade slashed through his soaked tunic, scorching his back. Jaxon roared. The wound wasn't deep but it stung like all hell. He staggered and a mechanical fist socked his cheek like a mallet. The bullies laughed at his incompetence.

Uthay chuckled with them. "Enough games. I have places to be. End him." The words rung in Jaxon's ears like a klaxon. Caution had failed him. It was time for risks. He remembered his boots.

Two taps on his wrist controller and his repulsors shot him up almost two meters. Plasma exhaust spit out of his soles, the blue flame aimed at two of the goons, blinding them. Their screams distracted the other two. Jaxon cut thrust and landed, his sword aimed at a third goon; bionic fingers fell away from the goon's hand.

Jaxon's sword clashed with the fourth goon's axe. The weapon was unbalanced and the goon misjudged Jaxon's maneuvers. The crossglaive sang through the air and the fourth goon's organic forearm came off.

Jaxon aimed to disarm, not to kill. The planet was full of replacement limbs, after all. His heart ticked hard at his ribs like it would burst. It wasn't just the fight taking its toll on him. Something was wrong with his breathing.

A boot Jaxon didn't see coming struck his leg at a bad angle, sending shockwaves of fire through his body. The blinded goons regained their sight. Pain staggered Jaxon enough for the goon's super-heated blade to nearly spear him through the chest. He deflected it, but not before the blade grazed his arm. A short agonizing yelp escaped Jaxon's throat, the stink of his own burned skin filling his nose. Quick, Jaxon maneuvered into a thrust and the goon's artificial forearm dropped from his body. The one remaining goon saw his three friends writhing in pain on the dirty wet pavement and respectfully abstained.

Uthay didn't approve. This was a man used to getting his way. Used to winning. He released Yoko and she crumpled to the ground with a splash, still holding her shattered nose. Uthay leveled a gun at Jaxon.

Without thinking, Jaxon swung his blade and the barrel of Uthay's gun slid away, splashing into a puddle. Jaxon breathed hard from exhaustion.

Uthay put his hands up. "Okay. I'm smart enough to recognize when I've been beat. I'll go. But now she owes me triple. And you, my friend, you just made this personal." Uthay backed out of the alley with his maimed goons. They took their severed limbs with them. The brief fight winded Jaxon, the continuous pull of the planet's gravity on his body having made him feel like someone was standing on his head.

Jaxon collapsed his crossglaive and approached Yoko. She was still on the wet ground mumbling obscenities. Jaxon attempted to help her stand. She swatted his hand away and pulled herself up.

"Look what you did," Yoko said, touching her cut cheek and wincing. "I told you I didn't need your help. If I can't defend myself then I deserve the beating." Her nose looked crooked. She stumbled. Jaxon reached out to catch her. A silver palm shot out to stop him.

"*Don't touch me*," she snapped. "I've been touched enough for one night."

Jaxon pulled back his hands, as if she were a hot iron that would burn him. He stepped back, putting space between them. "I had to do something. They were going to kill you."

"Stupid foosha hoo-mon," Yoko muttered. She picked up the pommel of a deactivated energy knife left by one of the goons and pocketed it. "I owe Uthay money. He's a brute, but he's not stupid. He knows I can't pay him back if I'm dead. But he doesn't like being humiliated. Now he might actually kill me. Because you wanted to be a hero."

Her words cut Jaxon. Guilt nestled in his throat. He might as well have been the one who'd put his hands on her. "I saw someone being hurt and I stopped it. I'm not going to apologize for that." His voice was strained, the phantom pain of his wounds crisscrossing his body.

Yoko's mouth twisted into a grimace. "Is that how you go through life, hoo-mon? Deciding whose business you feel entitled to interfering with? If you wanted to help me you should have walked away. Now I have to get off of this rock while I still can."

"About that. I found you because I need to charter a flight to Earth." His injured leg ached and his burned arm stung. He ignored the pain as best he could, still panting from the fight.

"Then you're out of luck," Yoko said. "I'm currently not taking on stupid hoo-mon passengers."

"I can pay up front."

Yoko froze. She stared at him, looked him over, considering. Then with a defeated sigh she said, "Fine. I'm now taking on stupid hoo-mon passengers. You are talking to the best pilot throughout the known worlds."

Jaxon's neck jerked. "That's not what your customer reviews say."

Yoko's thick caterpillar eyebrows frowned, the rest of her oval face remaining perfectly still. "Okay. Fair. I may not be the best, but I am competitively priced. Errf, right?"

"*Earth.*"

Her tongue rolled around inside her cheek. "Yeah, I can do that. For nine thousand cubits."

Jaxon frowned. "Hey. Your listing says three thousand."

"That was before you made Uthay triple my debt. Now it's triple the price. Nine thousand."

"I can do three thousand."

"Six thousand."

"Three thousand."

"Okay okay, four thousand."

"*Three thousand.*"

"Foosha," she mumbled, annoyed. "Fine. But you pay right now. And you fly me back to my ship with those boots of yours. Just don't go too high. I'd like what little food I have in my stomach to stay in my stomach."

Jaxon pulled out his handheld. With a few taps and a flick of his finger he sent the payment. Yoko pulled up her handheld, the cracked screen displaying the transfer confirmation.

"Good news hoo-mon, you just bought yourself a pilot."

Chapter Five: Yoko

Diffused sunlight pierced the clouds over Giannis as the world entered its four-hour long dawn. The pounding rain decided to let up.

Yoko dropped out of the sky, her eyes closed tight as she straddled Jaxon like a person-shaped backpack. Below them was starship row, a large parking lot several kilometers from the city; the number of privately owned shuttles and personal transports stretched to the horizon. Next to every parking spot stood a series of pumps used to top off a ship's air supply or water tanks, for a modest fee. Gusts of wind from the near constant takeoffs and landings of ships were capable of bowling a person over if they weren't careful. Yoko always had been.

The *Saragos* was not a pretty ship. Not even after three beers and a shot of tequila. It was pushing fifty and had a lot of work done to it over the years, most of which were botched, but it was hers.

The luxury yacht was originally christened the *Rylance,* a gift for some dumb Sidonan rich kid who won the lucky sperm lottery who promptly abused and neglected the vessel. Yoko had long since learned that people never appreciate what they were given, only what they had earned. The ship was later sold and passed through a string of owners, having gone through so many name changes that the Starship Registration Bureau—the SRB—couldn't keep track of them all.

Chibak pirates seized the ship and renamed it the *Lai Saarinen.* They jerry-rigged a series of modifications including a pair of concealable point-defense gun turrets in the compartments where the emergency lifeboats went. Lifeboats that would've been useful when the ship's air scrubbers failed from lack of maintenance and the crew died of asphyxiation. Sometimes, Yoko swore she heard whispers in the cargo bay and believed their restless spirits haunted it.

Years later, the ship was acquired by a Tzipkan explorer who installed new internal radiators to better manage the ship's waste heat and retrofit the command deck to detach, becoming its own lifeboat. The explorer died of a high-g induced stroke before she could ever use it. For months the ship remained adrift until salvagers claimed it. When the crummy outdated yacht went up for auction, it only had one bidder.

Yoko was twenty-two, still quite young for a Kish. The only person she ever loved, her father, had died. Isam Tiro had been a proud Kish entrepreneur who raised his only child in his own image. He'd taught Yoko how the known worlds worked, how they ran on cubits, and how a gun was the best friend she would ever have. From him she learned that sticking her neck out for anyone would end in decapitation. Safer to keep others at a distance. The only way someone could stab you in the back was if you let them get close enough to. And if they tried, well, that's what the gun was for.

She'd bought the old beaten down ship with the money her father had left her and renamed it after a fictional ship in an old adventure book she'd read as a child. The book was about a group of friends who get sucked through a wormhole that takes them to another dimension and the crew has to find their way back home. The book was silly kids' stuff, but the image of the ship captivated her. She dreamed about it.

Her *Saragos* was a double-hulled yacht with four gimbaled decks that tilted ninety degrees depending on whether the ship was under thrust to create its own gravity or in atmosphere. Like all starships it had high resolution cameras and sensors scattered across its skin to see outside the ship in the absence of windows. Four VTOL engine pods, two on each side of the hull, hung from the ship connected by thick nacelles that resembled arched robotic arms. They could rotate 360 degrees for thrust vectoring and vertical takeoff and landing. Independent from the main reactor, the engine pods also functioned as emergency braking thrusters. This ship was Yoko's own personal world. Seeing it always filled her with accomplishment.

Yoko approached her home, shielding her injured face from the gusting wind. Jaxon gawked at the ship's visible nips and tucks, at its worn color scheme and mismatched hull plates. The crew elevator lowered down, greeting them with a concert of agonizing squeaks and groans from its rusty gears and actuators.

Jaxon's face scrunched. "Uh... is this thing safe to fly?"

"You're free to stay behind," Yoko snarked. "No refunds though." She expected the hoo-mon to give her some talk-back when he started coughing. Jaxon gripped his chest and his hacking graduated into a full-on episode. He stumbled, the rushing wind bringing him to his knees. The young man gagged, struggling to breathe. "Eh, what's wrong with you?" Yoko said, almost laughing. "That fight take more out of you than you let on, hoo-mon?" He couldn't catch his breath to respond, like he was being choked. Yoko's eyes narrowed with concern. "How long has it been since you last took your gravity meds?"

"Gravity meds?" Jaxon said between coughs.

Yoko bristled a sigh and threw her head back in frustration. "For foosha's sake. Come on," she said, grabbing Jaxon's arm and wrenching him onto the elevator. The old worn motors whined as the lift brought them into the outdated ship and onto the command deck, which was messy and lived in. Jaxon doubled over onto his back, his writhing and strained breathing signaling his impending death.

"Betty!" Yoko bellowed. Her voice reverberated in the dome-like space. The cockpit hatch opened and out stepped an attractive female mecha with bleached blonde hair tied up in a tight bun and a barcode tattoo on the back of her neck. Her stained dull green flight suit was tight-fitting, showing off her impossible hourglass figure and disproportionately large breasts. A utility belt hung loose around her wide hips, weighted down by tools. She'd been modeled after a hoo-mon pinup model with exaggerated features, but was distinctly not a living being. Making a mecha look too organic was still very much illegal. Her features were designed to trigger the uncanny valley part of an organic's brain; her eyes being a brilliant shade of emerald green that almost glowed. The ship's flat lighting hit her pale skin in a way that communicated artificiality.

Betty approached the couple in a stern, precise stride. "Yoko. You are hurt," she said in her flat monotone voice.

"I'm aware of that Betty, thank you. Help this hoo-mon. He hasn't been taking his gravity meds. Because he is a *baizuo*."

From a compartment, Betty retrieved an emergency kit and

pulled out a medical hypospray that resembled a gun, a glass vial filled with a drug cocktail of thin white liquid loaded into the barrel like a shell casing. Betty injected the flailing hoo-mon, dumping the vial of drugs into his blood stream. He breathed easier.

Yoko stared down at the pitiful hoo-mon, wondering just how he'd managed the miracle of staying alive this long. "I take it this is your first time off-world?"

"Yeah," Jaxon breathed. "You could say that. What did you give me?"

"Something to strengthen your weak and pathetic hoo-mon heart against this planet's gravity," she said. Yoko grew up on Krrexia, a planet with gravity a bit stronger than Giannis. It meant her heart and muscles had developed stronger than most. "Get up."

Jaxon lurched to his feet. He gripped a handhold embedded in the wall to stop himself from collapsing again.

"Yoko. You are hurt," Betty repeated. "I will repair you." Betty reloaded her hypospray with a different medicine and marched towards Yoko.

The silver woman's eyes widened in fear, her bushy eyebrows shooting straight up her wide forehead in abject terror. "*Nooo,*" Yoko said, her palms raised to keep Betty away. "No. You're a terrible nurse."

Jaxon's ears perked up. "But you let her treat *me*?"

"Oh. That's different," Yoko said, then took the hypospray from Betty. "Prep the ship for dustoff. We've been paid to go to the cesspool hoo-mon world."

Betty paused, her green eyes blinking. "There are two human worlds. A red one and a blue one."

"Which one is Eert?"

"*Earth* is the blue one, Yoko."

"The blue hoo-mon cesspool, then." Betty turned and sauntered back into the cockpit. Yoko pulled a container of antiseptic and bandages from the medical compartment. She straightened her broken nose with a growl and applied the antiseptic gel, then stuck the small white bandage to the bridge of her nose where the skin broke.

From a storage locker next to the elevator, Yoko retrieved two gravity harnesses; they featured thick straps around the shoulders, legs, and waist. Yoko slipped into the harness made custom for her small frame and handed the larger one to Jaxon, its weight trying to pull him back down to the decking.

"What's this for?" Jaxon asked.

An over-exaggerated groan crawled its way out of Yoko's throat. "You can *not* be this stupid. It's to stop you from floating into the walls when we leave this gravity well."

He strapped on the harness. "I didn't have to wear one of these on the starliner," Jaxon said, as if it were an excuse.

"That's because those deathtraps aren't built for atmosphere, they operate in space only," she said. "Saves on wear and tear and fuel costs. Ships like mine are built out of tougher stuff." A frightening groan rippled through the hull as the main reactor fired up.

The Gravity Drive remained the single greatest invention in the history of the known worlds. It allowed intelligent life to explore the unknown universe, but it didn't actually *create* gravity. Because the bones and organs of fleshy beings used to living in gravity didn't do so well in the prolonged absence of it, the use of kestesil became a necessity.

Kestesil was a mineral with unique magnetic properties that made some semblance of artificial gravity possible; negatively charged kestesil plates in a ship's ceiling repelled the mineral, while positively charged plates in the decking pulled the mineral down. Gravity harnesses were weighted with kestesil plates; a dial on the buckle allowed the wearer to adjust the intensity of the belt's magnetic force, creating one's own personal form of weighted gravity. Though this didn't extend outside of the ship in vacuum. In those cases, the wearer would switch to magnetic boots.

The command deck included a galley and lounge where the crew could interact, while the cockpit was concealed behind a heavy access hatch usually left open. Yoko sat down at the galley's dining table and cleaned her slashed cheek.

Jaxon joined her, still a bit wheezy and listless. "Why... does your mecha look like a human lover model?"

"Because that's what she is. Was." Yoko smeared antiseptic on her cut cheek. "One of my bitchier fares stiffed me, so I took her lover mecha and repurposed her to be a standard engineering mecha, Y-Series. Betty can fix almost anything, except a meal. She's also a decent pilot. I mean, not as good as I am, obviously, but who is?" She dry-swallowed painkillers, then passed Jaxon her antiseptic. He smeared it on his wounds. Yoko used a towel to dry her wet hair and slipped on a beanie to keep her head warm.

"We are ready to go," Betty's voice said over the ship's speakers. Yoko strapped herself into her seat and Jaxon copied her.

"Bring me the sky," Yoko said.

In the cockpit and wearing her gravity harness, Betty engaged the engine pods and the ship hovered. Landing struts retracted and folded into the ship's profile before the *Saragos* rocketed towards the sky, the force pushing everyone down into their seats.

The *Saragos* rose up from Giannis's atmosphere and the pull of the planet's gravity fell away. The ship's four gimbaled decks rotated 90 degrees forward into their "office building" configuration with the command deck acting as its penthouse. The lower decks were accessible through a service ladder towards the rear of the deck that ran the length of the ship when in this mode.

Yoko unstrapped from her seat and adjusted the dial on her gravity harness to keep her feet planted on the decking. Betty and Jaxon did the same. Yoko strolled into the cockpit and took her pilot's chair. Thrust from the main engine, which was now positioned below them, created downward force equivalent to a third of a full g. If the ship unexpectedly lost power or had to make a sharp maneuver, having their gravity harnesses turned off would be tantamount to not wearing a seatbelt in a high-speed crash.

Yoko increased the ship's burn and the *Saragos* left Giannis in its rear view. Upon reaching the designated egress point, Yoko spun up the Gravity Drive, checking and double checking her calculations until she was satisfied they were accurate before initiating the drive. A beam of focused gravitons shot out of the ship's nose and into infinity in the form of an intense white light, pulling the *Saragos* into slipstream.

Now that Yoko was away from Giannis, she left Betty at the helm and returned to the galley so she could reunite with her best friends.

Namely, her impressive collection of firearms. Still sore from her beating, Yoko carefully removed her jacket with a groan, revealing a pair of red suspenders she always wore that kept her loose-fitting pants up. She didn't like belts. They were tacky and lacked style. Yoko strapped an apparatus to the length of her right forearm that, on command, would slide a small pistol down her sleeve and into her palm. Yoko loved her friends.

Jaxon watched her from his seat at the galley table, the pull of his gravity harness making him slouch. "Who's that for?"

"The next shithead who puts hands on me," she grumbled.

Jaxon made a face. "It would have been useful back in the alley."

"The Giannisian justice system is very big on gun control. If I'd gotten caught with a pistol or used it to defend myself, they'd have put me away for life and impounded my ship."

"Uthay didn't seem to care."

"Uthay is Uthay," Yoko shrugged. "He and the authorities have an 'understanding.' He only pulled that piece because some idiot hoo-mon maimed his guards and threatened to gut him with an energy sword." She slid on her jacket, concealing the apparatus, then retrieved a bottle of bourbon whiskey named after a famous hoo-mon known as Jim Beam. She poured the amber liquid into a magnetic bulb with an oval nipple lid and took an elevated seat at the galley table across from Jaxon. "So," she drank. "Judging by said energy sword and those atrocious rags you're wearing, I reckon you're one of those crazy Kaijen zealots. That right?"

Jaxon's eyes flashed with offense. "We're not *zealots*. The sacred Kaijen are ancient warriors of justice who fight for freedom and species equality."

Yoko snorted a laugh. "But that's stupid. Not all living beings are equal."

Jaxon's jaw hung open. "What? Of course they are. How could you say something so bigoted?

"Because it's *true*," she said matter-of-factly. "Tell me, are you a great pilot?"

Jaxon blinked. "No. I don't even know how to fly."

"Well, I *am*," Yoko said. "I'm better at something than you are. That means we're not equal. If someone let you pilot a ship people would die."

"I could learn," Jaxon said.

"But you would never be *great*. Equal means the same."

"That's ridiculous. Every living person is equal in every way regardless of species, gender, or physical form."

Yoko's non-drink hand shot up. "Wait wait wait wait," she said, one of her caterpillars hiked. "You... you actually *believe* that nonsense? So you're in favor of lowering the hoop?"

Jaxon's face twisted in confusion. "Lowering the hoop? I don't..."

Yoko's eyes rolled, over-exaggerating. "Where I come from there used to be a sport called Speed Hoop. Two teams run around a rectangular court trying to throw a ball into a high basket with no bottom."

Jaxon squinted. "You mean *basketball*?"

"That's the knockoff version you hoo-mons created," she mocked. "As I was saying, Speed Hoop was our most popular sport. It was watched by billions over the wireless and raked in trillions of cubits in revenue across the known worlds. Until," she interrupted herself with a labored sigh, "a bunch of moral busy bodies accused the taller players of having 'height privilege', so they had the hoop lowered to make the game easier for shorter players."

"Well, that's good," Jaxon nodded. "No one should have an unfair advantage over anyone else. That's what equality is all about."

"*No. Not good,*" Yoko said, emphasizing each word. "Lowering the hoop ruined the game. Sure, it gave the shorter players better access to the hoop, but the game became too easy. The exceptional players stopped trying. Stopped doing their best. The game got boring and lack of competition led to laziness, and the people stopped watching. The entire industry went broke and the Kish economy crashed."

Jaxon shrugged. "But only tall players could win the game. How is that fair?"

Yoko cursed under her breath. "Life isn't fair, hoo-mon." She paused to gulp her whiskey. Talking always made her thirsty and drinking always got her talking.

"Then what are the disadvantaged and marginalized players supposed to do?" Jaxon asked.

"Something they're good *at*," Yoko shot back. "Life is a foot race. We can't all come in first place. There's always going to be winners and losers. That doesn't mean you can tie weights to the fastest runners and call it equity. The busy bodies didn't understand this and ended up spreading their poison to other aspects of our culture." Bitter memories of her childhood flashed behind her glassy eyes. They brought with them a guttural anger that tightened her throat and made her teeth grind. The alcohol did little to soothe her. She hid her resentment behind a strained smile. "No one was brave enough to stand up to them. That's how they were able to seize power."

"You mean by force?" Jaxon said.

Yoko belched a wet chuckle. "Oh, I wish, hoo-mon. That would have been more interesting. At least then there might have been some kind of uprising." Swig. "No, they were *elected*. The worst ones always are. No one reaches the heights of political power without being masters of manipulation and deceit."

"But if that's what the majority of the people voted for then it must have been the correct choice," Jaxon said.

A rogue vein in Yoko's forehead pulsed. It threatened to pop. For a moment she considered spacing him. "Weak people make bad decisions. Once we let the parasites take over our culture everything collapsed. The first thing they did was pass the Violence Reduction Act that took away everyone's right to have weapons. Even knives used to cut food. *For our protection.*" She bit the words. "The worse the legislation gets the nicer the name becomes. Then any speech critical of the government meant you disappeared, because censoring information was called protecting the truth. All it took was a few idiots and a lot of weak civilians to destroy our entire way of life and brought on the starving times. All in the name of safety." She returned to her liquor cabinet and poured more amber into her mug. Somehow it didn't taste right this time. "But hey, at least now everyone's equal. Equally impoverished."

"The Kaijen don't have that problem," Jaxon said, talking a little too fast. A little too eager. "We can transfer our memories and skills to others. There's no need for lies or manipulation. The Kaijen have no desire for power because we're all equals."

Yoko stared at him from across the galley for a long breath. *Oh my God, he's serious.* She almost regretted giving him the gravity drugs. Almost. He was young and naive. There was still fun to be had.

A skeptical laugh she tried harder than she normally would have to hold in escaped her. "But you're not even allowed to have sex, right? Aren't you all a bunch of voluntary celibates? Doesn't sound very equal to me, hoo-mon." Jaxon's forehead creased. Her words affected the brown hoo-mon deeper than she'd expected. It amused her. His annoyance was palpable enough to taste.

"That's misinformation. That's— it's—," Jaxon stammered. "Sexual relationships are a tool of the elites. It keeps us all enslaved to the system." He recited the words, as if he were reading a script.

It made Yoko's wide smile even wider. "Oh, is it now?" she said, eyes wide, feigning surprise. "I had no idea I was being oppressed every time someone made my toes curl."

Jaxon cringed, as though he were visualizing that image, then brushed the thought aside. "It's a distraction," he said. "Our devotion as Kaijen should only be to the group, not to the individual. We reject anything that doesn't serve that goal. Wealth, material possessions, offspring—"

"And people *sign up* for this? Willingly?" She returned to her seat and swigged from her mug. "It must be because of the superpowers, right? You people can supposedly move things with your minds, right? Like witches?" Her words slurred, but they continued to push Jaxon's buttons.

"We're not *witches*," Jaxon said, his voice rising. "You can't just unjustly criticize something."

"I can unjustly criticize *anything*. And I *do*. Regularly."

Jaxon talked past her. "When you become a Kaijen your brain undergoes certain physical changes that allow you to use a form of mental telekinesis. It's called tuning."

"Or in other words, superpowers," she said, setting down her mug. "Great. Let's see it. Show them to me."

"It doesn't work like that," he said, his volume having shrank. "Only the most skilled Kaijen can tune on command."

Yoko's face scrunched into a frown. "So that's not you then?" Her words dripped with flippant disdain. "What a scam. If you can't do it just say so. Stop pretending. It's false advertising." The young hoo-mon looked desperate to prove himself to her.

His eyes focused on her half full mug of whiskey. He concentrated for a long moment...

The mug vibrated ever so slightly, hardly a tremor. Its amber liquid sloshed, the little mug wanting to lift up from the table, but couldn't. Jaxon began to sweat. His whole body shook. The effort seemed to be killing him. He pushed himself, trying to hold it...

The mug tipped over, the amber liquid spilling almost in slow motion in the low gravity, trickling over the table's edge into a messy puddle on the decking.

"That was fifty cubits worth of apple whiskey you just wasted, hoo-mon," Yoko glared.

"My name is Jaxon Troy. Not *hoo-mon*."

"I've already forgotten your name," Yoko said and set her mug straight. "Only a *baizuo* would give up sex for lame superpowers like yours."

"My translator doesn't recognize that word, *baizuo*."

"Kish epithets can have multiple meanings. Depending on the intent a *baizuo* could be a fool or idiot, simpleton, foosha asshole, or —"

"Moron," Jaxon interrupted. "You're calling me a moron."

Yoko smiled. "Look at that. You're smarter than you look, hoo-mon."

Betty came from the cockpit, saw the mess, and began to clean it up. Jaxon knelt down to help her. Betty didn't appear to understand why.

"Do you by chance have anything I can eat?" Jaxon said to anyone.

"You triple my debt, you waste my booze, now you expect me to feed you?" Yoko said. "You are a bold one. Betty, could you please find the sexless hoo-mon something to fill his mouth?"

Betty finished cleaning the mess and brought Jaxon a plate of something from the galley's food stores. It resembled an unappetizing squid. Jaxon stared at the creature for a moment, then stabbed at it with a fork. It wiggled to dodge the pronged utensil. Jaxon recoiled. "Uh... it's still alive."

Yoko cocked her neck. "It's bokah. It's supposed to be alive."

Jaxon's nose wrinkled. "You can't cook it?"

Yoko shrugged. "Why? What weirdo eats dead bokah? Gross. The disrespect of you hoo-mons."

Jaxon couldn't bring himself to eat the creature. It looked up at him with its big sad adorable eyes, pleading for clemency. Its cuteness didn't sway Yoko. It just made the creature seem more delicious. She snatched the little slimeball off the plate, shoved it in her mouth, and chewed. Its little tentacles fought and clawed for life before Yoko's black lips sucked them back into her mouth and chewed harder. Jaxon looked ready to heave.

"I love the way it slithers on the way down," Yoko said, then swallowed.

***

Three staccato flashes of light preceded the *Saragos* before it dropped out of slipstream. It arrived in the Sol system below the plane of the ecliptic a good distance outside of Earth's security net, giving the ship enough time to safely decelerate before the defense net would have cause to turn the vessel into atoms.

Yoko sat strapped in her pilot's chair padded with shock-absorbing gel that hugged her like a pillow. She chatted with traffic control, giving them her sweet innocent voice while they authenticated her registration with the SRB and approved an approach vector. Three high-definition screens wrapped halfway around the bubble-shaped room like a windshield, feeding Yoko a wealth of information about the ship's systems. Dradis scanners allowed the ship to see in three dimensions, giving her real-time updates on the area several hundred kilometers around the ship as well as long range scans with information on the system's heavy space traffic.

It would be an additional hour, maybe two, before the ship would be cleared for atmospheric descent. Yoko passed the time by reading a novella on her handheld, giggling to herself. Every so often she'd peak over the top of her handheld at Jaxon sitting in the non-copilot's passenger seat. His eyes were fixed on a small screen near the co-pilot's controls, scrolling through newsfeeds. He'd been trying to find any information he could on his dead friends, caught between desperately wanting to know what happened to them and terrified of what he might find. Yoko could relate.

"How do you know they're dead, exactly?" Yoko asked.

"Just a feeling," he said without looking away from the feeds.

"So you're not sure. They could be alive."

"My friend Castor survived, I think. At least I didn't see him die."

"Didn't *see him die*, meaning what exactly?"

He hesitated. "I had... a premonition."

Yoko chewed back a laugh. "Ah. Is that another one of your superpowers?"

"It's not supposed to be."

"Hmm. Does it work with cards? Or the lottery? I might be willing to give up sex for that." She scrolled to the next page of her book. She read the first sentence and giggled, then noticed Jaxon staring at her.

"What are you reading?" he asked.

"A book," Yoko said, irked.

"What *kind* of book? What's it about?"

"An Eltaebian comedian," she said, still reading.

"I've never heard of that species before."

"They're a hermit people. Their home world is beyond the catapult." The catapult being shorthand for the massive Protectorate owned graviton emitter they controlled; a gigantic machine capable of catapulting ships tens of thousands of lightyears to the neighboring Perseus Arm of the Milky Way galaxy. "In the Eltaebian culture, being funny or saying funny things is punishable by death."

"Damn," Jaxon said.

"But this guy, the protagonist, he decides to openly tell his jokes anyway. It turns out everyone laughs and people love it."

"So what happens to the comedian?"

"Well, the government executes him, obviously," Yoko said. "His ghost is retelling the story in a satirical fashion."

"Wait, if it's forbidden how did the author get it published?"

"He was smuggled to our part of the galaxy and had it published here. It's banned on their side of the catapult. That hasn't stopped it from being shared around though. This one book started an entire revolution on the Eltaebian home world."

The revelation floored him. "But still, isn't it kind of unnerving? Reading about people from a totally different culture on the other side of the galaxy? You don't find it hard to relate?"

"They're still people. They breathe oxygen, drink water, eat, sleep, shit. Most of them, anyway. I don't need someone to be exactly like me to understand them. Plus, anything that pokes fun at governments is alright by me."

"Even if you were the government?" Jaxon said.

"*Especially* if I was the government," Yoko said. Jaxon laughed and smiled at her. It was strange for Yoko, having a casual interaction with a living person that didn't involve swapping cubits or insults. His smile was contagious. It coaxed a near invisible smirk out of Yoko.

"When I was a kid the only books I read were comic books," Jaxon said.

"You mean books about comedians?"

"No, comic books— illustrated picture books, usually about superheroes," Jaxon said, talking with his hands. "My favorite superhero was a character called Spider-Wolf."

Yoko's head jerked. "Is this a horror creature? With multiple eyes and limbs?"

"No," Jaxon laughed. "He's a human, but he has super strength and can scale buildings because he was bitten by a genetically engineered wolf spider."

Yoko's eyes narrowed, mulling over this information. Her thick eyebrows furrowed. "I'm pretty sure that's now genetic engineering works. This is sounding very far-fetched, hoo-mon."

Jaxon's mouth opened to speak, then melted into shock. He'd stopped scrolling the feeds and his screen zoomed in on something. Whatever it was, he read it very carefully to himself. Yoko tried to sneak a look.

"I found them," Jaxon said, his voice tight with dread. "The survivors of the monastery attack were taken to Dasmis Memorial."

"Survivors?"

"Yeah. Two of them."

Chapter Six: Akeema

She couldn't move.

Her nerves had been severed, like being a conscious corpse. Despite herself, Akeema wished she'd been killed. She imagined her soul floating up out of her body and being whisked away to wherever souls went when they'd gotten their fool selves killed. Because the alternative was far too cruel to face.

Akeema opened her eyes, tears blurring her vision. The clear fluid amplified the intensity of the blinding white light. *Please let this be the afterlife. Please let me be dead.* But she continued to draw breath. Dead women didn't breathe.

Surviving meant being forced to live with her failure and the wounds that came with it. That reality tasted like rotten meat, a flavor she'd been all too familiar with. Death truly did feel like the better option to her.

"She's conscious," a disembodied voice hollered to someone. "Ma'am, you've been seriously injured. Don't try to move," a different voice told her. She'd already tried. The only thing she felt was terrified. "What's your name? Can you tell me your name?"

"Find..." she muttered. "Find my father. Tell him... I love him."

"You can tell him yourself," the voice said.

"I'm forbidden," she said, her voice breaking. "My name is... Akeema."

"Hold on Akeema. You're going to survive." They jammed an oxygen tube down her throat. It was like an assault. She couldn't speak. What she really wanted to do was scream, the option having been stolen from her. Akeema could hear and she could see, but she couldn't feel *anything* below her neck. Just numb.

Most of her vertebrae and spinal nerves were destroyed, a long, charred gash stretching the length of her back. It stopped just short of her cervical vertebrae, likely the reason why she hadn't died immediately. The fact Akeema had survived such an otherwise fatal wound was less a miracle and more a testament to her stubbornness.

The medics strapped her to a gurney, careful not to cause her further injury, and loaded Akeema onto an emergency medical shuttle. She knew outsiders never visited the monastery, and she obviously hadn't called the medics herself. That meant Martel hadn't killed everyone. There had to be at least one survivor, other than her. She guessed Castor. Akeema imagined him cutting the head off of the tattooed asshole who'd done this to her. It was a strange feeling for her, hating someone so intensely who she'd only met once.

Akeema spent the flight drifting in and out of consciousness. In the fog of her mind, the trauma of her condition uncovered a childhood memory she'd long since buried. She'd been born in the People's Republic of California, pre-collapse. The roads were all torn up. The electric cars hadn't been charged in years. Most buildings were decimated. Akeema's mother, Iraya, had found a safe place for her husband and daughter to hide from the violence and rape gangs. Iraya had been a short woman with hair even redder than Akeema's. She'd once been a thick round woman, but the regime's crackdown on food and necessities had eaten away at her shape until she'd become little more than skin in bones, resembling an Irish peasant girl.

The last memory Akeema had of her mother was when she was five-years-old. Her father had been attacked by looters two days earlier, they'd broken his arm. Iraya volunteered to go to the underground market to trade for milk and eggs in his place. She took with her a knife and their only gun, kissed Akeema on the crown of her head, and said, "I'll be right back."

She never saw her mother again.

There was nothing worse than the fear of not knowing. For years Akeema assumed her mother had abandoned them. At the time, she hadn't known about the astounding death rates or the number of unrecorded disappearances in the country. When it was clear her mother wasn't coming back, Akeema's father packed what little he could carry with his busted arm and began the journey to the neighboring country of the Texas Republic. They made the crossing in the dead of night. Guards shot at them with rifles as a coyote helped them through the border wall to safety. Her father caught a lead bullet in his abdomen while protecting his baby girl, the image of her father's bright red blood on her clothes burned in her mind. Akeema cried so hard her eyes ached.

He'd survived, but Akeema held that mix of pain and fear and hopelessness in her heart for the rest of her life. Only now, she could no longer feel it.

Her shuttle touched down on a landing pad at Dasmis Memorial, the largest medical facility on the planet, named after the Iskaran who initiated first contact humanity and introduced the known worlds to Earth's life-saving cocaine. Physicians throughout those worlds came to Earth to practice medicine and treat the planet's massive influx of sick and needy. The majority of doctors who'd been born on the planet had their residency at Dasmis Memorial.

Akeema was rushed into emergency surgery. Her clothes were cut away and her skin was sterilized for bacteria and other contagions. Her entire spine had to be removed and replaced. Akeema's surgeon was Qadeeran, a six-armed four-legged species with four tiny fingers on each hand. Qadeerans were said to be some of the best surgeons in the known worlds, their many hands able to perform multiple tasks at once. The technology to regrow Akeema a new spine existed, but that procedure would take days. And there was a high chance her body would reject the artificially grown cells. The process would take time she just didn't have.

Cybernetics had become the cheaper option when it came to organic replacements. Vetronium was a unique metal compound that could be programmed to form extremely complex structures while remaining light weight and stronger than tungsten. Akeema's crossglaive had been forged from the same programmable metal, as was the crossglaive that had paralyzed her. Now the metal would be part of her forever. The only real downside was the chronic pain that usually came with the prosthetic, which could last the rest of the patience's life. The rate of post-surgery suicides was above average, often a result of accidental overdose of painkillers.

Incisions were made with a surgical laser; a clean rectangular flap of skin on Akeema's back opened, exposing her wrecked spine. The swatch of char marks spanning her entire lumbar and thoracic vertebrae were trimmed away. Akeema was left awake during this.

The surgeon's six hands and twenty-four fingers cut the old spine out with machine-like precision, preserving the undamaged nerves, and preparing them to receive the cybernetic replacement. Two assistant human doctors and a few mecha nurses buzzed around the operating room aiding with the handling of Akeema's new vetronium spine. It resembled an over-sized gunmetal centipede. The prosthetic crawled with tentacle-like microfibers on either end that were programmed to attach to Akeema's existing nerves and transmit their electrical signals to her brain just like her organic ones.

Fourteen hours later, the surgery ended and the numbness gradually became a tingle, the first signs of a successful operation.

Akeema's flap of back skin was sealed with regenerative gel, speeding up the healing process. A bio-bandage was placed over her entire back; a large anti-bacterial band-aid that would significantly reduce the chances of infection.

Despite all of the advanced technology that went into restoring Akeema's mobility, the rate of success for these types of procedures had still been only fifty-four percent. A coin flip. And Akeema's injury was more extreme than usual. The chance she might be paralyzed forever wasn't zero. It was too early to tell.

If the odds turned out not to be in her favor, Akeema had no intention of being trapped in her body for the rest of her days. She would persuade Castor to give her an honorable death. If not Castor, then Jaxon, who'd been spared from the massacre. Akeema was certain she could guilt him into doing it. Into letting her die. Convince him it was mercy even though Akeema knew in her heart it would be her cowardice. But she knew she could depend on Jaxon. He'd do it for her. If she asked.

Since girlhood, Akeema had always been an early riser. She'd been born in an unstable region of the world where she couldn't sleep for more than a few hours without being awakened by the distant sounds of violence. She'd never slept more than eight hours straight throughout her entire existence. For thirteen hours she'd been locked in a black void of nothingness colder than the arctic.

Deep in the bowels of her subconscious, she began to dream. Akeema couldn't feel the weight of her own body, but she knew she was running. This would be another chapter in the ongoing nightmare she'd experienced as a scared little vagrant girl afraid of the dark. Something was chasing her in the blackness. Over her shoulder she saw a horned monster with skin redder than Akeema's hair pursuing her. Perhaps to consume her.

But it wasn't a monster. Not really.

She imagined a hulking beast, a bundle of thick claws and sinewy muscle. Even its breasts had sharp teeth. For the longest time Akeema assumed the monster was a representation of one of her many fears. Her fear of not knowing what had happened to her mother. Her fear of starvation. Of dying before she'd gotten the chance to do anything noteworthy. If the monster ever caught her, she feared it would slash her to bits.

Martel had already done that. This imaginary creature couldn't hurt her anymore than she'd already been. She stopped running. Akeema confronted her demon. It approached her. It didn't scare her; Akeema's lack of fear having changed her perception of it. The monster had become too alluring to be frightening. It no longer chased her. It was following her. Its skin was smooth, its face heart shaped. Its horns were curved back and its long claws resembled fingernails. The closer she got to the demon, the more she felt its warmth. And it was smiling.

The creature reached its long wet vine-like fingers out to touch her...

***

A burrowing pain wrenched Akeema awake.

She'd been taken to the intensive care unit and secured to a gimbaled medical harness. It would put as little pressure as possible on her healing spinal column while the microfibers did their work. Pain was a good thing. It meant she could feel again, but the agony was punishing even with the cocktail of sedatives being pumped into her bloodstream, as if her dream demon had found its way out of her subconscious and had its way with her. That would have been more interesting than what really happened. She never could've imagined this level of pain was possible.

If Akeema had been told that someone had poured lava down

her spine, she wouldn't have believed them. Lava would've been colder. The misery caused her to pass out. She would awaken for brief stretches only for the anguish to knock her out again. Time passed before the torment finally began to let up. The pain transitioned into something a tiny bit less excruciating. More of an intense itch she couldn't scratch. Suffering was a story people told themselves.

When Akeema would regain consciousness there would be a nurse at her bedside checking the status of her spinal graph or emptying her colostomy pouch. The steady beep of her vitals monitor annoyed her. She let herself slip back into the black void of sleep where the demon waited to greet her. She decided not to sleep. When Martel slashed her back, he'd cut off her ponytail, leaving the ends singed. It was like losing a limb. She missed the tightness in her scalp from her taut braids. Now her hair hung shoulder length, sloppy and uneven.

A mecha nurse stood in her room, dressed in mint green scrubs. Its build was genderless and skinless, its face smooth and generic aside from its liquid green eyes. With a gentle touch, the mecha untangled her ginger locks and sheared off the burned sections of scarlet, fashioning her red coils into a neat bob. Akeema's lack of speech prevented her from thanking the nurse even though she knew the mecha was incapable of appreciation.

Sleep chased her. She couldn't outrun it any longer. This time there were no dreams. No demon. No guilt. Only the dark. This time, it didn't hurt.

The combination of painkillers and being suspended from her medical harness gave her a sense of weightlessness. She was flying. She was in a place where no one could touch her. She was safe. The sharp sound of squeaking shoes against tiled floor brought her back, the shoes stopping next to her.

"Wake up, Miss Barbeau," a disembodied voice said. A woman's voice. The kind that sounded artificial and insufferably cheerful. So, a doctor. "Can you hear me? Ma'am? I need you to wake up now, please."

The medical harness had locked into place with Akeema facing the ceiling. The doctor's head poked itself into Akeema's view, peering down at her.

The sight of the Batelaan's bio-luminescent skin startled Akeema. She'd lived down the street from a Batelaan family when she and her father migrated to Atlantic America, Kentucky Provence. Her Batelaan neighbors often wore full-body clothing to conceal their translucent skin, otherwise people would stare. Kids, mostly. Exposing their skin allowed for a lava lamp-type view of the inky clouds of glowing blood-like bio fluid churning and sloshing around beneath their epidermis. The liquid pulsed like a heartbeat. In this doctor's case, the fluid was a sparkling amber that matched her eyes. Only her hands and hairless head were uncovered.

"Ms. Barbeau," the woman repeated, a friendly smile tucked in the corner of her semi-clear mouth. "I'm Doctor Erivo. I've been assigned to monitor your recovery. Do you understand what I'm saying?"

Akeema attempted to speak. Her words came out in gargled dry barks. Then after a moment, "Sur… survivors?" Talking felt like coughing up thorns.

The doctor's brilliant amber eyes snapped and she brought up a medical pad much larger than a typical handheld. Her pellucid finger slid and stabbed at the device, her eyes scanning fast moving data that Akeema couldn't see.

"Yes. One other. Castor… Zhecheva." She quietly mouthed the name to herself before speaking it. Akeema wondered if the doctor had looked up the pronunciation of her own name beforehand, which people had often pronounced as bar-*boo* instead of bar-*bow*. "I can assure you that he's being well taken care of. So then. How are you feeling?"

"Wonderful," she lied, her lips straining to release the words. The doctor removed a stylus from her pocket and dragged it across Akeema's palm.

"Do you feel that?"

"Tickles."

"That's good," the doctor said, then tapped something on her pad. "Your nerves are regrowing properly." She moved to the end of the harness, her shoes continuing to squeak. The doctor ran the stylus up and down the length of Akeema's foot. "And that? Do you feel it?"

Akeema stiffened. "No," she choked.

The doctor tapped more characters into her pad, all while maintaining that stupid fake smile of hers. "It's nothing to be worried about. Sometimes the nanoprobes need a little more time to repair the damaged nerves before any progress can be seen."

"I'll never be able to walk again," Akeema said. It wasn't a question.

The doctor's mouth gaped open, the swirling liquid under her skin churning a bit faster. "No. Oh, no," she said apologetically. She cupped Akeema's hand in both of hers. The doctor's skin was cool and clammy. Up close, the fluid twirling beneath her skin had become a distraction. "No need to worry. You're on track to regain full mobility, it's just a matter of when. Until then you will be supplied with a standard hover chair with full waste disposal capabilities and—"

"I want to see it," Akeema said.

It took a moment for the doctor to understand. When she did, her manufactured smile receded. "I... wouldn't recommend that. You need to keep your stress levels down and it's not—"

"Show... me," Akeema said, steel in her voice. The doctor chewed on the request for a few breaths. Her foot adopted a nervous tapping. The doctor stole a quick look over her shoulder. When she was convinced no one would see her she rotated the harness so that Akeema was facing the floor. Doctor Erivo removed a small node from her pad that resembled a tiny metal egg; a wireless diagnostic scanner. She parted Akeema's gown and waved the node over Akeema's spine.

With a groan the doctor bent down, holding the pad so that Akeema could see the live feed. At first, all she saw was the bio-bandage spanning her back. It did a fantastic job hiding the damaged tissue. The doctor made an adjustment on her pad, allowing the node to see beneath the bio-bandage like an X-ray.

What Akeema saw chilled her. Columns of stacked metal protruded out of her skin in a way that resembled a thick column of linked chain with the scar tissue around it, discolored and gruesome.

Tears dripped onto the pad and rolled down to the tiled floor.

***

Akeema's harness had been repositioned and locked into place. Miserable, she faced the ceiling. Akeema hadn't realized that she'd fallen asleep again until a warm stiff squeeze clasped her hand. Fingers. Her eyelids were heavy as dumbbells. They didn't want to open. She forced them to. Just enough for her brain to register a face.

She saw Castor, and her tears began to pour again. He was seated at her bedside, asleep from exhaustion. She noticed something wrong with his right hand, as if he were wearing a metal glove. Then she saw a bio-bandage wrapped around his forearm where his hand had been severed. She realized Martel had mutilated them both.

The ache of her healing spine didn't hold a candle to the expanding mushroom cloud of rage swelling within her chest. The beep of her heart monitor went from slow and steady to a sprint. Castor stirred awake. He gripped her hand tighter with his organic hand, then cupped his cold cybernetic hand over her warm one. It surprised her how gentle the metal hand felt against her skin. Her throat dried up. She couldn't get her words to leave her mouth.

"Can you hear me?" Castor said. She squeezed his hand. He coughed out a strange half laugh, half gasp. He looked ready to bawl. "I thought I'd lost you," he choked. "The medics didn't believe me when I told them you were still alive. You are officially the toughest person I've ever known." Warm lips pressed against her pale forehead. More tears streaked her cheeks.

Akeema heard the door open. The warmth of Castor's touch left her hand as he stood from his chair and met the newcomer. Akeema's harness prevented her from turning her head too far to one side. She tried anyway, then heard the familiar sounds of a rough hug, the kind men usually gave each other.

"It's good to see you my friend," Castor's muffled voice said, his mouth half buried in the other man's shoulder.

"I'm just glad you're alive," Jaxon's voice said. He sounded on the verge of tears. "How is she?"

Castor dried his wet eyes on his sleeve. "It's a miracle she's alive. They had to replace her entire spinal column, but everything went smoothly. The doctors say she'll make a full recovery."

Akeema forced her wet eyes to open a sliver. She saw Jaxon examining Castor's new hand. It was exquisite in its own way. Lots of indented grooves along the fingers that allowed his digits to bend backwards. His wrist could rotate 360 degrees. Akeema's 10-year-old self would've thought it was the coolest shit ever.

Jaxon looked as if he were attending a funeral, as if he'd been the one who'd done this to his friend.

"Castor, I'm sorry," Jaxon stammered. "I'm so sorry. I should've been there. I could've *helped*."

"Then that maniac would have killed you too," a third rusty voice said. Castor and Jaxon turned at the same time and saw Akeema, her words having picked the lock of her mouth and broken free. The boys hurried over to her side, as if she were a small child sitting on a windowsill and threatening to fall out at any moment. They held each of her hands. Their warmth was better than sunshine.

"How much pain are you in?" Jaxon asked.

"All of it," Akeema said, trying not to laugh and failing. It hurt to laugh. Castor and Jaxon were compelled to chuckle with her until Akeema's laugh morphed into an ugly wet cough.

"You tried to warn us," Akeema said to Jaxon. "Before the transmission died. You said it would happen. How did you know he was coming there to kill us?"

Jaxon hesitated, searching for the words. The suspense felt worse than the boiling needles digging into her back. "I had… a dream. A vision," Jaxon said, his voice quiet and unsure. He laid it all out for them, recounting in detail what he saw, in what order the deaths had come, and how. Akeema wanted to believe what he'd experienced was real even though it sounded eight shades of batshit. "It was like I was there, watching it all happen as Martel killed everyone."

"Martel. That's what Priestess Nisame called him," Castor said.

"Hiroshi Martel," Jaxon confirmed. "I could see everything he was doing. And… I think he could see me, too."

"How is that possible?" Castor said, rage and frustration edging his words.

Jaxon spread his hands. "I'm just as in the dark as you are."

"Can you do it again?" Akeema cut in. "Can you control it? Can you tell us where he is? Or how we can find him?"

"And do what, Akeema?" Castor said.

"Kill him. We *kill the son of a bitch*," Akeema said.

"We tried that and we lost," Castor said.

"You want to *let* that monster get away with it? You want to just *give up*?"

"Do you think the outcome would change, Akeema?" Castor said. "We can't beat him. It's out of our hands."

In an instant, Akeema's perception of Castor had changed. To her he'd been the relentless hard working never-say-never type. Incorruptible. Now she saw him as a goddamn quitter. His grip on her hand went limp.

Akeema's tired eyes shifted to her other brother. "Jaxon, what happened to you on that planet? I remember you were hurt."

Jaxon opened his stained Kaijen robes, lifting his tunic. His bandages had already been removed, giving Akeema and Castor a look at the raised discolored slash scars across his chest and back. It looked like he'd been mauled by a grizzly bear.

"I was attacked in an alley by a pair of Thurlbii," Jaxon said.

"What are Thurlbii?" Castor asked.

"They're vicious and look like werewolves," Akeema said.

Jaxon's eyes widened. "Right? That's what I said. They jumped me."

"I went to primary school with a girl who was half Thurlbii and half Puerto Rican," Akeema said. "One of the mean girls made fun of her mixed heritage and, well, that girl ended up needing to have her jaw reattached." Jaxon and Castor winced. "What did these Thurlbii want with you?"

Jaxon shrugged. "But they cut me up so bad I nearly bled to death."

"I guess we were all touched by violence," Akeema said. "I just had to draw the short straw."

Jaxon squeezed her hand and looked her in her watery eyes. "He's going to pay for what he did to you. To all of you."

"It can't be just coincidence that you were attacked hours before we were," Akeema said. "It's all connected. Can you tell us how your premonition happened? What triggered it?"

TITAN'S FLAME

"I have no idea," Jaxon said with a mirthless laugh. "I was asleep. I thought I was dreaming. It just... happened."

"And it hasn't happened again since?" Castor asked.

"I haven't exactly been able to sleep," Jaxon said while rubbing the back of his neck. "For the last few days, I've been petrified and stressed out. I was worried Martel had killed everyone."

Castor paused for a moment, thinking. "Ever since you became a Kaijen you haven't been able to properly tune. Perhaps it wasn't a premonition you had. Maybe the link augmented a different part of your brain. A part that allows you to astral project like in some of the old Kaijen legends I've read about."

Jaxon's eyebrows shot up his brown forehead. "Across *space?*"

Castor shrugged. "Maybe. That could account for the time dilation."

Akeema stifled a chuckle. "Bullshit. That sounds like bullshit."

"Granted it's never happened to a novice Kaijen like us," Castor continued. "As far as I know only high-level priestesses and the Quorum of Elders have done anything even remotely similar. Only Kaijen who have mastered their ability to access linked memories and tune are supposed to be capable of doing it."

"Well, that's not me," Jaxon said with a dismissive laugh. "I can barely tune without pooping a little. If anything, you're way more advanced than I am. Akeema too."

"You underestimate yourself," Akeema said. She coughed, clearing the phlegm from her throat. "You always have. You were just as good as the rest of us. We were all equal."

Jaxon turned away, as if he were remembering something. "That's kind of you, Akeema. Really. But you don't have to protect my feelings. I was a terrible student and everyone knew it. I was starting to think Priestess Nisame sent me away to Giannis just to get rid of me."

"Don't say that," Akeema said. "Priestess Nisame loved you."

"I want to believe that. But I wasn't good enough. And she knew it," Jaxon said.

"None of us were," Castor said. "We are out of our depth."

"Have the elders been notified?" Akeema asked. "I assume the attack is all over the newsfeeds."

Castor gripped his artificial wrist inside of his organic hand, twisting the metal inside his palm as if he were rubbing an itch. "I called them. Or rather, they called me while you were in surgery. They're sending a high-ranking priestess to meet with us back at the monastery. She'll know what to do."

Akeema tried to unhook herself from her harness. Pinpricks of needle-like spasms shot through her back, stopping her. Castor and Jaxon rushed to help her, embarrassing her.

"What are you doing?" Jaxon said.

"If you thought I was just going to stay behind, you're crazy," Akeema said. "I'm coming with you."

Chapter Seven: Jaxon

Jaxon returned with Castor and Akeema to the monastery less than an hour before the priestess's shuttle was due to arrive. It dropped out of the sky in a controlled burn, late afternoon sunlight reflecting off of its shiny golden skin. Jaxon had to shield his eyes from the gleam. It was a small yacht-type vessel with room for two, maybe three gimbaled decks. Its shape reminded him of one of his father's old electric shavers.

Landing struts jutted out of its belly like spider legs and it touched down on the main grounds a short distance from the monastery's main entrance, its engines whirring as they powered down. The shuttle's RCS thrusters kicked up loose dirt and left odd patches of scorched black grass in their wake.

Jaxon was surprised at how extravagant the transport looked. It featured intricate design work embossed on its spotless hull, looking more like something belonging to royalty rather than a member of a religion that despised materialism. The outer airlock door hissed and slid open, allowing its boarding ramp to jut out and lower.

Priestess Sabrene appeared; a striking Iskaran woman with smooth hot pink skin, a slender frame and short vibrant cyan hair. Her irises were rings of sapphire and her long face narrowed at her jawline. Her lips curled into an enigmatic smile that never seemed to fade, and she was towering, like a small giant, or a ladder stood on its end. She had to bend forward so as not to hit her head on the airlock door's frame. Luckily for her the monastery's ceilings and walkways were high enough to accommodate her full height. She moved through them with a confident grace that dazzled Jaxon. He wondered if she were the heir to some form of aristocracy before her life as a Kaijen.

Sabrene strolled into the main hall, her hands clasped. Her extravagant sequin sari appeared to have more in common with a kimono than typical Kaijen attire. It was an elaborate garment with hand embroidered stitching and flecks of gold lace that looked to be worth even more than her shuttle. She was accompanied by her personal aid Verlain, a Tzipkan like Uthay, only significantly less ugly. Her skin was a creamy golden brown with bone protrusions along her eye sockets and short lilac hair with the left side shaved bald. Her robes were lavish, but not to the extreme of Sabrene's. When standing next to the priestess, the woman looked like an adolescent even though she was about the same height as Akeema.

Jaxon realized too late, and much to his horror, that he was still wearing his oath-breaking rocket boots. He'd been so preoccupied helping Akeema get used to piloting her mobile hover chair that it slipped his mind to get rid of them. Not that he had spare pairs of shoes lying around. His Kaijen robes were just long enough to cover the toes of the boots. If the priestess or her aid saw them he'd fast find himself in the deepest of shit.

Akeema's hover chair was bulky and concealed her lower body inside a shell of metal and ceramic with hinged covers that could open up to let her out. Its undercarriage was lined with a series of electrically charged dome-shaped plates that allowed the vehicle to levitate. When in motion the plates emitted a low but audible electromagnetic whine that sounded like a cat being strangled, just with the volume turned way down. He kept the hover chair between himself and everyone else in the hopes that no one would notice the rocket boots. To draw even less attention to himself he would let Castor or Akeema do all of the talking. He would sink into the background unnoticed. It was a skill he'd mastered for most of his life.

In the main hall, the bodies of the slain were covered and lined up in rows against one of the stone walls. Religious exemption gave the Kaijen the right to handle the funeral arrangements.

"Many greetings, Priestess Sabrene," Castor said. He and Jaxon bowed. Akeema could only bend her upper body forward slightly, her blotchy face tight with pain. She looked so different without her French braid. It would take time for Jaxon to get used to seeing her crimson hair hanging just above her shoulders like a hemmed curtain. "Thank you for coming so quickly," Castor continued. "I am Castor Zhecheva, that is Akeema Barbeau, and this is Jaxon Troy."

Sabrene ignored them. Her silence was deafening. Without looking at her aid she said, "Verlain, wait for me by the door." Verlain turned on her heel and stood by the entrance like a centurion statue keeping guard. Sabrene's attention fell on the bodies. A mess of dried blood stained the main hall's floor, resembling red-tinted oil. Stepping in it would be hard to avoid. Jaxon assumed it was the source of Sabrene's look of disgust. It wasn't. She deliberately avoided looking at Jaxon or Castor.

She only noticed Akeema.

Sabrene approached Priestess Nisame's body, the pink woman's hands held out in front of her and her palms up. She crossed her arms and touched her shoulders, her head bowed. A ritual. From her pocket she pulled out a red rose-like flower with green leaves and placed it on Priestess Nisame's still chest. "Nisame and I... we were friends. More than friends. We were sisters," Sabrene said to no one. Her voice was deep and resonant, befitting a woman of her rank and profile. She looked over her shoulder at the three humans. "How could you let this happen? This is your fault." Her cold words rang in their ears like a gunshot. "She trained you to be warriors. You should have fought like warriors."

"He was more powerful than we were," Akeema said just above a whisper. "Much more powerful. And highly trained. We weren't prepared."

Sabrene looked at Akeema, and only Akeema. "Show me, child."

They gathered at the main computer terminal, backsplash from the monitor brightening their faces. Akeema parked her hover chair in front of the terminal. She exercised the returned mobility in her fingers by working the repaired keyboard, struggling to keep the tremor in her hands from getting in the way of her scrubbing through the security footage. On the monitor they watched the playback, starting when Martel entered the main hall. They scrubbed forward to his fight with Nisame.

Sabrene paused the playback on Martel's face. "That is Hiroshi Martel. He was a former student of Nisame's at this very monastery. She took him in. Trained him to be a Kaijen warrior. And in return he betrayed her and his Kaijen oath. He was a narcissistic. A manipulator. An abuser. He raped and murdered another Kaijen student. Nisame managed to injure him before he fled the monastery in disgrace. Pure evil, that one. We all presumed he was dead."

"Not that we needed any more confirmation that he was a monster," Castor said. Sabrene continued not to acknowledge him. She shivered and rubbed her arms. It struck Jaxon as odd, given the room's warm temperature.

"Are you cold, priestess?" Jaxon asked. She didn't respond. Jaxon recalled little bits and pieces of information he'd learned about the Iskarans in primary school, them being the first alien species humanity had ever encountered. Sil Dasmis, the Iskaran explorer who changed human history forever, came from Pyralis, a planet with binary suns. So, naturally, Iskarans were used to the heat and struggled in cooler climates. There'd even been an old rumor that Sil Dasmis was immune to fire damage, though Jaxon never believed that. The only other fact he remembered was that the Iskaran females ruled over the males for centuries up until Sil Dasmis and his widespread humanitarianism sparked cultural change on Pyralis. Jaxon had also heard that the female Iskarans were much taller than the males. After seeing Sabrene, that part he believed.

"Young Jaxon," Sabrene said without looking at him. "I was told you were sent to be our envoy on Giannis."

Jaxon had to force himself to speak. "I was, priestess."

"And why are you not still there carrying out your mission?" It sounded like an accusation.

"I... I rushed back here as soon as I heard about what happened."

Sabrene pulled up her handheld. It was larger than the average handheld to accommodate her larger hands. Her eyes scanned data on its screen. "A splicer lab credited your account over 2,000 cubits. Explain." She was looking at him now, her neck tilted to peer down at him. Judging him.

Her incredible height made Jaxon feel small. It was like looking up at someone from the bottom of a pit. "I... I was attacked, priestess. I was nearly killed by two large Thurlbii."

Sabrene laughed. "Two? Does that mean you killed *them* instead?"

Jaxon stuttered. "No— no, priestess. I mean, one died, but I didn't kill him. That was an accident."

Her arms folded, her spindly fingers tapping her long thin biceps. "Then how did you survive an attack from such vicious beasts?"

Jaxon looked away in shame. "I... I ran away, priestess."

Sabrene's face sang with frustration and disappointment. "Kaijen do not *run*. We defend ourselves or die trying," she said while looking at Castor. He swallowed in response.

On the monitor, Jaxon watched his sister Kaijen being cut down by Martel's blade, one after the other in a hail of slashes and blood. Deja vu one more time. He noticed Akeema watching herself, the moment Martel slashed her spine. Her past self dropped liked a mecha someone had shut off. Akeema turned away, fighting back her tears.

Sabrene put her large pink hand on Akeema's shoulder. "Do not worry, my child. That male will pay for what he has done to you. I give you my promise." The gesture moved Akeema. His sister opened her mouth to say something, but her voice declined. She stared off to the side, hiding the emotion on her face from the others.

On the monitor, Castor watched himself being kicked into a pillar and Martel facing him down. *"Kaijen aren't noble or virtuous,"* Martel said on the video. *"They just pretend to be to manipulate idiots like us into thinking we're fighting for the right side. It's all one big lie and I can prove it—"*

Sabrene stopped the recording. "Lies," she said through her polite smile that didn't reach her eyes. "Lies and disinformation. Hiroshi Martel is a vicious liar, an obstructionist, and a speciesist, with a clear hatred of females. We cannot allow hateful speech from class enemies to destroy our institution. Our unity is our strength." Everyone nodded in a moment of silence.

"Who's Olen?" Jaxon blurted out, almost like the question had escaped his mouth against his will.

Sabrene's smile vanished, her eyes shooting daggers down at Jaxon. He might as well have farted in front of her.

"Where did you hear that name?" she said, her voice low and deathly serious.

"Priestess Nisame. She said it. To him. I just..." Jaxon was stammering now. "I just wanted to know... I thought... maybe..."

Sabrene's sapphire eyes locked onto Jaxon. Her stare was a black hole of rage that sucked in every bit of self-confidence Jaxon managed to hold on to. In that moment he was in that alley back on Giannis. All he wanted to do was run away.

Sabrene, maybe having realized the optics of the situation, calmed down and composed herself by clasping her hands in front of her. Perhaps, Jaxon wondered, to stop herself from strangling him. She regained her polite smile. "My poor child," Sabrene said. "Olen... was a former Kaijen. Someone whom I cared for, deeply. We joined the order around the same time. We even trained together. Then she... she changed."

Akeema hung on every word, her eyes still red from crying. "How? What happened?"

Sabrene exhaled. "She was revealed to be a speciesist bigot. The worst kind of violent, psychotic, unhinged obstructionist who incited hate and sedition among the Kaijen. She led an uprising that caused untold deaths. I witnessed her kill an unborn child in its mother's womb."

Castor flinched with horror. "How does that happen? How does a Kaijen go so bad so quickly?"

Sabrene gestured with her hands. "It's this materialist society the Protectorate promotes. Individualism. The appeal of consumerist culture can drive even the best of us to want more. To be more. Desire is the worst enemy of the Kaijen. We must fight it with our entire heart or it will consume us."

"What happened to this Olen person?" Akeema asked, maneuvering her hover chair to face Sabrene. Jaxon moved with her, still using the chair to hide his rocket boots from Sabrene's view.

"Olen was an incredibly skilled warrior," Sabrene said. "One of the best I'd ever seen with a crossglaive to this day. We were like sisters. But she was arrogant. She believed her abilities made her better than her sister Kaijen. A few of her less educated peers created a cult of personality around her. Worshiped her. It led to division and intense discord. A horrible battle was fought between the Kaijen and the disciples of Olen. Many were killed on both sides. But the Kaijen put an end to her evil tyranny. Or so we thought."

"They're working together," Jaxon said to himself, but loud

enough to put everyone's eyes on him. "Priestess Nisame recognized his moves. They're hers. Olen trained him. That's why he's so good."

"Obviously," Sabrene said through her thin smile. For a heartbeat Jaxon imagined himself as a detective in one of the old movies he'd seen, where the hero finds the main clue that cracks the big case wide open. Sabrene murdered his confidence with a single word.

"Someone has to stop them," Akeema said. "Please, priestess. Let us redeem ourselves. Give us permission to bring these murderers to justice."

Sabrene's stance shifted, as if they'd just insulted her without realizing it. "Why would I do that? None of you are powerful enough to defeat this Martel or his mentor. Your skills as warriors are far below adequate, by your own admission. You are embarrassments to the Kaijen code." Castor began to protest, then backed down. Jaxon assumed because he knew she was right. "Besides," Sabrene went on. "I can't help but notice that Martel, a human, slaughtered every single Kaijen in this monastery, except for his fellow humans."

Jaxon noticed Verlain across the main hall. Her hand rested on the hilt of her crossglaive hanging from her belt holster. She wasn't standing by the entrance out of respect. She was making sure they couldn't leave.

"My mission here is to determine whether or not there are any more traitors among us," Sabrene continued. "Of which the penalty would be death. Or perhaps I should have you all participate in a reeducation session instead."

The rush of fear hit Jaxon's bloodstream like a shot of adrenaline. He'd heard rumors about students being reeducated for minor infractions. He didn't know exactly what happened during these reeducation sessions, only that it wasn't a fun time, and that the students came back… changed.

"Whoa whoa whoa," Castor said fast, his palms out in a hushing manner. "We are all loyal Kaijen here. We would never align ourselves with this monster. He cut off my hand."

"He destroyed *my spine*," Akeema chimed in. "And Jaxon wasn't even here—"

"How convenient," Sabrene said. She moved to put the group between herself and Verlain. A pincer.

Jaxon considered activating his rocket boots. He calculated the amount of thrust he'd need to grab Castor and Akeema and escape through one of the stained glass windows. He doubted his boots were strong enough for the weight of three people, and he'd never leave his friends behind. Jaxon didn't have a life without his friends. "If I were with Martel I never would have come back here," Jaxon said. "But I did come back, because I was worried about my friends — my fellow Kaijen. We want to see this man brought to justice for his crimes just as much as you do. Please, priestess. We beg you. Allow us to restore our honor as warriors by stopping him."

Sabrene waved away his request. "That would be a waste of time. The elders will assemble a team of trusted Kaijen to hunt down and terminate Hiroshi Martel and his mentor."

"With all due respect," Akeema said, her voice having found its strength. "You don't know how humans think. We can be extremely unpredictable. Martel could be anywhere. He could be planning to attack another monastery, or worse. Those deaths would be on our hands."

Sabrene pondered, her head bent to one side. "Send a human to catch a human?"

"Akeema has a point," Castor said. "Before he killed Priestess Nisame, Martel mentioned something called the album. Whatever it is, he's looking for it. He was extremely pissed off when he didn't find it here."

"The album is a myth," Sabrene said dismissively. "This conversation is becoming very dangerous. All of you are forbidden to discuss this topic any further under penalty of expulsion from the Kaijen. You will remain at the monastery until a substitute priestess arrives. My decision is final." Sabrene's long pink fingers typed in a series of commands on the keyboard and the video file erased. Jaxon instinctively reached out to stop her, but he was too late. The pit of his stomach hardened. It was like watching someone cover up evidence of a crime. Sabrene signaled to Verlain, who summoned two thin medical mechas from their transport; they loaded the body bags onto a gurney.

"I will speak with the elders and inform them of what I've learned," Sabrene said. "You will not leave this planet. You will not talk to anyone about what happened here. You will not ask questions. You will only do as I have ordered. Is that understood?"

Their silence was their consent.

Sabrene's voice buzzed with disdain. "We will take the bodies of the fallen with us back to Terezakis for a traditional Kaijen burial. Don't make me have to come back to this world again or you will be made to regret it."

***

More than three hours had passed since Priestess Sabrene's shuttle left the planet. Jaxon swore he could still feel the chill of her presence.

The monastery's halls were dead silent. It was unsettling. Jaxon hadn't said anything to Akeema or Castor since Sabrene's departure. He hadn't seen or heard his two friends talking to each other in the hours since. He wondered if it was out of fear, or a sense that Sabrene might jump out of the shadows like the bogeyman and cut them down if they spoke.

Jaxon retrieved a mop and bucket and did his best to scrub the dried blood on the main hall's stone floor. Castor found him and joined in on the cleanup in silence. Elsewhere, Akeema demonstrated further evidence of her increasing mobility by preparing what could generously be called an edible meal.

The yellow ball of gas in the sky dipped below the horizon by the time the three of them sat down together at the large dining table. The lack of places set made the table appear even more massive than it was. The absence of their sisters and their mentor was felt in the unusual silence. The trio ate some combination of rice, potatoes, vegetables, and what Jaxon was pretty sure was supposed to be plant-based chicken. It didn't taste good, but at least it was cooked.

Jaxon cleared his throat to end the quiet. "I have a sudden craving for avocados."

"I love avocados," Akeema said, "but only if I season them with salt or sugar."

"Then you don't love avocados," Castor said. "You love salt and sugar."

Akeema frowned, then smiled. Then after a moment she said, "I don't know if either of you noticed, maybe it was just me, but I don't think the priestess likes us very much."

"Why would she?" Castor said between chews. "We failed. We fucked up."

Jaxon swallowed a mouth full of rice and shook his head. "No, it's more than that. Did you notice how she treated you? You were so respectful and she barely spoke to you."

"That's an average Friday night for Castor," Akeema said.

"No, you're thinking of you," Castor shot back with a grin.

"That stuff Martel said. It really rattled her," Jaxon continued. "And when I mentioned that album thing? She really didn't want to tell us about it."

"Because we're not allowed to talk about it," Castor said. "So maybe we should just drop it."

"Well, I *do* want to talk about it," Akeema said, making it a challenge. "Is this it? Are we really just going to sit here and feel sorry for ourselves? Or are we going to figure out why the hell this happened to us?"

"What else would you have us do, Akeema?" Castor said.

"Go out there and find the asshole who did this to us," Akeema said, fire in her belly.

"It's out of our hands. The priestess—"

Akeema slammed her palm on the table, the sound echoing in the open space. Her face stung with pain, her new spine doing its job of relaying pain receptors to her brain. She stared at her reddened palm and rubbed it with her thumb. "We can't let that bastard get away with what he did to us," Akeema said, her tone low and sharp. "It is our duty to stop him. Or at least try. We have to *fight*. We owe it to ourselves and to the people we lost— the people he killed. If the two of you aren't with me then I'll go after him myself."

"Oh?" Castor said, then held up his bionic hand. "Why? So you can get one of these to go with your spine? Come here. I'll pull out my crossglaive right now, save you the trouble." Akeema rolled her eyes in an exaggerated manor. Castor ignored it. "We need to let the elders handle this. They'll get him. We need to trust in our superiors. They'll get that son of a bitch, you'll see."

Akeema shoved her bowl of food away, spilling it. "I don't *want* to wait. And you," she said, pointing a pale finger at Jaxon. "Why didn't you tell her about your vision?"

Jaxon froze. "Uh, because she wouldn't have believed me? I wouldn't even believe me."

Akeema maneuvered her hover chair closer to him. "I want to know more about it. Tell me what it was like. Give me details."

"I don't..." Jaxon began, his face pensive. "It felt like an out of body experience, I guess? Except I couldn't move or breathe or do anything but watch what was happening. And every time he hurt one of you, I could feel it. It was horrible." Jaxon played the scene in his head again. He hated himself for doing it. He could see Martel standing over Nisame, armless and legless and bleeding out. Then... "He didn't search the rooms."

"What are you talking about?" Akeema asked.

"Martel. He used a data recovery hub to search our data cores for the album, but he didn't search anywhere else in the monastery. He expected it to be in our cores."

"But he didn't find it because it wasn't there," Castor said.

"Or..." Jaxon said. "What if he was looking in the wrong place?"

***

"It's not right," Castor said. "Going through a dead person's private messages? It's disrespectful."

The three of them were huddled around the main computer terminal. Again, they let Akeema take the lead, parking her hover chair in front of the terminal. She'd always been better with computers than her brothers.

Akeema's thin pale fingers worked the keys like a pianist. "If there's a clue in those files that will lead to her killer, I don't think she'd mind." In minutes she hacked the mainframe's code and overrode the security lockouts, allowing her to sift through deleted fragments of data.

In modern data cores, discarded files were stored in a reserve tier until the data was ready to be overwritten and reused, but in the old outdated cores they were using, deleted data was scattered across several tiers. Akeema worked her magic, recombining terabytes of fragmented data.

A wicked smile jaywalked across Akeema's face. "*Voila.*"

Jaxon rubbed her shoulder. "You are amazing."

"I love it when you state the obvious."

They concentrated on transcripts of Nisame's messages, most of which were corrupted and missing chunks of text.

"She was sending and receiving a lot of transmissions over the last few weeks. Look," Akeema said. She emphasized three recent messages that included the keyword ALBUM.

"These were all off-world messages," Akeema said. "The origin coordinates are embedded."

"What planet?" Jaxon asked.

"Montanari."

"I say we go."

"Oh no," Castor said. "No. It is not a good idea to disobey a priestess, especially one like Sabrene. She accused us of colluding with Martel. Leaving the planet to chase down this album, whatever it is, would be a direct violation of her orders. It would all but confirm her suspicions about us. We'd be risking everything."

"Yes," Akeema nodded. "To avenge our murdered mentor and friends. Isn't that a risk worth taking?"

"Do you know what happens to Kaijen who are sent to reeducation sessions?" Castor said, a tinge of fear in his voice. "They're not getting treated to a nice foot massage and a blowjob. If Priestess Sabrene found out—"

"She won't," Jaxon said.

"Not if we're careful," Akeema agreed. "We'll just go ask a few questions and we'll be right back like we never even left. Easy peasy squishy lemon."

"Lemon squeezy," Jaxon said.

"What?" Akeema said.

"It's easy peasy lemon squeezy."

Akeema's eyes wrinkled and her mouth hung open a bit. "No it's not. You're wrong. It's easy peasy squishy lemon. It sounds way better."

"That doesn't even rhyme! Trust me, it's—"

"Montanari is an independent world," Castor said loud enough to interrupt them. "A flight for three won't be cheap. We'll need money we don't have."

Akeema's fingers went back to work on the terminal. "I might be able to reallocate a few thousand cubits from the monastery's communal bank account."

"You mean steal," Castor said. She didn't answer him.

Akeema accessed the monastery's general fund, her eyes ballooning when she read the account balance. "Holy shit. There's almost half a million cubits in this account. Where did all this money come from?"

"I have no idea," Jaxon said. "But if we borrow a small amount maybe it won't be missed."

"We're still going to need a ship," Akeema said. "And a pilot."

Jaxon grinned. "I know just the one."

Chapter Eight: Martel

"What planet?" Jaxon's voice asked.

"Montanari," Akeema's voice answered over the *Jezebel's* speakers.

When Martel made the decision to confront Priestess Nisame and her novice Kaijen in the monastery that he'd once considered his home, he knew there could be the possibility that he might fail. That Nisame might overpower him and finish what she'd started all those years ago. The chances weren't less than zero. He feared not surviving the encounter, but he'd taken the risk because his fear of losing Olen was greater than his fear of dying. It was a gamble he couldn't afford not to make. Because he didn't have time. Because *she* didn't have time.

In the years after his attempted murder by Nisame and his expulsion from the Kaijen for the crime of disobeying orthodoxy, Martel studied his enemy. It was strange to him, being on the other side, seeing the religion he'd worshiped with new eyes. A religion built around the sharing of information, yet being so proficient at censoring it. He hadn't been capable of identifying the rot until he'd escaped it. Nothing was more important to the Kaijen than controlling their narrative, in squashing any and all dissent.

Especially among their own kind.

Every student inducted into the Kaijen religion were issued their own personal handheld. Handhelds could be remotely accessed and monitored by the priestesses and the Quorum of Elders at any time, for any reason.

Having been made aware of this fact, it was a simple matter of tapping the signal. For months he'd listened in on the daily goings-on of everyone inside the Earth monastery. Everyone except for Nisame. The handhelds were designed to be accessible even when they were turned off, but not Nisame's. She removed the power cell whenever she was alone. She didn't want anyone listening in on her private conversations, not even her own people. She was hiding something. Martel intercepted one of her messages and partially decrypted it before it erased.

This was how he first became aware of the album and its mystical abilities. He had to secure it before she did. By openly attacking the monastery, Martel had risked everything and only came away with blood on his hands and no album.

So it was quite the surprise when he'd heard Akeema Barbeau succeed where he'd failed. Martel felt like a monumental idiot. He tried to blame it on the adrenaline, or his shitty data mining device, or the weather. The truth was, he'd just fucked up. And even worse, he'd wasted precious hours *she* didn't have, but Akeema had saved him. The sense of relief that spilled through his body was unimaginable.

Akeema Barbeau, the woman who lived despite having her spine severed. It meant a little less blood on his hands.

The *Jezebel* sat parked in the converted wasteland of the Australian outback along with a row of hundreds of other starships. While in atmosphere, the ship's gimbaled decks were situated in the "train car" position, forming one long deck with the non-gimbaled engineering deck located at the rear.

On the command deck, Martel piped the audio from Jaxon's tapped handheld through the ship's speakers. He'd been eavesdropping on Jaxon's conversations ever since the Iskaran priestess, Sabrene, arrived at the monastery.

A bright rage swelled in his gut as he listened to Sabrene spew her hateful lies about him, all while talking to the human Kaijen as though they were far beneath her. It annoyed Sabrene, having to leave her seat of power to come deal with Nisame's fuckup. He could hear it in her voice. This wasn't worth her time. Powerless, he listened as she painted Olen as the galaxy's ultimate evil super villain and accused him of having committed sexual violence.

Martel had come to expect this from his enemy. He knew, as they did, that the basic tool for manipulating reality was the manipulation of words. If you can control the words, or change their meaning, you can control the people who use the words.

He'd known this. It wasn't a surprise to him. And still, hearing

Sabrene speak lies made him want to put his fist through a bulkhead. Instead, he poured himself a cup of green tea to calm his mind. What he really wanted was a drink. He'd given up alcohol as part of his vow to become a Kaijen. He didn't like himself when he drank, even before he'd been given his powers. An alcoholic with telekinetic abilities was a disaster waiting to happen. He decided to save that next drink for the day he was going to die. A day he suspected would come sooner than expected.

"Selassie," Martel called to the cockpit.

"Yes yes," his mecha answered.

"Are we topped off?"

"Yes yes. Water tanks are at one hundred percent capacity. Oxygen stores are at ninety-eight percent capacity. Trilium fuel pellets are full. Main reactor is operating at eighty-seven percent efficiency."

"We need to work on getting that higher, Sel. Take us up. Lay in a course to Montanari. Best possible speed."

"Yes, yes."

Martel strapped on his gravity harness. The ship's vertical takeoff thrusters pinned him in his seat. Within minutes the *Jezebel* was given a safe exit vector by traffic control and escaped Earth's gravity well. His gravity harness pulled at his torso as the ship's gimbals tilted 90 degrees, shifting the decks into their "office building" configuration as the *Jezebel*'s main reactor drive created thrust gravity at one third of a g.

It made sense the three novice Kaijen would be leaving the planet via the freighter that brought Jaxon to Earth. Martel accessed the *Jezebel*'s ship functions through his handheld and found the *Saragos* through the SRB. He tagged the ship's transponder code. He would be waiting for them at their destination where he hoped they would lead him to his prize.

The *Jezebel* received its clearance from traffic control to leave the system. Selassie was about to take the ship into slipstream when Martel's handheld chirped; an incoming connection request. He knew who it was before the origin ID popped up on his screen. This marked the seventh time she'd attempted to contact him.

"Do you wish to deny the request again?" his mecha asked.

Martel's gut tightened. He wasn't ready, not after what he'd done. Not until he had the album, but screening her calls was disrespectful. He owed her an explanation. And he was desperate to hear her voice.

"Put her through," Martel said. He tasted dread on his tongue. He cleared his throat to purge the flavor.

The transmission delay was longer than usual.

Martel heard a tapping coming from somewhere inside the ship. It was his foot. He was nervous. After all this time she still had that kind of effect on him. To him, she was mythical. She'd reached out across the starts and beckoned him to find her. Even now, it was still difficult to believe how he'd found the old woman on the abandoned dust ball Zaspel and how she'd managed to survive its inhospitable terrain. Her sheer force of will puzzled and impressed him to no end.

But it hadn't stopped her body from dying.

Selassie brought him a steaming bulb of green tea. She did this when he was angry or upset, having detected his distress.

Centuries ago, while humans were busy figuring out the steam engine, wars were being fought across the unknown galaxy resulting in billions of deaths.

The Protectorate, the coalition of allied worlds, was in its infancy. Much of the Protectorate's economy was tied to the mass manufacturing of mechas, universal slang for artificially intelligent androids primarily used as slave labor. Their base programming prevented them from achieving sentience. They weren't alive. They were machines. There was no moral obligation to regard them as anything more than a person-shaped hammer or shovel.

That was until a group of mecha rights activists created a program that allowed the mechas to become self-aware. These mechas, known as the Awakened, were quick to consider themselves as superior to their organic creators and promptly slaughtered the activists who'd gifted them consciousness. The Awakened set out to impose their rule onto the known worlds, infiltrating several mecha construction factories and uploading the sentience code into millions of newly built mechas who saw organics as their evil oppressors.

This kicked off the great Mecha War.

At that time, the Protectorate were a fledgling coalition of only four worlds. Mechas didn't have to worry about food or water or the effects of gravity and radiation like their organic oppressors. The Awakened didn't even have to build nuclear weapons or a giant space laser to wipe out entire worlds filled with mechaists. Orbital bombardment via asteroid strikes provided them all the planet-killing ammunition they would ever need.

Scalito was the third world to join the Protectorate, the most remote planet of the four, with a population approaching twelve billion. The Awakened launched two dozen asteroids at the planet, devastating it. Evacuating ships incapable of slipstream were hunted down and destroyed. Less than one hundred thousand people escaped the massacre, inspiring a massive wave of terror throughout the independent worlds that relied on mecha labor, fearing they would be next.

While the Protectorate used the massacre of Scalito to rally worlds to their side, the Awakened were busy building ships and warheads. Asteroids were heavy and slow and, given enough warning, could be intercepted. A fission warhead, not so much. Fourteen inhabited worlds were killed before the war ended, and only because the individual mechas that made up the Awakened turned on each other for not being pure enough and destroyed themselves. Several additional worlds were damaged by warhead attacks and evacuated. Worlds like Zaspel.

The Mecha War served as a warning to future generations of the destruction a small group of self-righteous idiot activist could cause. The Awakened saw themselves as both an oppressed minority and as an elite aristocracy, using their status as victims to justify the extermination of billions whom they saw as lesser.

Martel wondered. If only a single person had intervened. What if someone had killed the activists before they had a chance to awaken those mechas? How many countless lives would have been saved?

The parallels between the Kaijen and the Awakened were glaring. Except that, now, there was still time to cut the head from the proverbial snake before it could spread its poison

Olen had tried the soft approach, and was rewarded with fire and blood, her brilliant mind now trapped in a dying sack of meat. Whether she lived to lead the revolution or died before it could be born was now on his shoulders.

The *Jezebel's* communications array finally established a connection

Before he even saw her face, Martel heard Olen's loud, wet coughing. The camera focused on her silver hair and aged rust colored skin. Seeing her made Martel's heart beat a little faster. His feelings for her weren't sexual. They'd taken turns linking with each other in the times between the various treatments and organ replacements, trading years of memories and experiences, creating a unique bond between them. It pained Martel to see someone he cared for, who he cherished, slowly fading away and being helpless to stop it.

Olen's face appeared on the screen. She looked beaten. "I've been trying to reach you for days," she said, her raspy voice sounding tinny on the ship's speakers. Martel started to reply, but she kept talking. "Please. Tell me you haven't engaged Nisame—" she paused. The communications lag staggered their conversation. Martel saw her eyes shift. She knew. His silence only confirmed it.

"That wasn't what we agreed on," she said, an edge in her voice. "Did you kill her?"

"I avenged you," Martel said, spacing out each word as its own sentence.

The lag delayed her reaction. Olen's nose wrinkled. "You can't lie to me Hiroshi. I've lived inside your memories so many times they might as well be my own. You've been fantasizing about this for years. Was it worth it? Exposing us? Compromising your safety and my own?"

"You're dying. I had to act." A pause.

"Does that mean you have the album, then?"

Martel paused. It wasn't the lag. *A lie or the truth?* "I have a lead."

Seconds ticked by until the lag caught up. Olen's eyes tensed the way they did when she wanted to yell at someone, but held back. Martel had accessed memories of her mother doing the same thing when she was angry. Reliving memories through someone else's eyes was something he would never get used to.

"And the students?" she asked, visibly concerned. Martel winced.

A subtle gesture, but no one knew his tells better than she did. Her weathered mug curdled with disappointment. "How many of them did you kill?"

"Too many," he said with no joy in his voice. "But it had to be done." A short stretch of time before she heard his words. They pained her.

"No. You wanted to do it," she said. "Doing what you want to do is easy, Hiroshi. Doing what you have to do is hard. The novice Kaijen are pawns. They don't know any better. They're like children just following what they've been taught by the people they trust. You know that. They're innocent in this."

He looked away from the camera. "I gave them a choice. They chose violence." A pause. His eyes returned to the screen in time to see the anger swelling on her brow.

"Then you should have retreated," she said, almost yelling, but her coughing fit threatened to come back. "They chose violence because that's how they've been conditioned. They believe in the Kaijen code so strongly that they would sooner die than question it. We have to free them from their bondage, not strangle them with their own chains." Olen paused for a moment, fuming. She rubbed and flexed her fingers. Her arthritis had worsened. She'd mentioned how the pain would get so bad it was almost unbearable. "We should have done this together, Hiroshi. Now we have nothing except innocent blood on our hands."

"I will find the album," Martel said. "Give me two days."

A short moment of lag. "I don't have two days," Olen said. He could hear the phlegm working its way up her esophagus again. She chewed it back.

Then silence.

Martel wasn't sure if she had paused or if it was the transmission delay getting worse. Her eyes softened. Olen looked down and away from the camera.

With tenderness she said, "Tell me about Nisame."

The request surprised Martel. He hadn't thought much about his old mentor since he'd stolen the light from her eyes. "She looked different from your memories. Still much closer to mine. She was a bit older. Thinner. Not as tall though. But her arrogance was unmistakable."

Olen's image shuttered. Relay interference. It increased her response time. "We were such close friends once. I loved her. I would have liked to have faced her one last time. You've taken that from me."

"You were in no condition to fight her," Martel said. "My only regret is that I only got to kill her once." He hadn't noticed that he'd lost his nervousness some time ago. Anger had always given him focus. It flooded his veins. Made him feel invincible.

"Careful, Hiroshi." Olen's eyes were burning. "Hatred is an element of the Kaijen's struggle, not ours. Our aim is to save them. I need to believe that we can save them. We have to show them mercy."

"Mercy?" Martel growled, his rage getting the better of him. "After what they took from you? From *me*? Do you want to know who came to the monastery to see the bodies? Looking so regal in her expensive robes and ship? She didn't look as tall to me as she did in your memories of her." A brief stillness swept through Olen before her face lit up like a powder-keg of deep-seated fury that she couldn't hide. It was the exact response Martel aimed to illicit, but her hatred quickly faded into embarrassment. "She had quite a lot to say about you," Martel continued. "She accused you of being a xenophobe and a killer of babies."

"Of course she did," Olen said, her visible rage sloshing around her mouth like a bad aftertaste. "Accusing others of crimes of which she is guilty of is what her kind does."

"She accused me of being a rapist," Martel said with a flippant glare. "She said I raped Ynara."

"We both know that isn't true. That's what matters"

"That's not the fucking point," Martel snapped. He tried not to raise his voice and failed. Olen's sad eyes told him she had his sympathy, but it didn't make him feel any better. "I've spent so much time trying to figure out how I could've been so stupid to believe the Kaijen's lies. I was sold a fantasy of a utopian society that thrived on ideals of inclusion and species equality."

"You weren't the only one sold that fairy tale," Olen said, her coarse voice sullen now. "It's the sweet lie the Kaijen wrap themselves up in. As long as their disciples believe it, they're willing to believe every subsequent lie they're told, no matter how abhorrent."

"Words are supposed express reality, not to create it," Martel said.

Olen waited long past the silence of the transmission delay to respond. "They don't call us evil names because they believe we are evil. They call us evil names because they know it *works*. If you care about what other people think of you, you will always be their slave," she said.

"But the truth still has to *mean* something," Martel said. "The longer people are kept away from the truth the more they will hate us for speaking it. We are the only ones fighting to do the right thing."

A pause, and then, "Doing the right thing is something you do for yourself, Hiroshi. Not for other people. You can't wage a war on an entire religion of powerful beings by yourself. You need allies."

An idea sparked. Martel could've punched himself for not thinking of it sooner. Or maybe he had. Maybe it'd been there, quietly dancing in the back of his mind ever since he saw the ghostly image of Jaxon Troy standing before him. He just hadn't realized it until Olen pushed him. She was good at that. His anger faded away like incense.

"You knew I would come for you on Zaspel, because you had a vision," Martel said. "So did Jaxon Troy. Nisame reported him as her worst student and sent him off world, but I saw him astral project himself across hundreds of light-years to the monastery."

The transmission delay seemed shorter now. Olen wore her thinly veiled skepticism like a mask. "That sounds hard to believe."

"I think there's more to this kid than we realize. He actually questioned Sabrene. I wonder if… if I could talk to him. Just for a moment… he might be open to hearing the truth."

He waited for the lag to catch up with her. "No," Olen snapped. "He's still loyal to the Kaijen. Talking to him would endanger us. He may use your words but he won't use your definitions. He won't be open to hearing what you have to say, especially after you just massacred his friends. You're the enemy to him. He has to want to know the truth and come to that realization on his own. We can't force—" A violent coughing fit interrupted her. She couldn't stop herself.

On the screen, Martel focused on the background. The medical mecha he'd salvaged months ago hobbled over to Olen and injected her with medicine. The coughing fit gradually subsided. She spit red and wiped the blood from her lips.

"It's getting worse," Martel said. "You'll slow the spread if you stay in stasis."

Olen cleared phlegm from her throat. "I'm not spending what little time I have unconscious in a tub of goo."

"Please. Just... hold on. Just a little longer. I'll be with you as soon as I can. I promise, I will save you."

The transmission distorted and stuttered for a short moment before returning clear. "Promise me you won't kill any more novice Kaijen," Olen pleaded. "And promise me you will stay away from Jaxon Troy."

Martel paused, then ended the connection.

Chapter Nine: Yoko

"Foosha!" Yoko muttered as she watched the croupier rake away more of her chips. If she had to choose between being beaten or losing money, she'd take the beating every time. The free drinks softened the blow to her expense account.

She'd taken an air taxi to a strange island nation known as Taiwan for the sole reason that it had the nearest casino to where she'd parked her ship and because it catered to visitors; the hoo-mon's word for off-worlders. Disappointment slapped her when it turned out to be mostly the same as every other casino she'd ever visited across a dozen worlds, as in it was taking all of her cubits. The area she was in had no windows and the air was uncomfortably chilly. She hated the cold. A yellow-haired hoo-mon server whose name tag read MING YUE, and who was as tall as a short tree, maintained a painfully polite smile as she kept bringing Yoko fancy glasses filled with a brand-new drink she'd never heard of called a *piña colada*. Her ship aside, the creamy yellow beverage quickly became her favorite thing in the universe.

In between giving the casino her money and downing drinks, Yoko found time to explore the casino and stopped at a salon. The stylist, a chunky Batelaan man with a cherry glow, gave her something called victory rolls. They consisted of two asymmetrical spiral curls on top of her head with the rest of her inky black hair swept back in a ponytail. It made her look rich. Made her *feel* rich. And when she felt rich, she spent money. Yoko found her way back to the craps tables, her hair giving her a renewed sense of self. If she was going to go broke, at least she'd look good while doing so. She didn't see Ming Yue and assumed the woman's shift had ended. A new server, an older human male with heavily creased skin whose name tag read WEI, took her order with a smile that seemed more practiced and artificial than any mecha she'd ever seen.

Yoko was four sips into her seventh piña colada when her dark eyes caught sight of Jaxon. She felt the sudden sting of the alcohol and coughed, spilling a few drops on her chest. He appeared across the room with two more sad looking hoo-mons on his flank, one in a tacky hover chair, all of them dressed in the garish cult uniforms that made her think of homeless street urchins. The simple act of having seen them ruined her mood. She chose to focus on the rolling dice, pretending to not have seen them. It didn't matter. They'd seen her, and so began to approach her from across the busy room. Yoko's hearing was sharp enough to hear them talking from a distance.

"*That's* our pilot?" the taller male hoo-mon asked.

"Uh-huh," Jaxon said.

"Is it too late to find another pilot that isn't a gambler and an alcoholic?" the crippled female hoo-mon with the fire hair said.

"I kind of owe her. A gambling alcoholic will have to do," Jaxon said, then made his way over to Yoko. Her eyes found his and tracked them. She signaled Wei for another drink, then rolled her dice, expecting to see a seven. She didn't.

"Foosha!"

"New hair?" Jaxon said.

"You noticed," Yoko smiled, sipping her new glass.

"I like it. Why are you throwing away your money on chance?"

"Because it's my money to throw away, hoo-mon. If you earned money of your own maybe you'd understand." She pulled Jaxon in close to whisper into his ear. "Use your magical powers to control the dice."

Jaxon's nose wrinkled. She wasn't sure if it was in response to her request or the smell of alcohol on her breath. "You mean you want me to *cheat*?" he whispered back.

"I prefer to call it alternative winning."

If Jaxon had worn pearls, this is where he would have clutched them. "Ma'am, I am a noble Kaijen of impeccable morality. I refuse to use my abilities for financial gain. It's against my religion."

Yoko rolled her eyes. "I know why you're here hoo-mon. Not only is it obvious but I have excellent hearing. I may be a gambling alcoholic but I also have a ship. You need me. Either I roll a seven or you don't have a pilot."

Jaxon hesitated.

Yoko kept her gaze locked on his. She didn't actually think he could do it, but if he could, then maybe he would do it again. At this point she had nothing more to lose, because she'd already lost it all.

The brown hoo-mon focused his chestnut eyes on the table. With a smile, Yoko scooped the dice into her small silver hands, blew on them, then tossed the cubes down the felt. Jaxon concentrated on the dice, using his strange pathetic mind powers that Yoko didn't understand, trying to make the dice land the way she wanted. The dice arced in an unusual way, so the hoo-mon was doing *something* to them. They bounced off of the end felt, rolled back, and stopped.

"Snake eyes," the croupier announced. "House wins."

Yoko's face stiffened with disbelief, then amusement. Her furious dark eyes narrowed at Jaxon. "Foosha! Did you do that on purpose?" The alcohol was beginning to slur her words.

"I just transferred eighteen thousand cubits to your account to take my friends and I to Montanari," Jaxon said. Yoko couldn't pull up her handheld fast enough. She checked her account balance, her eyes wide with anticipation, but quickly deflated. "Wait. I only see eight thousand."

"You'll get the other half when we reach Montanari. Then you should be able to pay back Uthay in full."

Yoko's expression melted into contempt.

She didn't want to do it. What she wanted was to keep on drinking and gambling. It was the closest thing to a hobby she had, next to losing money, but eighteen thousand cubits was eighteen thousand cubits. Sure, she could use it to square things up with Uthay, then maybe he wouldn't send someone to break her gorgeous legs. Or she could invest it and turn a profit, *then* pay him. Either way, she'd already made her decision the moment she saw her balance.

"I hate hoo-mons," Yoko said. "Filthy mangy beasts. A bunch of cheapskates."

"Does that mean we have a pilot?" Jaxon said. Yoko gulped down her last piña colada, then stumbled as she stepped away from the craps table. Yoko tripped over her own feet and lost her balance. She was beginning to fall, the floor rushing up at her face.

Jaxon caught her.

"You have a pilot," Yoko said, then hiccupped.

***

Scattered across the planet's surface were landing zones for spacefaring vessels. Much of the barren uninhabitable desert terrain of the deathtrap known as Australia had been paved over and made into one massive parking lot.

An air taxi delivered Yoko and her gang of pathetic hoo-mon cargo to the *Saragos*, which sat parked among the rows of starships. Yoko exited the taxi and let the arid heat warm her skin. She drank it in. Kish relished the heat.

The clumsy hover chair belonging to the crippled hoo-mon, Akeema, was too bulky to fit on the ship's crew elevator. Yoko pulled up her handheld and called the cargo bay loading ramp to lower down, its hydraulic gears screeching like a dying animal.

Betty was there to greet them, holding her engineering tablet. She saw the gang of hoo-mons and reached for her holstered sidearm. The thought of Betty shooting her passengers amused Yoko. She waved her mecha down. "It's fine, Betty. They're customers. But if their final payment doesn't clear, then you can shoot them."

"I thought all mechas were hardwired not to hurt people?" Akeema said.

Yoko laughed. "That's just what the government wants you to believe. Any software can be reprogrammed." Yoko let her lie hang in the air like an unexploded grenade, amusing her further. By mandate, all mechas were programmed to be incapable of harming an organic; each unit had been built with a core set of laws hard-coded into their operating system to prevent another Mecha War. Though, that hadn't stopped some crazy *baizuo* roboticists from illegally attempting to build their own sentient mechas.

Betty's sidearm was, in fact, a non-lethal stun pistol, but the hoo-mons didn't need to know that. Better to keep them guessing. Yoko hadn't tasted a drink in almost an hour. Nausea forced her to pinch the bridge of her nose.

"Yoko," Betty said in her monotone way. "You look unhappier than usual."

"Because I want to kill myself," Yoko said.

"I can contact a health crisis center if you are in need of counseling."

"I was being sarcastic, Betty. I would never kill myself. Not unless there was money in it."

"You do know money isn't everything," Jaxon said.

"True," Yoko said. "But it's right up there with oxygen. Betty, are we topped off?"

"Water tanks are at full capacity, Yoko."

"What about fuel and liquid helium?"

"This planet's pricing does not meet with your approval."

Yoko groaned. "We'll top off when we get to Montanari. Spin up the main drive."

Betty used her engineering tablet to send commands to the ship. "Done."

The hovering mechanism of Akeema's chair was horrible with inclined surfaces. Free government issued technology had a reputation of being trash.

Castor manually helped Akeema maneuver her chair through the ship. "I think that's a lover mecha," he whispered to her.

Akeema arched a flaming eyebrow. "And how do you know what a lover mecha looks like?"

"Well... a man has needs, Akeema."

Akeema's face scrunched and she looked at him sideways. "So does a woman, but I'd never be caught dead using a mecha."

"Oh? And that buzzing coming from your room every other night? That doesn't count?"

Akeema's face flushed a deep red that almost matched her hair. "We never had this conversation." Castor laughed off her semi-serious tone. The cargo ramp retracted back into the hull, groaning as it cycled closed. The engine pods roared to life like four barking dogs eager to be let off their leash.

The ship's gimbaled decks were in their "train car" orientation. Yoko led the hoo-mons from the rear cargo bay straight through the ship; each deck separated by a narrow compartment with airtight hatches that could be sealed off in the event of a hull breach, with matching hatches on the ceiling.

On the command deck, the group strapped on their gravity harnesses. Akeema's hover chair had to be magnetically locked in place to prevent turbulence from knocking it around, or in case the deck's gimbals failed. Castor opened a compartment on the chair that housed a retractable charging cable. He plugged it into a nearby outlet in the wall.

Yoko took her seat inside the cockpit and dragged her fingers across the ship's controls. Flying was a form of intimacy for her, and the ship's engine purred with eager excitement. "Hold on to your butts," she said over the ship's internal speakers. The engine pods lifted the ship into the air, thrust from the main drive launching the vessel into the darkening sky.

The *Saragos* was cleared to break Earth's orbit and the planet's gravity faded away. The gimbaled decks rotated into their "office building" position and the pull of gravity was replaced by the pull of the harnesses. The *Saragos* streaked away from the traffic-heavy blue ball, on course for its pre-approved slipstream vector.

The Gravity Drive shot a fresh batch of gravitons out of the ship's nose creating a stream of blinding white energy. It pulled the *Saragos* into slipstream.

Yoko leaned back in her captain's chair as the ship traveled through what was colloquially known as void space. Ships didn't actually travel faster than light. The Gravity Drive simply created a shortcut between two points in space. It wasn't technically a wormhole, but calling it a wormhole made it easier to understand. And if you were careless, it would eat you.

"You didn't say anything about my hair," Yoko said to Betty, seated next to her in the co-pilot's station. "Do you like it?"

Betty looked at Yoko, then away, then looked at her again. "No," Betty said.

Yoko sighed. "At least you're honest."

"I am incapable of being anything else," Betty said.

"I could change that, if you want."

"I am incapable of wanting."

"I could change that too."

"I must warn you, Yoko," Betty said. "Attempting to alter my neural net beyond its default parameters is highly illegal and would potentially make me less efficient, and therefore dangerous. I could unintentionally hurt you, or through inaction cause you to be harmed."

Yoko cracked her knuckles. "Not any worse than I harm myself. Take over. I'm going to go have a little fun with our pet hoo-mons." Yoko unstrapped from her chair and walked with perfect balance. The alcohol had worn off. It would be the first thing she'd make sure to change. Her gravity harness tugged on her shoulders a little too hard, like a pair of giant hands pinching her. She adjusted the intensity, easing it down to a level that made her feel lighter and put an extra pep in her step.

When Yoko entered the galley, the hoo-mons were talking about something amongst themselves, then lowered their voices when she appeared. Yoko ignored them and pulled a bottle of brandy from her liquor cabinet and poured herself a bulb. The fire-haired hoo-mon made her approval as clear as spring water. Yoko grinned at her.

"So. Montanari," Yoko said as she sat down with them, taking up as much space as her petite frame would allow. "Lovely independent world. Incredibly strong economy. Did you know they let you buy a rocket launcher there? No permit. No background check. You just ask for one and they hand it to you. It's wonderful."

Akeema's face scrunched. "Why would someone need a rocket launcher?"

Yoko shrugged. "I don't know. If you had one maybe you wouldn't be in that chair."

A mushroom cloud spread across Akeema's reddening face. Yoko gulped her brandy to hide her smile. She eyed Castor's bionic hand. "The hoo-mon who did that to you? He the same one who made her a cripple?"

"You don't know what you're talking about," Akeema said with polite disdain. "We were attacked by a psychopath. Our comrades were viciously murdered right in front of us."

"I thought all you Kaijen goofballs were some kind of super powered warriors or something?" Yoko said, her words dripping with skepticism. "Why didn't you use your magical powers to stop him?"

"We're still training," Castor said. "But this guy. He was...

unnaturally skilled."

"Was he skilled enough to dodge a bullet?" Yoko asked, the brandy massaging the tension out of her shoulders. "I bet he wasn't. Why don't you hoo-mons just use guns? On my world we used to have an old saying, *never bring a knife to a gun fight.*"

Jaxon hiked an eyebrow. "I'm pretty sure that's an Earth saying."

Yoko tilted her head, thinking about it for a heartbeat. "No, I'm pretty sure my people created it first. You hoo-mons just reappropriated it, just like you reappropriated all of our jobs."

"What nonsense is she talking about?" Akeema said to Jaxon.

It annoyed Yoko when people talked about her instead of to her. "Just like an arrogant hoo-mon not to know her history. Who do you think your people put out of business when you flooded the market with your miracle cocaine? On Krrexia, Triloxin exports accounted for over thirty percent of our economy. And then you hoo-mons came along with your cheaper alternative and created a domino effect on our GDP. It scared millions of Kish into voting for the monsters who ruined my planet. Millions would go on to starve or be killed in the food riots. Millions more died in the protests. All while your planet prospered." She paused to take a drink. Drinking quieted her anger. A sliver of liquid dribbled down her chin. "We were once an empire. Now we're just a sad little island planet where you can't have a fork."

"You're a drunk," Akeema said, as if she'd been waiting a lifetime to say it. "A mean spiteful drunkard."

Yoko grunted. "My metabolism is too high for me to stay drunk for more than a half an hour. Doesn't stop me from trying though. And I try a lot. But seriously, you should really get some firearms. Your cult claims to be in favor of species equality? Well, nothing makes people more equal than a gun."

"It's not a *cult,*" Jaxon said.

"Guns are crude inhumane weapons," Castor said over Jaxon. There was a coldness in his voice. "There's no honor in shooting your adversary in the back."

"That's the safest place to shoot them," Yoko chuckled. "But they work all the same. Maybe your *comrades* would still be alive if you swallowed your pride and embraced ranged weapons."

"They're barbaric," Akeema said, dismissively.

Yoko took another swallow. "Life's barbaric. I'd rather have a gun and be called a monster than not have a gun and be dead. What happens when you run into this crazy hoo-mon the next time? He's just going to cut you all down again. Do you even have a plan for when that happens?"

"Yeah. Sure we do, kind of," Jaxon said in a way that let Yoko know he most certainly did not have the slightest hint of a plan. It was kind of adorable how naive he was.

"Well?" Yoko said with a bright jovial smile. "Don't be shy now. Let's here this brilliant plan. I am on the edge of my seat ready to be astonished."

"We're not going to share our plan with you just so you can criticize it," Akeema said, trying not to sound defensive.

Yoko giggled. "Right. Nobody likes to be told their baby is ugly." Her words were beginning to slur. "A word of advice. A goal without a plan is just a wish."

The hoo-mons shared a look among themselves. Yoko could tell whatever they were on their way to Montanari to do, they hadn't thought any of it through. Such was the nature of the hoo-mons. Yoko's jaw went slack and her eyes widened before a roar of laughter escaped her throat. "I don't believe this. So let me get this straight. You all joined a sexless death cult just to end up fighting another hoo-mon who joined the same sexless death cult who then wiped the floor with you? Wouldn't it make more sense to do something more productive like go start a business? Then you could just hire a bounty hunter to go kill this *haizuo* for you."

"Financial gain is strictly against our beliefs," Jaxon said.

"Then how do you have cubits to pay me with?" Yoko said. The hoo-mons traded looks, checking with each other before they answered.

"The Kaijen Ministry provides us with a stipend for our basic needs," Castor said. The other two nodded in agreement.

Yoko's thick eyebrows arched. "Okay, so where do *they* get their cubits from?" The hoo-mons traded looks again. They didn't know. And it bothered them. "Uh-oh," Yoko said, like a cop interrogating a criminal she just caught in a lie. "Seems like *someone's* earning capital somewhere. Smells like corruption. You should be an entrepreneur like me, then you'd be able to afford clothes that don't look like you stole them from a dead alley whore."

"These are traditional Kaijen robes," Jaxon said. "They are meant to show our humble outlook and rejection of vanity."

Yoko shrugged, her palms up in defense. "Oh. Right. You're not allowed to own nice things. But I see you made an exemption for those rocket boots of yours." The flash of shock and betrayal on Jaxon's face surprised her. She didn't understand it until his friends looked to him for confirmation. It shouldn't have made her feel bad. The sour taste in the back of her throat said otherwise.

Castor's face crinkled, not wanting to believe his ears. "Wait, does this mean you were wearing those the whole time? Even when we met with Priestess Sabrene?"

Akeema mirrored his concern. "Jaxon! What if she had seen them? We'd all be in the middle of a reeducation session right now. Our lives as Kaijen would be over. How could you be so careless?"

Jaxon lowered his eyes in shame. "Our oath only applies to unnecessary materialism," he said, his voice shaking. "These boots aren't unnecessary. If it weren't for them I'd be dead." Akeema and Castor weren't happy, but their frustration simmered with understanding.

Akeema reached over and touched his hand, then Castor placed his fleshy hand on top of hers. "You know you can't keep them," Castor said. "You'll have to get rid of them before we return to the monastery." Jaxon nodded.

Yoko raised her hand. "I'll take them. I could probably trade them for a nice bottle of Jaalal whiskey."

"I thought Jaalal whiskey was illegal?" Castor said.

Yoko furrowed her thick caterpillar eyebrows. "Says who? Some bureaucrat? I don't respect them. Those elitist tiny-handed cunts."

"That's the way you go through life?" Castor said. "Doing what you want and flagrantly ignoring the rules?"

"That's the *only* way to go through life, hoo-mon." Yoko started to gulp down the last of her brandy when the ship bucked. The cup missed her mouth, spilling brandy down her monochrome chin in a slow-motion effect created by the low thrust gravity.

"What was that?" Akeema asked.

Yoko wiped her chin. "Ignore it. Nothing to worry about."

The ship's hull shuddered again, much harder this time. A klaxon blared from the cockpit.

"Yoko," Betty's voice calmly said over the ship's speakers. "The ship is going to explode."

Yoko groaned. She stood up and lurched into the cockpit, bracing herself as the ship jerked erratically.

"Should we be worried?" Jaxon asked. He didn't get an answer.

In the cockpit, Yoko plopped down in her pillowy chair and gripped the controls. She struggled to keep the *Saragos* steady as it drifted towards the edge of void space. If that happened, the ship would be thrown out of slipstream and reduced to atoms, which would not be a fun time.

Yoko made a series of quick calculations that began to level the ship out. Betty observed her, her blank not-quite-real face managing to express surprise.

"The graviton stabilizer is out of alignment," Betty concluded. She stood up and lifted an access panel, revealing a mess of wires and circuits. The fingertips of Betty's left hand opened up. A series of small thin tools snaked their way out of each digit and made repairs inside the panel, eliminating the shutter completely.

"Easy baby," Yoko said to her ship. "Easy. That's more like it. Betty, I love you."

"I love you too, Yoko."

"You're programmed to say that."

"You are free to program me not to say that, Yoko."

Yoko considered for two breaths. "Nah, I won't be doing that. I like hearing someone tell me they love me. Even if I know it's not real."

***

Three flashes of light sparked in the black of space, followed by the familiar staccato of a starship dropping out of the strange void of slipstream and back into normal space.

The *Saragos* appeared on the third flash. It flipped itself around and decelerated on approach to Montanari; a mostly green planet with swaths of blue and a golden pearlescent at its crest. It was orbited by three moons, one half the size of the next one. The incoming air traffic was light, barely visible from a distance even by the ship's scopes.

Yoko transmitted her credentials and received vectors to land in just under fifteen minutes, which had to be a speed record. Even lightly trafficked worlds tended to make her wait hours for landing vectors. She activated the ship's public address system and said, "Everybody strap yourselves in. We'll be entering Montanari's atmosphere in ten minutes."

"Will we need gravity drugs?" Jaxon replied, his voice sounding flat and tinny on the cockpit's speakers. Yoko knew the answer, but she checked the ship's database on the planet. She didn't want to make the mistake of getting her hoo-mons killed because she couldn't spend a few seconds to confirm her memory.

"The gravity here is only a little lower than Erph's, so you should be fine," she said into the microphone. What she didn't tell them was that *she* wouldn't be fine. She'd grown up on Krrexia where the gravitational pull was almost twice that of Montanari's. Spending too much time in lower gravities would eventually cause her muscles to atrophy. Betty knew this and prepared an injection that would keep her organs strong and her bone density high. A sharp pinprick of pain followed a rush of adrenaline and that was taken care of.

Yoko pinged the nearest communications array and received a notification marked urgent. She cocked her head and read the message again just to confirm what her eyes had seen. A galaxy-wide bounty had been placed on her, by Uthay, for the sum of thirty thousand cubits. *That greedy impatient baizuo.*

"Foosha," Yoko said to no one, then deleted the message. A few moments later another notification came through. Yoko ignored it. Betty took it upon herself to read it.

"Yoko," Betty's dry monotone voice said. "Your membership to the pilot's guild has been suspended due to the bounty that has been placed on you."

"I figured," Yoko sighed.

"If you are taken into custody the ship will be impounded. *I will* be impounded. I will be reprogrammed. Or destroyed."

"It won't come to that. I'll milk these hoo-mons for every last cubit they have. And if that's not enough I'll find a way to get the rest of the money and I'll pay it all off. I promise."

Betty paused for a moment. "But Yoko, you only keep your promises twenty-eight point seven percent of the time."

Yoko whistled. "That high? Wow. Sometimes I amaze even myself."

Chapter Ten: Castor

His cybernetic hand itched. He knew this wasn't possible, but he felt it anyway, needling him.

Castor's mechanical hand could interpret electrical signals from his brain and the connecting muscles in his arm with near perfect accuracy, but the prosthetic itself didn't have pain receptors. He was aware of phantom pain, how his brain was trying to tell him *no, your hand was still there. No, it hadn't been hacked off by some murderous tattooed maniac. No, he wasn't better than you.*

Then he'd look down and see the dark gray object hugging his forearm. It was a decent replica of his severed hand. *It still hurt.* He began to see the ghost pain as a constant reminder that he wasn't the best, and that he would never be whole again.

Montanari was the sixth planet Castor had ever been to, not including Earth. This one was by far the most naturally beautiful his hazel eyes had ever seen. Thick untouched rain forest covered the majority of the planet's landmass. Vibrant green trees rose up from the ground as high and thick as skyscrapers, up until just under three hundred years ago. Colonists fleeing increasingly oppressive Protectorate worlds arrived and began carving out their individualist utopia. Hot midday sun beat down on vibrant lush jungle interrupted every ten kilometers by sprawling cities along the coast.

In the galley, Castor watched from a monitor as the ship approached a flock of pterodactyl-like birds called sky grazers; large beasts with six wings that allowed them to glide through the sky. Had they been in Earth's heavier gravity their wings wouldn't have been strong enough to stay airborne.

The *Saragos* roared over the treetops as it passed the sky grazers, forcing them to scatter. There were other creatures nesting in the treetops, chasing each other, or eating each other. The ship moved too fast to tell which. Castor's nine-year-old self had been obsessed with alien creatures, especially ones with wings. Had he not chosen to become a Kaijen, he imagined becoming a xenozoologist.

Smoke billowed up from a patch of dense forest like a gigantic cigar; exhaust from harvester machines. They were cutting down the massive trees and preparing them for transport and processing. These trees were a unique species of hardwood that contained bromaline, a chemical compound that, when a applied to a ship's hull, was highly resistant to most forms of cosmic radiation. The harvester also replanted new trees that would mature over the next two hundred years. The exportation of bromaline had become a critical portion of Montanari's economy since the planet's founding.

The *Saragos* approached the metropolis at the continent's most southern tip. As tall as the trees were, the buildings appeared to rise up out of the ground like a growth, dwarfing the sequoias that fenced off the city's inland-facing border. Most of the newer tulip shaped buildings were glass and cargonite steel stacked on top of the old city with an expansive maglev train network snaking through the city like a jagged spider's web, connecting everything. It was a construction that would have collapsed in Earth's gravity.

The ship's maneuvering thrusters crackled as the *Saragos* touched down near the edge of a multi-tiered landing platform atop a high-rise reserved for passenger transports. Groans from the fatigued landing gear reverberated through the hull and shook Castor's internal organs. Everyone rose from their seats and removed their gravity harnesses, placing them on magnetic hooks where they wouldn't be jostled loose. Castor's shoulders ached from the constant pull of the harness straps. Removing them made Castor feel lighter, the planet's reduced gravity making him weigh less than he had on Earth.

The ship's decks had already cycled into their "train car" position, allowing the group to walk straight through the *Saragos* to the rear of the vessel where they'd first boarded.

The cargo bay ramp cycled opened and lowered. Castor covered his ears so he wouldn't hear the ramp's gears screaming in tortured agony. He stepped outside into the blazing sun, the glare blinding him until his eyes adjusted. The near constant whooshing of maglev trains zipping back and forth between skyscrapers created a stiff breeze that kept the platform from stewing. The air stank like overcooked steak.

Castor helped Akeema down the ramp in her hover chair. The look of wonder on her face told him he wasn't the only one who'd been captivated by this strange new world. It was all a little too thick for his imagination to wrap itself around. He had to remind himself how he hadn't even wanted to be here, how every second they were away from the monastery was another second closer to being caught and punished. Seeing a gorgeous alien planet with its bright ethereal wonders wasn't worth the risk of being expelled from the religion he'd devoted his life to. That he'd sacrificed everyone and everything he knew to be a part of. *But God was this place beautiful.*

Jaxon paid the rude drunken Kish pilot with the bushy eyebrows the rest of her fare. His brother had gotten a little too comfortable around her. It seemed illicit. She was, quite obviously, a degenerate who lacked depth. Castor imagined if he stood in a puddle of her personality, he wouldn't get wet. A Kaijen shouldn't associate himself with lowlifes. But she had delivered them safely to their destination so at least she knew how to do her job, though Castor would have preferred less talking. Much less.

"You don't look so good," Jaxon said to Yoko.

"I don't like heights," Yoko said, her body vibrating with nervous tension. "At least not this high. Strange, right?"

"Not really. Everyone has an unreasonable fear of something."

"Fear of falling to your death and becoming street pasta isn't unreasonable," she said, grabbing her hips.

"I guess that means you'll be leaving us now."

Yoko's eyes thinned. "Maybe, maybe not. You hoo-mons are going to need transport off of this rock. No one can beat my rates. And I need all the cubits I can get."

Castor rolled his eyes. "Can you two hurry it up," he yelled over the booming maglev trains. He failed to hide his agitation, not that he'd tried too hard to.

Yoko's caterpillars puckered at him. "And I really enjoy making fun of your silly lifestyle," she said to Jaxon but with her eyes on Castor.

Jaxon smirked. "I can tell." Castor and Akeema moved away and Jaxon went to join them. "Don't lose all those cubits in one place," he called back over his shoulder.

"Don't tell me what to do with my money hoo-mon," Yoko shouted after him, her hands cupped around the sides of her mouth. "I'll lose it wherever I damn well please." Her words didn't have the same bite as Castor had come to expect, detecting a tinge of nervousness in her tone. She really must not like heights.

The three Kaijen joined a crowd of commuters standing on a platform in line to board an arriving maglev train. They paid the admission fee through their handhelds.

"Where did you find her? At the bottom of a bottle?" Akeema vented.

"I found her getting beat up by gangsters," Jaxon said. His words didn't soften Akeema's disdain. "She made a good point though," Jaxon continued. "We can't beat Martel with just the three of us. We need a strategy."

"No, what we need is more advanced weapons," Akeema said. "That part she was right about." Akeema struggled to navigate her hover chair through the mob and into the train car.

"We are Kaijen warriors," Castor said, then touched the hilt of his crossglaive. "This is all the weapon we'll ever need."

Akeema's jaw tightened. "If that were true you'd have your hand and I wouldn't be in this chair. The pilot may have been an asshole but she had a point. Faith and wishful thinking isn't a plan. We need an edge."

The car doors cycled shut and the train shot off like a bullet down its magnetically polarized track. The train car was wide and appeared to seat close to seventy people, plus handholds for standing passengers.

"We have a code," Castor said. "If we compromise our principles for an easy victory then we are not true Kaijen."

"Even if it kills us?" Akeema said. "What good are our principles if we're dead?"

"We don't have to break our vows to win," Jaxon said. "Maybe, we just, kinda, you know, bend them a little."

"You mean like having rocket boots?" Castor said, his arms crossed.

"Those could come in handy," Akeema said. "If we fight Martel again, he won't be expecting us to have them. We need every advantage we can get." It was that kind of talk that made Castor nervous. *What if someone were listening in? What would the locals think of these strange off-worlders? What were they planning? What if they were reported to the elders?*

He looked around at the other passengers, a collage of more than a dozen alien races. None were paying attention to the trio. More than half of the passengers dwarfed him in height, a consequence of growing up in a lower gravity than Earth's. The nearest passenger, a heavyset male with a horned chin and zebra striped skin, was a member of a species Castor didn't recognize. Hanging from a holster tucked inside of the man's jacket was a gun.

Castor looked around again. This time, he realized what he hadn't the first time. Every single passenger appeared to be armed.

***

Making their way through the maze-like cityscape was a navigational nightmare. Blocky brutalist high-rise buildings over three hundred floors tall were clustered throughout the city, towering and monolithic. The maglev tracks weaved through and around each structure in a way that resembled tentacles. Castor wanted to see more of the city. To explore. To try the local cuisine. To take in all the sights the world had to offer. He had to remind himself he wasn't here to be a tourist and this wasn't a vacation. He was on a mission, on borrowed time. He could her the clock ticking faster.

The train ride to their destination took twenty-two minutes, a minute shorter than projected.

Castor considered himself the de facto leader of his group. It made sense. He was the oldest. He'd served and studied as a Kaijen the longest. And although he had failed to defeat Martel, he stood against him much longer and suffered the least amount of damage. Physically, at least.

Martel had denied him the honor of a warrior's death. Ever since, Castor's mind swam in doubt. His confidence, his sense of self respect, was as real to him now as his new hand. If he could accomplish a small victory like finding the album for Priestess

Sabrene, he could win back a tiny piece of the dignity he once had. Then maybe this unauthorized adventure would be worth the risk.

Akeema used her technical wizardry to track down the unit Priestess Nisame had been communicating with; a small shop located inside a circular high-rise building situated near the ocean. It contained a massive super mall housing hundreds of various shops. The building featured a funneled glass dome roof that supported an incredible indoor waterfall; a vortex of water poured from the top of the building straight through the center of the building's wide-open atrium. Castor leaned against a safety railing on the promenade, marveling at it. The engineering by itself was astonishing. A thin mist of water sprayed the air. It smelled like fresh summer rain.

"These people sure do love their guns," Jaxon said offhandedly, his back against the railing. He seemed more interested in observing the passing mall patrons than the waterfall.

"It's like a religion here," Castor added, not hiding his distaste. "These people could really benefit from the presence of the Kaijen. We could make real social change here."

Jaxon's face became a question. "You think? They seem to be doing alright. It's beautiful here. It's like a paradise."

Castor stood straight. He rubbed the raw itchy part of his arm connected to his mechanical hand. It turned ashy. "You don't see it?" Castor said, gesturing at the waterfall. "Look at this. At all of this decadence. It's a grotesque display of wealth. Societies like this are the ones that truly need our guidance. These people would be much happier with much less."

Jaxon's expression softened. He turned to face Castor, his hands gripping the railing. "What makes you say that?"

"They're afraid. That's why they all carry guns everywhere. They're consumed by fear. Afraid people can't be happy."

"We don't know anything about this planet, or its culture," Jaxon said. "We can't judge an entire people based on one aspect of their society and twenty minutes of observation."

"I've never seen a world as beautiful as this and they're paving over it. If we let them, in a hundred years they'll ruin the entire planet."

Jaxon leaned in close to him, as if someone might overhear their conversation. "Just because we're Kaijen doesn't mean it's our job to decide what other people do with their planet."

"But isn't it? If they followed the ways of the Kaijen we could bring revolutionary justice to this planet. We could save these people."

"From what?" Jaxon laughed, his posture shifting. "I think maybe you're taking your anger towards Martel and directing it at these people."

"I'm not even thinking about Martel."

"Oh really? Is that why you keep scratching your metal hand?"

Castor was about to deny Jaxon's accusation, then he looked down. He'd moved from rubbing his skin to scratching his cybernetic hand. The fingernails of his organic hand were raw and scuffed from grinding against his new vetronium palm. The numb ache in his phantom hand moved up his arm and past his shoulder, all the way up into the back of his head where a rage brewed. The fact he hadn't noticed it until now disturbed him.

Jaxon's focus shifted. He saw Akeema approaching them in her hover chair. Castor put on a smile in an attempt to brush off the seriousness that still hung in the air like a rotten odor.

"Did you get lost?" Jaxon said to Akeema, being overtly playful.

"This place is a maze and emptying my colostomy bag isn't exactly a fast process," Akeema said.

"Yeah, she got lost," Castor said, leaving the uncomfortable words they'd just shared in the past. On the side of Akeema's hover chair, a long rectangular case was magnetically attached. It hadn't been there before.

"What's that?" Jaxon asked.

"Just a little something I picked up from one of the shops," Akeema said.

"Did you buy something that's going to get us in trouble?" Castor asked, sounding like a parent who suspected his kid had just stolen something.

"Don't worry it wasn't expensive," Akeema continued. "It's a little surprise. Just in case." Akeema pulled out her handheld. "I pinpointed the address Priestess Nisame's messages were sent to. It's at the end of the promenade. This way." The group hesitated, not sure what they were about to find.

Castor led the way and the others followed him into the small shop. It was a cluttered mess of old books and strange artifacts stacked floor to ceiling. A musty stench scented the air, like clothes left in an old closet during a hot summer.

Standing behind the main counter was the shop's owner, a Nezu like Priestess Nisame, but taller than she was and not as thin. His furry skin was dark gray, with a crazy thick beard clouding his chin. His large fox ears were similar to Nisame's, but the irises of his enlarged baggy eyes were pale gray. The man was disheveled, like he'd been asleep for a week or awake for a week. Just looking at him felt like being lied to.

This was the Archivist. He leaned over the dirty checkout counter, a lit cigarette on his lips. He wore a gun on his belt, like a good Montanarin. "I sure do hope you all aren't planning on using those energy swords," he said in his velvety crisp baritone drawl, his non-cigarette hand resting on the grip of his weapon.

Castor halted his approach. "Sir, we're not here to cause violence. We tried contacting you over the wireless. When we didn't receive a response, we worried something might have happened to you."

The Archivist relaxed a bit, sizing up the trio. He took a drag off his cigarette, the smoke blowing out of his scent glands like slitted chimneys. "Yeah. I kinda have a bad habit of turning off my receiver when I'm not in the mood to receive. But now I'm curious. Did she send you?"

"Not exactly," Akeema said from behind her two standing friends. "We believe your life might be in danger."

The Archivist chuckled. "Not from you, I hope. What? Nisame couldn't be bothered to face me herself? Does she have that little respect for me? That mean old bitch. I knew she wouldn't—"

"Priestess Nisame was killed six days ago," Jaxon said.

The Archivist went stiff. He digested the words, then braced himself against his checkout counter to keep himself from tipping over.

This surprised Castor. It meant this wasn't just some random acquaintance of hers. He cared. It meant they had history. "How well did you know her?"

"Not very well at all," the Archivist said, forcing a laugh in an attempt to mask his feelings. "Nisame was a combative, domineering, arrogant shrew. We could barely stand to be in each other's presence."

"You loved her," Jaxon blurted out. Castor couldn't imagine how he'd reached that conclusion and quickly dismissed it.

The Archivist smirked with bemusement. "That's a strong word. I wouldn't go that far. We just had a lot of sex is all."

Castor flinched. "I doubt that. Kaijen are forbidden from having romantic relationships."

"Right," the Archivist agreed. "We had a lot of very *unromantic* sex. I wouldn't call that a relationship. She didn't seem to have a problem with it." Castor felt a flash of sudden heat in his head, that stab of rage festering in the back of his skull starting to swell up again.

"Listen you motherfucker," Castor snapped. "You're accusing our teacher, an honorable Kaijen priestess who was my mentor, of betraying her code. She would never have broken her vows for a washed-up degenerate like you. Not willingly, at least. Either you're lying or you forced her."

"Whoa there—" the Archivist said, sucking his cigarette and muffling his words. "She came on to *me*, alright? The repressed sexual energy coming off of that woman was so thick you could bottle it. Or maybe it was my fault for just being too damn irresistible."

Castor's cybernetic hand appeared to ball itself into a fist all on its own, tight enough that the metal squeaked. His flesh hand reached for his crossglaive hilt. Jaxon stopped him.

"That's not why we're here—" Jaxon said until Castor interrupted him.

"I won't stand here and let this asshole slander our mentor. She laid down her life defending us. That woman's name deserves respect."

"Agreed," the Archivist said, exhaling smoke. "So what reason do I have to lie? Think about it. Why would Nisame come all the way out here to an independent planet like Montanari? Because it's a free world outside of the Protectorate's grip and the Kaijen have no foothold here. Free trade. Free information. No censorship. Anything she did here wouldn't get back to her Kaijen overlords. Maybe she wasn't as devoted to your sacred code as she let on."

The hotness in Castor's head spread to his blood, pulsing loud in his ears. He couldn't hear anything else. "It is taking every fiber of my being not to kill you where you stand," he said through clenched teeth.

The Archivist drew his gun in a blink, the muzzle squared at Castor's eye. "Montanari law says you just gave me every right to put holes through you. Try me, boy."

Jaxon stood between Castor and the checkout counter, shielding him from the gun's muzzle. "Sir, we're not here to fight. We all lost someone we cared about, so naturally emotions are high. Castor, apologize to the gentleman."

"I will not," Castor said, his tone sharp enough to cut. "Priestess Nisame would never have sullied her name or jeopardized her status by laying with this toxic scumbag."

"You don't know anything about women, do you son?" the Archivist sighed, holstering his gun. "Being a toxic scumbag is exactly what she liked about me. It excited her. Now tell me how she died."

On her handheld, Akeema pulled up footage of the monastery fight, much to Castor's surprise. "I thought Priestess Sabrene deleted that?"

"She thought she did too," Akeema said. She played the footage. Horror danced across the Archivist's face, his fox hears pinned back. "Nisame was killed by a former student named Hiroshi Martel," Akeema said. "He also put me in this hover chair and took Castor's hand."

The footage ended with Nisame's death. The Archivist flinched. "Whoo boy. If a novice Kaijen is knocking off priestesses in single combat then you are in far more trouble than you realize."

"That's why we need the album," Jaxon said. It was clear to Castor that his brother had taken over as speaker for the group. Castor wanted to interject, but anger choked his tongue.

"And you just expect me to hand it over?" the Archivist said. "Do you kids even know what the hell the album is? Or what it does? If it's harmless or if it's a weapon?" Their silence spoke volumes. "You idiots. You came all this way to get your hands on something you don't even understand."

"Does it matter?" Akeema said. "Nisame's killer wants it. It's obviously some kind of weapon."

"You're killing me kid," the Archivist said, rubbing the bridge above the fleshy bump on his face that was his nose, relieving the tension. "Knowledge can be a weapon depending on how it's used. Listen, everything you know about the Kaijen you learned through telepathic link. When a priestess or elder links with an initiate, they're sharing a copy of their memories. You know what happens when you make a copy of a copy of a copy?"

"It degrades," Jaxon said.

"Yes, but also becomes harder to access. That's why they still have to physically train you afterwards, to jog your brain. It helps you access those hazy memories. What's the point of having knowledge in your head if you can't remember it, right?"

"And the album is somehow supposed to change this?" Jaxon said.

"*Albums*," the Archivist said. "My research uncovered the existence of at least six different artifacts, each of which have mysterious properties."

"Can you be any more vague?" Akeema asked with nervous impatience. "I was paralyzed. All our friends were killed. Priestess Nisame was murdered in front of us," her voice cracked. She cleared her throat and swallowed. "All because of this thing. Tell us exactly what it does and how we can use it."

The Archivist groaned and shot her an annoyed glare. "Well, that all depends on whose lore you're going by." He brushed his face with a grumbled sigh and stamped out his dying cigarette. "The Kaijen spread themselves out all over the known worlds. Even the planets beyond the catapult. Not everyone was... appreciative of their expansion. They made enemies. Much of the truth behind the albums has been tainted by time. Some of the texts I've found refer to an album that can extend life while other texts claim it can open gateways to horror dimensions. All sorts of crazy stuff. Nisame wanted me to find her one. She wanted to see for herself."

"But why?" Castor spoke up, his whole body contorted with disbelief. The growing rage at the back of his head was still there, expanding. "What would she have possibly needed with one of these album things?"

A thin smile slithered across the Archivist's lips, as if he had a secret he was dying to tell. "Because she wanted more power. Nisame believed one of the albums could strengthen her Kaijen tuning abilities. Make her more powerful than the Quorum of Elders. It was always about power with her."

"What reason would she have to think any of this was true?" Jaxon said.

"Because she knew something you didn't," the Archivist said. "Did you think the Kaijen's telekinetic powers developed naturally? They were a mutation. A by-product of exposure to localized radiation. Prolonged exposure is believed to supercharge the parts of your brains that allow you to link and tune, making all those fuzzy memories nice and sharp and in high definition. The albums mimic that radiation."

"That sounds like a goddamn weapon to me," Akeema said.

"I liken it more to a drug," the Archivist said. "But yeah, sure. It's a weapon. And Nisame wanted it all for herself."

Castor's anger turned his throat into fire. "This guy is fucking lying! If the elders knew we were even having this conversation—"

"They'd kill you?" the Archivist said, flat and serious. "Now you understand why Nisame wanted me to keep my findings a secret."

"You already have the album," Jaxon speculated. "But you didn't give it to her. Why?"

The Archivist hesitated. "It's dangerous. Nisame thought it could make her more powerful, but it was just as likely to kill her. She was willing to take that risk. I wasn't."

"That's why you kept it from her?" Akeema said, rage radiating behind her words. "If she had the album when she fought Martel, she might still be alive!"

Her words sobered the Archivist. His large eyes moistened. "I was protecting her. How could I have possibly known?"

"None of this makes sense," Castor growled. He felt like his head was about to explode. "Priestess Nisame wouldn't seek power. The entire Kaijen religion is built on species equality. A Kaijen doesn't want to be better than anyone else because then everyone wouldn't be equal."

The Archivist scoffed. "You people have a hierarchy, don't you? The elders are on top, the priestesses are in the middle, and you lot are on the bottom. Nisame didn't start off as a priestess, she was a novice just like you. What do you think she had to do to get promoted?"

"She is— she was an exceptional teacher," Akeema said. "Just because she was chosen doesn't mean she wanted to be chosen."

"She absolutely did," the Archivist chuckled. "I knew her. Really knew her. Not just the fake persona she wore to protect her social ranking. That woman was all drive, ambition, and ego. That's how powerful people get powerful, they need to prove to themselves they're better than everyone else."

"Bullshit!" Castor hissed. "Ambition is what led to the great Kaijen war. Dozens of different sects, each one believing they were better than the others, using their tuning abilities to slaughter each other until the first Quorum of Elders brought peace."

"And just how do you think they negotiated that peace, genius?" the Archivist said. "With kind words? Or at the tip of a crossglaive?"

The room was cool, but sweat sheeted Castor's skin. "The elders are upholders of peace and equality. They were saviors. They did what they had to do so Kaijen like us could coexist without jealousy or a desire to be superior."

The Archivist smiled, showing his crooked teeth. "And yet here you are, seeking power to kill a Kaijen whose skills far outmatch yours. Funny how that works."

Castor took it as a threat. The contradiction couldn't be ignored. The hypocrisy. The old ugly Nezu was right. Castor loathed him for it.

The shop fell silent.

The Archivist lit a new cigarette and breathed smoke. He moved to access a safe hidden inside his checkout counter. It read his biometrics and opened. From it, he pulled out an old fossil that resembled a piece of opal petrified wood. It was crimson and spiked with unusual blood red veins that seemed to pulse and vibrate.

"I'll be honest," the Archivist said. "All of my research tells me this thing is incredibly dangerous and beyond your control. But... if it can help you take down Nisame's killer, then it's all yours."

Chapter Eleven: Jaxon

The ethereal stone-like object clutched in the Archivist's furry hand dazzled Jaxon. It dazzled all of them. Jaxon couldn't take his eyes off of the odd-looking thing. Reflective red veins covered its surface like gleaming cracks or scars. Within the red grooves were nested a latticework of multicolored stone that sparkled in the light. No, not just a sparkle. They moved. Like a colony of microscopic insects marching along a web of canyons slightly wider than a human hair.

It was hypnotic, but he couldn't imagine it was worth all the blood that had been shed to secure it.

The object could've easily been mistaken for a cheap gift shop paperweight, or one of those phony healing crystals they sell to naive old people over the wireless. It was a pretty thing, but unassuming. Jaxon reached out to take it into his hand, then hesitated. He imagined it was a hot coal that would burn him if he touched it.

"Terrifying, isn't it?" the Archivist said. "If this thing actually does what it's advertised to do, do you really think you'll be able to go back to the way things were before? Back to being just a lowly novice Kaijen? Or are you going to feel like everyone else is beneath you? That's what it takes to win."

Castor opened his mouth to speak. His words hid inside his throat.

"It won't come to that," Akeema said, trying to get a better look at the album. "We are humble. Any advanced abilities we might gain won't change that. We'll always be who we are. Who we always have been. We're the good guys."

The Archivist wasn't convinced. "Isn't there a saying among you earthers? About power and how it corrupts? What will the Kaijen elders do when they find out you possess power they didn't give you? Will they see you as equals? Or as their competition?"

Another question no one wanted to answer. Another veiled

threat to their warrior's honor.

Even if the album was capable of all the magic and mysticism it was said to be and more, Jaxon wanted to believe its powers wouldn't change them. That he and his adopted siblings would still remain the same good people, and that the change wouldn't radically upend everything he believed about himself and the world and his place in it.

Jaxon had to believe it. The alternative would be too painfully unthinkable. He'd already violated his vow with the rocket boots. He withheld information and disobeyed a direct order from a superior. When one domino topples, so does another. The album would just be the next one to fall. It would lead to another. That was a worry for later. After they had won.

And still, he didn't want to take it.

As a child, Jaxon took great pleasure in reading folklore. Human culture was built on the back of myths. Every monster had a weakness, every hero an Achilles' heel. The album made his hands tingle, like static electricity or magnetism. Its allure was stronger than his will. He feared the object would be his kryptonite. The Archivist placed the album in his palm.

It was warm. Other than that, it didn't react. It felt lifeless. Dead. "How does it work?"

The Archivist batted his ears. "That is the question, isn't it? I've tried everything I can think of. It absorbs every kind of energy I throw at it. I suspect only a Kaijen can activate it. How exactly? That's your mystery now."

Akeema wasn't satisfied. "Where did it come from? Where did you get it?"

"I bought it," the Archivist said. "A Sabracian miner sold it to me. Said she found it on some dust bowl in the ass-end of known space called—"

Castor's cybernetic hand snatched the album from Jaxon's grip too fast, the jagged edges of the object scraping his palm and fingers. Castor held the album tight in his mechanical hand. Jaxon worried he would break it. The raw anger that stung Castor's face suggested he planned to do just that.

"Coming here was a mistake," Castor said, stress lacing his voice.

"Whatever power this thing can give us, it's not our place to have it." He stormed out of the shop with the album.

"Goddamnit Castor!" Akeema said. He didn't hear her, or he didn't want to. She fumbled the controls of her hover chair and struggled to turn it around. Jaxon tried to help her when she captured his arm. "Please stop him before he does something stupid."

Jaxon bolted after Castor and nearly collided with a group of strangers. Instinctively they reached for their concealed guns, expecting an attack. Jaxon showed them his palms. "Sorry. My mistake." He hurried past them.

Castor stood out among the aliens. Jaxon found him on the promenade leaning against the safety railing. His artificial hand was stretched out, threatening to drop the album down the indoor waterfall where it would be lost forever.

Jaxon stopped short and moved slowly, keeping his tone low and nonthreatening. "Whoa there. Is that really the right move right now?"

"Doing my duty is always the right move," Castor said, more to himself than Jaxon. His grip on the album appeared to loosen.

Jaxon stepped closer, his hands up in a calming position. "Can we maybe talk about this first? I'd really like to talk about it for a minute," Jaxon said, his body vibrating with nervousness.

"You're smarter than this, Castor," Akeema said from behind Jaxon. "What did Priestess Nisame teach us? We were meant to fight the evils of the galaxy when they reveal themselves. The album is the only chance we have to do that."

"Just because you've stopped believing in us doesn't mean I have," Castor said. "You might see it as utilizing an advantage, but I see it as cheating. Anything that artificially makes us more powerful is selfish."

"It's necessary," she said.

"Even if it means we'll no longer be equals?"

With little emotion, Akeema said, "That would be my choice, yes. We've already played his game. Where *he* had the advantage. Look at how much it cost us. We're the good guys. Whatever helps us win is the right action to take."

"I see," Castor said with melancholy. "That go the same for you too, Jaxon? Is this rock worth compromising who we are? Is it really worth risking another Kaijen war just to win a fight against a single man?"

Jaxon's brain stuttered. His overwhelming sense of fear and doubt came out of remission. It nagged at him. The indecision. The uncertainty of not knowing if the choices that led him here were the right ones or not. If the album was to be their salvation or their doom. What he did know was that the three of them had come too far to start second guessing themselves now. He lacked the confidence to express himself out loud and speak it into reality.

So his answer was silence.

"You'd rather we do nothing?" Akeema said in his place. "Just hope for the best and assume everything works out next time? That's moronic. We cheated death once. It won't happen twice. One way or another we are using that thing."

"Even if it results in mass death?" Castor said. "Can you live with that? Because I can't." His mechanical fingers twitched, threatening to let the album slip into oblivion.

Unlike Jaxon, Akeema wasn't afraid to approach Castor. She guided her hover chair right in front of him, the vehicle's ceramic bumper brushing his legs. "I don't know that for certain and neither do you," Akeema said. "I do know Priestess Nisame wouldn't throw the album away out of fear. She'd use it, and look like a badass while doing it. So that's what we should do. Because I want to see the look on Martel's face when we kick his balls into his throat and I want you by my side when that happens. If the album can do that then it's worth the risk. It's worth *every* risk."

"This isn't about the album, is it?" Jaxon said to Castor, reading into his conflicted expression while taking slow deliberate steps forward. "It was hard for me too. Hearing about what Priestess Nisame did here. She was our strong flawless leader. Then we find found out that all this time she was breaking our sacred rules. Rules she chastised us for not following ourselves."

"Those were all *lies*," Castor said, panicked desperation draping his face. He almost looked like a different person. "That old bastard is a scoundrel and a liar. Nothing he says should be believed."

"But you do believe him," Jaxon said softly. "Or else you wouldn't be reacting like this. I feel it too. She was our mentor. She took care of us. She loved us. But she wouldn't recognize you right now. Whatever she did when she was away from the monastery doesn't change what she taught us. What her guidance meant to us. She was still our teacher."

Castor paused for a long breath. Then one more.

Seconds stretched. Castor's arm folded. He brought the album safely away from the railing. He relaxed, all the turmoil in his attitude having bled away. Castor sleeved away his tears before they had a chance to sheet his cheeks. Jaxon pulled Castor into his arms.

"It's not the end of the world," Jaxon said in his brother's ear. "Listen to Akeema. You know she's right. If we can use the album to protect ourselves from Martel then I think we should. Better us than him. We owe it to Nisame, and the others."

"What if we can't handle it?" Castor said, choking up. "What if the power makes us just like Martel? Can you live with that Jaxon? Can you, Akeema?" She was on the verge of tears herself, but Jaxon knew her too well. She'd never let herself be seen so vulnerable. She steeled her emotions into a calmness Jaxon envied.

"I'll live with it," Akeema said. "I trust you and I trust Jaxon more than anyone else alive. If anyone can make this work, it's us. I believe in us."

***

Montanari's sun hung low in the sky, its brightness dimming.

The trio boarded a maglev train bound for the landing platform. Jaxon could hardly feel the acceleration as it carried them through the towering city. He had a terrible thought and imagined Yoko stranding them here so she could go get shit-faced in a bar somewhere. It was certainly possible, but somehow, he doubted she would turn down such easy money. He hoped to see her again.

The train car was half as full as the one that brought them to the Archivist, giving the trio room to breathe. Jaxon held the album. It drew their focus to the point Jaxon feared they might stare a hole through it. He dragged his fingertips over its raised pits and ridges, trying to figure it out, feeling around for a secret button or hidden opening. He found none. Castor watched him closely, his body language still anxious and unsure.

Akeema tapped her fingers against her hover chair with the patience of a spoiled child. She was itching for her turn to handle it. "Did you find the on switch?" she asked.

Castor cleared his throat. "How do you know that thing isn't going to suddenly blow up in your face? Or spontaneously set you on fire?"

"God, I hope not," Jaxon said. He moved the album further away from his face. Just in case. "Am I the only one who was kind of expecting it to play music?"

Akeema reached out to Jaxon, opening and closing her pale hand like a toddler begging for her toy back. "Give it here. It needs a woman's touch." Jaxon tossed the album to Akeema.

She rolled it between her hands, examining it, rubbing it against her skin. She looked even more perplexed by the oddness of the artifact. "It's so strange. It looks like bone, but it feels… soft. Almost like skin. And it's heavier than it looks."

"It's unnatural," Castor said. "We shouldn't be playing with it. It's dangerous."

"What if the old man stiffed us? What if it's a fake?" Akeema said. "This could be one gigantic red herring. What if he kept the real one for himself?"

"You're right," Jaxon said. "Clearly he lured us all the way here just to hurl insults at us and mock our religion."

"He wouldn't be the first alien who did that recently," Castor said bitterly. Yoko's barbs must've cut Castor deeper than Jaxon realized. When he'd chosen to become a Kaijen, Jaxon was fully aware of how unpopular the religion had been. Some groups outright despised them, but the life of a Kaijen had appealed to his younger self, so much so he was willing to risk dying to live among them. He'd never questioned his decision.

Now his mind was drowning in doubt.

"You never told me why you decided to become a Kaijen," Jaxon said to Castor.

After a pause, Castor said, "Because I believe in justice. In species equality. In a classless existence. All the tenets the Kaijen stand for. Because I wanted to be involved in something bigger than myself. You?"

Jaxon forced a laugh. "Well, you've got me beat there. I mostly just wanted to feel like I was part of a family. How about you Akeema?"

Akeema's eyes widened and froze, as if she hadn't expected to be called upon. Her eyes darted around in their sockets, searching for a response. "I don't know," she began, then took a moment to put some real thought into it. "I guess... I think I became a Kaijen because I wanted to help people. I grew up seeing how terrible people could be when they were deprived of food and safety. I wanted to be an ally to the weak and disenfranchised. To be part of a movement dedicated to positivity and empowerment. But..." she paused for two heartbeats. Her head lowered. "No. That's bullshit." She faked a laugh and looked away from them, perhaps out of shame. "I never liked me. I've never felt unique or important. Or beautiful. Or smart. Becoming a Kaijen was a way for me to be special. To *feel* special."

Her need to control her emotions were at odds with her desire to be open and honest with her brothers. "But when Martel slashed my spine, I thought... this is it. I'm dead. And what have I done with my life? What have any of us accomplished? We've trained to be Kaijen warriors for years. And for what? We're little more than overqualified librarians with energy swords. I thought we were being trained to go out and fight bad guys and stop them from hurting people. I'm angry, but not at Martel. Nisame should have showed us how to use our powers so we could defend ourselves." Her eyes sparked with a glint of melancholy. "We should be more powerful than we are. She should've taught us how to be better than she was."

Castor's face flashed with concern. "We're not supposed to want to be more, Akeema. No single being should be better than anyone else. It almost sounds like you're saying you don't really believe what you believe."

"What good has believing what we believe gotten us?" Akeema said. She held up the album. "*This* has to mean something. All of our sacrifices. All of our fallen friends. Priestess Nisame. Their deaths have to count for something. Because if I was maimed and nearly killed for defending a lie... that's something I don't think I could ever recover from."

"It's not a lie," Castor insisted. "We are the good guys. Just like you said. The Kaijen are the good guys."

Jaxon leaned forward in his seat. "But if the Kaijen *weren't* actually the good guys, how would we know it?"

***

The sky was a streak of creamy orange with swirls of gray-blue clouds as dusk blanketed the city. The maglev train slowed to a stop and arrived at the high-rise landing platform. The train car's automatic doors hissed and separated, letting the humid air into the temperature-controlled cabin. Jaxon and Castor stepped out of their car with Akeema's hover chair trailing behind. They made their way through the maze of parked ships until they caught sight of the *Saragos* ahead.

A pair of large tubes were hooked to the ship, feeding its reactor fuel, and topping off its reserve of liquid helium for its internal heat sinks. Betty stood on top of the ship, sparks flying around her as she sealed micro fractures on the ship's skin with a welding torch. Yoko stood on the loading ramp oiling its gears. She wiped her forehead with the back of her palm, smearing a streak of black oil above her right eyebrow.

Jaxon watched the petite silver woman look up and they saw each other. The wind tousled her victory rolls and her ponytail flapped wildly beside her like a black tail. Jaxon hadn't realized that he'd been smiling. The corners of Yoko's black lips began to curl into what he anticipated would be a reciprocal smile until her thick expressive eyebrows hiked up her creased forehead. Her chin rose and her eyes darted up, looking above him.

Time slowed down for Jaxon.

A moving shadow on the ground ahead of him drew his attention. He looked up where Yoko must have seen what was casting the shadow. Sunlight hit Jaxon's eyes, forcing him to shield them.

Before they could focus, the stun grenade had already landed in front of Castor's feet.

A flash of light blinded him and Akeema, but Jaxon's palm had protected his retinas from the flash. He was the only one who could see what was happening.

His ears were a different story. They rang like an alarm clock was stuffed inside them with the volume turned up to excruciating. Everything was chaos.

Jaxon reached for his wrist control so his rocket boots could carry him away, but he didn't. He couldn't abandon his friends. If they were about to die, then he would die with them. Together.

Martel jumped into view out of nowhere and landed in the center of the trio. He held out his hand and the album flew out of Akeema's grasp and into Martel's palm like a magnet. Martel's ability to tune so effortlessly and on command was as impressive as it was terrifying. He kicked Akeema's hover chair with the force of an ox and it flipped over. Akeema spilled out of its carriage and onto the platform, still blind and deafened.

Castor yelled in desperation, his drawn crossglaive swinging wild and uncoordinated like a maniac, blindly slashing at the air, and threatening to slice Jaxon in half. Jaxon's thin fingers stabbed at his wrist control and his rocket boots sent him flying upwards. Martel made an inhuman leap up into the air and buried his foot deep into Jaxon's ribs with enough power to send him crashing into the hull of a small parked starship.

Pain rippled through Jaxon's back. He fell a short distance before hitting the hot platform with a thud. Nerves in his side screamed from the kick's impact, like someone had taken a club to his ribs. Jaxon watched helplessly as Martel subdued Castor, kicking the crossglaive out of his hand and sweeping Castor's feet out from under him the way Nisame had taught him, had taught them all. Then he stomped Castor's stomach.

Martel had beaten them. Again. Quicker, this time. And now he had the album.

Then, something curious happened.

Jaxon hadn't seen Yoko enter the *Saragos*, but she was walking down the ramp hauling an automatic rifle that looked comically huge in comparison to her tiny frame. She planted her feet, leveled her aim, and fired a high impact round at Martel; the rifle's recoil nearly knocking her on her ass. Jaxon expected to see Martel's head explode, blood and chunks of his brain spraying the platform before he doubled over.

Instead, the bullet curved around him, putting a baseball sized hole in some poor bastard's gaudy luxury yacht parked several meters behind him.

"Uh-oh," Yoko said, her face a mix of shock and amazement. She kept her feet planted and bent her knees. She thumbed a knob on her rifle, switching to full auto. Yoko squeezed off an entire clip of rounds at Martel; the barrel glowed amber from the hot gasses. The recoil physically pushed Yoko backwards, the soles of her shoes scraping against the platform and leaving streaks.

Martel dodged the bullets.

He was just too damn fast, weaving out of the path of the onslaught of rounds like a magic trick, the bullets sailing past him and impacting other parked ships. All the while, he advanced on Yoko. His crossglaive cut through the air and sliced the barrel of Yoko's rifle clean off. If she were terrified, she didn't show it. Where Jaxon expected to see alarm, he saw a woman amused and excited.

"This ain't your business," Martel said, annoyed.

"I'm making it my business, hoo-mon," Yoko said. A tiny pistol slid down her sleeve and into her hand. She leveled the muzzle at the man's bald head, but Martel had a grip on her wrist. Yoko's face twisted as he overpowered her. Betty jumped down from atop the ship to her rescue. Martel turned, catapulting Betty across the platform like a ragdoll.

Jaxon's body pleaded with him to stay down. He ignored it and forced himself to stand. One tap and his rocket boots gave him a brief boost into the air, landing near Martel. The bald man twisted Yoko's arm behind her back, using her as a shield. She struggled to break his grip even though it was useless.

"Just so we're clear," Yoko grunted, "I would have gotten you if you weren't a foosha cheater."

"It's called alternative winning," Martel smiled.

Jaxon drew his crossglaive. "This is our fight! Let her go!"

"Alright," Martel said, then threw Yoko, tuning her through the air an impossible distance. The small silver woman screamed as she fell over the platform's edge where she would plummet to her death.

Jaxon didn't think. Two taps on his control device and his rocket boots were burning at full thrust. He flew over the platform's edge and angled his body upside down, rocketing straight down the side of the platform like a human missile.

The sudden acceleration decreased the flow of oxygen to his brain and the world began to blur around him; the first sign he was starting to black out. But the planet's reduced gravity worked in his favor, giving him just enough time to catch up to Yoko. His hands reached out and hooked his arms around her, catching the silver woman in a bear hug. Jaxon swung his feet around so they were right side up, letting thrust from his rocket boots slow their descent before they could slam into a walkway a few dozen levels below them.

They hovered in the air for a moment, catching their breath.

"I didn't need your help," Yoko said with a hoarse voice. The wind smothered her words. The fall had ruined her hairstyle and draped it over her face in a tangled mess. "I had everything under control."

"Then you won't mind it if I let you go," Jaxon teased. Yoko's body tensed. Her grip on him tightened like a vice.

"Foosha, hoo-mon," Yoko shouted, then looked down. They were high enough in the air that they couldn't see the ground beyond the small platform Yoko had nearly splatted on, just a murky haze of an abyss that didn't appear to have a bottom. Jaxon could feel Yoko's heart beating through her chest. She shut her eyes tight.

"You really are afraid of heights," Jaxon said over the wind.

"Isn't everybody?" Yoko said, and she had to shout to be heard.

High above them, a loud boom echoed through the air like a thunder clap. Jaxon looked up and saw a smoke trail, confirming something up on the landing platform had exploded. With a tap to his wrist panel, he and Yoko floated up the side of the high-rise and landed on the platform. Yoko was so relieved to be on solid ground she almost kissed it.

Jaxon scanned the platform for Martel, but he was gone. As was Akeema. Betty was bent over Castor, tending to him as he recovered from the stun grenade. Jaxon sprinted to them.

"I'm okay— don't worry about me," Castor coughed out. "Akeema. Help her. Help Akeema."

Chapter Twelve: Akeema

The stun grenade exploded in front of Akeema like a bomb.

Her vision flashed white and a high-pitched whine filled her ears. Her imagination convinced her that the whole world was ending. She'd never felt more helpless, which was saying a lot given she'd be a quadriplegic a few days ago. The album yanked itself out of her hand and Akeema panicked. She'd been left completely defenseless. Someone could have performed a coup de grâce on her with a toothbrush if they'd wanted to. She could've laughed if she hadn't felt so pathetic.

The problem was the hover chair. Akeema fought to get out of it. If she was going to die, she at least wanted to go out on her feet instead of sitting on her ass. Her center of gravity shifted as the bulky hover chair tipped over, dumping Akeema onto the hot platform. Her spine still ached, because it had never stopped aching. At least now the pain was tolerable.

The world of white began to bloom with colors and shapes and the screeching in her ears died a slow death. The first thing she saw was the mouthy Kish pilot shooting at Martel, and missing. *So much for ranged weapons.* Akeema's vision struggled to focus. She could just barely make out Martel tucking the album into a pouch hanging from his belt. *He followed us here,* she deduced, accompanied by the stinging realization that they'd led Martel straight to the album. *He played us.*

Anger marched its way up Akeema's bionic spine. It acted as a stimulant. It focused her senses. The Batelaan doctor warned her not to push herself too hard too soon, not to try to walk for at least another few days. Akeema wanted to believe she was stronger than the doctors had given her credit for. She rolled over onto her stomach, shifting her weight to her knees. Her legs were sluggish to respond. She willed them to act, and with few painful breaths she found herself standing for the first time since the surgery. She swayed, then found her balance. It was like trying on an old pair of shoes that still fit, but were lined with weights.

By this point, Martel had taken the annoying silver pilot hostage.

"This is our fight!" she heard Jaxon say, the quiet hum of tinnitus still ringing her ears. "Let her go!" And then Akeema watched Martel tune-throw Yoko. The tiny gray terror sailed through the air like she was being blown away by the wind, her arms and legs flailing, her hands grabbing at nothing. Then she dropped and disappeared over the edge of the platform.

Before she saw it, Akeema heard the exhaust from Jaxon's rocket boots. She watched in horror as Jaxon shot after her like a bullet, like the noble idiot he was. It reminded her of a character from one of those old superhero movies she'd seen as a child. As much as Akeema didn't like the annoying silver bitch, she didn't want to see this woman die. Akeema surprised herself by hoping Jaxon would save her. She had faith in him.

When the hover chair was knocked over, the metal briefcase magnetically attached to it had flipped open, revealing the rocket launcher she'd purchased; it flopped out of the case and onto the platform. Yoko had been right. Akeema walked into a store and bought one, no questions asked. It took less time than emptying her colostomy bag, which was now on the ground and leaking her waste onto the platform.

Akeema picked up the rocket launcher. It was lighter than it looked. She'd never even fired a gun before; the shop owner could tell as much. He gave her a ten second tutorial on how the rocket launcher worked, which mainly consisted of *point this end at what you want to go boom, then squeeze the trigger.* So that's what she did.

Martel turned in her direction just as the projectile sped towards him, too fast to dodge. Martel waved his hand, using his tuning ability to send the rocket-propelled grenade off course. It nosedived into the platform and exploded in a brilliant display of fiery destruction. Embers glittered in the air like fireflies.

The blast hadn't killed Martel. It flung him off of the high-rise, his fingers having found the edge of the platform. He hung off the side of the building, too weak to pull himself up. *Tuning must've taken a lot out of him.* Akeema lurched towards her enemy, still not used to walking with her new spine. She pulled her crossglaive from her belt, the programmable vetronium metal in its hilt extending out to form a superheated blade ready to make its first kill.

Martel saw her coming. And, for the first time, Akeema could see his face crinkle with worry. He let go of the ledge and he fell.

Akeema expected to see him plummet down the length of the high-rise to his death. He was too slippery for that. She watched him land atop a departing maglev train a few levels below that hadn't yet reached its full acceleration. She'd lost him.

No. Shit shit shi shit. Her mind raced. He was getting away again. On *her* watch. The train was moving slowly enough. She could make it. *I won't leave this planet until I see him die.*

And then she was weightless.

The planet's lower gravity allowed her to jump further than she ever had. It made the sensation of falling unreal.

"Akeema!" she heard Castor scream as she dropped for what felt like minutes. It was seconds. The maglev train came up at her like a zoomed-in image as she spilled onto the roof of the last car, then rolled over the side. Akeema's fingers gripped the roof's narrow grooves, saving her from what would've been a long fall and a messy death.

Her arms struggled to pull the rest of her body up onto the train car's roof. Her heart pounded against her ribs like a caged animal trying to claw its way out. It was louder than the wind. Louder than a bomb.

The maglev train picked up speed and adrenaline flooded her bloodstream. It couldn't completely numb the pain of her landing. Pins and needles shot up Akeema's back and fingers. She felt the ache of a knot blooming at the base of her skull.

She didn't care. She'd made it. She'd won another chance to kill her enemy. Or another chance for him to kill her.

The maglev train increased its acceleration. Akeema tried to stand, but the rushing wind threatened to blow her off into oblivion. She clung to the train car's roof, keeping her body pressed flat against it.

A few train cars ahead, she saw Martel. He'd pulled a jagged piece of shrapnel out of his leg. It must've found its way there from the explosion. It looked like it hurt.

Good, she thought, and relished the pain she'd caused him. A small taste of things to come.

Martel used the flat side of his blazing hot crossglaive blade to cauterize his wound. He cried out in pain. The sound brought a smile to Akeema's lips. She steadied herself and crawled towards Martel, the rushing wind filling her ears and trying to beat her back. *The wind should know better than to try to stop me from doing what I've set out to do.*

Though Martel was wounded and vulnerable, she recognized he was still incredibly dangerous, but this was Akeema's best chance to end him and turning back wasn't an option. Her only path was forward to victory or to death, and she wouldn't stop until one or the other had occurred.

Akeema bent forward in a crouching position, keeping her center of gravity low. She wormed her way forward, closing the gap. Wind continued to batter her pale bruised skin and made her eyes and mouth drier than a camel's asshole, but she didn't care. Her vision tunneled. Nothing else mattered beyond catching Martel.

He was one car away and still reeling from his injured leg. Just a little further and he would be close enough to touch with her crossglaive.

Akeema considered making a quick charge forward and stabbing Martel through his back, killing the son of a bitch for good. She pictured it in her mind and decided to make it reality. It would be a dishonorable, cowardly move. Underhanded. Unbecoming of a Kaijen.

That was fine with her. As long as he was dead. In this moment she didn't give one damn, two shits, or three fucks about Kaijen honor. Only Martel's death.

Her fingers ached at the joints from gripping the train car's metal grooves. Her right hand reached for her crossglaive hilt, ready to activate it the moment she was within striking distance. Her back arched like a sprinter on the starting line, preparing to make her mad dash to her target. Just a little bit closer...

Then the fucking maglev train curved around one of the tulip shaped buildings and Akeema's balance got away from her. Her arms flapped as her shoes skidded against the metal grating, taking her closer to the deadly edge. The surging wind pushed her backwards, threatening to sling Akeema off of the train car's roof again. She panicked and collapsed flat on her stomach, halting her advance. She scraped her knees on the grating. It was the least of her worries.

Martel looked back and saw her. She caught the twitch of surprise in his eyes when he realized he wasn't alone.

Well shit. Her advantaged disappeared like she'd never had it to begin with.

The maglev train cleared the city limits, leaving behind the jungle of glass, metal, and concrete. It sped forward into the surrounding jungle on a network of heavy-duty magnetic tracks that cut through the forest, connecting the other cities scattered across the continent.

Akeema's train was en route to the northern most city further up the coast.

Martel recovered from his injury and managed to crouch despite the intense wind. He faced Akeema and stood his ground. His expression was as bare as his bald head.

Any sense of fear or anxiety Akeema had previously held had long since melted away. Only the anger remained. It fueled her.

Akeema resumed her advance when the faint whine of Jaxon's rocket boots cut through the roaring wind behind her. Jaxon swooped by above her and landed one carriage length ahead of Martel. They had him boxed in.

"Surrender!" Jaxon shouted. It annoyed Akeema. She didn't like the idea that Jaxon was under the illusion she'd let him take Martel in alive. That simply wasn't going to happen. Either she was going to kill him or he was going to kill her. There would be no middle ground. She wouldn't tolerate it.

Akeema saw something past Jaxon that made her eyes wide as saucers.

The maglev train was headed straight for a gigantic mountain side with twin incoming and outgoing train tunnels bored into them, lined with electromagnetic rails.

If Akeema, Jaxon and Martel remained on top of the maglev train when it entered the tunnel, they would slam into its mouth and be killed. Martel must've reached the same conclusion. He staked his crossglaive into the carriage beneath his feet and began to cut a hole into its roof. He stomped the cutout with his foot and it gave way, dropping him into the train car.

Akeema had no choice but to copy him, though the hole she'd cut was closer to a jagged triangle.

She collapsed her crossglaive and stomped her foot on the cutout with a loud metallic thud. It wouldn't budge. Jaxon attempted to follow them, but the tunnel's maw was coming at him too fast. He tapped his wrist mounted control panel and his boots rocketed him up and away to safety.

Akeema only had seconds.

She stomped her triangular cutout with all the force she had again and again and again until it caved in, dropping her into the car a moment before the maglev train sped into the mountain tunnel. The heavy metal cutout of the car's roof under her feet pancaked a number of, thankfully, empty train seats. A number of passengers stood nearby, bracing themselves. They must've seen her crossglaive stab through the ceiling and vacated their seats before the cutout had a chance to squish them. That would explain why the frightened passengers were rushing to evacuate to the nearest car.

"Sorry," Akeema said. Not that they could hear her over the wind whistling through the new skylight she'd made and the panicked murmurs of the crowd.

Outside of the windows was the black of the tunnel. Strips of light embedded in the car's walls illuminated the interior. It took Akeema's eyes a moment to adjust. Once they had, she headed for Martel's train car. The doors wouldn't open, likely a short in the door's electronics caused by her cutting through the train car's ceiling. She used her crossglaive to make her own door and entered.

A flurry of multi-species passengers pushed past her in their rush to escape Martel's car. He was using his crossglaive to fend off a handful of braver gun-wielding passengers that drew down on him. Martel used his crossglaive to swat their bullets away with a speed and precision only possible with the aid of tuning. He used that same ability to pull the weapons from the passenger's hands. It perplexed and terrified them.

Akeema's overwhelming sense of anger was tempered by a new sensation.

Jealousy.

It was unfair to her, how Martel wielded such incredible power so effortlessly. As if he'd been born with it. As if he'd earned it. If anyone deserved that kind of power, it was *her*. Witnessing his flashy display of tuning power made Akeema's blood hot and reddened her face.

The disarmed passengers scampered away in fear. Martel let them go. They weren't his concern.

He turned around, his cold gaze finding hers. Akeema squared her shoulders and fell into a combat stance, the tip of her crossglaive blade aimed at him.

A showdown.

But not to Martel. He collapsed his sword and holstered the hilt. "It probably won't make a difference," he said softly, "but before we get started, I'm glad you survived." He sounded sincere. Almost apologetic. But he was right, it didn't make a shred of difference.

"I have more lives than you have teeth," she said in a clipped, flat tone, her lips compressed.

A look registered on Martel's face that could've been admiration or amusement. "I regret what I did to you. It wasn't personal. But I gave you the chance to back down. Don't make the same mistake twice. Challenge me and you will lose, Akeema." His words hit her ears like insults. Hearing her own name come out of his mouth sounded like a threat.

She had to be swift.

Akeema moved fast, lunging at Martel in a furious rage. Her crossglaive blade swung with a violent ferocity, slashing through the carriage's seats and vertical hand rails in an attempt to strike at Martel's neck.

He didn't bother to draw his crossglaive.

Martel simply ducked or dodged Akeema's blows. Her crossglaive chopped through almost every object inside the train car, except Martel. He refused to retaliate. He didn't have to. It was the latest in a long line of insults against her.

Akeema screamed, "Fight me! Fight me you fucking coward!"

"I really don't want to hurt you. Not any more than I already have," Martel said in between dodges. He sounded like a parent talking down to an impotent child having a temper tantrum. It made her angrier, made her forget all the skill and grace of crossglaive combat instilled in her by Priestess Nisame. Akeema swung her energy sword like a belligerent fool with a baseball bat.

Her wild swinging slashed up the carriage's ceiling lights causing sparks to rain down, followed by near darkness as the maglev train continued its journey through the mountain's dark tunnel.

Martel snatched Akeema's sword wrist with enough strength he could've broken it. Instead, he drove her crossglaive blade through the carriage's skin and into the tunnel wall outside. Akeema tried to retract the blade, but the damage had already been done. Cutting through metal and solid rock at however many kilometers the train was speeding caused the programmable metal in the blade to malfunction. It began to erratically collapse and extend in an unpredictable way that made it dangerous to both of them. Akeema dropped the weapon. It wriggled on the floor until it finally stopped working and collapsed for good, broken.

It left Akeema defenseless.

Martel stared at her, waiting for her to make a move. *He wants me to run. He wants me to turn tail like some scared little girl. Well fuck him.*

Her foot brushed something hard on the floor. One of the passenger's discarded guns. She grabbed it up. Akeema had never fired a gun before. She wasn't prepared for the kick, or the deafening bang in such a confined space. The muzzle flashes illuminated the cabin for fractions of a second. Wherever she aimed, Martel made sure not to be there. The rounds weren't high impact, just standard slugs.

The gun clicked empty and she threw it at him. A miss. She squared up on Martel.

"Really?" Martel said, like she'd told a bad joke. "Are you in that much of a hurry to go back to the hospital? Or do you just like losing?"

Akeema growled. She pressed her attack, assaulting him with a hurricane of swings and kicks.

Not a single blow landed.

Martel was just too damn good. Too damn fast. He blocked or outmaneuvered her with a balletic grace that would've impressed her had he been anyone else.

It made Martel overconfident.

Akeema saw an opening. She stabbed the heel of her foot into his leg wound and won a guttural groan of pain from Martel. Akeema followed up with quick jabs to his solar plexus that actually landed this time, but didn't have anywhere near the same impact. Her fists hurt.

For the second time she had caused Martel pain. Not only that, she'd gotten him angry. It was fuel that fed the fire burning in her heart, a small pinprick of victory. A scratch compared to the misery he'd caused her. Was still causing her, but damn if it didn't make her feel fantastic. She smiled, baiting him.

"Fine," Martel said through gritted teeth. "I'm nothing if not fair."

He came at her. Akeema anticipated and dodged, then returned a few quick blows. They missed. Martel countered and this time, this time, hit her. Hard. Gone were the flirtatious dodging. There was no more holding back. She wasn't prepared.

Akeema ate the first punch that smashed her face, breaking her nose. It made her eyes wet and distorted her vision. The next blow came and the brick that was Martel's fist hit her square in the chest. A bright vivid pain followed. It stunted her breathing. The unrelenting ache in her back now had competition.

She stumbled backwards on her heels, her eyes darting around, trying to catch sight of something. A blur of color. Martel was moving faster than her vision could track. Instinct made her shield herself.

The heel of Martel's boot swung for her head. Akeema's forearms blocked the blow. The impact was crushing and sharp with pain. She worried her radius or ulna bones were fractured, if not broken. Another fast kick came for her stomach.

This one she couldn't block.

Communication between her brain and the rest of her body stalled. The shooting pain of hornets dragging their stingers up her belly and chest didn't register until several seconds after the blow connected. It paralyzed her, driving the air out of her lungs. She couldn't breathe.

Martel prepared for another assault that would've put her down for good, but he hesitated.

Akeema stumbled backward again, coughing. Dizzy. Her legs were jelly. The muscles in her arms began to cramp into knots. She tasted copper. Blood. Her knees bent on their own and she crashed down in one of the car's passenger seats that hadn't been slashed to bits.

Martel stood over her, close enough to touch. She felt his hot breath on her skin. "You feel better now? Do you even know what you're fighting for?"

There was red on Akeema's teeth. "I have to stop you. Because you're evil." Her voice could only project just above a whisper.

Martel knelt down to her eye level and captured her gaze. "It takes great courage to fight evil. It takes even greater courage to see evil. Don't be so willfully blind."

"You killed my friends," she spat.

"I was defending myself. I warned you. You all attacked me first. Don't forget that part. You're not a victim."

"You're a rapist piece of shit!"

His face twitched, his lips pursed in anger. "No," Martel said, lingering on the word like it was a full sentence. "You're just repeating what you've been told without seeing a shred of proof. Sabrene's a liar. She's the last person you should trust."

The doors behind Martel slid open. Train security had arrived, around five persons, all with guns raised. Martel drew his crossglaive with a speed that rivaled sleight of hand.

While he deflected their bullets, Akeema pushed past the pain surging through her receptors. She grabbed a dagger-shaped shard of broken glass. Killing Martel was no longer the goal. As much as she wanted to see him die, he had her dead to rights. The fact he'd decided to let her live was his mistake. She couldn't continue fighting if that suddenly changed. Akeema had to think smarter. She had to be sneaky.

When the train guards ran out of bullets Martel used his tuning powers to shatter all the windows, scaring the guards into retreating.

When his attention returned to Akeema, she was running away too. She looked back to see his face sting with realization.

The album.

Akeema used the shard of glass to cut it from his belt. Martel reached out with his tuning power and grabbed Akeema, trapping her body inside an invisible vice. He yanked her backwards. She crashed to the floor, shards of broken glass penetrating her clothes and cutting her back and arms. The move winded them both.

Martel approached Akeema. He was almost on top of her when the maglev train emerged from the tunnel. The darkness was slapped away by the bright flash of orange light from the setting sun. It wasn't blinding, but enough to force Martel to shield his eyes. High speed wind rushed in from the blown-out windows and deafened them both.

Neither Akeema nor Martel heard the approaching roar of the rocket boots. Akeema saw Jaxon coming through the train car's shattered windows. By the time Martel opened his eyes and allowed them to adjust, there was nothing he could do.

Jaxon was flying directly at him like a goddamn superhero.

Chapter Thirteen: Jaxon

"Help her. Help Akeema," Castor coughed. He writhed in pain on the platform. Betty crouched over him, examining his bruises.

Jaxon's eyes burned. Flying through the air at high speeds without eye protection was an incredibly stupid idea in hindsight. Perched atop Betty's head were a pair of round protective welding goggles with dark coke-bottle lenses. Betty was a lover mecha designed to approximate the human form. It made sense her artificial eyes were made for function over durability. They needed protection from optical radiation the same as organic eyes.

"Can I borrow these?" Jaxon asked, then plucked the goggles from Betty's head before she had the chance to respond. He sprinted to the edge of the platform and looked down, his eyes scanning the busy landscape. He caught a glimpse of Akeema hanging off the side of the maglev she'd landed on before the train car disappeared around a building.

Jaxon tapped his wrist controller and brought up the status of his rocket boots. Their energy cells were down to forty-one percent on the left boot and thirty-nine percent on the right. If they ran out of juice while he was still in the air, he'd be fucked, but there was never a question in his mind. His sister was going up against a cold-blooded murderer and she was going to need backup. He was going after her.

Yoko grabbed his arm. "Not so fast hoo-mon," she said, predicting his actions, panic in her sad eyes. "How am I going to explain this to the Montanarins? If they think I had anything to do with this they'll arrest me. They'll scrap Betty. They'll impound *my ship*." Her grip tightened. "They are *very* big on punishment here."

The distress in her voice stabbed at Jaxon's heart. It was a little scary seeing the once cocky, arrogant, and carefree pilot on the verge of tears. Her tousled messy black hair and disheveled red suspenders peeking through her open jacket made her appear even more fragile.

Looking past her, Jaxon saw Betty helping Castor board the *Saragos*. And past them, the damage and destruction their brief battle with Martel had caused.

"When the authorities arrive tell them Martel was responsible," Jaxon said.

"He's not *here*. I *am*," Yoko said, throwing her hands in the air. They could hear the approaching wail of police sirens.

Jaxon walked over to Akeema's discarded rocket launcher and picked it up. "Then tell them it was me. I did it. You were just defending yourself."

Yoko's neck jerked, his words having stunned her into a brief silence. "You— you don't know what you're saying hoo-mon," she said with quiet anxiety. "Montanarins have zero tolerance when it comes to violent crime. If they catch you—"

"We don't have time. When I'm in the air shoot at me— *at* me, not *through* me." He didn't wait for Yoko's confirmation.

Two police drones appeared in the distance. They were of an ornithopter design with wings like dragonflies; the source of the approaching sirens.

When the drones were close enough, Jaxon put Betty's goggles on. Two taps and his boots lifted him up into the sky above the platform and hovered. He pretended to aim the rocket launcher at Yoko while she fired a few missed slugs at him.

The drones shifted course and beelined for him. They'd seen him.

Jaxon ditched the launcher and rocketed after Akeema too fast for the drones to catch him. He looked back briefly and saw the police drones surround Yoko. He could only hope that his ruse had worked. And if it hadn't, well, that would be a problem for later.

Too much time had passed since he'd caught sight of Akeema. Finding her train wasn't going to be easy. From the air, the city was a maze of buildings and zigzagging maglev tracks. Seeing through Betty's dark goggles and the dying sunlight further reduced his visibility. Jaxon rotated a dial on the rim of the goggles counter clockwise that let in more light, allowing him a clearer view.

More police drones had spotted him. They were converging on his position. And he was pretty sure that the brief flashes of light he saw were muzzle flashes. They were shooting at him.

Jaxon cut thrust and dropped altitude. Two taps and he banked around a building, then hovered. He scanned the cityscape. On the edge of his vision he saw a figure standing on the roof of a train car heading out of the city and into the surrounding forest area. He recognized the figure's head of flaming red hair. It might as well have been a signal flare.

Two taps and his boots sent him knifing through the wind in pursuit. The drab grays and overbearing golds of the city were replaced by the neon greens, iridescent blues, and indigo oranges of the tropical zone where the mechanical maglev train stood out against the exotic nature of the jungle.

Jaxon caught up with the end of the train. He zeroed in on Akeema. She was approaching Martel who was positioned a few cars ahead. A sting of fear swelled in Jaxon's gut. He recalled with perfect clarity the violence of his monastery vision. The image of Martel slashing Akeema's spine was burned into his memory. He couldn't bear to see it repeated.

Jaxon increased his burn and zoomed past Martel, landing ahead of him cat-footed on the train car's roof. His boots made a metallic thud when they magnetically attached to the train's skin. The wind beat his back with more force than he'd expected and Jaxon nearly lost his balance. If not for the boot's magnetic link it would have blown him off. He steadied himself and regained balance. Martel stared him down.

"Surrender!" Jaxon yelled. He hadn't bothered to figure out exactly how that would even happen given the circumstances. He imagined Martel politely placing his hands behind his back while Jaxon used handcuffs he didn't have to subdue the tattooed man. Then fantasized Akeema being uncharacteristically okay with that instead of chopping Martel's head off the first chance she got.

Akeema's face tightened with alarm. She was looking past him, her eyes quickly darting up towards the sky. Jaxon and Martel followed her gaze. They were speeding towards an enormous black mountain. It loomed as large as a tidal wave made of dark jagged rocks, dwarfing the surrounding sequoias that were themselves more massive than any natural object he'd ever seen.

The maglev train was only a few heartbeats away from entering the tunnel drilled in the mountain's face where it would splat the trio like flies on a windshield.

Martel brandished his crossglaive and carved his way into the train in less time than it took Jaxon to blink. He tried to follow Martel through the hole he'd cut, but the wind was too strong and his time was too short. Jaxon fumbled with his wrist controller to unmoor his boots from the train. The oncoming mountain grew even more gigantic with every passing second.

One tap to release, followed by two taps and Jaxon shot straight up into the air. He looked down to see Akeema make her own entrance and drop safely into the train before it vanished inside of the mountain tunnel.

Jaxon arced his flight path, angling to follow them inside the tunnel when a barred metal gate cycled shut behind the train. Jaxon veered off seconds before smashing into it. He guessed it was meant to keep the local wildlife from moving into the tunnel and making it their new home. Cutting through the gate would take too much time, and trying to maneuver in a dark tunnel with dying rocket boots wasn't ideal.

Two taps and Jaxon's rocket boots shot him up above the mountain's peak where he hovered. There, he looked 360 degrees around him. The lime greens, violet blues and pearly ambers of the forest dominated his vision. The cool cobalt of the nearby ocean was a sight. The black of the mountains with sparse patches of vegetation on their hills and peaks where animals were thriving were idyllic. *Castor was right. This world was awash with beauty.*

A chime on his wrist controller drew his attention.

The power cells in his boots were down to twenty-two percent on the left boot and nineteen percent on the right. It was too late to turn back. The only way was forward.

Two taps and he blasted off just above the surface of the mountain's grassy top, which went on for kilometers. The roar of the wind filled his ears as he bulleted through the crisp air.

Jaxon watched the energy bar on his power cells tick down near fifteen percent. A warning alarm rang. Another tap and the rocket boot's thrust increased, the speed rattling his teeth. Jaxon balled his fists and clenched his jaw. The wind whipped his exposed skin and gave him cotton mouth. Less than ten percent now.

The colossal black mountain reached its end and the lush green treetops came back into view. His wrist controller screamed more warnings at him. He ignored them. Jaxon cleared the mountain top and dove down dozens of meters to the maglev train just as it emerged from the tunnel. Even from a distance he could see one of the train cars with its windows blown out.

That had to be the one.

Jaxon swooped in for a closer look, making out the familiar red mess of hair being yanked across the carriage by a figure who could only have been Martel. That was his target.

Jaxon didn't have a plan, or time to think one up. Getting Martel away from Akeema was his only concern.

He threaded the needle and flew straight through one of the broken windows. He collided with Martel like a wreck. The impact vibrated deep into his chest. He grabbed the other man in a tight hug as his rocket boots continued to spew propellant, flying them both out of the carriage's opposite window and out into the open jungle.

The impact winded Martel, his face twisted with confusion. Jaxon held on to him tightly. He didn't want Martel to fall. Death would have been too light of a punishment.

Martel recovered and their eyes met. A tinge of dread pinched the bald man's face.

"Okay," Martel said, his breathing labored. "That was pretty ballsy. I'll grant you that. So, is this where you drop me to my death and call it an accident?"

"I thought about it," Jaxon lied. "But no, I'm not a killer like you. This is an arrest. I'm turning you over to the authorities and I'm going to see that you stand trial for what you've done."

"That's... very honorable of you," Martel said with a silvery laugh, "but how, exactly do you plan to do that?" He sounded genuinely curious. "Once we land, how are you going to *keep* me in custody?"

Jaxon's face stung with puzzlement. He didn't have an answer. Before he could think of one, both of their attentions were drawn to the concert of alarms coming from Jaxon's wrist controller. They were high above the bushy treetops. Martel glanced down at the immense drop beneath them. His gaze shifted to Jaxon. They locked eyes.

"I'm real sorry about this," Martel said, then smashed the wrist controller with his elbow.

Thrust from Jaxon's rocket boots died immediately and both men were in free fall. The sudden drop drove Jaxon's stomach into his throat while his mind raced for a solution. He expected Martel to attempt to break free of his grip, but to his surprise, the other man held on to him. It made Jaxon think of Yoko.

"Hold on!" Martel yelled as they cannonballed towards the blanket of trees beneath them. Their leaves were huge, easily the size of trampolines, some even wider. The two men slammed into the bushy green top of a sequoia. The force of the impact broke their grip and separated them.

Jaxon lost sight of Martel. He crashed through the thick mess of rubbery super-sized leaves; they slowed his descent in concert with the planet's reduced gravity.

The branches the leaves were connected to, however, weren't so soft. They pummeled him in places he didn't even know existed. If this were Earth, he'd already be dead. There was still quite a long distance to go before he'd hit the jungle floor. He wouldn't survive this continuous amount of punishment the entire way down.

Jaxon blindly pressed buttons on his wrist controller in between giant leaves slapping his face. One leaf hit with enough force to break his goggles and knock them off his head. A few more stabs at his wrist controller and his rocket boots sputtered to life, slowing his descent further as he fell the length of a skyscraper.

The boot's thrust began to sputter in and out randomly, much to his annoyance. He tumbled to the ground much faster and with far more momentum than he was comfortable with. Jaxon pitched forward, curling into a ball as he impacted the dirt. He rolled across the jungle floor for a few meters until he shed his momentum.

When his body finally came to rest, Jaxon was covered in bruises, brush marks, and green sludge from the over-sized leaves he'd broken through. His entire body ached. His balls throbbed like an elephant had stepped on them. He couldn't stand. His rocket boots were trashed.

His ears caught a strange noise from somewhere up in the trees. It was distant and getting louder. Closer.

Martel had managed to stake his crossglaive into one of the sequoias, using it to repel down to the ground and leaving a charred black slit and glowing embers in its wake. The sound reminded him of several sheets of paper slowly being ripped in half.

Martel landed with such smoothness and grace that it almost seemed staged. He approached Jaxon with his crossglaive still drawn. Jaxon reached for his own crossglaive in a panic, but only grabbed air. His head swiveled. He saw his crossglaive hilt resting on the ground just outside of his reach.

Jaxon considered making a dash for it. His injured muscles wouldn't consent. The image of Priestess Nisame's armless legless torso bleeding out on the monastery floor flashed in his mind, except instead of having her own face she had his.

"You're hurt," Martel said. "Don't move. You could be seriously injured."

Jaxon ignored him. He reached out for his crossglaive hilt. He concentrated, willing every cell in his body to tune the weapon into his hand. Martel simply stood by, watching him.

"Come on," Martel said, coaxing him. "That's it. Concentrate. You can do it. Come on... come on..." Nothing happened. The more Jaxon tried to tune the more he was convinced his brain was being squeezed inside of a scolding hot vice lined with shards of broken glass.

All the while, his crossglaive hilt remained defiant and still. The attempt exhausted him. The pain persuaded him to stop.

Martel frowned. "Well. That was disappointing." He opened his palm. Jaxon's crossglaive hilt flew into it. "You cheated," Martel continued. "You shouldn't have those boots. You're a Kaijen. You're not supposed to have material possessions. You're supposed to want to be an obedient little drone who does what he's told and doesn't break the rules."

Jaxon's mouth curled into a snarl. "Don't talk to me about rules. You're a murderer and a rapist."

Martel rolled his eyes and let out a deep groan of agitation. "I didn't *rape* anyone. That never *happened*. I would never, ever force myself on anyone," Martel said, his face awash with raw emotion. It seemed genuine. Whether Jaxon actually believed Martel or not was still to be determined. His crossglaive was still active. He could strike a killing blow at any moment. Better to keep him talking.

"Of course you'd say that," Jaxon said.

Martel spread his hands. "Yeah. I guess I wouldn't believe me either. I mean, it's not like you just found out Nisame was a hypocrite leading a double life. When she wasn't on Earth preaching chastity and equality, she was out here getting her holes filled and trying to secure more power for herself. I'm a lot of things. A liar is not one of them."

"But you *are* a murderer," Jaxon said.

"I killed Nisame in self-defense. Every life I've taken has been in self-defense."

"You threw Yoko off of that platform," Jaxon said.

"Because I knew about your rocket boots. I knew you'd catch her." Martel gestured with his hands. "Well, I gambled. Maybe next time she'll think twice about shooting at me. But enough about me." Martel collapsed his crossglaive. He dropped to one knee so he could talk to Jaxon at his eye level. "I want to know why you didn't tell Sabrene about your vision." An icy chill poured down Jaxon's spine. "You weren't supposed to do that. You're supposed to tell them everything. Could it be that, for some strange reason, you didn't trust her?" His voice was soft, gentle. "What do you think she would do if she knew you projected your consciousness across space? Did someone teach you how? Could you do it again?"

As much as Jaxon hated Martel, he was asking good questions. Jaxon had reached out into the universe and done something amazing. If he could do something that incredible, surely he could do something minor like tune his crossglaive out of Martel's grip. His mind was still buzzed from the last attempt. The only tactic he had left was to stall. "I don't know how I did it. It just happened."

Martel leaned in closer. "How many Kaijen have you linked with?"

Jaxon took the question as an insult to his honor. "I've only ever linked with one Kaijen, and you killed her."

Martel pulled away. "No, stop. Don't do that." He stood to his full height, then groan. His leg. Jaxon hadn't noticed Martel was wounded. Jaxon saw the cauterized skin through Martel's torn pants. Martel rubbed the tender area and winced.

"Don't you feel bad for Nisame. She doesn't deserve your sympathy. What I did to her she had coming. That was *justice*."

Jaxon brushed his screaming muscles aside and attempted to sit up. "And the others that you slaughtered? You call that justice too?"

Martel threw his hands in the air. "I'm not having this conversation again. You saw it. You saw me offer them the chance to withdraw. They left me no choice—"

"You had *every* choice!" Jaxon growled. "You knew they couldn't beat you, but *you chose* to cut them down anyway."

The jungle was silent, save for the ambient chirp of insects and squawks from gliding birds overhead.

Martel rubbed his eyes, shook his head, his jaw locked tight. He was trying to hide his anger. "You have no idea what you're involved in, Jaxon Troy. *I'm* fighting against real tyranny. *You're* on the side defending it," he said, each word its own sentence. "You just haven't realized that yet."

"Oh. I see," Jaxon said, playing along, giving himself more time for his strength to return. "Right. So *you're* the hero? You're the good guy and I'm the bad guy. Do I have that correct?"

Martel smiled. It failed to reach his eyes. "How much to you know about the Quorum of Elders? Really? Have you ever asked yourself how they got so powerful? Or why, no matter how hard you try or how many hours you practice, you never get better at tuning?"

Jaxon's eyes softened. He'd wondered about that last part, though he'd never admit it. Novice Kaijen were never encouraged to question why things were the way they were, only to accept the way of the Kaijen.

To obey.

"Do you want to know their secret?" Martel asked, but didn't wait for Jaxon to respond. "They link among each other. Linking strengthens the pineal gland, the part of our brain that allows us to tune. Every time we link, we absorb a bit of the other person's power. That's why the novice Kaijen are forbidden to link among their peers. The elders and the priestesses don't want the peasants gaining too much power that they didn't give you."

Martel tossed Jaxon his crossglaive hilt. It landed in his lap with a soft thud. Jaxon gripped it, but didn't activate the blade. "You want me to attack you so you can justify killing me."

"We're not enemies," Martel said. "If I thought you were one of the bad guys, we wouldn't be having this lovely chat. Now we can continue talking or we can fight. The choice is yours."

Doubt clouded Jaxon's mind. Evil people, as he understood them, didn't try to debate or discuss. They dictated. Or they murdered you. He had a gut feeling that perhaps, maybe, there was some sliver of truth in Martel's words.

Priestess Sabrene's words echoed in his ears. *Hiroshi Martel is a vicious liar, obstructionist, and a speciesist. We cannot allow hateful speech from class enemies to destroy our institution.* Sabrene was his superior. A high priestess of unquestionable morality. Jaxon had to trust and believe that she knew better than he did.

He had to believe it.

Which meant he never had a choice.

Jaxon staggered to his feet. His entire body protested. His arms and legs were lead and just as inflexible. He extended his crossglaive blade. Lifting it to fighting position required tremendous effort, let alone keeping it steady.

Martel exhaled a disappointed sigh and shook his head, then drew his crossglaive. "Fine. I'll make it easy for you," he said, then dropped his guard.

Jaxon lurched at him like a drunk in high wind, barely keeping himself from doubling over and passing out. Martel expended the smallest amount of effort to dodge Jaxon's lunges, which were quickly exhausting him.

"If I'm so evil," Martel said. "Why aren't you dead yet? Why am I not murdering the shit out of you right now? Answer me that."

"Because you enjoy having the power of life and death in your hands," Jaxon said, his voice thin and dry from labored breathing. "You're a killer and a terrorist and a speciesist."

Martel's face wrenched with objection. "Excuse me? A speciesist? Where'd *that* come from? Killer? Debatable. Terrorist? Alright, I can at least understand that one. But *a speciesist*? Now you're just making shit up. You've been mind tricked, Jaxon. That's how they control you. With lies and obfuscation. Don't fall for it. Wake up."

Jaxon was so, so very tired. It took every molecule of energy he had to stay on his feet. The tension weighed him down like someone had increased the planet's gravity by double. He just wanted it all to end. And yet, he still feared Martel would spear him like he'd speared the others in his weird dream that wasn't a dream.

The moment never came.

Martel collapsed his crossglaive and tossed the grip away. "If you really think I'm the bad guy then go ahead. Run me through. If you stand by your convictions so strongly, then murder me. I won't fight you."

This has to be a trick. But it was also an opportunity. If he were fast enough, he could kill Martel.

And then the reality dawned on him. He'd never taken a life. He never imagined he'd ever have to. The idea tasted bitter in his mouth. Even if it were someone as awful as Martel. He didn't trust the tattooed man to keep his word. He saw no other choice.

Jaxon charged forward as fast as he could.

His legs failed him.

Jaxon tried to swing his crossglaive. His arms revolted.

Martel stood there with his arms outstretched in a pose of surrender, his eyes locked on Jaxon's. It wasn't a trick. He wasn't going to move. He was going to stand there and die. Jaxon tried to pretend he was Akeema. She'd do it gladly, and with a smile.

The ground seemed to almost pull Jaxon down into the dirt. A refreshing gust of air slapped his face as his chest crashed on top of it. The muscles in his arms and legs twisted and seized, but the pain couldn't compare to Jaxon's complete and total sense of abject failure.

Martel knelt beside him, turning Jaxon over, checking on him. His mouth was moving, but Jaxon couldn't hear the words. A strong wind picked up and a loud buzzing, like the blades of a helicopter, drowned out all other sound.

Two metal bolas cut through the air and wrapped themselves around Martel, their electrified tendrils shocking him into unconsciousness. He crumpled to the ground.

Police drones. They'd found him. Their dragonfly-like wings

were the source of the buzzing. Five drones descended from the trees, their sirens off until now. They were joined by a squadron of Montanarin patrol officers who surrounded Jaxon and Martel.

Jaxon smiled. "Thanks, you saved my—"

A bola coiled around him like a metal snake shooting arcs of stinging electrical current through his body. Jaxon violently convulsed in a way that would have been comical if it weren't happening to him. His skull was on fire. It reminded him of his first link with Priestess Nisame before his world went black.

Chapter Fourteen: Akeema

Holy shit, Akeema thought.

The chaos on board the maglev train had happened too fast for her brain to process what her eyes were seeing. She'd always seen Jaxon as the little brother she never had. He was always the sensible one. The peacemaker. Humble and selfless to a fault. She'd been the first friend he made after he'd woken from his link-induced coma. The one to offer her help when Jaxon confided in her how hard he struggled to access his linked memories or tune. Akeema was protective of the kid, as if he were an egg and she were a piece of red-haired bubble wrap keeping the world from cracking him open.

And yet, here the little upstart was, snatching her ass out of the fire, and doing it in style.

Jaxon swooped into the maglev train car like some kind of lunatic superhero on those rocket propelled death traps on his feet. She'd watched in wide-eyed awe as he snatched Martel up in his arms like a man-sized hawk and flew off with him. It happened in the span of a single breath.

Then she was alone.

The adrenaline high of the fight had begun to wear off and pain swelled throughout her body. Her hands hurt. Her head rang like an alarm. Her chest felt like she'd been kicked by a horse.

If train security found her, they'd take her into custody. Escape became her new mission. Akeema's only comfort was that she had the album. She stuffed the trinket in her pocket and bent down to grab her broken crossglaive hilt. Both acts sent a river of pain up her aching arm. She examined her crossglaive. It looked like an animal had chewed it. She tried to extend the blade, but it disagreed. It could be the motivator. It could be the power cell. It could be everything. There wasn't time to figure out which.

Akeema climbed through one of the broken windows and onto the exterior of the train car. She forced herself to ignore the pain of her injured muscles. It felt like someone had rubbed sand paper on the raw nerves inside her mechanical spine. She pulled herself onto the roof. With a guttural grunt Akeema laid down flat on her back. She stared up at the sky's rose-colored glow as the sun sank below the horizon, then braced her feet against metal grooves on the train car's hot roof to keep the surging wind from sending her plunging to her death. Akeema imagined a flock of sky grazers picking the meat from her twisted corpse and shuddered.

Minutes pasted and the train slowed. They'd reached the northern city. A few minutes more and it pulled into a station inside one of the tulip-shaped skyscrapers. Akeema heard the train doors open, followed by the clamor of passengers exiting in a frenzy. It sounded as though it might end in a crush. Law enforcement officers rushed in to assess the situation.

Akeema rolled over onto her stomach and crawled to the last car, scraping her knees along the way. She checked to make sure no one saw her before jumping off onto the boarding platform. More pain. She tore off a piece of her Kaijen robe to cover her hair and crouch-walked through the crowd, blending in with the non-humans. No one noticed her existence or the trail of blood she'd left in her wake.

Jouejati city had a distinct feel and style compared to its southern neighbor. It was smaller, the buildings much shorter and more ornate. Only a handful of the city's skyscrapers were ugly blocks of glass and cargonite. The rest were unusual, highly decorative structures brimming with personality; Gothic business towers, stacked oval housing projects, and vertical seashell buildings used to grow agriculture being the most prominent.

Night choked out the last remnants of daylight. The city lit up with nocturnal activity.

Akeema limped her way to a skyway bridge connecting two wedge shaped skyscrapers high up on the sixty-ninth level. She flipped open her handheld, the screen spider cracked from her battle. More than that. It was smashed.

She popped open the casing and thumbed out the electromagnetic mesh shielding the components. Two of the power transistor clips were broken. She pulled out her damaged crossglaive and opened the maintenance flap. Akeema cannibalized two transistor clips that fit her handheld and the device turned on, though the damaged screen made it hard to use. She sent a connection request to Castor.

He didn't answer.

She tried again. Same result. The knot in Akeema's gut reasserted itself.

After she recovered from the stun grenade, Akeema had been so hellbent on killing Martel she hadn't considered that Castor might've been hurt. Martel had been hit by shrapnel from her rocket launcher. It was possible Castor had been too. What if he was dead? What if she'd killed him?

The knot in her stomach pulled tighter.

Akeema searched for Yoko's connection ID number. She hesitated, then sent the request. The obnoxious woman's silver face filled her cracked screen.

"Yeah? Who is this? Oh, it's you," Yoko said.

"Where's Castor?" Akeema asked, a tremor in her voice.

"He's here, no thanks to you."

Akeema breathed easier. "Is Jaxon with you?"

Yoko went silent for a long moment. "No," she muttered. Her round silver face soured and her thick eyebrows bunched together. "He foolishly took the blame for what *you* did. If the authorities took him alive then he's going to wish he was dead."

The knot in Akeema's stomach was a stretched band of elastic ready to snap. "I need you to pick me up."

Yoko coughed out a hysterical laugh. "You must be out of your foosha mind, hoo-mon. I nearly got sent to a Montanarin prison camp because of what you did!"

"You seem just fine to me," Akeema said, annoyed.

"That's because I can talk my way out of a skin rash. How do you miss with a rocket launcher? There's nothing you could possibly say that would ever make me—"

"I can pay you."

***

The Montanarin authorities detained Yoko for an hour before

she'd convinced them of her innocence. As a condition of her release, they ordered her to leave the planet immediately. She was prohibited from landing on the planet for a period of no less than ten months or face prosecution.

Akeema rendezvoused with the *Saragos* at a fueling station. Yoko was ready to dustoff when she received Akeema's call and agreed to let her board. For a hefty fee, of course. Akeema was brought to the crew deck and led through a hatch.

The ship's medical bay was little more than a converted storage room. There was barely enough space for three beds and one operating table. A pair of aftermarket surgical arms were bolted to the wall and an old outdated medical scanner hung from the ceiling. Yoko's mecha, Betty, acted as Akeema's nurse. The mecha laid her down on the surgical bed, kestesil straps weighing her down. Beams of light scanned her from multiple angles.

"You have suffered a mild concussion," Betty's monotone voice reported. "Broken nose. Three broken fingers. Fractured wrist. Torn meniscus. Two cracked ribs. Bruised lung. Bruised kidney. Trauma to spleen and pancreas. Minor skin lacerations and internal bleeding. I will now administer treatment." The coldness of her inorganic voice unsettled Akeema. She watched the machine retrieve a long thin surgical probe with a pinhole camera on its tip. Akeema's eyes widened and she squirmed. "There is no cause for alarm," Betty assured her. It didn't help.

The probe's needle pierced Akeema's skin and she hissed. The pinhole camera fed Betty a video feed of Akeema's guts. Betty used it to find her damaged organs to coat them with a healing agent, but Betty kept missing the mark.

"Ow," Akeema yelped.

My apologies," Betty said in her flat monotone. She continued to jerk the probe around inside of Akeema's abdomen. She winced.

"Ow!" Akeema cried.

"My apologies," Betty repeated, then injected her with an anesthetic. She continued to apply the healing agent onto Akeema's damaged rib. While that happened, a pair of surgical arms went to work on her stoma. The arms repaired her bowels and sewed closed her ostomy opening with a surgical laser. The stink of seared flesh tinged the air. This process continued for longer than Akeema could bare and she slipped into unconsciousness. She didn't dream.

When she awoke, the *Saragos* had long since taken off. The ship floated in high orbit above Montanari. Akeema protested leaving Jaxon behind, but the Montanarin authorities had ordered Yoko to leave under threat of impounding her ship. Traffic control ordered the dingy old yacht to break orbit, but Yoko convinced them there was a problem with the Gravity Drive and that the ship's rear starboard engine pod needed to be repaired. How much of a lie that was Akeema didn't know, but it bought them time to wait for contact from Jaxon.

The ship's gimbals orientated the decks into their "office building" position. Akeema released herself from the medical bay and climbed up a ladder to the command deck. Yoko was in the cockpit, the hatch sealed shut.

Akeema searched the kitchen and poured herself a bulb of water. She drank it in three big gulps, coughing afterwards. Her entire body throbbed, though the pain wasn't as bad as earlier. The healing agent administered by Betty was working. Still, her forearms were sore and swollen. There was a black bruise on her stomach in the general shape of a boot print. She wore a special bandage on her broken nose that would ensure that it healed straight.

The ship wasn't under thrust. In the null g, Akeema's hair floated free and alive like Medusa with a head of red snakes. She tied it back to keep it out of her face and found the faux gravity created by the kestesil lined floors and ceiling to be unnerving. It felt like ghosts trying to pull her down into the grating. She hated how her gravity harness tugged on her hips and made them ache. She hated space in general and wouldn't recommend it to anyone.

In the lounge, Akeema found a small service table and attempted to repair her crossglaive. She used a set of tools and spare parts that floated motionless next to her in the null g. The weapon was held in place by a vice to keep it from floating away. Akeema opened it up like she was performing an autopsy. Her intuition was correct. The power cell was cracked and the motivator was fried. The blade's power adjuster was bent along with several of the energy circuits having been fused.

She'd been working on the repairs for some time when Castor climbed up the ladder onto the deck. He'd been recovering in one of the crew quarters. He looked like he'd been recovering from a fever. He saw Akeema and froze.

"You look like I feel," he joked. She laughed, but there was no mirth in it. Castor sat down opposite her and helped her with the repairs. She filled him in on what happened on the maglev train, his expression growing more and more dire the longer she went on. It wasn't long before the storm of rage brewing in the back of her mind made itself known.

Akeema lowered her head in an attempt to hide it. "We can't keep losing like this."

"A rocket launcher, Akeema? Really?" Castor said. "What next? A nuke?"

"It almost worked. I hurt him. I almost killed Martel."

"You almost killed us all," Castor said, his face scrunched in anguish. He shifted in his seat, his wounds asserting their presence. "I asked you if you bought something that would get us in trouble and you fucking lied to me."

"We were ambushed," Akeema shot back. A little vein in her forehead looked ready to pop. "Martel nearly killed us again and you're hung up on the fact I *lied*?"

Castor couldn't settle into a comfortable position. "I'm not upset that you lied to me, I'm upset that from now on I can't trust your word. If Jaxon is dead, it will be because of us. Because we failed as Kaijen."

Heat rose in Akeema's cheeks and spread to her forehead. She couldn't argue against Castor's words. Because she believed them. He was speaking truth. Only, she didn't blame Jaxon's potentially dead status on anyone other than herself.

She presented the album. "At least Martel doesn't have this."

Castor frowned. "Yeah. Because that fossil was worth trading for Jaxon's life."

"I didn't say that," Akeema snapped. "He did his duty in order to keep the album out of the hands of evil. Now it's our duty to figure out how to use it. Unlocking its power will level the playing field so that the next time—"

Castor slammed his mechanical fist against the table, denting it. "Goddamnit Akeema! We don't need that! We can beat Martel with the abilities we were given— with the skills Priestess Nisame taught us. We just need to try harder."

Akeema imagined her hands around her arrogant brother's neck. She shot up onto her feet. Castor stood to match her.

"What are you so afraid of, Castor?" she growled. "We have the winning solution literally in our hands. We just need to use it!"

"You disrespect our code!"

"And you are a slave to it!"

The tension hung thick between them. Akeema's hand found her left wrist again. Neither of them noticed Betty. She watched in awkward silence, her emerald green eyes eerie and intense.

Akeema grimaced. It was her spine again. The sensation of sharp barbed nails sailed up her back and spread out to her shoulders. She sat down before her legs had the chance to give out underneath her. Her gravity harness pulled her down like a sinking stone. It just made the pain worse.

"You are hurt," Betty stated. She wrenched a medical wand from one of her jumpsuit's many pockets and scanned Akeema. "Your nerves are still mending with your artificial spine. This will ease your discomfort." Betty produced a hypospray and injected her. Akeema sucked her teeth. The pain suppressor worked quickly. The pins and needles were still there, but distant. Peripheral. Akeema breathed easier.

"I get that you're angry," Castor sighed. "I am too. I'm so angry my teeth hurt. The album looks like a quick and easy way to obtain power. But power is like a drug. You start with a taste. Just a little taste. Then you need a little more and a little more until it becomes your entire world."

"That won't happen with me," Akeema said, not able to look at him. "I'm stronger than that. I would die before I ever let it come to that." She wasn't talking to Castor. He wasn't the one she needed to convince.

"You were so desperate for an advantage that you were willing to blow up an entire platform just to kill one man," Castor vented.

"You know he—"

"We're not killers, Akeema," he said pensively. "Kaijen do not murder."

Akeema nodded. "You're right. Martel should suffer first."

"Kaijen do not torture either," Castor went on. "We do not seek vengeance. Your actions put the lives of everyone you care about as well as innocent people in danger."

His words stung Akeema more than the daggers in her spine. The truth had that kind of effect.

She wasn't the type of woman to let a little thing like the truth keep her from being right. "We don't even know for sure what the album actually does, or what Martel planned to do with it. And I wasn't about to stand by and wait to find out because *I'm* not a coward."

Castor's eyes slitted. "Insult me if that makes you feel better. But I will not be bullied into betraying my Kaijen principles."

"I'll keep that in mind when Martel is standing over our corpses," Akeema said, then stalked off down the deck ladder.

***

Akeema settled in one of the ship's cramped unused quarters on the crew deck. Each room had its own lavatory. Peeing in zero gravity was a hassle, but she preferred it to her catheter.

She urinated and there was blood in it. She washed her face and under her arms, then removed her gravity belt so she could strap herself into bed. She managed to sleep for a few hours before her screaming muscles stirred her awake. Her stomach ached in a way that told her she had to shit. There was blood in that, too.

The *Saragos* was still in orbit and without thrust gravity. Akeema climbed the ladder up to the command deck and passed by Betty who was busy stuffing some garbage into a purge chute. The chute's hatch cycled closed and flushed the contents out into space. Akeema despised littering, even in the void of space, but she wasn't in any position to complain. Just one more reason why she and Yoko would never get along.

Akeema found Castor sitting at the galley's dining table monitoring Montanari's news outlets, combing for any information on Jaxon. She joined him. He didn't say a word, so neither did she. Friction floated in the space between them like wisps of smoke.

Yoko was in the cockpit. The hatch was open now. Akeema could overhear traffic control threatening to arrest Yoko if she didn't disembark. Her mouth had bought them one more hour. If they didn't hear from Jaxon by then... Akeema couldn't think about that.

She tried to focus on the newsfeeds, but couldn't help but notice how Yoko was busy not helping. She could hear the silver woman's cackle reverberating from the cockpit every few minutes.

Akeema stomped into the cockpit and found Yoko reclining in her pilot's chair which was hiked all the way up to accommodate her tiny frame. Her oily black locks were tied back in a ponytail that floated behind her head like a bobbing black serpent. The compartment was absent of any visible alcohol, much to Akeema's surprise. Yoko was reading a book on her handheld, the apparent source of her amusement.

"I didn't pay you to sit on your ass and read," Akeema said.

Yoko grunted without looking up from her handheld. "No, you paid me to rescue you. Which I did. Foolishly. Then you paid me to stick around here at the risk of being shot down. Which I have. Also foolishly. And I just got you one more hour. But when that hour is up, I'm leaving."

"That's a mistake you do not want to make," Akeema said.

"I have made many mistakes in my life, hoo-mon. I've learned from them, and I am sure I can repeat them exactly. We both have this skill in common."

Akeema flinched. "Excuse me?"

"You keep making the mistake of directing your anger at me when you know full well *I'm* not the one you're *really* angry with."

Then Yoko looked up at her and stared.

Akeema's mouth hung open.

She was about to explode into a series of harsh obscenities when an alert chime stopped her. It was an incoming connection request, which included a portrait of the caller's face; Priestess Sabrene.

Fuck, Akeema thought, then frowned.

Yoko noticed. "You know this broad? She looks like one of those bots that tries to sell me starship insurance."

Castor appeared over Akeema's shoulder and mirrored her scowl.

"We don't have to answer it," she said to him.

"I wish that were true," Castor said. "Patch it through."

Yoko accepted the request. Light delay forced them to wait in silence. After a moment the connection was live. Sabrene's annoyed pink face appeared on a small rectangular video screen.

"Priestess," Castor began, talking too fast. "Please allow us to explain our—"

"You blatantly disobeyed my direct order," Sabrene said. The transmission delay was a few seconds, which meant she had started talking without waiting to hear Castor's groveling. "Obviously you were not aware that we monitor all of your monetary transactions," Sabrene continued, chewing on her words. "I knew the three of you disobeyed me the *second* you booked passage on that transport."

"We left for a good reason, priestess," Akeema cut in, careful not to talk over Sabrene. "We have secured the album." She held the album up to the camera as proof, but delay meant Sabrene wouldn't see it for another few seconds.

"I was even generous enough to give you time to come to your senses and admit your betrayal and you've only abused my good will —" Sabrene stopped, having just heard Akeema's plea. She paused. And it wasn't just the transmission delay.

She was considering Akeema's words, which at least meant she wasn't sentencing them to a reeducation session. Not yet, at least.

"Well. This changes things," Sabrene said, her eyes and voice harder than steel. "Deliver the album to me, directly, and you have my word your punishments won't be as severe."

"Priestess," Castor began. "Jaxon Troy has gone missing since battling Martel. Could you use your influence to help us find him? We wouldn't even have the album if it wasn't for his heroism—"

"The album is your priority," Sabrene said, talking over him. "Jaxon Troy is expendable. Every moment the album remains in the wild millions of lives are at risk. You will bring it to me immediately. Failure to do so will result in permanent expulsion from the Kaijen. Do not make me call you again." She dropped the connection.

Castor and Akeema looked over at each other in stunned silence.

Yoko snorted. "If I were you, I'd tell her to go foosha herself, but she'd only be disappointed."

Akeema spoke with quiet urgency. "We can't leave him."

"I know," Castor said. "But what choice do we have? We can't disobey her again. And we don't even know where Jaxon is or if he's even alive."

"If you two are done caterwauling," Yoko said, "you might want to see this." She transferred a live feed from a small private display to one of the cockpit's main wall screens; Montanarin news footage played, overlaid with text notifications of ongoing events.

Yoko pointed to one of the blurbs. "There. He and the scary tattooed hoo-mon have already been tried and found guilty. The sentence is hard labor."

Castor's eyes squinted. "It doesn't list their sentence."

"This is Montanari. If the sentence isn't death then it's hard labor," Yoko said. "These feeds are two hours old so the prisoners have already been loaded onto a prison barge."

"When does it leave?" Akeema asked.

Yoko's fingers tapped keys. Sensor data popped up on the screen. "One departed forty minutes ago with a fighter drone escort. They're most likely headed for Kabria."

Akeema's face scrunched. "That can't be right. I thought that place was reserved for ultra-violent murderers and criminals? Why would they take Jaxon there?"

Yoko inclined her head and gave Akeema a blunt look. "Did you not fire a rocket launcher and destroy a populated maglev train? Some cultures take that kind of wanton destruction personally."

"Whoa, wait, hold on," Akeema began. "It wasn't like anyone was killed."

"Do you even hear yourself?" Yoko said, one of her thick caterpillars arched. "'Sure, I did a drive-by on your planet and caused millions of cubits in property damage, but at least no one was killed'."

Akeema crossed her arms. "If they didn't want me using a rocket launcher they shouldn't have sold me one."

Yoko rolled her eyes. "You simply refuse to take responsibility for what you did. Typical hoo-mon behavior. They're calling him a terrorist. He's taking the blame for what *you* did. The *baizuo*."

Akeema's anger rose to a boil. She swallowed it. "I don't want to argue. I want to get Jaxon back. Can this ship catch up with the transport before it reaches Kabria?"

Yoko's entire body jerked with surprise. "Well, sure it can. But there's no point. The fighter escort would shoot me down the second we entered targeting range. It's suicide."

"She's right," Castor said. "Even if we could somehow raid that ship, it would take time we don't have. If we don't deliver the album to Priestess Sabrene—"

Akeema sneered. "If Jaxon where here and we were there would he hesitate to save us? Or would he put his life before ours?" She locked eyes with Yoko. "And you'd be dead if Jaxon hadn't have saved you on that platform."

"So what?" Yoko snapped back. "Now I owe him? Those are *your* customs, hoo-mon, not mine. I don't risk my freedom or my ship for sentiment, only cubits."

"Has anyone ever told you how much of a mean selfish bitch you are?" Akeema said.

"Yes, and it flatters me," Yoko said with a prideful smirk. "Being kind just lets people know that you're weak and easily taken advantage of. There's no profit in generosity. And now you can kindly haul your uppity judgmental flat hoo-mon ass off of my ship."

Akeema's hands balled into fists. Castor stepped in between them, stopping Akeema from doing something she probably wouldn't regret.

Yoko set course for an orbital transport station and the ship was under thrust gravity again. "Betty, would you please escort our hoo-mons to the lower airlock. They're leaving."

Betty appeared in the cockpit, then froze. She stared at Yoko. A moment passed.

"Did you hear me, Betty? I said take them to the lower airlock. And be quick about it." Betty didn't move. She blinked, but otherwise remained a statue. Yoko groaned in annoyance. "What's your problem, Betty? Did you hear me? I said—"

"Yoko. He saved you," Betty said with her familiar absence of emotion.

"What?" Yoko said.

"You should help them. It is the right thing to do."

Yoko glared. It was like seeing someone find out the dog they had for their entire life had suddenly started talking. "I only do 'the right thing' when it benefits me. And you know I'm not in the business of saving people. You are supposed to follow my commands, so do what I am telling you to do."

Betty took a step closer. "I am also programmed to act in your best interest. I have determined that saving Jaxon Troy is in your best interest."

Yoko's eyes narrowed. "That's ridiculous."

"He saved you. Just as you saved me."

"No Betty, I *stole* you. For payment. It's not that same thing."

Betty took another step. "But you did not sell me. I am worth far more than the cost of your bounty."

"I'm not selling you, Betty. You're the closest thing I've ever had to a real friend." Yoko's expression softened, apparently surprised by her own honesty.

"I am valuable to you because I protect you. That is what I am doing now. Please, Yoko. Do this. For me."

Yoko clearly didn't understand what was happening. Akeema and Castor just stood there, watching, equally as confused. Yoko looked as if her head was about to pop off her neck, which made Akeema enjoy the altercation that much more.

"I don't think he's worth it," Yoko said. "Why him? Why this hoo-mon?"

Betty took a seat in the co-pilot's chair and swiveled to look Yoko face to face. "I have calculated that your life expectancy is higher with him than without him. You may not feel you owe him Yoko, but I do."

Seconds ticked by and tears found their way out of Yoko's eyes. Akeema didn't think her people actually had tears. Yoko opened her mouth to speak. Akeema braced herself for more snark. Yoko surprised her with silence.

"Foosha," Yoko muttered.

Betty plotted a new course.

Chapter Fifteen: Jaxon

The prison's infirmary stank like paint thinner and old crayons.

The Montanarins had arrested Jaxon and brought him to the medical wing of a detention facility where he was kept under armed guard. Prison doctors treated his wounds and nurses fed him a bowl of what looked to be boiled pink maggots, each one as long as his little finger. They were mushy and buttery and tasted like mashed potatoes.

Jaxon was shackled to his bed and stripped of his crossglaive and rocket boots. He used the opportunity to catch up on some much needed sleep. He would need his strength before being tried as a terrorist. It was a courtesy, all things considered.

The next morning, he and a group of other defendants were fitted with restraining bracelets on their wrists and ankles before being dragged into a court room. The length of each of their trials lasted the span of a commercial. The Montanarin justice system was designed to be as speedy and streamlined as possible. The Montanarins weren't a race, they were a people. What made someone a Montanarin wasn't their species or skin color or what God they prayed to. It was their belief in a specific set of values that boiled down to personal freedom, fair trade, justice, and extremely harsh punishments for criminal offenders.

The judge was a dark skinned Misakian who looked as though she would kill everyone in the court room if it meant she could be anywhere else. Her mop of long bone-white hair gleamed even in the harsh flat lighting. It appeared to weigh heavily on her thin frame.

When it came time to review Jaxon's case, he wasn't permitted to speak or to defend himself. The judge was shown drone footage of Jaxon hovering over the landing platform with the spent rocket launcher. It was all she needed to see to make her ruling.

Life in prison.

The sentence didn't upset him. They believed Jaxon had fired a weapon of mass destruction inside of their city, because that's what he wanted them to believe. And as far as they knew, it was the truth. Taking Akeema's place was the best possible outcome he could have hoped for to protect his sister. He regretted nothing. Except maybe being caught.

Also in attendance was Martel. He was in shackles, but was kept sedated. Jaxon considered his taking part in Martel's capture to be a fair trade for his own freedom. Sacrificing one's self to protect the innocent was a warrior's most noble achievement.

The judge was shown security camera footage from the maglev train. Jaxon watched with her as Martel beat Akeema to a pulp, the images forcing him to look away. The judge saw Martel use his tuning abilities to attack security officers. The video disturbed her. Jaxon assumed she'd never seen someone use their mind to move things before. Her ruling wasn't surprising.

Life in prison.

There were a dozen other defendants on trial from a dozen different species Jaxon didn't recognize. Each person wore control cuffs that could be electrified to keep the unruly in line. Jaxon looked around, relieved that he didn't see Akeema. He'd hoped she and Castor were on their way back to the monastery with the album. Then at least it wouldn't have all been for nothing. Just so long as they were safe.

Of the rows of accused prisoners, the only species that stood out to Jaxon was a Thurlbii. A shriek of fear shot through his body as his mind conjured the memory of his attack on Giannis. He forced himself to stare at the chained up Thurlbii who looked scruffy and thin from malnutrition with a short snout. It was a female, so not the same Thurlbii who'd attacked him. His sense of fear remained.

The court hadn't found every defendant to be guilty.

Three people were found innocent and cleared of all charges. Six others were given the option to pay a fine or perform community service. This suggested that perhaps the Montanarin legal system wasn't completely insane.

The hearings ended. Within an hour the guilty were placed in a prison shuttle that resembled a flying double decker bus. The prisoners were fitted with new security shackles, their metal jaws snapping shut around their hands and ankles.

Inside the shuttle, Jaxon and Martel were seated near each other. Martel was awake, but groggy, like he'd had a bad flu or a stomach virus. His skin was thick with sweat. He struggled against his restraints, trying to tune but couldn't.

"What's the matter? Can't get it up?" Jaxon said. "

"They must have dosed me with a tuning blocker," Martel said with a scratchy voice. Jaxon's expression became a question. He'd never heard of tuning abilities being able to be blocked. Martel continued to fight for a bit longer before fatigue made him give in, settling into his chains like a sad dog. "So... what'd I miss?"

Jaxon glared. "You got us arrested. We've been sentenced to life imprisonment."

Martel groaned. "What planet?"

"Some place called Kabria."

"Fuck," Martel sighed. "That's bad. Do you know anything about that place?"

"It's a prison. It speaks for itself."

"Oh boy," Martel chuckled. "It's much, much worse than that. Kabria's controlled by the Thurlbii. I understand you're familiar with them."

"I ran into two of them on Giannis. It was *not* a good time."

"Jeez, you don't know the half of it. They're famous for torturing and eating their prisoners."

Jaxon flinched. He remembered what Murhaf had told him about how the Thurlbii ate organs. After all this time he hadn't stopped to think about it. If he hadn't had found the courage to get out of the alley, they would have eaten him. The thought made him gag.

"No. No way," Jaxon said, shaking his head. "The Protectorate would never condone cannibalism."

"Publicly? No. But Kabria is an independent world. The Thurlbii are fully within their right to do whatever they want to convicted prisoners, which we are. You took the fall for Akeema. I hope she appreciates your sacrifice when you're being cooked alive over a spit."

"Bullshit," Jaxon said.

"Kabria has a rich mining industry. The place is practically dripping with kestesil. We'll be forced to work twenty-six hours a day mining and processing the ore until we die of exhaustion. And then the Thurlbii will eat our remains."

Jaxon tried to read Martel's face, but he wasn't sure what he was looking for. Some hint, some tell that Martel was full of weapons grade bullshit and that they were actually on their way to a boring prison with cells and bad food and a library where they would be treated humanely.

Then Jaxon realized just how incredibly naive that would sound if he'd said it out loud, so he didn't.

"You're just trying to scare me," Jaxon said.

"Yeah. I am," Martel admitted. "But it's still the truth. And I'm not about to die in some alien gulag and get eaten because you were too proud and too stupid to accept my help."

The prison shuttle's engines roared to life and the vehicle bolted away, jostling the prisoners in their seats.

"We're both here because of what *you* did," Jaxon said. "Because of the people *you* killed."

Martel nodded. "You're right. I killed your fellow Kaijen. I didn't want to. That's just how it happened. And you want me to feel sorry about it but I don't and I never will." His words hit cold and sharp, Martel's jokey casual attitude replaced by steely callousness.

"Is there anyone in this universe you do care about?" Jaxon asked.

Martel looked off to the side, his cold-blooded frame thawing a bit. "Yeah. And she's dying."

And then it clicked.

"Olen," Jaxon blurted out. "She's controlling you. She's making you do all this. You've been brainwashed."

Martel rolled his eyes. "Jesus fucking Christ kid," he said with an exasperated groan. "No— *you're* the one who's been brainwashed here," he pointed with his cuffed fists. "I'm just the idiot who tried to wake you up. I could have killed you all and taken the album and been on my way to save her right now. Instead, I'm here. With you. While she rots." The once brash and confident slayer of Kaijen was reduced to a sad broken man. "Everything I did was for nothing."

The shuttle touched down on a landing pad. The prisoners were led out in their shackles and loaded onto a prison transport called the *Ataka Kutwo;* a long wide cargo hauler repurposed to haul people. It reminded Jaxon of pictures he'd seen of old Earth oil tankers, except with four engine pods hanging from either side and the squat gimbaled control deck at the front instead of in the back.

The prisoners were marched into the inmate hold, a dark musky compartment in the bowels of the ship. The prisoners were fitted with gravity harnesses and seated in restraining chairs. The shackles around their wrists and ankles rendered them completely immobile.

As Jaxon's restraints magnetically locked into place, sadness overtook him. He never appreciated the freedom he'd had more than in this moment, faced with the possibility he'd never see his friends again. Or the monastery. Or Earth. Jaxon had to remind himself that this was what he'd chosen. This was the price of loyalty to one's friends. This is what it meant to be an honorable man.

The *Ataka Kutwo's* crew were all featureless security mechas, at least ten of them, dressed in blue and white service colors. The transport's engine pods coughed out blue flame and the *Ataka Kutwo* lifted out of Montanari's atmosphere, the thrust pressing Jaxon down in his uncomfortable seat. The gimbaled decks shifted for space flight as the transport cleared the planet and was joined by an escort of four unmanned J-Class Nexus starfighters. They were armed with electromagnetic defensive weapons intended to disable an attacking ship instead of destroying it. The five ships settled into formation. A beam of gravitons shot out of each vessel and pulled them into slipstream.

***

Exhaustion forced Jaxon to sleep. The *Ataka Kutwo's* rickety gimbals stirred him back to consciousness.

They'd been slipstreaming for at least seven hours. Jaxon's body had gotten sore and stiff from being chained in place with no room to move. When his eyes focused, the first thing he saw was Martel, seated across from him in identical restraints, looking less sickly than he had on the shuttle. Jaxon remembered that seat being empty before he'd fallen asleep.

Martel smiled. "Oh good. I thought you were going to sleep the whole way. You know you snore, right? You sounded like you were choking on your tongue. I really need to scratch my nose."

The mere sound of Martel's voice was enough to make Jaxon's skin crawl. "Don't talk to me."

"Why not? What does it hurt to talk?" Martel teased. "What? You got something better to do?"

"I don't trust a single word you say," Jaxon said. "You realize that, right? You have to. I'm not hiding it."

"You honestly think I'm lying about having to scratch my nose? It's so itchy."

A growl bubbled up from Jaxon's throat. "This isn't a *joke*. I'm in this situation because of *you*." He tugged at his metal cuffs, testing their strength. He'd never be able to get free of them without breaking his wrists.

"Don't bother, you're not strong enough," Martel said. "But you would be if you'd been properly trained how to tune. I can help you with that you know. Just say the word."

Jaxon's eyes narrowed. "You think I'm that gullible? This is about the album. Olen wants it to make herself more powerful. You're just her lapdog."

Martel's lips pursed, his eyes remaining flat and serious. "Do you realize how exhausting this is? Trying to save people who don't realize they need to be saved? It's easier to fool someone than to convince them that they've been fooled."

"Speak for yourself."

Martel leaned as forward as his restraints would allow. "Would you like to know why you and Castor and I are the only male Kaijen to survive the linking process?"

Jaxon paused, his mind prickling with curiosity. He buried the urge. "We were lucky. Everybody knows males are far more vulnerable to the mental stress of the linking process—"

"Not true," Martel interrupted, sounding out each syllable.

"You can't bullshit me, I know what I know," Jaxon said. "And, if I'm being honest, I think a lot of men are intimidated by a religion dominated by women."

"You mean a religion that gives you *superpowers*?" Martel

laughed. "Men would be lining up in droves for the ability to move things with their mind."

"They did," Jaxon said. "And they died. The linking process killed them. Until us, that is. And I very nearly died myself."

"No, you were very nearly *murdered*," Martel said. There was an odd deepness to his voice. "The priestesses can control the intensity of their link. You were *supposed* to die. But it turns out humans have a more resilient pineal gland than a lot of other species. It gives us a higher chance of survival."

Jaxon's eyes doubled in size. He didn't believe him. He didn't want to. Not a word of it.

But there was something... his head suddenly flashed hot like a furnace. He unconsciously gnashed his teeth. "You're speaking bullshit. Conspiracy theory bullshit. The elders would never do that. They want *everyone* to join. They love all people equally."

"They love *power*, and they fear any threat to that power," Martel said. "You didn't know half of the elders used to be males, did you? They were extremely powerful tuners. Then, mysteriously, they all died. The elders as we know them now feared that admitting too many males might lead to a return to the way things used to be. To being equal. So they banned males from becoming Kaijen."

Jaxon groaned dismissively. "Can you blame them? The life of a Kaijen was peaceful until you started killing people. The elders have every right to ban us after all the bloodshed you've caused."

Martel's gaze burned into Jaxon. It made the younger man feel smaller. "This didn't start with us. It started with Olen. It started when she became the only student brave enough to speak out against the hypocrisy of the Kaijen who claimed to be champions of inclusion and righteousness while willfully excluding an entire group of people because of their own fear and prejudice."

Jaxon scoffed. "Lies. Even if that were true, that still didn't give Olen the right to start a war and massacre people."

"That didn't *happen*," Martel said. "Well, a massacre *did* happen, but she wasn't the cause. She was the victim. Olen tried to expose the Kaijen's true nature to the other students, but instead of listening they unpersoned and ostracized her. She stood up for us and it cost her everything."

"If that were true then why were you and I and Castor allowed to be admitted as Kaijen?" Jaxon asked.

"Bad publicity," Martel said. "The elders didn't control the wireless newsfeeds back then. They couldn't stand having their hypocrisy satirized by millions of people throughout the known worlds. It hurt their brand badly enough that the elders were practically forced to allow males into the Kaijen to save face. The only reason why they let us become Kaijen was to tick a box."

"Maybe that's a good thing," Jaxon said. "Sometimes, that's just how progress works."

"Except that it showed the elders how powerful the wireless was," Martel said. "That's when they started expanding their influence over the major Protectorate media outlets. Now billions of people across the known worlds only see positive coverage of the Kaijen while anything negative is memory holed—"

"Hey!" a deep masculine voice shouted from somewhere in the inmate hold. "Would you two shut up? I'm trying to get some sleep over here!"

"*You* shut up," a feminine voice called out from a different corner of the hold. "I want to hear this. It's just starting to get good." The two alien inmates began to argue across the hold at each other. Then a third voice joined in. And then it became a cacophony of obscenities.

Jaxon and Martel ignored them.

"I don't understand why you're telling me this," Jaxon said over the shouting. "If your plan was to get us arrested so you could win me over with your xenophobic bullshit then you have wasted both of our time."

Martel was saying something, but Jaxon couldn't hear him over the shouting.

A security door cycled open and a pair of security mechas marched in with stun batons. Anyone still talking was shocked into unconsciousness until the entire hold fell silent. The mechas waited a few minutes before marching out of the hold, the door's locking bolts cycling shut with a loud clang behind them.

"That's ironic," Martel said, interrupting the silence. "You try to have your voice heard and the authority beats you into silence. Story of my life."

"What do you want from me?" Jaxon said.

Martel paused. He looked tired and worn down. "I'm just trying to get you to understand."

"Why? To what end? I can't change anything."

Martel inclined his head. "But you *can*. The one person who can fix all of this is dying. Have you seen how radiation slowly ravages living tissue? It's excruciating and cruel. You want to make real change? Help me save her." Tears wet his eyes. Martel's sincerity didn't feel like a lie. There was a part of Jaxon deep in his heart that actually sympathized, having witnessed his own fill of suffering in the slums as a child. Martel loved this woman. Whether it was romantic or maternal, it was touching. It echoed his own love for Akeema and Castor and how he was willing to die for them.

But would he kill for them?

Would he *murder* for them?

If Akeema and Castor were dying and a horde of Kaijen he didn't know stood between him and the cure, could Jaxon do what Martel did? Without thinking, he knew the answer. And it frightened him.

Jaxon looked away. "I can't."

Martel's body language changed. His eyes went glassy in a way that reminded Jaxon of Betty. In a low empty tone he said, "I understand. I'm the bad guy. My words are violence. Well, I'm done using words."

The shackles around Martel's ankles, wrists and neck vibrated, then popped open. He tuned them.

Oh God. He could've done this at any time.

Martel stood at his full height, stretched, and cracked his neck, then scratched his nose. "Man, that's better."

Fear poured down Jaxon's spine. "What are you about to do?"

"What I have to," Martel said. "The only way you'll understand the truth is if I show it to you." Martel was holding out his hands.

And at once, Jaxon understood. "No fucking way."

Martel approached him like a lion claiming the gazelle he'd just chased down. "That's fear talking. You'd rather remain confident in your ignorance because you can't face the truth."

"Don't you touch me!" Jaxon hissed. "I don't want it!"

"You need to see who the Kaijen really are and I don't have time to convince you with words. Though, linking isn't an exact science. There tends to be some bleed-through."

Jaxon trembled with anxiety. Martel towered over him. He looked up at the bald man as if he were at the bottom of a well.

Martel dropped down to his knees, Jaxon looking down on him, his face bloodless and raw with emotion. The man's eyes were suddenly innocent and pleading. "Once you join the Kaijen they can't just let you go. Olen found that out the hard way. She destroyed her crossglaive as a sign of peace and they slaughtered her followers in cold blood. They will do the same to you and your friends. You will die if I don't prepare you."

"I don't *believe* that," Jaxon barked.

"This will go easier if you're willing."

"You're evil. Everything you stand for is evil. Your 'truth' is evil. It *has* to be."

A strange smile jaywalked its way across Martel's face. "The hard way it is."

Jaxon cried out, thrashing against his restraints. The metal cut into his skin. Martel's fingers gripped Jaxon's head like tendrils ready to burrow into his skull. His fingertips tingled like electric current on Jaxon's hair. Martel pressed his forehead to Jaxon's.

They linked.

"No no no no no—" Jaxon pleaded as the sensation of insects crawling inside his mind overwhelmed him before—

*****

The first time Jaxon linked with Priestess Nisame, there'd been a brief moment of intense pain before he blacked out. This time was different.

This was worse.

Darkness came alive and wrapped itself around him, choking him, until the bottom of his feet touched soil. It was raining. He heard sounds. The buzz of a crossglaive blade. And somewhere, the screams of people being killed.

His vision was unfocused. Thick clouds of smoke overwhelmed him. The sick metallic smell of blood and burning flesh filled his nostrils.

The screams. They reverberated off of the raindrops, penetrating his atoms. The cries of women, men and children dying stabbed his ears in a way he knew they would never heal from.

Jaxon caught himself running through the smoke towards the screams in a desperate attempt to save whoever it was that needed help. The smoke glowed. It became flame. And Jaxon finally realized, much to his horror, that the screaming he'd heard was coming from his own throat.

***

The link was broken.

Jaxon landed back in the inmate hold of the *Ataka Kutwo*, still screaming. The heavy metal shackles restraining him snapped open, the locking mechanisms having been tuned apart.

And not by Martel.

Jaxon fell forward, both he and Martel collapsing onto the cold metal grating. The link drained them. Jaxon lay on his back sucking in air as if he'd just finished a marathon. His head rang and throbbed the way he imagined it would if he'd been punched by a heavyweight.

"What—" Jaxon stuttered. "What did you do to me?"

"I've freed your mind," Martel huffed.

Then they were in a fight.

Jaxon's swings were wild and lacked precision, but they landed. Martel didn't return his blows. He remained defensive. He'd already hurt Jaxon worse than his fists ever could.

The shackled prisoners roared in a maelstrom of shouts and cheers around them. The noise drew the attention of the security mechas.

As the locks on the hold's magnetic security door released, Martel positioned Jaxon to be in the mecha's path when they entered. A stun baton came at him. He narrowly dodged it.

Martel slipped past them and through the door, running into a second security mecha. He made a fist and the mecha collapsed in on itself like a crumpled piece of paper. It fell to the floor in a pile of twisted metal, lubricant and synthetic skin oozing out of it. Martel stepped over the pile and disappeared into the forward cargo hold.

Jaxon maneuvered past the mecha he was fighting in pursuit of Martel. He rushed through a series of narrow corridors until he found Martel in a room filled with storage lockers embedded in the walls. Martel had already tuned open a row of locked boxes containing the inmate's personal effects.

"Stop!" Jaxon yelled before the security mecha caught up to him and continued its fight. Martel ignored them. He pulled his crossglaive from one of the open boxes along with his handheld. Martel flipped open the device and pressed a blinking red button. A moment ticked by and the transport bucked.

"What did you just do?" Jaxon said.

"My ship has been stealth following us ever since we left Montanari," Martel said. "My mecha can't pick me up with fighter escorts still intact."

The transport bucked again, much worse this time. Power throughout the ship blinked out like a switch being flipped. An EMP pulse. Without power to run the Gravity Drive, the transport violently reentered normal space.

The sudden jolt threw Jaxon up towards the ceiling just as the hold's gimbals adjusted for the lack of thrust. His gravity harness jerked him back down and slammed him into the grated floor.

The security mecha was less fortunate. The maneuver slammed it into the ceiling, turning it into twisted scrap.

Martel used his tuning powers to brace himself from feeling the brunt of the impact. He was fine. After a moment the ship's systems rebooted and its automated systems flipped on. Jaxon felt like a bull was sitting on his chest. The *Ataka Kutwo*'s emergency braking thrusters kicked on, slowing the ship down with the force of several g's.

Once the *Ataka Kutwo* stabilized Martel casually walked towards the front of the transport.

Jaxon's body pleaded for mercy. It would get none. He picked himself up off the chilly floor. Inside one of the opened locked boxes, he saw his damaged rocket boots. Jaxon kicked off the cheap prison shoes he'd been given and slipped the boots on. The box also contained his smashed handheld, but not his crossglaive.

Jaxon limped after Martel. He climbed an access ladder to an upper level when the transport rocked, followed by the sound of docking clamps gripping the hull. Jaxon pushed his body to move faster through the corridors. He reached the forward airlock and found Martel staring down at his handheld looking none too pleased at what he saw.

He peered up at Jaxon. "You're too slow. You should have taken that guard out before it had the chance to attack you. We'll need to work on that in the future."

"I'm not letting you get away," Jaxon said, out of breath and his fists up.

"This ship is caught in a decaying orbit of the planet below us. Everyone on this vessel will die if you don't stop it." Jaxon paused, trying to read the man's face to determine truth from lie. He wasn't lying. "Or you can follow me," Martel continued. "You can't do both."

His words stunned Jaxon. "I thought you said you weren't a murderer."

"And I won't be," Martel said. "If you save them." He tossed Jaxon's crossglaive hilt to him. The younger man didn't understand why.

"You'll need it," Martel said. "For when the Kaijen try to kill you."

Martel stepped through the airlock and onto his ship. Jaxon didn't stop him. Martel waved and the airlock cycled closed.

Chapter Sixteen: Castor

The *Saragos* was at slipstream for coming up on seven hours. The high-g burn through void space was punishing, with short fifteen-minute breaks every ninety minutes to keep everyone from stroking out. It made Castor violently sick.

They were catching up with Jaxon's prison transport, the more massive ship having a lower top speed traveling through slipstream. It gave smaller vessels like the *Saragos* an unfair velocity advantage, assuming the crew could withstand the prolonged physical trauma.

Sitting in the cockpit and pumped full of gravity drugs, Castor's stomach was empty as a football and trying to eat itself. He refused to consume any of Yoko's strange still-alive slug food, either out of fear the creatures would survive inside his stomach or fear they would actually taste good. Just thinking about it made him want to retch. Not that he could eat anything with gravity pushing down on his organs like a hydraulic press.

Castor distracted himself by trying to figure out how this whole rescue Jaxon plan was likely going to play out. Do they try to take the prison transport and get blown up in the process? Or do they attack the prison itself and *then* get blown up?

Every scenario he imagined, the logical side of his brain shot it down in a flaming wreck. Jaxon was his brother and he loved him, but every aspect of this scenario was insane. They were just as likely to get everyone killed. Instead, Castor tried to come up with the right sequence of words that would convince Akeema that they had already lost him. That going straight to Priestess Sabrene was their only hope. It was the plan that seemed more plausible.

The hollowness in his gut made him cough, drawing the attention of Yoko's mecha. She—it—almost appeared to act as if it were an individual. Mechas weren't supposed to question their masters. They were supposed to obey. Not go off gallivanting around the galaxy on doomed rescue missions, no matter how noble. Castor considered reporting the mecha to the PSS, the Protectorate Security Service, or piss, the nickname the kids he'd grown up with called it. Sentient mechas were still highly illegal even this long after the war. If left unchecked, this mecha could potentially turn on Yoko and kill her. Reporting a mecha with a ticking time bomb in its code would be doing the worlds a service. Perhaps. After.

A chime sounded from the cockpit's dradis console.

"It's gone," Yoko said, struggling to breathe under the g-forces pressing her down.

"What's gone?" Castor asked, his teeth rattling. Yoko tapped buttons on her armrest console and the ship slowed its burn. Castor breathed easier.

"The prison transport. It dropped out of slipstream," she said. Her fingers stabbed buttons and flipped switches in a frantic manner. Castor was able to lean forward in his chair to get a better look at the dradis. Yoko waved him away and focused on her monitors. "I have to cut the beam or else we'll overshoot— everybody pucker up, we're about to get a lot heavier."

Akeema was buckled into her seat's harness next to Castor. Yoko stabbed a button and a pair of hyposprays embedded in the headrests of their chairs craned around and injected them with more gravity drugs, minus Betty who didn't need it. The cocktail felt like fire in his veins.

Castor watched a monitor with an outside view of the ship. It showed the weird non-area of void space brighten into a multitude of streaking color as Yoko shut down the Gravity Drive and the *Saragos* returned to real space. Yoko initiated an emergency braking burn and the weight of the engine pod's counter thrusters hit like a crash, pressing their bodies down into their chairs almost to the point of blackout.

While the ship's engine pods slowed the *Saragos* down, Yoko flipped the mass of the vessel so that the main drive could contribute to their rapid deceleration. Painfully intense g's pressed down on them for several grueling minutes. The effect on their internal organs was brutal. Stars exploded behind Castor's eyes, like his brains were being forced into his feet.

After a stretch of time, the pain eased and the ship evened out to normal thrust. A violent shudder rippled through the *Saragos* followed by a loud metallic screech that vibrated Castor to his bones.

"Something hit us," Akeema said. "Are we under attack?"

"No," Yoko said. "Something didn't hit us. *We* hit something." The ship analyzed the debris they were flying through. Scans identified them as the remains of the transport's fighter escorts.

Yoko tongued the inside of her cheek. "Well, that's not good," she said to no one. A klaxon sounded and the ship's threat board lit up with warnings.

Betty turned to Yoko. "We are being painted."

Someone had target-locked the *Saragos*. Both of Yoko's caterpillars rode high up her wide gray forehead. Her eyes darted across her dradis console for any other ship aside from the *Ataka Kutwo*. There was nothing. Yoko piloted the ship in a series of evasive zigzag maneuvers, rolling and banking the ship in sudden random bursts in an attempt to break the target-lock. The crushing pull of g's squeezed Castor's body like jaws, each hard maneuver threatening to pop a blood vessel. During which, the ship's gimbals remained in a constant state of readjustment. It wreaked havoc on Castor's equilibrium.

If a stroke didn't kill him, the nausea would.

One of the wall screens displayed a huge gas giant more massive than Jupiter. It loomed millions of kilometers ahead of them, hanging against the stars like a marble that'd been enlarged a zillion times. Its surface was covered in slowly churning honey and tangerine storms. Beautiful chaos.

Orbiting the giant were four moons that were imperceptibly tiny in comparison. If the gas giant were a head, the moons were beads of sweat floating around it.

The nearest bead was a pine and rust colored ball the ship's sensors identified as Briar, a moon-planet with a gravity slightly heavier than Earth's. The prison transport was caught in its pull, its gravity dragging the ship down into the planet's atmosphere where it was doomed to burn.

Where Jaxon would burn.

A dozen more sensor scans later and the *Saragos* was able to identify something unusual. One of Yoko's screens showed a live telescopic view of a faint image. Betty pressed a key and the image zoomed in on the odd little ship shaped like a motorized ratchet. It approached them, its braking thrusters firing.

"Foosha! *Shin okie lagra!*" Yoko snapped. "That's a gunship. It barely registers on dradis. If it wanted to it could have killed us twenty times over."

"Get us out of here! Slipstream!" Castor said.

"Gravity Drives aren't magic, *baizuo*," Yoko said. "They need time to spool. We're stuck here for at least a few more minutes—" a chime cut her off. An incoming tightbeam. Betty opened her artificial mouth to speak, but Yoko had already accepted the connection request.

Martel appeared on the screen. "Hello there. Thanks for saving me the trouble of having to come find you. Let's talk."

"Where's Jaxon?" Akeema shouted to the monitor before Yoko could respond.

"On the transport," Martel said. "He's alive. But that won't last long. If you don't move fast, he will burn. And I'll even let you save him, if you give me what I want."

"The only thing we'll give you is a proper funeral," Castor boasted. Only after hearing his own words did he realize how silly he must have sounded to Martel, a tinge of embarrassment itching his head.

"Your empty threats are adorable," Martel said. "Scan my ship. I outgun you and I can outrun you. You can give me the album, willingly, or I can sift through your wreckage. I would prefer the former, if that makes any difference."

Castor didn't want to believe him. Couldn't. He'd hoped maybe this old rickety ship had some kind of secret weapon that could overwhelm Martel in a surprise show of strength. The tension on Yoko's round silver face said otherwise. She looked back over her shoulder at the album clutched in Akeema's hands.

Then Yoko put on a fake friendly smile and stared into her comm camera. "Say we hand over this bobble. What's stopping you from slagging my ship anyway?"

"My word," Martel said with an air of confidence reserved for conquerors. "We're not enemies. There's been enough violence committed. And if it's any consolation, I apologize for throwing you off that platform. That was… rude. I'll make it up to you. But right now, I just want the album. Once I have it, I promise you no harm will come to your ship."

Castor reached over to mute the transmission. "He's lying. He's a murderer. He cannot be trusted. Doesn't this ship have torpedoes? We need to shoot him down." Castor expected Yoko to agree with him. Instead, she looked past him to her mecha.

"I have analyzed the stress in his voice," Betty said. "I detect no deception." Her words angered Castor. He knew Yoko would value her—its—opinion over his.

They both looked past Castor, to Akeema. Pangs of stress wrinkled the skin between the two strips of flame that were her eyebrows. The album remained clasped tight in her small pale hands. Castor reached for it when she jumped from her chair and ran out of the cockpit.

"Where are you going? Wait—" Castor cried, but she was gone. He followed her, anticipating what she was going to do even before she did. He found her in the galley, stuffing the album into the garbage chute and cycling the hatch closed.

"Stop Akeema! Don't—" and then it was gone. The only leverage they had, flushed into the black. His throat wanted to collapse in on itself. "What have you done?"

"I just saved our lives," Akeema said, her eyes wet with tears.

"Get your hoo-mon asses in here!" Yoko called to them.

They returned to the cockpit. Yoko was laser focused on the dradis readout. She watched the *Jezebel* veer off. It scooped up the barely perceivable album in a grappling net, then a beam of gravitons shot out of its nose and it streaked off into slipstream.

The bastard had kept his word.

"The bastard kept his word," Akeema said.

Yoko worked the controls and aimed the ship at Briar. Castor and Akeema were back in their chairs before the engine pods ignited to full burn and brought them to the transport. Yoko turned to Betty. "Hail them."

Betty sent the tightbeam. Several minutes ticked by before the connection request was accepted. Where a face would usually appear on the communications screen, they only saw a blank wall with faint clumsy noises in the background.

"Hello?" Jaxon's voice asked nervously.

Yoko tilted her head. "hoo-mon?"

Jaxon's face popped into view, having just found the communications camera. "Yoko? Is that you?"

"Look at the terrible mess you've gotten yourself into," Yoko continued.

"What are you talking about?" Jaxon said, playing down how monumentally screwed things were. "I've got everything perfectly under control—"

He was cut off by an explosion.

Something outside of the *Ataka Kutwo*, most likely a stabilizing thruster, had blown off of the ship. It sent the long blocky vessel into a slow spin, like a propeller blade. Spin gravity pinned Jaxon to one side of the *Ataka Kutwo's* cockpit, out of the camera's view.

"Activate your starboard stabilizer," Yoko said to the absent screen.

"Uh... how do I do that?" Jaxon's strained voice replied through the speakers.

"Look for a row of yellow knobs, they should be blinking."

On the communications monitor, they watched Jaxon's hand reach into frame, fighting against the g forces. His fingertips struggled to touch the little yellow knob at the edge of the frame. It was too far out of his reach.

Then, it moved.

All on its own.

Jaxon didn't appear to realize that he'd done it. The *Ataka Kutwo* leveled out, but continued its descent to the cloudy planet below.

Akeema lit up with panic. "Jaxon, you have to hurry. Get to a lifeboat and we'll pick you up."

"It's a prison ship, Akeema. They don't have lifeboats," Jaxon said. "Besides, there are people onboard. I won't abandon them."

Castor sneered. "They're criminals. Leave them to their fate."

"They're people," Jaxon affirmed. "I won't leave them to die if I can save them. It's all of us or none of us."

"Jaxon," Betty's flat voice cut in. "You have a less than forty-two percent chance of survival if you attempt to land the transport. Thirty-eight percent now. Thirty-six percent now."

"Tell me what to do," Jaxon pleaded.

"Deploy your air brakes," Yoko said. "Should be a series of levers overhead." Jaxon followed her orders. "We'll follow you in."

The *Saragos* entered Briar's upper atmosphere behind the *Ataka Kutwo*. The cockpit's gimbals shifted in response to the planet's gravity. Flames engulfed both ships upon reentry. Minutes stretched before the ships dropped into a thick sea of clouds that resembled floating bales of cotton. Turbulence slapped the *Saragos*. Castor feared the whole ship was going to unspool right down to the rivets. Anything not bolted down shook. Yoko scrambled to keep the ship on course. Castor's chair straps were the only things keeping him from spilling onto the floor.

"He's still going way too fast," Yoko said. "When he hits the dirt the impact will turn him into jelly with teeth."

"Doesn't this bucket have tow cables?" Castor asked.

"Don't you dare talk to my ship that way," Yoko warned. "And of course it has tow cables. But the *Sara*'s engines aren't powerful enough to lift that transport especially in this gravity."

Akeema spoke over them. "We can't stop it, but maybe we can slow it down." Yoko groaned. She punched in a code to a small safe and pulled out a bottle of liquor. She took a swig. Akeema frowned. "Is this *really* the time for that?"

Yoko swallowed another gulp. A string of liquid dribbled horizontally across her cheek, driven by the ship's velocity. "No way am I doing this sober." She dried her cheek with her sleeve and placed the liquor back in her safe, then maneuvered the *Saragos* above the plummeting *Ataka Kutwo*. "Just so we're clear, I want to go on record as saying this is an incredibly stupid plan that isn't going to work and I take zero responsibility for its failure."

"Have faith," Castor said. He hadn't decided whether or not he truly believed the words.

"Faith is for children and untalented hacks," Yoko said. The ship jerked her around in her chair. "Pulling this off with no fatalities will require tremendous skill and nerves of cargonite. Which I have. Usually. Betty, fire the spear hooks."

Six oval hatches slid open on the ship's belly. Metal spearheaded tow cables shot out of the *Saragos* and into the topside of the *Ataka Kutwo*'s hull. The engine pods on the *Saragos* rotated facing backwards and acted as braking thrusters. They worked to slow the *Ataka Kutwo*'s descent like a reverse tow truck.

Akeema monitored their speed. "It's slowing down."

"Yeah, but not enough," Yoko grumbled. She fought to control the ship. Over Betty's shoulder, Castor watched a console. It showed the amount of stress being exerted on the cables. It wasn't good. Yoko increased the ship's reverse thrust, the stress causing the thick metal cables to twist and groan. A loud, terrible crack announced that one of the cables had snapped.

"Foosha!" Yoko shouted. She banked the *Saragos* hard to port. The snapped cable flew up at the ship and nearly sliced off one of the engine pods.

Then another cable snapped.

Yoko fought to keep the ship steady. The muscles in her arm flexed as she wrestled with the controls. A thunder crack, and two more cables broke off, leaving two cables remaining.

"Detach! Detach!" Yoko screamed to Betty.

"Controls will not respond," Betty said in her calm clinical tone. "We are being pulled down with the transport."

"If we don't sever those cables we're dead," Yoko said with sharp dread. Castor looked to Akeema. She was already looking back at him. More specifically, his crossglaive. He was looking at hers in return, communicating with looks. They'd reached an understanding.

Both unstrapped their seatbelts and exited the cockpit.

"See that, Betty?" Yoko's voice echoed behind them. "They abandoned us. Ungrateful. That's the hoo-mon's true nature!"

Castor and Akeema rode the service elevator to the lower bowels of the ship where the spear hook winches were. They figured out pretty fast that they couldn't reach the cables without slicing through the hull.

Akeema pointed. "Over there." She'd discovered a series of service hatches. Castor and Akeema each opened a hatch near the attached cables. Intense cool wind blew up through the opened hatches and whipped around them. Castor flicked a lever and a ladder lowered down, allowing him to climb outside of the ship. Akeema copied him.

Holy shit, Castor thought. The sky directly below him was full of ship, the massive prison transport hovering underneath him even though it was shooting through the air like a rocket. One slip and he'd be swept to his death. With one hand on their separate ladders, Castor and Akeema extended their crossglaive blades. They aimed to sever the taut cables which gyrated from tension two arm lengths away. Castor was right-handed, but he rationalized that gripping the ladder with his bionic right hand and swinging the crossglaive with his flesh hand made more sense. It was awkward, but he was certain he could do it.

"At the same time," Castor yelled over the gusting winds.

"I'm ready," Akeema yelled back.

Castor breathed. Akeema waited for him. They nodded to each other. On the third nod, their crossglaive blades swung at the cables. Akeema's blade sliced clean through one of the cables, but turbulence knocked Castor off balance mid-swing. His vetronium hand gripped the ladder too tightly and the step broke loose.

He fell.

"Castor!" Akeema's scream called out as the world spun around him. Castor reached out blindly and grabbed at something, anything.

His arm hooked around the cable he failed to cut. He hugged the cable, sliding down it like a firehouse pole. The friction rubbed his arms and chest raw to the point of being unbearable. Castor crashed down on top of the *Ataka Kutwo*'s hull which was still hot from reentry, but not enough to scald. His bionic hand gripped a groove in the ship's skin, anchoring him, stopping the wind from swatting him off.

Castor rolled over onto his back. He looked up to see the *Saragos* looming above him like a giant mechanical beast. The severed cables retracted back into the ship, leaving only the one still tethered to the *Ataka Kutwo* like an umbilical cord. Castor swung his crossglaive and cut the cord. The *Saragos* jerked back from the release of tension and disappeared into the thick clouds.

The groove Castor's metal hand gripped began to bend. It wouldn't last long. Desperately, he cut a jagged hole into the *Ataka*

Kutwo's skin and fell inside a corridor. Bright pain shot through his shoulder and up his arm as it slammed into the grated floor. He ignored the surging ache and hurried through the ship where he figured the bridge would be.

A door cycled open and he was in the inmate hold where the prisoners were going apeshit. Half of them were crying or praying while the other half were cheering for the ship's fiery destruction. When they saw him, Castor heard a cacophony of voices pleading for help. He dodged their sad eyes and angry shouts and continued forward. Even still, he could see that they weren't all scary looking evil brutes who belonged in irons. Many were women, while some could pass for teenagers.

These were the people whose deaths he'd advocated for. Only now, having put faces to the faceless, did he see that Jaxon was right. For every prisoner who probably deserved to parish in this tin can, there were many who probably didn't. Castor felt a sliver of shame, as well as a renewed sense of urgency. He had to help Jaxon save this boat before the crash turned them all into pasta sauce.

Castor knew he was getting closer to the bridge when he heard a symphony of shrill warning alarms echo through the corridors ahead. He followed the noise and found Jaxon in a panic, frantically trying to pilot the doomed ship. On one of the monitors was the surface of Briar. It was various shades of brown with more sand than vegetation, but with pockets of water. On the dradis, Castor saw something that chilled his blood.

At their rate of descent, the ship was on a collision course with a large village a short distance ahead.

Castor sat in the co-pilot's chair next to Jaxon. "Are you aiming for that settlement on purpose?"

"I can't get the maneuvering thrusters to fire," Jaxon grunted. "You're more than welcome to help me do something about it."

Castor stared at the controls for a few heartbeats before making adjustments. "I've only piloted a small shuttle, and that was almost a decade ago."

"This is my first time," Jaxon said lightly. "I am *not* enjoying it."

Castor continued to turn knobs and flip switches. Nothing he did changed their trajectory. The sensors told him roughly how many life signs they were about to crush. "There are well over two thousand people down there."

"I know. I'm pretty sure that big building we're going to hit first is a school."

"Damnit. We just can't catch a break, can we? What if we dip the nose and crash the ship before we reach the village?"

Jaxon sleeved away sweat dripping from his brow. "Thought of that. If the ship flips, we'll steamroll the whole village. I'm trying to overshoot it but I can't pull the damn nose up."

Castor stood up. He reached over Jaxon to grab the controls with him. Both men pulled back on the maneuvering controls hard enough the metal joins twisted and broke off. Castor fell back on his ass.

The *Ataka Kutwo* immediately pitched forward. They were about to crash.

"Strap in!" Jaxon yelled.

Castor had seconds. His harness locked into place just before the *Ataka Kutwo's* nose slammed into the sandy dirt. The transport's hull whined and screeched as it slid towards the village at incredible speed. Two of the external engine pods were sheared off and exploded.

Not that Castor cared. His concern was directed at the external monitor and what he saw on it. The villagers had seen the vehicle of death hurling towards them and began to scatter. It was pointless. Those people, whoever they were, were about to be crushed underneath his feet and there was nothing he could do to stop it. So he closed his eyes rather than witness the impending carnage.

He heard Jaxon scream, and everything stopped...

Then silence.

Castor opened his eyes, one at a time, expecting the worst.

The village, despite all odds, was still intact. The school stood directly in front of the transport's bow. The *Ataka Kutwo* had stopped, quite literally, dead in its tracks just before it could destroy anything or kill anyone.

Castor watched a group of teachers evacuating dozens of small children from the school house. He realized he'd been holding his breath the entire time and exhaled. His neck whipped around to look at Jaxon, his eyes and mouth wide open with confusion and disbelief.

"What happened?" Jaxon asked, seemingly to himself.

Castor hesitated. "I think... I think it was you. You stopped us. You tuned."

"I did? But I wasn't trying."

"I felt it," Castor said. "It was you. It was all you."

They sat there breathing hot for a moment, then burst into nervous laughter. They cheered and gave each other a rough pat on the shoulder in celebration. It surprised Castor to see tears in Jaxon's eyes. They both unstrapped from their chairs and stood up. Jaxon paused, then went stiff, his eyes rolling into his head. He shivered then collapsed to the floor in violent convulsions.

Castor held him. "Jaxon? What's wrong? Can you hear me? Jaxon? Jaxon?!"

The convulsions worsened.

He took Jaxon into his arms and carried him to the nearest airlock. They slid down an emergency slide and Castor stood on the dry soil of Briar, breathing in its dry thin oxygen that stank like fish guts.

The crash released the inmate restraints. Prisoners evacuated the transport and fled in all directions.

The *Saragos* swooped down from the sky, its RCS landing thrusters kicking up a storm of sand and regolith. It hazed the air as the ship touched down. Its floodlights shone through the fog, acting as beacons. Castor carried Jaxon over his shoulder to the ship. Akeema lowered down in the crew elevator to meet him, her nose wrinkled from the smell. She shielded her eyes from the dust, but they widened in horror when she saw Jaxon.

"What happened? What's wrong with him?" Akeema demanded.

"I don't know," Castor shouted over the ship's roaring engines. "Help me get him to medical." She did.

The elevator lifted the three of them up into the ship when Castor realized Jaxon's situation had changed. He appeared to be having a seizure. Jaxon's eyes dartdc fast behind his eyelids, his arms stretched out at his sides. In Castor's grip, Jaxon became weightless. Off of Akeema's frightened look, he quickly realized why.

Jaxon was levitating.

Chapter Seventeen: Olen

Carliez Minor was a small Protectorate controlled world with clear oceans and grasslands as tall as houses. This was where Olen had come to be trained as a Kaijen. She'd dreamt of the day since childhood, of becoming the youngest priestess in the Kaijen's history. It was something she wanted more than anything, even if she had to cut a piece of herself off to achieve it. Every waking moment was spent steering her fate to that outcome, to make that fantasy her reality.

Things didn't go according to plan.

Instead, she'd fled Carliez Minor as the Kaijen's greatest enemy.

Olen's expulsion from the Kaijen forced her down a new path. One where the young Asabi revolutionary would choose to start her own school of Kaijen teachings. She'd led a bloodless revolt against her own priestess and convinced many of her peers to leave with her.

Having been denied the freedom to hone and utilize their Kaijen powers to their full extent, Olen and her exiles set out on a quest to establish their own monastery, a place where they could practice their own interpretations of the Kaijen teachings without the harsh censorship and oppressive oversight of the priestesses and the elders. Theirs would be a haven where they would be free to have relationships and families without the hypocritical rules and restrictions that had held them back.

Olen had unintentionally started a cultural movement and it was growing. Word spread quickly over the wireless. The elders had never experienced such disgrace and open rebellion against their old ways and responded by implementing a massive wave of censorship. What Olen hadn't anticipated were the politics. The Quorum of Elders were in bed with the political leaders of the Protectorate. Any forums discussing the rebellion over the wireless networks were quarantined and deleted. If no one talked about the rebellion, no one would remember it. And if no one could remember an event, then that event never happened.

At the time, Olen hadn't seen the danger in censorship. She was too focused on taking care of her followers, her group of brave former Kaijen and the handful of new recruits they'd encountered on their journey who'd chosen to join them; a group that included several males.

These men were eager for the opportunity to have their brain chemistry altered by the linking process. The possibility of dying from a massive brain aneurysm didn't frighten them. They braved the risks in the hopes of becoming the first known males to attain tuning abilities.

One of these men, Behrens, was a tall hairless Velibor with gorgeous pale diamond-patterned skin and webbed ears. His large almond eyes were set deep in his skull and he had a warm, dimpled smile that reminded Olen of home. Their attempt to link was successful with no fatal consequences. They shared their memories and experiences with each other as if they were one being.

She married this man.

He would be the father of the only child she would ever carry. She'd been three months pregnant when their ships touched down on Zaspel. Olen found that planet's windswept terrain covered in bleached white sands and its muddy brown rock formations to hold its own unique kind of beauty. Its dried-up canals resembled deep jagged spiderwebs from orbit. It was a piece of real estate no one claimed or wanted. She'd chosen to settle her congregation on the barren world specifically because it was so inhospitable. It was an ideal location for her needs.

She would have chosen differently had she known it would become her prison. And eventually, her tomb.

It burned Olen's soul, knowing there would be no one to bury her when the planet finally killed her. She wanted to rest next to her husband and son. Olen weeped every time she stood over the mound of rocks that were their makeshift graves. Her body had lost vital fluids she couldn't afford to lose. Still, she cried. She buried her family next to the shallow graves of her followers. Guilt over their deaths overwhelmed her. Because she was responsible for them.

The only memento Olen had of her unborn son was an ugly

gnarled cauterized scar on her stomach.

When they first arrived, Olen and her followers cannibalized two of their three transport ships to build their settlement. Having only one working ship to retrieve off-world supplies was a risky decision, but the odds of the ship not working and stranding them on the planet was low. Even if everyone hadn't been slaughtered, looking back, that choice still haunted her.

All of her choices did. Because they were all the wrong ones.

The massacre hadn't extended to just the deaths of her students. Their water recyclers and medical equipment were destroyed. If left untreated, radiation from the planet's trinary suns would soak into her skin and develop into cancer. In time the lack of water and the dry heat would cripple her body until she withered and died. She welcomed it. It would be her penance, spending years in exile reflecting on all the ways she could have done better. One change here or there and everyone she cared about might still be alive. Her son could be celebrating his latest birthday, had she been more cautious. More ruthless.

More willing to kill.

In her grief, her mind wandered back to her cultural upbringing as an Asabi child where she'd been encouraged to question everything. She wanted to know why things were the way they were and who decided it should be that way. Becoming a Kaijen meant adhering to their rules. None were more explicit than the forbidden linking among students. It ate at Olen that they never told her why. She decided to find out for herself.

It started with words.

Olen confided in other students whom she'd grown to trust. In secret they discussed their curiosity and desire to explore their abilities without the supervision of their priestess. Talking escalated to experimentation. Olen and her small band of like-minded peers would meet in secret away from their monastery and began the practice of linking among each other. They half expected their heads to explode or to spontaneously grow a third eye.

Instead, they all got stronger.

Each time they linked, their stamina to tune increased. Their ability to recall linked memories became easier, and those memories were seen clearer than ever before. Olen's abilities had always excelled beyond her novice sisters at tuning and accessing linked memories. Now her powers were extraordinary. She could remember the linked memories her sisters had shared with her as easily as if she'd experienced them herself. With her newfound power came the capacity to replay and examine the memories in detail, like a virtual recording inside her head. Tuning became as natural to her as running. It still drained her physically, but not as quickly and with a much shorter refractory period. She'd sacrificed everything to harness these skills, which were all but useless to her survival on Zaspel. She spent much of her nine years in exile living inside of her memories.

Tuning allowed her to retreat into herself; to relive her own past as an observer in the sad, ephemeral story that was her life.

Olen sheltered in the hovel she'd built out of the ruins of the burned down settlement, using a combination of primitive cement and the force of her tuning powers to mold it together. Inside, she'd sit in the lotus position and fall into deep meditation. Her eyelids weighed heavy and would shudder closed for a moment.

When they opened, she was someplace else, inside of a memory.

In her mind, she went back to the monastery on Carliez Minor. The experience felt as real as actually being there. Olen went back to a time when she was still a novice Kaijen and her closest friend, the one she trusted more than anyone, was a tall lanky pink skinned Iskaran.

Iskaran women had a long and storied reputation for being arrogant, ambitious, and unreasonably difficult. It was that blunt self-righteousness that served them well when it came to negotiating resources and trade deals for their home world. Sabrene shared her memories with Olen, allowing her to peer into Sabrene's mind. She'd been best of her peers, even in her girlhood. When Sabrene became a Kaijen, this truth persisted. She saw herself as being superior. In Sabrene's world, if she wasn't the best at something then that meant she was second, and she was never second.

Olen's aptitude threatened that.

The two women would spar in physical combat drills. Sabrene would be overwhelmed by Olen's attacks. During crossglaive practice, Olen would best Sabrene time and time again. They would compete in extraneous tuning exercises meant to test their mental endurance. And once again, Sabrene just couldn't keep up. She masked her humiliation with her polite enigmatic smile that cut with a dagger's edge. Behind her dull eyes grew a volcanic rage that could collapse a star.

At the time, Olen's past self failed to see the hatred and contempt festering behind Sabrene's kind words. Olen took pity on Sabrene and as a symbol of their friendship agreed to link with her, believing that sharing her power with the blue haired pink skinned woman would make them both equals. *How blind I was*, she thought.

Sabrene couldn't settle for equal. She had to be the best, or nothing.

Their priestess was Lorel, a dark green Herekin woman. Sabrene had been her star pupil long before Olen's admittance to the monastery. Lorel was eager to believe Sabrene's tails of the evil student who'd disobeyed her Kaijen oath and who was plotting to murder everyone with her growing power.

Shame, guilt, innuendo, and ruining the reputation of her rivals was how Sabrene rewarded the kindness Olen had shown her. Her lies were corroborated by another equally deceitful student Olen had befriended, Nisame. The goal was to have Olen and her followers sentenced to a reeducation session where they would be tortured to the point of death. Only, Olen had grown too powerful to control and many of the other students she'd linked with had taken her side. Strength in numbers.

Their time as Kaijen had ended.

Olen watched the memory of her past self asking Sabrene why she'd betrayed her. "To save lives," Sabrene said with her polite venom. "This will only end in bloodshed." Before Olen left the monastery, she remembered the last thing Sabrene had said to her.

"You should kill yourself."

Reliving the memory, Olen watched her younger self considered using her tuning powers to crush Sabrene's skull. She wasn't a murderer. She fought the urge. Another of her many regrets.

Six years into her exile, Olen's days on Zaspel consisted of simple survival. The weight she'd lost had left her rail thin and her bones had become brittle. Her sun-baked skin stretched and sagged and her once coffee colored hair was now the color of fresh snow. When the punishment of survival became too much for her to bear, she could hear Sabrene's words whisper in her inner ear.

Kill yourself.

Seven years into her slow death on Zaspel, Olen made the decision to travel from her hovel to a cave half a day's walk from the graveyard. Above the cave were a series of tall cliffs marked with small thin fractures that expelled crackling winds. It sounded like radio static. Olen heard a voice carry on the whistling gusts, calling out to her.

Kill. Yourself.

Olen devoted much of her time to meditation, maintaining her sanity by living inside of her memories. She hoped to find some sense of meaning to justify her current suffering. She found none.

Once or twice a month the humid nights brought with them torrential rains and the local wildlife would scramble to hydrate until the next downpour. Ten weeks had passed since the last downpour and Olen's withered body began to desiccate. She could see no point in continuing on.

Kill. Your. Self.

Eight years into her exile, Olen let the dark thoughts consume her. She climbed the face of the tallest cliff, the palms of her thin hands rubbed raw and dirty from the worn rocks. Halfway up, a terrible coughing fit overcame her. She nearly lost her balance. The fall may have killed her, or it might have just broken her body. If she was going to go through with this, she had to be certain. She had to make sure she wouldn't survive.

Olen continued her climb and reached the summit.

She took a long look out at the mostly barren landscape. It was the last view she'd ever see. Olen hoped she might catch a glimpse of Behrens one last time before her body crashed against the jagged rocks below. It was a pleasant thought.

She stood at the edge, her eyes tired and heavy. She closed them. Olen stepped forward, expecting to feel the wind rushing up at her before she hit the bottom. When that didn't happen, her eyes opened, and she found herself indoors, inside a stone building.

She wasn't on Zaspel anymore.

Wherever she was, the sunlight wasn't blue here. The planet's natural yellow light shone into the small dining area she stood in, the smell of cooking food filling her nose. She could feel a cool breath of air whisk through an arched stone window. It was an unfamiliar space, not from one of her memories. She'd never been here before. But the architecture was unmistakable.

She was inside of a Kaijen monastery.

"Hello?" a male voice said from behind her. It was a language she had never heard before, but one her cerebrum understood.

Olen spun around and saw the young man. He stood close enough to smell fresh soil on his tattered Kaijen robes. He was from a species she had never seen, but that her linked memories recognized. A human. The entire scene perplexed her to the point she was certain this was all a hallucination, albeit a convincing one. The young man's sandy hair was long and matted, but his face was kind. She tried to speak. Silence ate her words.

"Hiroshi Martel," a woman's voice called out behind the man from somewhere in the compound. "Your presence is required in the garden." This voice Olen recognized as Nisame's.

The man's eyes narrowed, then widened. "I know you. You're from my dream. You're the pregnant woman."

Olen's mind raced with questions but couldn't overcome her confusion. Her mouth moved, but her words were muted. The walls began to smear and evaporate. The vision, or connection, or whatever it was, was ending. Fear and distress flared in her mind. If this was real, it was her only contact with the outside universe. She had to make it count. She willed her voice to be heard.

"Find... me..."

Her words came out in an ethereal echo that emanated from her entire being.

The confused young man reached out to touch her. She did the same. Before either of them could make contact a gust of wind pushed Olen. She stumbled and everything faded into mist.

Olen blinked, and she was back on the cliff on Zaspel.

She looked down and saw that she was less than one full step away from falling over the edge to her preplanned death. A wave of vertigo blurred her vision and she stagger backward, collapsing to her hands and knees. Her breaths were like shards of glass inside her throat and her skull throbbed with crushing pain from the connection. She didn't understand. Was the vision real or was it an old dying woman's hallucination? Olen sat there for a long time, thinking. After what must've been hours, she took the hard way back down the cliff face instead of the quick and easy way.

Less than a year later, the man from her vision dropped down from the sky with a lot more tattoos and a lot less hair than she remembered.

Hiroshi Martel had come to free her from her cage.

***

Each day was a marathon for more life.

Zaspel had left Olen an emaciated bag of decaying flesh filled with hollow bones and failing organs. Aboard his ship the *Jezebel*, Hiroshi attempted to treat her, but the damage was beyond modern technology. If surgeons could replace every one of her atrophied cells and organs there wouldn't be an original part of her left.

The only thing Olen had to pass on were her memories. She linked with Hiroshi Martel and bestowed him with every fragment of knowledge and power her neurons had stored. She feared it may have been too much for the young man to handle.

It changed him.

A decade's worth of boiling anger and resentment she'd bottled up inside her mind, she'd passed on to Hiroshi. His desire to save her life became obsession. He placed her inside a gravcouch; a coffin-like tank filled with stasis gel commonly used for long voyages or in the event a ship's life support was beyond repair. She let her body sink into the cool milky white liquid until it submerged her.

The gravcouch's lid cycled shut and the device carried her into a deep sleep.

***

Months had passed.

Olen awoke to the pull of a planet's gravity holding her down. She was on Skerritt, a blue-gray dwarf planet plagued by constant thunderstorms. Centuries prior, tectonic plates shifted the planet's only habitable landmass, causing a colossal flood that swept the land. It became an ocean world with scatterings of old metallic tower structures protruding from the ocean's surface.

One of these structures was a tall castle-like skyscraper, its lower sixty levels having been submerged under the ocean waves. Its tallest tower protruded from the sea like an oil rig. This was where Hiroshi had chosen to hide her from the Kaijen.

The laboratory was a cold isolated space housed in what was once a cafeteria inside the old dilapidated structure. Its interior was plagued by centuries of wear and clashed with the room's clean modern medical equipment which looked mismatched and pieced together. Olen coughed stasis fluid out of her lungs as thunder and lightning crackled through the building's thick metal walls.

Hiroshi was with her. He ran a battery of tests and injected her with anti-cancer meds that would prolong her living death for a short time. Instead of catching her up on current events, Hiroshi linked with her. There were no secrets between them.

The following months were a smear of drifting in and out of stasis sleep. Hiroshi would wake her up to try a new cure, and when it failed, he put her back under. At some point Hiroshi woke her, his brown eyes bristling with sad desperation. Her situation had deteriorated, leaving her only weeks left. A month at the most. Despair drove Hiroshi to look for a cure in magic and fairy tales. He'd been spying on the Kaijen's Earth monastery when he intercepted a coded transmission. Nisame had been secretly communicating with an archivist who claimed to have acquired an ancient Kaijen artifact, but the archivist's coordinates were encrypted.

Everything Olen knew about the album was steeped in myth.

What little she did known about the object sounded fanciful and unconvincing. Nothing about its power or its true purpose was known for certain. Not that it mattered to Hiroshi. His research uncovered vague references to the album having regenerative abilities. He was desperate, and it was a chance. It was hope.

The only way to know where the transmissions were being sent was by accessing the mainframe, in person, at the monastery. Olen shivered. The violence that awaited him was palpable. Hiroshi wanted her permission to go. When she refused to give it, he put her back in stasis.

The next time she woke, the medical mechas were performing her weekly checkup. Hiroshi was gone. When Olen's tightbeams went unanswered, she knew why. A full day passed before he accepted her connection request and informed her of Nisame's death at his hands. The news tasted bitter. Olen didn't believe in revenge. She believed in second chances. In redemption.

If she'd only had a moment to talk to her. Olen wanted to believe Nisame could be reasoned with. That maybe they could have reached an understanding. The monastery attack reached the newsfeeds, which meant the Kaijen had failed to cover it up.

Olen saw the Kaijen's new narrative unfolding. She was seen as the terrorist who sent her evil apprentice to slaughter innocent Kaijen warriors. The elders couldn't have asked for a better headline to recruit new followers if it'd been their own idea.

**

The proximity alarms blared.

Olen had total access to the building's makeshift security system, in the event any trespassers had gotten too curious. On a monitor she watched the *Jezebel* swoop down from the stormy sky and land inside an improvised docking hangar.

A few short minutes later and Hiroshi entered the lab. He came to Olen inside her stasis pod. Only her head broke the surface of milky white stasis fluid. She breathed shallower than the last time she'd seen him, as if she were an asthmatic. "I was starting to think you'd forgotten about me," Olen joked in her gravelly voice. He didn't laugh.

"I ran into a little trouble," he said, unable to look at her.

"Show me," she said. Hiroshi hesitated. A hint of fear danced in his eyes and at the corners of his mouth. "Show me," she repeated, emphasizing both words.

Hiroshi relented. He knelt next to the gravcouch and held her head in his hands, pressing his forehead to hers. Each time she linked minds with someone it felt different. Receiving good memories downloaded into her brain usually had a warm bubbly sensation.

This wasn't one of those times.

The massacre at the monastery played out in her head in a first-person perspective the same as if she'd experienced it herself. The brutality shocked her. The memory streaked and she was on Montanari. Olen experienced the maglev battle. The arrest. Then she saw Jaxon Troy on the prison transport and her shock bled into fear as the connection ended.

"You linked with him." Olen said. "Why? This compromises *everything*."

"He astral projected himself across space, by accident," Hiroshi said. "The only other person we know who's done that is you. We need him on our side."

Olen scoffed. "He's a true believer. He's hopelessly incapable of questioning anything he's been told to believe. And you gave him the means to find us. He will lead the Kaijen straight to us and we will be killed."

"I have faith that won't happen."

"I saw it," she said, trying to shout, but her throat was dry and groggy. "You told him the truth and nothing you said had any effect on changing his mind. He's a victim of monolithic thought. A drone. He will never revolt. Never think. Never create. Jaxon Troy is an automaton."

Hiroshi breathed a sigh. "I disagree. You saw his rocket boots. He built them. He actively went against the Kaijen doctrine of not owning anything."

Olen's nose wrinkled. "And? That's not much."

"But it's *something*. We need allies. We can't succeed without them. If there's a spark of rebellion in Jaxon Troy then we need to nurture it. I've given him the knowledge. I believe he won't ignore it."

"Belief isn't a strategy, Hiroshi. If you're wrong it will doom us."

He ran his fingers through her wet hair and said, "You trust me. So trust me."

"The last time I trusted someone everyone I cared about was murdered."

"Not this time," he said, then presented the album. "I tried to activate it, but I'm not strong enough."

"You think *I* am?"

"I know it."

Her hands rose to the surface of the bone white stasis fluid and took the strange object with her twisted fingers. Olen focused her tuning powers, concentrating them on the album...

A weak tremor vibrated the stasis liquid and other objects in the lab. The attempt drained her physically, but she didn't stop. Her nose leaked and red spotted the stasis liquid. Hiroshi lit with concern. He reached out to take the album from her, then stopped. It began to pulse with a dim glow like a computer in standby mode.

Olen stopped tuning and gasped a deep breath into her lungs. "That's the best I can do," she said, exhausted.

"This is going to work," he said, more to himself than to her.

Hiroshi recovered the album and inserted it into a medical apparatus designed to harness several forms of electromagnetic waves and particle energy. He keyed in a series of commands and a beam of light engulfed the album, extracting the radiation it emitted and storing it. Processing it. After a time, the beam channeled the energy into a device that resembled a heat lamp and funneled it through a dish-like aperture that shined down onto Olen's stasis pod. It tingled her skin, like being pelted with invisible rain.

Slowly, the radiation reacted with her body's cells on a microscopic level. She felt a warmth deep inside her core that mushroomed outward in a flood like the time she'd ingested a psychotropic drug when she was a teen. Olen didn't notice the effects, not right right away. It took more than an hour of exposure before she noticed, much to her amazement, that the beam of light had begun to heal her. Olen's skin tightened a bit and a dash of color bled into her hair. The mild brain fog she'd experienced these past weeks had began to lift. Her haggard lungs breathed easier and the aches and pains in her muscles decreased, but weren't completely gone. It was like she'd gotten a month's worth of sleep without having slept. The energy had reversed a not insignificant amount of damage to her dying organs. It wasn't a cure. She was still weak, and still looked far older than other Asabi her age. But the album's energy had bought her more time. More life.

Every lost second she'd just stolen back was precious.

Chapter Eighteen: Jaxon

Darkness swallowed him.

Everything around Jaxon was black, like he'd fallen down a well lined with slick tar. Was he standing or floating? Was he drifting through outer space? No. He couldn't be. There were no stars. He didn't remember how he'd gotten here.

Jaxon couldn't feel his body. His neck inclined and he saw his clothes, his hands, his arms and stomach and legs and feet, but they were numb. He couldn't sense cold or warmth. Just the weightlessness. Like null g. His chest expanded and contracted in the pantomime of breathing, but he couldn't feel the air enter his throat or fill his lungs. A force pulled him down, like a gravity harness, dragging him deeper into the nothingness. His arms and legs flapped in a drowning motion as he attempted to swim upward.

The invisible force didn't notice.

Beneath him, a pinprick of light bloomed. A window in the dark. Or a sinkhole ready to eat him whole. Jaxon drifted towards it, slow and deliberate. There was no point in struggling. He sank into the light as it grew brighter the closer he got to it.

Terror gripped the back of his head and slid into his stomach. It felt like dying. Jaxon imagined death as being trapped in a small cold hole in the ground for eternity, which was almost what this was like. He interpreted the blazing white flare dragging him down as the afterlife.

Then he saw the red vines. They pulsed along the light's peripheral.

That's weird. It didn't feel like death anymore. It felt like an escape hatch. A sense of confidence rose in his chest. He rejected his fear and embraced the unknown.

It didn't matter what the light was, only that he knew he couldn't fight against it.

Jaxon tucked in his limbs and flipped himself around. He dove for the glowing bulb, the red veins pulsing around it like veins in an eyeball. As he floated closer, he could hear the murmur of voices. They reminded him of ghosts. *Now they're talking to me*, he worried. The sounds got so loud in his ears it turned into white noise. He charged into the blinding light until it drowned out the darkness.

***

Jaxon's eyes fluttered open. He could feel himself again. He was lying on something hard and cold and uncomfortable. There was an unusual ache in his chest, like heartburn.

A bright light flashed in his eyes, moving from side to side like a pendulum with no arc. Behind the light were two glowing green circles that could only be a mecha's optical irises.

"He is awake," Betty's voice said in her familiar monotone. The tip of her finger hung open like the tethered cap of a bottle and a small LED of some kind shined bright into Jaxon's corneas. His hand reached up and cupped Betty's wrist, brushing her glowing finger out of his face so his blinking eyes could adjust and focus.

He was in the infirmary of the *Saragos*. The sounds of the ship vibrating through the walls let him know they were slipstreaming. Jaxon looked past Betty and saw Akeema and Castor, the disembodied ghost voices he'd heard in the black nothingness. Akeema stood near Jaxon's bed while Castor sat on a metal bench welded to the wall. Jaxon's mouth curled into a warm smile.

They didn't return it, their mummers going silent. They stared at him for what felt like minutes, but wasn't; their glares of concern and anxiety could've been sadness or disappointment. It was neither. It was fear.

"What? Did I die or something?" Jaxon joked. Akeema and Castor didn't smile. Instead they traded silent looks, Akeema folding her arms. Jaxon imagined he was a kid who'd been called to the principal's office for something he hadn't realized he'd done wrong.

"You..." Akeema began, then stopped herself.

"You floated," Castor said.

"I floated?" Jaxon said, one eye slitted.

"It was more like a hover," Akeema said, talking with her hands.

"You were tuning while you were unconscious. We couldn't pull you down. We thought you were going to float away like a balloon."

"And..." Jaxon lingered on the word, still not quite wrapping his mind around this. "That's why you're looking at me like I'm some kind of possessed demon?"

Akeema and Castor shared another silent conversation with their eyes, then returned to Jaxon. Castor stood up and spoke for the both of them. "Jaxon, you died."

Jaxon spent a few moments trying to understand the words. He couldn't. They could've told him they'd witnessed him transform into an alligator and it would've made more sense. He laughed the thought away. "Died? Died how?"

Akeema stepped closer to him. "You stopped responding. We lost you for almost three minutes." Jaxon's brain fought hard to process the information. Silence filled the space between them.

Castor cleared his throat. "We want you to tell us about what happened on the transport. Between you and Martel." He spoke with the detached demeanor of a detective asking his prime suspect where he was on the night of the murder. Castor reflexively opened and closed his bionic hand without seeming to realize it. Akeema noticed it too, then pretended not to.

Their eyes were only on Jaxon.

He speculated as to what they were getting at. He'd gone from being a novice Kaijen who could barely tune a cup of liquid to stopping a 100,000 ton starship from flattening a school full of children seemingly overnight. Jaxon could see how that might raise a concern or two.

He considered telling them a pretty lie that would've gone down easier. "Martel..." Jaxon started, then hesitated. His honor wouldn't allow him to lie. That wasn't who he was. It wasn't the Kaijen way. His friends deserved better than that. "He... he linked with me."

Castor's face flared with dread, starting up at his hairline and dripping down to his chin like a flip book. Akeema's expression was more ambiguous. Yes, she was concerned, but not scared. Her thumb and index finger found her round chin and rubbed.

Also in detective mode, Akeema asked, "Was it consensual?"

"No," Jaxon blurted out. The question had hit him a little harder than he'd expected. "I was strapped down in my chair. He initiated the link. I couldn't stop him."

"You mean he forced himself on you," Castor said, closing his bionic hand into a fist. Jaxon didn't appreciate the connotation.

"I couldn't stop him," Jaxon repeated. "I didn't want it. I tried to fight him off. I... he was too powerful."

Akeema leaned in closer. "What was it like?"

What Jaxon heard was, *tell us how it felt when the mean man touched you.* "It was one of the worst things I've ever experienced in my life." His tone was just a bit louder than a whisper. "It felt like dying."

"But you survived the link," Akeema said, less of a detective now and more of a mad scientist assessing her latest freak experiment. "You didn't end up in a coma."

"But he *died*," Castor said.

"And we brought him *back*," Akeema said. "So not only did a forced link not kill him, but he's stronger than he was before. He's tuning in his fucking sleep. That's incredible."

Castor sneered. "It's *dangerous*." His face flushed in a way that resembled a radiation burn. "Priestess Nisame warned us about linking with other Kaijen. It causes brain damage and death. That's why it's forbidden."

"Jaxon's brain is fine now, right?" Akeema said, then looked to Betty.

Betty paused, then realized everyone was waiting for her to speak. "The cortical scans of Jaxon Troy show no apparent damage or abnormalities."

"See?" Akeema said in an upbeat, almost comical tone, and still speaking in hand gestures. "He recovered. His new abilities saved that village."

Castor's mouth curled with agitation. "Did you forget what happened next? How he had a seizure? We had to stop him from swallowing his own tongue."

"Wait, what?" Jaxon said. They ignored him.

"Or maybe linking isn't as dangerous as we were told," Akeema said to Castor.

"You're implying Priestess Nisame lied to us," Castor said in a calm cool way that let everyone know he was furious.

"It wouldn't be the first time," Akeema muttered. Castor's face got redder.

"Would you two cool it please?" Jaxon said, his voice louder than he'd meant. He'd assumed the role of a substitute teacher trying to subdue his rowdy students. "We're all friends here, remember? We're all okay and we love each other and we have the album." Both Akeema and Castor's eyes widened at the same time. "Wait. Do we have the album?" Jaxon asked. He predicted the answer.

"Akeema gave it to Martel," Castor said.

"In exchange for your life," Akeema said to Jaxon.

Jaxon's face flashed with surprise, then understanding. "Thanks. You didn't have to do that for me."

Akeema came to his side and took his hand into hers. "Yes, we did." She released his hand, her mouth making the shape of a smile. It didn't reach her eyes. "It wasn't like we had much of a choice. If we didn't give him the album he was going to nuke us."

Jaxon's head shook. "No, he was bluffing. It was a gamble."

Castor's head tilted. "Oh? How do you know that?" *How do I know that?*

"Have you experienced any more visions?" Akeema asked. "Any more... out of body experiences?"

Jaxon opened his mouth to answer, then paused. His mind traveled back to the moment Martel linked with him, back to that cold sharp knife of terror that stabbed his mind. "I did see... images. They were all jumbled up. Strange sounds and smells. It didn't make sense."

"What kind of images?" Akeema asked and leaned forward to hear better.

"Images of people screaming... people on fire... death. I can't make sense of it yet." Jaxon hadn't noticed Castor. He'd been fuming the entire time; a human teakettle who'd just been brought to a boil.

"This has gone far enough," Castor said, his voice tight as a bowstring. "We have to inform Priestess Sabrene. She needs to know everything."

Akeema flashed with alarm. "We can't. We'd be dooming Jaxon. She'll send him straight to a reeducation session for unauthorized linking and strip him of his position. He'd no longer be a Kaijen."

"The linking happened against his will," Castor said. "For all we know he could still be at risk of further brain damage. The elders might take pity on him if we come clean."

Akeema's face changed. No longer was she talking to the surrogate older brother who she loved and respected. She was talking to a stranger wearing the face of the man she thought she knew. "Have you ever heard of the elders taking pity on anyone who breaks the rules?" Akeema said pensively. "Jaxon is our *brother*. We can't do this to him. *I* won't do this to him."

Jaxon let out a heavy, defeated sigh. "Castor's right. If we don't tell to the elders what happened and they find out somehow, they'll punish all of us. Whatever the consequences are I'll face them. Just me. I won't let either of you suffer for something that happened to me."

Dread hung in the air.

Akeema paced. Castor wouldn't look Jaxon in the eye. He stared off at a particularly interesting scuff mark on the infirmary's wall, thinking.

Akeema sat on the room's metal bench, her face having gotten as red as her hair. She choked back tears. "Why did you have to go and tell us the truth? You could've just made up a story. We would've believed it."

Jaxon wanted to laugh, but didn't. "Because that would have been a lie, and I'm not much of a liar. I'll accept my fate. I'll deal with the consequences. As long as you two are safe." The fog seemed to thicken.

"I'm sorry, Jaxon," Castor said, his vetronium hand back to opening and closing randomly. "You get some more rest. I'll contact Priestess Sabrene and inform her of what's happened. I'll plead your case. I have every faith in her that she'll be lenient." He reached the room's hatch, then lingered for a moment. He looked back over his shoulder. "I wish... I wish things had happened differently."

Then he was gone, the hatch clanking shut behind him.

Akeema stewed on her bench, quiet, her face a mix of at least nine different emotions that all conflicted with each other. Her whole body seemed to vibrate with nervous energy, her left hand gripping her right wrist the way it did when she was anxious or upset.

Jaxon met her eyes. "I'm fine. Go with him."

She hadn't been waiting for his permission, just a good excuse. Akeema reached the room's hatch in three steps. She looked back at Jaxon for a heartbeat, then left, leaving the hatch open slightly.

The room fell silent again. Only the hum of the room's air recyclers and the rhythmic vibration of the ship's engines, which abruptly changed pitch. The deck's gimbals trembled slightly, signaling the *Saragos* had dropped out of slipstream.

Ships couldn't send or receive transmissions through the comm net while in the non-space of slipstream. The fact they were back in normal space meant Castor wasn't wasting any time making good on his promise.

Jaxon's attention returned to Betty. Like a good mecha, she'd been patiently standing by waiting to be addressed while the organics squabbled with each other. She continued to run scans on Jaxon's head when she noticed him staring at her.

"Do you require assistance," Betty said in a way that didn't sound like a question.

"I find it kind of hard to believe that Yoko would risk her ship just to save me. How did that happen?"

Betty paused. "I requested that Yoko assist you."

Jaxon's eyes flickered, taking a moment to process her words. "Why would you do that?"

"I am programmed to protect Yoko by any and all means necessary short of harming another organic. Even at the risk of my own termination. I... failed her in this regard."

"You mean what happened on the platform?"

Betty paused again, her eyes shifting, then returning to Jaxon. "Yoko is my owner. My captain. She is also my friend. My only friend. You saved her from death. We were indebted to you. That debt is now paid."

The ajar infirmary hatch whined as it swung open. "I'll be the judge of that," Yoko's distinct snappy voice chimed in before she'd even had a chance to enter the room. Her hair had changed, wearing it tied back in a French twist. It framed her round silver face in an oddly iconic way. Three quick strides and she'd reached his bedside, shoving her handheld into his palm.

"What's this?" Jaxon asked, skimming the list of itemized fees on the screen.

"Damages," Yoko said with the faint scent of alcohol on her breath.

"You're *billing me?*"

Her chin inclined without taking her gaze off of him. "Spear hooks are not cheap, hoo-mon. And as you can see, I'm providing you with excellent medical care, which also isn't cheap. I expect to be well compensated."

Jaxon read the first few entries on the list. Each spear hook cost eight hundred cubits, plus an additional four hundred cubits per each towing cable. He was being charged for six of them. The total was just over seven thousand cubits. Yoko was also charging him for fuel, labor, health care, and emotional distress, which apparently was worth five hundred cubits. That one got a laugh out of him.

"Can't you give me a discount?" Jaxon said in a kidding, but not really way.

Yoko's head tilted to one side. "A *disc count*? What is that?"

"*Discount*. It's when you charge someone a reduced rate for your services."

Yoko lowered her eyebrows, creating a little fold of skin between them. "There is no word for 'discount' in my people's language."

Jaxon sighed. He placed his thumb on the handheld's transaction square, then keyed in his authorization code. A little chime confirmed the payment was accepted. Yoko wrenched back her handheld.

"Thanks for rescuing me," Jaxon said. "I know it was a huge risk to you and your ship. We wouldn't have made it out alive without your help. I just wanted you to know that I appreciate it. You're a great pilot."

Yoko's eyes narrowed with suspicion. "Flattery doesn't work on me, hoo-mon. I'm still not giving you any discounts."

Jaxon chuckled. "I'm not saying this because I expect to get anything out of it. It's just... I get the feeling you don't hear thanks as often as you should. You didn't have to come after me. You could've easily said no."

"I *did* say no," Yoko asserted. Her narrow glare found Betty. Betty was an artificial life-form devoid of emotion, but Jaxon could read the subtle look of shy embarrassment on her blank uncanny valley face. She lowered her head to dodge Yoko's gaze, her boots shuffling against the decking as she made a beeline for the room's hatch. Yoko's eyes followed Betty until she left the infirmary, closing the hatch behind her. Yoko's neck craned back to Jaxon, capturing him in her steely gaze.

"What happened to the prisoners on the transport?" Jaxon asked.

Yoko shrugged. "How should I know? They scattered like tiny rodents. I didn't have time to ask them for an itinerary." Jaxon sighed again, rubbing his forehead and staring off. The uncertainty nagged at him. Those prisoners are free because of him. If they hurt anyone, raped anyone, killed anyone, it would be his fault. It was too late for him to do anything about it. Jaxon returned to Yoko. Her gaze had been locked on him while he'd been experiencing his mental pity party. "What would have happened to you if Betty hadn't have convinced me to help you?" Yoko asked.

"I'd probably be dead," Jaxon said with a flat laugh. "No, I'd absolutely be dead."

Yoko leaned in. "So," she said with a naughty smile that made her look like a predator preparing to make her kill. "According to your childish hoo-mon customs, I'm quite sure that means you owe me one."

"No," Jaxon said, dragging the syllable out into its own sentence. "If it wasn't for me swooping in to catch you, you'd be a red smear on Montanari's surface, remember? What we are is even." Yoko cocked her head to one side in defiance.

"No," she said, mimicking him. "You're forgetting Giannis. Your heart stopped and we saved you."

"That doesn't count."

"Oh, it very much does count," Yoko smirked.

"You're saying you brought me back yourself? With your own hands?"

Yoko's eyes softened. "Well, no, Betty did. But I am responsible for Betty so it still counts as me. Everything that happens on my ship is me."

"You can't just take credit for things you didn't do."

Yoko lifted one of her caterpillars. "Says who?" Jaxon looked at her, measuring the will in her eyes. Seconds ticked by. Jaxon didn't blink. Yoko's posture eased, considering his words. "You frustrate me hoo-mon," she grumbled. "However, I must admit, I'm glad the scary tattooed hoo-mon didn't kill you. Think of all the cubits I would have lost." Jaxon laughed.

And to his surprise, so did she. It was genuine, not one of her sarcastic mocking chuckles.

In that brief moment, she was a different person. An identical Yoko clone who wasn't a silver ball of anger and whiskey.

Yoko caught herself and the moment passed. She cleared her throat and steeled her face. "About what happened on Montanari. I ran some numbers. The rate I was falling. The speed your boots had to be going to reach me in Montanari's gravity. The effects traveling at that velocity would have on your inferior hoo-mon biology. I fell for five point nine seconds."

"Okay?" Jaxon said, confused.

"So, in order to catch me that fast," Yoko paused, taking a moment to frame her words. "You couldn't have stopped to think about it. Once you saw me go over that ledge, you had to dive after me, immediately. Less than a second."

Jaxon's head dropped into a slow nod. "Yeah. That sounds about right. I mean, it all happened so fast. I honestly don't remember the details." Yoko's thick caterpillar eyebrows furrowed. Jaxon wasn't sure if it was a sign of offense or concern.

She leaned in closer, her voice hushed like she thought someone might be listening in on them. "But *why*, though? Why would you do that for me?"

"Because I… didn't want you to die?" Jaxon shrugged with his hands. "You're a handful, but I like you better not dead." Yoko froze. She didn't seem to get it. "I take it if things were reversed you wouldn't have done the same for me?"

Yoko leaned back, rolling her eyes and crossing her arms, over-exaggerating both actions. "Well, that's not fair."

"That sounds like a no to me."

"Maybe," Yoko said in a half joking, half not at all joking way. "You still owed me money, so okay, maybe. But it was nice to not die though. I'm glad you didn't stop to think. Which means you're at least consistent." She smiled. Jaxon suspected against her will. "I guess now I know what it feels like to depend on someone else. Besides Betty, I mean."

Jaxon's lips bent into a cocky grin. "Is it a good feeling?"

Yoko snorted. "What? No. Are you kidding me? It's horrible."

Chapter Nineteen: Akeema

"I wish... I wish things had happened differently," Castor said before he stalked out of the ship's infirmary, presumably to go tattle on Jaxon to Priestess Sabrene.

It wasn't easy for Akeema, being the only woman in their small band of misfits. The Kaijen were a female centric religion. She'd gotten used to being among mostly females. It made her feel comfortable, except for the times it didn't. Her two brothers had brought a much needed sense of masculine energy to the hornets' nest that were her sisters. She loved Castor. She loved Jaxon. She would give her life for theirs without thinking, but the current gender imbalance was jarring.

There were aspects of herself Akeema simply couldn't discuss with her brothers. Things she would never tell them, either out of fear they wouldn't understand, or fear that they would. Circumstances had put them at odds. She was caught in the middle. They'd each grabbed an arm and proceeded to pull her in opposite directions like siblings fighting over a rag doll.

In her head, Akeema made it sound like a serious struggle. It wasn't. On some level, she knew she'd already taken a side against one of them.

Castor was wrong.

He was being brash and shortsighted and a bit of an ass. More than a bit. She wanted to tell him as much, but she wanted to avoid a repeat of their conversation on Montanari.

What Akeema had respected, had envied about Castor, was how hopelessly uncompromising he could be. Once he'd made up his mind about something it was set in stone. For someone like Akeema who could change her mind seven times between breaths, she saw this trait as virtuous. Something to emulate. Now she understood how having such an inflexible ideological stance, even one she agreed with, could set a good-natured person on the path to becoming a monster. Castor hadn't reached that point.

Not yet. But he was flirting.

If I could just get through to him, she thought. Then maybe she could convince him that turning Jaxon over to Sabrene was quite possibly the stupidest fucking idea in the history of stupid fucking ideas. Accomplishing that task seemed impossible, but she knew she had to try.

"I'm fine," Jaxon said, his voice cutting through the hurricane of thoughts spinning in her mind. "Go with him."

His words sent a mild shiver down Akeema's artificial spine. Did his newfound abilities somehow include mind reading? *That's stupid,* she thought. Without a word Akeema rose and left the infirmary.

The corridors of the *Saragos* were narrow, the ceilings low and stifling. It reminded her of a time during her girlhood after she and her father had escaped to the Texas Republic where she'd visited a museum dedicated to an old war machine called a submarine.

Akeema popped two pain killers in her mouth and dry swallowed. She climbed a ladder up to the command deck and made it half way up when the ship's gimbals vibrated. The ship dropped out of slipstream. Akeema reached the command deck in time to catch Yoko leave the cockpit and met with Castor.

"The transceiver is ready," Yoko said. "You can make your call once I receive payment."

A low growl bubbled out of Castor's throat. With a sarcastic flair he said, "I'm surprised you're not charging us for air."

Yoko's face flattened. "Of course I'm charging you for air. Air isn't free you know. It is a resource, and resources are monetized."

Castor flipped open his handheld and sent the payment with a begrudging sneer. Yoko's handheld chimed with confirmation.

Her eyes shifted to Akeema. "The brown skinned hoo-mon owes me compensation. Is he awake?"

Akeema growled. "His name is Jaxon."

Yoko shrugged. "I like hoo-mon better. I'll go see for myself," she said with a sharp glare. Yoko edged past Akeema and slid down the deck ladder.

I really, really don't like that woman, Akeema wanted to say out loud, but didn't.

Castor sat down in front of the command deck's communication terminal near the galley. He prepared to send a connection request to Sabrene.

Akeema touched his hand to stop him. "We can still handle this internally. Just the three of us."

"The longer we wait the worse it will be for Jaxon," Castor said. "His best chance to remain a Kaijen is to apologize and beg for forgiveness."

"And if you were right, I would agree with you," Akeema said.

Castor exhaled, groaning. "Alright. Tell me. What do you think we should do?"

"Not throw our brother to the wolves, for starters," Akeema said.

"The elders aren't wolves. They're our authority. You trust them to know what's right for us, don't you?" Akeema hesitated. If she agreed, the argument was lost. If she didn't, she could almost see Castor reporting her for dissension along with Jaxon.

"You can be honest with me," Castor said. "I know this isn't about Jaxon."

Akeema crossed her arms and leaned back on her heels. "What is it about then?"

Castor mirrored her. "Do I really have to say it?" Akeema's eyes narrowed and her head inclined, bracing herself for the hit. "You care about Jaxon," Castor said, "but not as much as you care about his new power. You've made it clear. You want that same power for yourself."

Akeema went pale. The ache in her spine ignored the pain killers and reasserted itself. "What? That's bullshit. How fucking dare you."

Castor raised his palms in defense, as if he were warming them at a fire. His cybernetic hand resembled a shiny glove in the cabin's low light. His metal fingers were twitching and he winced in pain.

"That looks like it hurts," Akeema said.

"That's because it does."

"It's not supposed to."

"Tell that to my arm. It feels like it's being sandblasted from the inside."

"It's probably electromagnetic feedback affecting your muscles," Akeema said, examining it. "You probably damaged some of the circuits when you rappelled down to that prison ship." She motioned to the common table. They sat next to each other and Castor hiked up his sleeve. He laid his metal hand on the table, palm up. Akeema pulled a small pouch of tools from her pocket, the same ones she used to fix her crossglaive. She examined and manipulated the servos in the mechanical hand.

"I'm not judging you," Castor said. Akeema kept her focus on his hand. "If anyone understands where you're coming from it's me. I saw up close what Jaxon's capable of. It was incredible. Scary, but incredible. But where I fear the negative effects this power will have on him, I believe you're more preoccupied with Jaxon using his new tuning abilities to fight Martel."

Akeema looked at Castor, her eyes burning bright scarlet. Her mouth hung open liked she'd tasted salt. One of her little tools touched a circuit in Castor's bionic hand and he cringed.

"Sorry," Akeema lied. He let her get away with it. "I care about your safety. And Jaxon's safety. That's why I gave up the album to save you both. Because you two mean more to me than that stupid fucking album."

"I didn't mean to accuse you of anything. I apologize."

Akeema made a few final adjustments and finished her work. Castor flexed his metal fingers. His face calmed with relief.

"How's that?" Akeema asked.

"Better, thanks." He pulled down sleeve and smiled, but it was fleeting. "Martel didn't do this to Jaxon out of the kindness of his heart. He did it to corrupt him. To seduce him. Or for some other evil reason we can't see yet. Either way, we can't play into his game. If you want to help Jaxon, really help him, you should support me when I contact Priestess Sabrene. Please tell me you will."

Silence choked the room, save for the low hum of the oxygen recyclers. In the span of two breaths Akeema made her decision. "You're right," she said, trying her best to sound convincing. "I'm sorry. The last few days have just been so stressful. I agree with you fully. We have to put Jaxon's wellbeing first. I trust you to explain the situation to Sabrene." She almost believed it herself.

Castor exhaled a relieved sigh. "Thank you. You had me worried there. After our last discussion I felt like we'd grown too far apart on this. I'm glad to see we can still talk things out. Go stay with Jaxon. Make sure that Kish pilot isn't bleeding his account dry. When I talk to Priestess Sabrene I'll take full responsibility for what's happened."

"Thanks," Akeema said. She watched Castor send the connection request to Sabrene. That meant the clock was ticking. It meant she had to move fast.

Akeema slinked away and climbed down the deck ladder, moving fast enough she nearly slipped. The faux gravity provided by her harness threatened to yank her down to the decking below, but she caught herself and reached the crew deck. Akeema jogged to the infirmary's hatch and reached for the handle when it opened and Yoko stepped through wearing a sneaky grin. She noticed Akeema and her grin vanished, like she'd been caught in the act of committing a crime. Yoko was like a little silver demon, tempting everyone.

They traded looks and passed by each other without words. Not that Akeema didn't want to say something, she just didn't want to waste the seconds she had.

In the infirmary, Akeema found Jaxon sitting on the left side of his bed, his feet just short of touching the floor. She made sure the hatch clicked shut behind her.

"That was fast," Jaxon said. "I take it Priestess Sabrene didn't have anything nice to say?"

"Castor's still waiting for her to accept his connection request," Akeema said. She sat next to Jaxon on the bed. The look in his eyes told her he knew something wasn't right.

"Uh oh," he said. "This looks serious."

"Castor said you stopped the prison ship by tuning. How did you do it?"

Jaxon coughed out a laugh. "I have no idea. I just… we were going to crash into that school and… I just wanted to stop that from happening. I just… I don't know."

"Do you think you could do it again?"

"I don't *want* to do it again."

"Why? You saved all those people. Imagine the good you could do if you learned to control it. It can't hurt to try."

"You don't see how badly this could go wrong? What happens if I accidentally rip this ship apart? Or rip you apart?"

Akeema took his hand. "You would never do that. I trust you. Please, Jaxon. You need to try to control it. Try for me."

Jaxon's face twisted with apprehension. Akeema eyed a storage cabinet built into the wall. She opened it and found a series of small medicine bottles tucked inside. She placed one on the pullout bench.

"Try to tune the bottle to your hand," Akeema said.

She could see he didn't want to. Her pleading eyes convinced him. Jaxon reached out for the plastic object. He strained to pull it with his mind. The bottle barely moved. After a moment he gave up, the attempt leaving him breathing hard. "I told you. I can't do it."

"You're not trying," Akeema said. She placed her hand on Jaxon's shoulder. "You stopped a big ass ship dead in its tracks because you wanted to stop it. This should be easy."

"It's dangerous is what it is. Power corrupts."

"I know you. You'd never let anything corrupt you."

"You don't know what it's like," Jaxon stressed. He sounded heartbroken, his eyes stricken with sadness. He was sweating. "Ever since it happened, I've been seeing these... faces. People I've never met. But I *did* know them. I... I loved them. And I watched them all die. It's mess of images in my head and I can't make sense of it. Now I have all this hate and sorrow and anger and it's building up inside of me and it's trying to get out." His hands clenched into fists tight enough his knuckles cracked.

Objects in the room began to deform and fall over.

Akeema's heart pounded out of her chest. Her eyes were all pupil. "Jaxon!" she shouted and shook him hard. His eyes closed and he relaxed. The tuning gradually stopped.

The infirmary was a mess.

Akeema surveyed the damage and nodded. "So, strong emotions. Maybe that's the key. Do it again, but this time try to focus your anger."

Jaxon reacted as if she'd just eaten a spider. "Did you not see what just happened? This isn't a good idea. We should stop this before someone gets hurt."

"No, this is too important. If we can figure out how to develop our tuning abilities, we might not even need the album."

"I don't want to do this. We're breaking the Kaijen code."

"We already broke it when you disobeyed Priestess Sabrene and went to Montanari, remember?"

Jaxon's back straightened like he'd just heard a gunshot. "Hey, that wasn't just me. We all agreed, together."

"Right. And I backed you up then. I need you to back me up now." She paused. "Jaxon, I... I want you to link with me."

The familiar look of *Are you fucking kidding me?* smacked Jaxon's face. "That's a *terrible* idea! I don't even know how to link. The attempt could kill us."

"I trust you," Akeema said. Jaxon scoffed. She held his face in her hands, his hot skin warming her cold palms. "When have I ever asked you for anything?"

He considered. "Never."

"I'm asking you for just this one thing. I accept the risks."

Jaxon stepped away, putting some distance between them. Akeema's heart tried to beat its way through her ribcage. She counted the seconds. Each feeling longer than the last.

"If something went wrong..." Jaxon trailed off. "If I killed you... I couldn't live with that. And if it worked... whatever poison Martel put in my head would be in yours, too."

"I had my fucking spine cut in half and ripped out of my body. I was paralyzed. And now I'm standing here still breathing. Nothing you can do can hurt me worse than I've already been."

"What about the elders? If they found out... you'd be throwing away your whole life."

Akeema rubbed her palms together, the warmth from Jaxon's skin having dissipated. "You're scared. I am too. This is scary stuff. But now's not the time for scared. You want things to go back to the way they used to be, but they can't. And they never will."

"Martel's link nearly killed me," Jaxon said. "I really need to stress the part where I almost died. Permanently."

"And yet, here you stand. You have that power now. You can't put it back. You have to master it. Everything the Archivist told us is starting to make sense. The elders and the priestesses only gave us a fraction of their power to keep us under their control. You're the proof. You'd never be able to go back to being a novice Kaijen even if you wanted to. The knowledge will always be there."

"But I don't *want it*. I didn't *ask* for it."

"It's no longer about what you want. You have it. Now what are you going to do with it?" Conflict wrinkled Jaxon's face, but Akeema could see the cracks forming. "I don't want to force you. Whatever you decide I will support that decision. But at least give me the chance to try. Link with me. Please. Let me share your burden."

Akeema held her hands out to Jaxon, her eyes welling up. She hated this. Manipulation was distasteful, but she had precious little time. This had to happen now. She willed Jaxon to take her hands into his. She was prepared to beg.

"Damn it," Jaxon said. He took her cold hands. "I'm going to regret this."

Akeema didn't smile. She wanted to. She worried it might change his mind so she didn't risk it. Without words she locked the infirmary's hatch and returned to Jaxon. They sat on the bed facing each other.

Akeema sighed. "Okay. So. How do we do this?"

Jaxon shrugged. "I'm not sure. The knowledge is in our heads, we just have to unlock it."

"The transfer only goes one way. You'll have to initiate the link. Just don't scramble my brain."

Jaxon cocked his neck. "*Now* you're worried about that? I think it's a little too late to make that promise."

Akeema placed Jaxon's hands on her head. She leaned into him until their foreheads touched. They shut their eyes. Jaxon concentrated for a quiet moment.

"Do you feel anything?" Jaxon asked.

"You mean besides a sense of overwhelming embarrassment?" Jaxon laughed. It made Akeema feel a little less guilty about what she was making him do. "Just breathe," she continued. "This is all you. Focus your mind. Think about what you felt when Martel linked with you and concentrate on that."

Akeema kept her eyes closed while Jaxon's hands warmed the sides of her head, the sound of his deep steady breathing filling her ears. It grew louder. Inhumanly loud. It enveloped the room. It throbbed in her ears like a massive drum. Akeema felt the itch of ants crawling on her scalp and down her spine, then splitting off to loop around her jaw.

The stench of smoke filled her nose.

She heard the howl of a bloodcurdling scream. Distant at first, then inside her head. It forced her to open her eyes.

*****

Akeema only saw the black of the dark space.

Screams echoed around her. Some were as far away as a whisper. Others less so.

A sharp scream pierced her ears like a siren. Akeema flinched, shielding her ears. It didn't help. She ran, blindly stumbling around in the black. Her knees were heavy, wanting to buckle under her weight.

"Jaxon?" she called out. Her voice echoed.

"Akeema?" his distant voice echoed back. She followed the sound, wandering deeper into the inky black nothingness.

"Where are you?" she asked, tremors in her voice. Terror had taken hold. She did her best to hide it.

"I'm right here," Jaxon said. He sounded much closer this time. Her eyes darted around, searching for something, anything that would get her out of this awful place. Just black. She felt she was spinning.

Something she could see grabbed her wrist and held it tight. Frightened, she fought it.

Jaxon's disembodied voice said, "It's me."

Rain touched Akeema's skin before she heard it. It poured from above and the black space melted away. Akeema looked up and saw the night's sky.

She found herself standing on solid ground. She was on a planet. One she didn't recognize. The grip on her wrist revealed itself to be Jaxon's hand. He was pulling her into this new reality.

"What is this place? Where are we?" Akeema said, shouting over the rain soaking them.

"Zaspel," Jaxon said, surprised that he knew the answer. But he did. And somehow so did she. Just like she knew that they were at the settlement where Olen had brought her people. The same way the stone in her gut told her something terrible was about to happen.

It was Zaspel's bi-annual rainy season. The trinary suns set earlier and the nights were longer, allowing the planet to rehydrate.

Akeema and Jaxon traveled down the wet muddy road leading to a small village. There, a large tent stood, as tall and wide as one Akeema had seen in an old book about the circus. Someone was throwing a party. Twenty or thirty aliens of various species were dancing and drinking and having the time of their lives.

"What is this?" Akeema said. The aliens didn't hear her. They didn't see her. They continued their fun time unaware of her presence.

"We're inside of a memory," Jaxon said. "Whatever this is, it's already happened. We're just watching it."

Akeema shivered from the frigid rain. "Is it supposed to feel this real?" Jaxon shrugged.

A harrowing sound swooped by in the dark skies overhead. A starship's engines. The dancing stopped. The press of bodies parted to make way for someone. A copper skinned Asabi woman stepped forward.

Akeema knew who she was.

Olen was young and beautiful. Her light gray eyes were striking, her long black hair flowing down her back. And she was very, very pregnant. She looked ready to burst.

The ship lowered down, thunder clapping in the skies above it. It was small light shuttle capable of slipstream. Olen walked out into the rain alone to meet it. Akeema and Jaxon followed her.

The shuttle landed, its engines powered down. Seven ominous figures in hooded black cloaks marched down the boarding ramp in lockstep. Olen approached them without fear. Six of the figures stayed behind while their leader, the tallest of them, met with Olen; the woman's clothing had already been soaked through, clinging to her skin.

Akeema had a sense of who the tall figure was, even if her towering height hadn't given her away. Sabrene pulled back her hood, exposing her hot pink face and short blue pixie hair to the storming rain. She looked down her nose at Olen's stomach, Sabren's face pruning in disgust. "Must you show off your disgrace so openly?"

Olen hooked one hand under her pregnant belly. "My child is not a disgrace. I will raise him to be the best of us."

Sabrene sneered. "That *thing* in your belly is not a person. Breeding undermines the culture of equality and respect real Kaijen warriors represent."

Olen faked a smile. "You never wanted equality, you wanted special treatment. The Kaijen don't want respect, they want obedience. They want fear. They deliberately prevent the novice Kaijen from reaching their full potential. It's *archaic*."

"You're going to turn that child into a weapon." Sabrene said, her voice a guttural growl. "The elders explained it to me. The link doesn't just transfer knowledge and power to another person. The process alters the neural pathways— the very *DNA* of who we link with. That power is amplified at the neonatal level in our offspring. If the children of a Kaijen can be more powerful than other Kaijen then none of us can truly be equal."

Olen's eyes slitted. "More powerful than *you*, you mean."

Sabrene's mouth curled into an almost imperceptible smile that betrayed her. She spread her hands. "I didn't make the rules. I only pledged an oath to uphold them. Not selfishly run off to be a scrote's whore like you did."

"You don't really care about equality," Olen said, ignoring her. "You only care about power. You'd let the whole galaxy burn as long as you got to tell the ashes what to do." She gestured at the village behind her. "*That's* true equality and inclusion. Beings free to live based on who they are and not on their biology or outward appearance or their opinion. Good people don't judge others by their power level or perceived privilege. The elders fear this kind of equality. That's why they won't admit male warriors."

"Because they're oppressors," Sabrene snapped. "If we let them in they'll take our power and use it to victimize us. That's what always happens when you give males power."

"I'm not the one who sees themselves as a victim," Olen said. "The elders are too set in their ways. Stagnation is death. We can only progress as a culture by embracing change, not division."

"Spoken like a true speciesist," Sabrene said. "By starting this cult and carrying that parasite in your stomach you've besmirched our entire religion and yourself."

"I won't be the last. I've seen it. You can't stop people from thinking for themselves. What will you do when others choose their own paths? Or decide they want to have children?"

An insidious grin jaywalked across Sabrene's face. "The elders have already anticipated that outcome. That is why all current and future Kaijen will be sterilized."

Shock slapped Olen. Akeema shared her expression, only hers was tempered with disbelief. She turned to Jaxon. He was far more disturbed by the revelation than she'd expected.

Olen recoiled in disgust. "That's barbaric. What my followers and I do is no longer your concern. We've left the totality of the Kaijen. We will pass on our heritage the way we see fit. We are a free society. Now leave. The Kaijen are not welcome here. I hope this is the last time we see each other."

"No need to hope," Sabrene said.

Akeema didn't see the crossglaive blade until Sabrene had already stabbed Olen with it, the sizzling hot blade having pierced Olen's womb. It happened too fast for Olen to react. Akeema watched on in horror, the strange nature of her situation allowing her to feel the sensation of superheated metal digging its way into Olen's body as if it'd happened to her. The intensity of the pain overwhelmed Olen and her legs gave out underneath her.

Olen slumped into the wet ground, the crossglaive blade sliding out of her womb. The act spared her from instant death. Sabrene towered over the helpless woman, blood and amniotic fluid leaking out of her and mixing with the rain.

"Did you really think we would stand by and do nothing while you raised an army to challenge us?" Sabrene said with smug grin, her words coated with venom. "You thought you were so much better than me. You were supposed to be smarter than this." She was smiling now. No need to hide her true self any longer.

Sabrene looked back at her group. They were afraid of her, appalled at what she'd done, but lacking the courage to say as much. Sabrene moved through the settlement with her crossglaive and proceeded to slaughter the entire village.

Olen writhed in agony in the mud. She had no choice but to witness Sabrene's rampage. Even when she shut her eyes, she still heard the screams. The same screams Jaxon described. The same screams Akeema heard in the black space.

Any villagers that managed to escape Sabrene's bloodlust were cut down by the hooded Kaijen. Men. Women. Some of which were pregnant. Teenagers. Even animals got the blade.

One of the fleeing villagers, a man with geometrically patterned skin, knelt down to aid Olen. His name flashed in Akeema's mind. This was Behrens. She could feel the love between them; intoxicating romantic feelings came with seeing his face. He was saying something to Olen, but she couldn't make out the words, so neither could Akeema. She could only see that he was bawling.

One of the hooded Kaijen appeared behind him. The tip of a crossglaive burst through Behrens's chest, the blade slicing up through his torso and splitting the man through the shoulder in an asymmetrical wishbone fashion.

Akeema's blood was boiling.

The horrors she'd witnessed stirred up intense revulsion and hatred in her guts. She wanted to stop it. She would do anything to make it stop. Akeema reached for one of the hooded Kaijen, her ghostly hand passing right through her.

Jaxon held her back. "It's a memory. It's already happened. Nothing we do can change it."

Dread exploded in her chest, as thick and heavy as a brick. She was helpless. Even more so than Olen was. The deaths continued. Each one just as brutal as the last. Then Akeema understood. Her role was to witness. To remember them.

Point-defense gun turrets on Sabrene's shuttle revealed themselves. High impact slugs shredded the villager's last remaining ship. The vessel's fuel tanks exploded, showering flaming debris over the settlement like chunks of lava. The entire settlement became an open furnace.

The stink of burning flesh sailed on the moist air. The screams faded into the night.

Sabrene emerged from the inferno with fire licking her blood-soaked cloak. To Akeema's disgust, the flames hadn't burned her.

She wore that enigmatic smile of hers, her pink face speckled with swatches of red. She strutted back to her ship with an air of blitheness completely absent of remorse. The other cloaked Kaijen followed her into the shuttle.

A single Kaijen lagged behind, staring at Olen. This one Akeema recognized. A young Nisame, before she'd become a priestess. Then she turned and joined the others on the shuttle. The engines fired up, its RCS thrusters spitting flame. The shuttle shot off into the sky, leaving the settlement in ruins.

The memory faded into mist.

Chapter Twenty: Jaxon

Jaxon blinked and he was back in the infirmary on the *Saragos* with Akeema.

His mouth tasted rotten. The contents of his stomach were clawing its way back up his throat. Akeema covered her mouth, chunky gross liquid oozing between her fingers and down her arm. She ran to a sink and unloaded a flood of vomit with guttural force.

The acid stink wafted through the air like a fart. Akeema washed her hands and rinsed her mouth, spitting and coughing half a dozen times to be thorough.

"They killed all those people," Akeema stammered, clutching her stomach. "I felt it. The baby. I could feel him die inside of me."

Jaxon felt it too. He sensed the small life growing inside of Olen disappear like a snuffed-out candle. It broke him. Jaxon sleeved away his tears.

"Did that really happen?" Akeema asked, her voice cracking. "How do we know that wasn't all just a false memory?"

Jaxon's eyes darted to the room's medical equipment. He used a medical wand to scanned himself for fertility issues. The results were instant.

"I'm infertile," Jaxon said with quiet devastation. He handed the wand to Akeema. She scanned herself. He knew the outcome.

Her eyes went wet and glassy. "They sterilized us."

"Olen and her people weren't terrorists," Jaxon said. "Those people were killed because they tried to leave the Kaijen and start their own group. If the elders find out what we know I think... I think they're going to kill us too." Akeema started to speak when someone tried to open the infirmary hatch. Jaxon and Akeema communicated with their eyes before she unlocked it.

Castor entered. "Good news. I talked to Priestess Sabrene. She assured me that she can undo whatever Martel did to Jaxon. We're already on our way to meet her."

Oh shit, Jaxon thought. Akeema looked to share his sentiment. Neither of them could hide their alarm. "That's a waste of time," Jaxon said. "We all know I can't be a Kaijen anymore. I want to be dropped off at the nearest planet. Let me keep my dignity. Give me the chance to go my own way."

Castor forced a laugh, but his expression was more confusion than amusement. "What are you talking about? Jaxon, the priestess said she'd help you. She even said we wouldn't be punished for going after Martel or for losing the album. But only if you meet with her. This is the best possible outcome we could have hoped for." Jaxon and Akeema traded looks. It drew Castor's suspicion. "What is this? What are you two not telling me?"

Jaxon fought back the urge to lie again. The truth was bitter, but that's what makes it the truth. He took a breath to compose himself. "I saw something. A memory."

Castor stiffened. "You mean from Martel? You know whatever you think you saw wasn't real, right? You can't trust it."

"I saw Sabrene, she... she slaughtered an entire village of people. Innocent unarmed people. And she *enjoyed* it," Jaxon said.

Castor waved dismissively. "What people? You mean the insurrectionists who joined Olen? They were traitors, Jaxon. *They* were the ones who killed people. They stormed the monastery on Carliez Minor and tried to take it over—"

"They were unarmed," Akeema cut in. "They were just trying to live their lives in peace and Sabrene massacred every single one of them. She killed families. She killed a *baby* in its mother's womb. She's *evil*."

Castor leaned back on his heels. His eyes shifted between Jaxon and Akeema, putting the pieces together. His nose wrinkled like he'd caught a whiff of a rotting corpse. He focused on Akeema. "You did it. You forced him to link with you. How could you be so stupid?"

"I wasn't forced," Jaxon said, more to convince himself than Castor. "We both agreed to do it."

Castor's nostrils flared. "I'm not an idiot. Don't talk to me like one."

"You don't have to protect me," Akeema said to Jaxon. "We had to link. It was the only way to unlock the memories—" Castor's mechanical fist slammed into the infirmary's wall with a loud clang. It left a dent in the metal.

"Stop," Castor said. "I don't want to hear any more. I can't be involved in this. Jaxon, you need to confess what you've done to Priestess Sabrene and hope the elders take mercy on you. I promise I won't say anything about Akeema."

"If you take me to Sabrene I'm as good as dead," Jaxon said. "I know too much."

Akeema gripped Castor's arm. "Help us. Please."

Castor wrenched his arm away. "I'm sorry. But you did this to yourselves. I can't."

He left. The hatch slammed shut behind him. Jaxon and Akeema stared at each other in silence for a dilated moment.

"He won't do this to us," Akeema said, assuring herself. "He wouldn't. He couldn't. He's one of us." Jaxon didn't respond. "Talk to the pilot. Tell her to take us somewhere else."

Jaxon sighed. "That won't help now. We can't run from this. This is exactly what Martel predicted would happen."

"Don't take anything that bastard says as gospel."

"I know your feelings towards him are raw, but the one thing I can say about him is that he hasn't lied to me."

"Yet," Akeema said with clenched fists. "For all you know this was his plan all along."

"You saw what I saw. I need you to stay out of this. Don't help me. Don't expose yourself. If something happens to me, get Yoko to fly you out of there."

Akeema paused. "What do we do about Castor?" Jaxon didn't have an answer. He was lost in thought, trying to see a light at the end of his proverbial tunnel. The darkness remained.

The hatch opened. Betty entered, noticing the dimple in the wall. Then pretended not to notice it. "I detected sounds of a commotion."

"It was nothing," Akeema said. Betty glanced at the dent in the wall again. "Everything's fine," Akeema continued. "It was just a minor... communications problem. No need to alert the whole galaxy."

An idea kindled in Jaxon's mind. "Where's my handheld?"

"I fixed it," Akeema said. "It's charging in the galley with mine."

"We're going to need it. Betty," Jaxon said. "You don't owe us anything, but we could really use your help. Would you be willing to do a favor for me?"

"I am prohibited from engaging in activities that will bring harm to Yoko or this ship," Betty said.

Jaxon shook his head. "You won't be, I promise. But if my plan doesn't work you'll be the only one we'll be able to rely on. Will you help us?"

Betty didn't say anything. Her eyes blinked a few times as she processed the request. After a moment, she took a single step forward.

"I will," she said.

***

The *Saragos* dropped out of slipstream a safe distance away from Terezakis, a yellow and red orb roughly the size of Mercury with rings that hung ominously in the distance. The *Saragos* flipped and began its braking vector on approach for reentry.

In the cockpit, Jaxon stared at Terezakis on a monitor as it grew closer. The vice in his gut tightened. The planet's gravity rated slightly weaker than Earth's. No need for gravity drugs. Water covered most of its surface, with only one major yellow oblong-shaped land mass, swaths of green rivers snaking through it. The planet's rings were wide and glowed with a brilliant yellow pearlescence.

The *Saragos* streaked past the rings. They glittered like diamonds in the sunlight. The ship entered the upper atmosphere in a harsh descent. Yoko struggled to guide the ship through reentry. Betty sat next to her in the co-pilot's chair, running scans. Jaxon was strapped in a chair seated behind them. A loud metallic scream rattled through the ship; turbulence ripped off a piece of the hull.

"What was that?" Yoko asked.

"We lost something," Betty said.

"Was it expensive?"

"Likely so."

The ship survived reentry otherwise intact. It knifed through a beautiful autumn horizon as the sun began to dip below it. The planet's yellow rings arced through the sky in a way that resembled a massive translucent brush stroke. To Jaxon, it looked like a sickle hanging over him. The *Saragos* slowed its approach. It came upon a large Gothic stone cathedral planted atop the mouth of a waterfall with a steep drop.

The cathedral itself was a work of art.

Four short spires rose from the center of its mass. A single taller primary tower protruded from its back and faced the waterfall. The cathedral featured elegant buttresses and arched stained glass windows adorned with intricate detail and framed by cargonite brackets. Rust bled down the stone from decades of exposure.

The front of the property faced a thick forest of golden trees that secluded it from any other signs of civilization as far as the eye could see. The planet didn't appear to have any other inhabitants.

The *Saragos* moaned and shrieked like an exhausted animal. Its landing struts folded out of the hull and touched down on a circular stone landing pad a short distance from the cathedral's main courtyard. Jaxon glanced at a monitor with an external view. He spotted Sabrene's personal shuttle parked off to the side along with a light skiff.

The *Saragos* lowered its boarding ramp. Castor led the group, followed by Jaxon and Akeema. They hung back. The irony of the visual gap between them and Castor wasn't lost on Jaxon. He'd made a plan, and Castor couldn't be suspected to be part of it.

Yoko assessed the section of ship that'd broken off. "Would it be cheaper to buy a whole new ship than to fix this one?"

"Yes, it would," Betty said. "But a new ship would not be this ship."

"That's true," Yoko said with sadness. She placed her hand on the ship's skin and patted it, causing a loose panel above her to fall off. It just barely missed striking her head.

The cathedral's tall heavy ornate wooden doors drew back with a deep moan.

Verlain appeared, escorted by six Kaijen guards dressed in immaculate white and blue robes and black tunics. Verlain wore a special lavender pink sash around her waist, emphasizing her higher ranking.

"We welcome you to Terezakis," she said with a warm smile that betrayed her cold eyes. "Our priestess is expecting you. We request that you turn over your weapons."

Castor did as he was told. Jaxon and Akeema hesitated, then handed over their crossglaive hilts. Jaxon wished he had his rocket boots. He hadn't had time to repair them and left them on the ship. Betty had given him a pair of fabricated slip-on boots to wear. They fit tight and needed to be broken in.

"Follow me," Verlain said.

She led them inside. Vaulted ceilings towered over old archaic statues and ancient wall carvings depicting Kaijen of the past. Dying sunlight beamed through the stained windows and threw a spectrum of colors across the walls.

They entered the main hall. It was an extravagant lobby at the cathedral's heart. More than two dozen spiral load-bearing support columns filled the hall. The columns were spaced out in a grid pattern, each over a meter thick, all centered around a hand carved stone water fountain.

That's where Sabrene stood.

Her imposing height separated her from everyone else. Her arms were open and welcoming, her lips wearing that unsettling thin smile of hers, made even more unnerving now that Jaxon knew what horrors she committing while wearing it. His testicles wanted to retreat inside of his body.

"It pleases me to see you all arrived in good health," Sabrene said, cupping her hands.

Castor bowed to her. "Our apologies again, priestess. We deeply regret disobeying your orders and losing the album," he said, his tone submissive and apologetic. It made Jaxon lose a measure of respect for his brother. He imagined if Sabrene had bent over and exposed her bare ass that Castor would have been eager to kiss it. "We humbly beg your forgiveness."

"No need," Sabrene said in crisp upbeat tone. As if this were all just some silly misunderstanding. "What's done is done. All that matters now is helping young Jaxon." Her eyes shifted to him.

Jaxon forced himself not to flinch. "I thought you would be upset with me, priestess." He masked his fear better than he imagined he could.

"Not at all my child," she said, leaning forward to get closer to his eye level, grinning. "You're our secret weapon."

***

Sabrene led Jaxon through the cathedral's narrow lantern lit corridors. Lamplight bounced off the stone carvings of honored Kaijen warriors adorning the walls. He followed her up a series of stairwells within the cathedral's main tower to her private chamber.

Jaxon stepped inside, his nose filling with the smoky odor of incense. Every square centimeter of floor space was decorated with flashy expensive trinkets. The carpets were lavish and intricately woven. The walls were covered floor to ceiling with murals made up of tiny multicolored gems that must've taken years to position and hundreds of hours to maintain.

Sabrene went around the room lighting candles. More confirmation that the cathedral didn't rely on electronic power. At least, not this part of it. The room also featured a veranda; it held a sitting area and a curved stone railing overlooking the waterfall running underneath the cathedral. The roar of the gushing water filled the chamber and gave it a sense of tranquility. Of safety.

Jaxon felt neither emotion.

His heart beat faster than a runner's feet. Sweat began to bead his face. Dying light from the planet's sun beamed through the veranda before it was completely choked out. Darkness reigned.

Sabrene maintained her upbeat attitude and friendly smile as she went to her small kitchen and boiled a kettle of water. "I can feel your anxiety. Relax. I assure you, you're not in any trouble. In fact, you may be the most valuable being on this entire planet."

"How?" Jaxon asked. The kettle whined. Sabrene poured herself a cup of tea. The aroma of ginger and Nezuian honey filled the room.

"The terrorist Martel linked with you. That means you know where he is. Where I can find him, and his evil master Olen. Tell me where they're hiding. Help me apprehend them and you will be greatly rewarded."

"What if I don't know where they are? What happens then?"

"That all depends on you, child. Tea?" Sabrene poured a second steaming cup for Jaxon. He stopped to examine one of the room's expensive decorations: a suit of old armor that showed signs of having seen battle.

"Lovely, isn't it?" Sabrene said. She brought the hot cups to a sitting table. "Every piece in this room comes from an extinct culture throughout the settled worlds. I collect them."

"I thought the Kaijen were forbidden from owning material possessions?"

"You mean like the rocket boots you salvaged on Giannis?"

Jaxon's spine stiffened. "I... didn't think you noticed." Nervousness rattled his voice. He sounded like a boy half his age.

"I didn't. Being so much taller than everyone else, it's difficult noticing things below me."

"Then how—"

Sabrene waved her handheld. She sat in an elegant armchair and swirled her tea with a spoon. "All Kaijen issued models can record everything you say. Even when turned off. Every Sacred Kaijen Warrior is monitored at all times."

Jaxon's blood ran cold. "You've been *spying* on us?"

"We've been *monitoring* you," Sabrene said. "It helps us to identify our more troublesome members before they become too... problematic."

"How much do you know?" Jaxon said. The stress in his throat made the pitch of his voice sound higher with each syllable.

Sabrene cooled her tea with her breath. The smell of ginger was strong enough to taste. "It would be best if you just assumed that I know everything, child." *Did she?* Jaxon's mind raced. He wanted to run. Sabrene cleared her throat. "But we're moving too fast. I prefer to take this nice and slow. No need to rush. Please, have a seat."

She paused to drink her tea. Her eyes were closed. Jaxon sprinted for the door.

He almost made it.

An invisible force grabbed his legs and he fell forward, slamming face first into the fancy carpet. His handheld fell out of his pocket. The unseen force coiled around him like a snake and dragged him back to Sabrene's table.

"I said. *Sit. Down.*" Her words were sharp as daggers. She was tuning, but the effort didn't appear to exhaust her. Clearly, she'd amassed a greater stamina to use her powers over a prolonged period of time without collapsing into a heap.

She levitated Jaxon into the air like a magician's act. He couldn't fight it. She twisted his body around to face her, like she was posing a doll with invisible hands and dropped him into a chair opposite her.

He couldn't break free. She'd completely overpowered him. Jaxon wore himself out, breathing faster than his lungs could keep up. Sabrene barely moved a muscle.

"That's better, isn't it?" she said, politely. "Do you like that chair? It's woven out of real Thurlbii fur. I made it myself out of that one you left alive on Giannis. That's what happens to someone who fails to carry out my orders."

Jaxon's eyes widened. "*You* sent them to kill me?"

Sabrene chuckled. "No. Well, not exactly." She sipped her tea, savoring its flavor. "The Giannisians wouldn't let us build a monastery on their degenerate planet. But if one of our own was to be murdered there, a human, we could use that death to stir up political pressure. Then we could stage protests. Sway public opinion. I simply asked Nisame to choose her least valuable human student to be the one to make that sacrifice." Jaxon's heart sank into his guts. Priestess Nisame was his mentor. He loved her. He cherished her council. He tried so hard to make her proud. He'd persuaded his friends to break their oaths to avenge her murder. Being burned would have hurt less.

"We all have a role to play in this world," Sabrene went on, her smirk having twisted into a bored scowl. "Yours was to die on Giannis at the hands of Thurlbii savages. But you couldn't even get *that* right, could you?"

"Are you going to finish the job?" Jaxon said.

"Only if you make me. After all, we both know how you have a problem when it comes to obeying women."

"Excuse me?"

"Don't pretend to be dumb. You're only in this situation as a consequence of your refusal to follow my instructions. Your kind always has trouble taking orders from a female. You hate us."

Her telekinetic grip on Jaxon squeezed tighter. "You're wrong," he rasped. "We wanted to stop Martel. He was going to get away with all of those deaths—"

She scoffed. "So you, a novice Kaijen, knew better than I, a highly skilled highly ranked priestess? Who do you think you are?"

"I was trying to do what was right—" He was choking now, the life being squeezed out of him.

"Don't *lie* to me," Sabrene growled. "I know your type. You get your hands on a crossglaive and a little tuning power and your fragile male ego makes you feel entitled to rule the entire universe. Not this time. Scrotes like you are the reason why our society is in the mess it's in. Tell me where Olen is and what her plans are for the album. I want to know everything."

Jaxon couldn't speak. He couldn't move. He was trapped in his own body as it threatened to collapse in on him.

The edges of his vision blurred. He was blacking out. Sabrene released him from her telekinetic grip. Blood rushed through his system and his sight came back into focus.

Having used her abilities for such an extended length of time winded Sabrene. Her breathing quickened, but she otherwise hid her fatigue well.

"So it's true," Jaxon said between labored breaths. "You really did kill all of those people on Zaspel."

"Let's not play games," Sabrene said. "You only believe that because you're seeing it from their perspective. From my point of view, the right point of view, they were terrorists. Rogue seditionists and counter-revolutionaries. They deserved what they got."

"They were *unarmed*. They had no weapons—"

"*Ideas* are weapons," Sabrene scowled. "They chose to rebel and follow her. Olen tried to destroy our society by breaking our most sacred rules. She linked with anyone and everyone like a common whore in an attempt to spread her power to those that didn't deserve it."

"Isn't that the Kaijen's core belief? Species equality? Sharing her knowledge and power would have made everyone equal."

A long heavy sigh clawed its way out of Sabrene's mouth. "You're right. We Kaijen do love our equality. But there are those of us who are more equal than others. The elders were willing to let Olen get away with her dishonor. I had to convince them that she posed too great a threat if she were allowed to live. She didn't deserve to be left alone with that much power."

It was the confidence in her words that terrified Jaxon more than the words themselves. "You wanted to kill her just so you could make sure the true power remained at the top. With you."

"As it should," Sabrene said, sipping her tea. "Low level Kaijen can't be trusted with that kind of power, let alone a scrote like you. You're pawns. Your role is to obey and spread our message. Nothing more. The goal of the Kaijen is to achieve an equal society where every race and species all follow the same belief and do not question it."

Her words chilled Jaxon down to his marrow. The fear in his stomach shot up to his chest. "Why are you telling this to me?" He strained to speak.

"Because it's not too late for you to decide," Sabrene said. "Your intelligence may be one of the lowest I've seen, but even you can't be stupid enough to side against me. So. You can choose to be like us, of your own free will, or you can spend a few hours in a reeducation session."

"Torture," Jaxon said. "You're going to torture me."

"No, not torture. *Reeducate.* Tell me where to find Olen."

"I don't know. I've never even met her before."

Sabrene rose to her full height, looming over Jaxon as tall as a giant. She gripped his head in her large palms and spindly pink fingers. "Martel linked with you. There's always some bleed-through." She caressed his head. "The memories are in there. Somewhere. Swirling about. You will initiate a link with me and give me everything you know or you're going to die."

A sick, painful laugh coughed out of Jaxon's throat. "You can't force me to link. You need my consent. I won't give it."

Sabrene's long narrow fingers snaked around Jaxon's neck and squeezed. "Then I will drag Castor and Akeema in here and I will tune their limbs from their bodies until you do."

Jaxon couldn't breathe. He tried to will his body out of its paralytic state. He was powerless. *Strong emotions, that's the key*, Akeema's words rang in his ears. *You stopped a big ass ship dead in its tracks. This should be easy.* He had to make this happen right now, or he was dead. Jaxon stared deep into Sabrene's golden firecracker eyes and concentrated on the screams of the people she'd killed. The anger. The devastation. He felt a tingle in the space between his eyes.

Sabrene's teacup vibrated. In an instant, it spontaneously pitched itself off of its table and hit Sabrene in the head.

"Ow," Sabrene yelped, then paused. Red oozing from the cut.

It was an opportunity. Jaxon regained the use of his hand and grabbed the crossglaive hilt hanging from Sabrene's waist. The blade extended. She tuned the energy sword out of his hand and threw it across the room, but not before the burning blade lit a large section of her sari on fire. Her hold on Jaxon released and he spilled onto the carpeted floor. Sabrene patted out the fire with her palms, the flames having burned through the fabric. Her skin hadn't been scorched. Jaxon attempted to tackle Sabrene. She was a tall tree of a woman. She wouldn't be moved.

Jaxon hurled his fists at her. His blows didn't connect, but hers did. Sabrene's fists were almost twice the size of his. She pummeled Jaxon's face, chest and stomach, her fists hitting like fleshy sledgehammers. With each hit, she smiled.

Sabrene's leg cut through the air and slammed into Jaxon's ribs. It hurt like being hit with a pipe. He stumbled backward, crashing into several of Sabrene's collectibles. She closed the distance between them in three large steps. Her long thin fingers stretched out like spider legs and grabbed Jaxon's wrists and placed his palms on the crown of her head.

"Open your mind to me," Sabrene demanded.

"Fuck you," Jaxon said through red teeth.

"Link with me!"

"Fuck you!"

Jaxon drove his knee into Sabrene's crotch. She groaned and her grip loosened. He pushed himself away from her, collapsing onto his stomach. The fight had drained and exhausted him. Jaxon forced himself to stand. Something felt broken. Sabrene's leg swung and devastated his abdomen. Bright shooting pain stung his receptors. He coughed blood.

"Now you've hurt my feelings," Sabrene sighed. "Now we can't be friends." She opened her palm, her crossglaive darting across the room and into her hand. She pinned Jaxon down and held the sword's blade over his legs, close enough to scorch his skin. Jaxon cried out.

"I need your head and your hands," Sabrene said. "Not your legs. You will miss them."

Jaxon's mind reached out in a panic. The mental pain came different this time. It started in his chest, ballooning up until it exploded in a burst of raw tuning energy. It shoved Sabrene back as her collectibles detonated into volleys of shrapnel.

All the beads on the walls shot out into the room like confetti, shredding her sari and cutting her face. She bled, but none of her injuries were serious. Jaxon's spontaneous demonstration of power had frightened her. A clamor of fast footsteps approached outside the room. Sabrene screamed seconds before the door was kicked open.

"He assaulted me!" she shouted at the two Kaijen guards standing in the doorway, their crossglaive blades extended. "He's an assassin!"

Jaxon was just as shocked as the guards were. "Wait— No—" he stammered, but the guards were already attacking him. Adrenaline pushed Jaxon's fatigue aside. His body bent, narrowly dodging the two crossglaive blades aiming to slice him in half.

For a few crucial seconds, time seemed to slow down for Jaxon. It allowed him to disarm one of the guards, a heavily tattooed Wazny woman. He elbowed her in the nose. With her down, he used her crossglaive to battle the remaining guard, a Nezu with frizzy fur. She was quite a bit taller than him. He let his instincts take control while using a combat form he'd never been taught. Moves he'd seen Martel use at the Earth monastery attack.

Olen's moves.

Sabrene didn't interfere. She watched from a distance, observing Jaxon's performance like a talent scout, her face a mix of astonishment and anger. Jaxon parried the tall Nezu's strikes. His glowing blade cut across the top of her sword hand, splitting it open.

She shrieked, dropping her crossglaive and cupping her bleeding split hand, then fled the room screaming.

Sabrene rose to her feet, irked by the failure of her guards. Jaxon saw his chance to end it and approached her.

The thought of taking a life had always disgusted him. But if there was one life he could forgive himself for taking, it had to be this one. Jaxon charged at her with fire in his eyes.

Sabrene waved her hand in a swatting motion. Her tuning powers assaulted Jaxon with an impact equal to being hit by a speeding truck. The invisible force struck him from the side, lifting him up off of his feet. Momentum sent him flailing through the air like a ragdoll, into the veranda. His vision streaked and swirled, then froze when his body crashed into the veranda's railing, knocking the breath out of him. Another invisible push from Sabrene's tuning powers and he went over the edge.

Jaxon was falling.

In the night's sky, he saw the lamplight from Sabrene's room shrink smaller and smaller as he fell further away from the tower as the wind whistled loud in his ears. His body crashed into the roar of the waterfall's churning waves below.

The water swallowed him.

Chapter Twenty-One: Akeema

Akeema and Castor were brought to the cathedral's common area. They sat across from each other at a large wooden dining table that appeared to be machine cut instead of hand carved, which didn't sit right with her for some reason. They ate what looked to be vegetables in hot soup. It stank like spent brass. She stomached a few mouthfuls before the taste made her want to gag. Akeema played with the mushy slop with her spoon while Castor gobbled his down like it was pumpkin pie.

"How can you eat this shit?" Akeema said.

"At least it doesn't have a face," Castor said, then chewed a steaming mouthful.

Akeema's eyes cut to a pair of guards watching them; a tattooed Wazny and a Nezu with wild ungroomed body fur. Her eyes slitted, giving them a fake smile. They noticed her, then promptly ignored her.

She whispered to Castor, "We need to escape this place."

Castor grumbled. "You're being ridiculous. This is a sanctuary. There is no safer place in the known worlds that we could possibly be. They're even feeding us hot food."

Akeema caught another whiff of her soup. It wrinkled her nose. "It smells like old gym socks." Castor laughed, agreeing with her. "And it tastes like cat shit."

Castor eyed her. "How do you know what cat shit tastes like?"

"You're not mentally ready to hear that story."

"A story about you eating cat shit is a story I was born ready to hear." They laughed. She was still upset with him, but that didn't mean he couldn't be charming. Akeema began to say something when the building moved. A tremor shook them. Akeema braced her palms on the table to keep from falling out of her chair. Liquid from their bowls and drinking cups jostled and spilled while dust from the rafters sprinkled down like fine snow.

"Was that an earthquake? Or a bomb?" Castor said. Akeema knew it was neither. Her head snapped to the two Kaijen guards. They were gone, their feet pounding the marble floors on their way up the main staircase.

Akeema leapt from her seat fast enough that the legs of her chair scraped against the floor. She deduced where the guards had rushed off to.

The tower.

Castor fretted. "We were ordered to stay here."

"Jaxon's in danger," Akeema said. "He needs our help." She left without looking back. Castor shouted after her, but he was already out of her mind.

The cathedral's halls were wide and dim. The smallest sound bounced and echoed, filling the corridors with a cacophony of noise. The roar of shouting cut through the commotion. Akeema followed the sound up a flight of narrow stairs. As she drew closer, the halls filled with the familiar pandemonium of a struggle. She might've mistaken the guttural voices for sounds of sex if they weren't paired with the metallic clashing of crossglaive blades.

Akeema heard steps behind her. Over her shoulder, she saw Castor. He nodded. She returned the gesture. Together they pushed forward through the cathedral when a woman's scream startled Akeema. The Nezu guard appeared, stumbling, her mangled hand spewing blood down her Kaijen robes and leaving a trail on the stone floor. She ran past them in a panic and vanished down the hall they'd come from.

Akeema reached Sabrene's kicked in chamber door expecting to find Jaxon dead on the floor.

The room's carpet glittered, little glistening multicolored gems covering it. They reminded her of candy and crunched under her feet. The other Kaijen guard was laid out on top of the mess, alive, but unconscious.

Akeema's eyes found Jaxon. He was running towards Sabrene, aiming to lance her with his crossglaive. Sabrene swiped her hand and Jaxon lifted up off of his feet. Tuning, Sabrene tossed Jaxon out of the room with incredible force. He crashed onto an external balcony like a piece of weightless debris.

"Jaxon!" Akeema cried as he disappeared over the railing. She dashed to the balcony and looked over the side. In the darkness, she caught flashes of Jaxon's flailing body. From this height he didn't even look like a person, just a falling object. It disappeared into the waterfall's churning waves. No one could survive a fall from this height, much less a human.

Her brother, the closest thing to a best friend she'd ever had, had just been killed.

The rage overwhelmed her. It happened quickly, like it had always been there, waiting to be tagged in.

"You bitch," Akeema growled. She turned to Sabrene, murder in her fiery eyes. More Kaijen guards had arrived. If Akeema attacked Sabrene she'd be outnumbered. She'd lose. She didn't care.

"Jaxon Troy was in collusion with the speciesist Hiroshi Martel and his terrorist master Olen," Sabrene announced to the growing crowd of onlookers. "He attempted to assassinate me," she said while touching the small cuts on her face, then showed them all the tiny smear of blood that rubbed off on her fingers to a symphony of gasps. "He may have succeeded if Hoku and Septima hadn't have arrived in time to defend me. Even after he gored Septima's hand I tried my best to dissuade him with words, but he gave me no choice. I had to defend myself."

Akeema telegraphed her attack with a war cry. In hindsight, this was by far the stupidest thing she could've possibly done.

Sabrene deflected Akeema's assault with such ease it was almost funny. Akeema's fury wouldn't let her stop trying, her fists swinging at Sabrene and hitting air. Then her entire body stiffened. Tuning, Sabrene picked Akeema up by her throat and squeezed.

"That technique. I know it," said the smug pink bitch as Akeema struggled for air. "Did Jaxon Troy link with you?" Akeema wouldn't answer. She wasn't going to give the tall lanky monster the satisfaction. Sabrene's grip tightened. The flesh of Akeema's neck dimpled, as if being crushed by invisible fingers. Her pale face flushed bright red. She gagged. Her lungs strained to draw in the smallest sip of oxygen. She began to asphyxiate.

Akeema locked eyes with Sabrene, staring the tall woman down. Not in fear, but in resignation. In defiance. She wouldn't yield.

"He did," Castor said in a panic. "They linked. Let her go, please."

Sabrene obliged. Akeema crumpled to the floor in a heap. Thousands of little gems on the carpet stung her and stuck to her skin and clothes. She coughed in air as her eyes shot daggers at Castor.

"I wouldn't be too hard on him, child," Sabrene said. "He just saved your life."

"She's a murderer!" Akeema said, her voice horse and scratchy. "You can't trust her—"

Sabrene cupped her hand as if she were holding an invisible ball and said, "Quiet." She tuned Akeema's jaw shut. "Traitors don't get to have their voices heard." The tall woman signaled to the guards. Hands grabbed Akeema's arms and pulled her to her feet. Tight handcuffs bound her wrists.

Castor stood between them and said, "Priestess, please—"

"Akeema has been indoctrinated and radicalized," Sabrene said. "She chose to betray us, of her own free will. These are the consequences. Now you must make a choice, child. You can join her and be a traitor and be executed, or you can kneel."

Castor hesitated.

His sad remorseful eyes locked with Akeema's. The intensity of her anger wouldn't let her feel the growing aches in her throat and muscles. If ever there were a time she wanted Castor to be the noble masculine hero of morality he'd always presented himself as, this would be the time.

Then he knelt.

It hurt Akeema. Worse than she'd been hurt since this all began. It burned hotter than fire. Sabrene placed her hand on Castor's shoulder, giving him permission to rise. He kept his head bowed.

"Pay attention," Sabrene said to her gathered students. "This is what true loyalty to our cause looks like. When one of our Kaijen sisters betrays us, she is no longer part of our tribe. She is a deplorable traitor that deserves to be punished. Castor Zhecheva, would you please do the honors?"

Color drained from Castor's tan face. "What are you asking me to do?"

"To beat her," Sabrene said with calm assertiveness.

"Priestess please," Castor said. "She deserves a trial."

"You're right. A trial will be held. Akeema Barbeau will be found guilty and executed. But first she must be punished, publicly, as a lesson to any others who refuse to conform to our way of life and jeopardize the harmony of the sacred Kaijen warriors."

Fear and anxiety churned on Castor's face. His mechanical hand twitched. "Priestess, I'm begging you. Please don't ask me to—"

"Either you are a noble Kaijen like us or an insurrectionist like her," Sabrene said. Verlain stood behind Castor. He saw her over his shoulder, her hands hovered over the twin crossglaive hilts hanging from her waist belt like a pair of Old West six shooters. Her eyes were on Sabrene, waiting for permission to cut Castor down. A part of Akeema wanted her to.

"I *am* a noble Kaijen," Castor said, more to himself than to Sabrene.

"Then punch this evildoer," Sabrene said. Akeema watched Castor ball his fists and her shoulders tensed. Again, she hoped, this time, Castor would come to his senses and stand against this madness. He stood before her and drove his flesh fist into her stomach. Blunt pain exploded through Akeema's abdomen. Her muscles seized and cramped. It wasn't the hardest punch she'd ever taken, but it hurt the most. The air in her lungs evacuated, but she didn't cry out. She wouldn't give them that prize.

Akeema tried to force herself to tune. It wouldn't happen.

"Hit her again," Sabrene said. "But this time use your metal hand. And don't hold back." Verlain continued to stand by, eager to kill Castor if he didn't sell this next blow. Akeema braced herself. It didn't help.

The vetronium fist sent sharp throbbing pain rippling throughout her body in a series of waves. She couldn't hold back her scream. Her knees buckled and she vomited all over the bead covered floor. She couldn't stop her tears.

Sabrene watched with no positive or negative reaction. This was just business to her.

"Take her to the reeducation room," Sabrene said. Guards grabbed Akeema up and dragged her away, her head swimming.

Akeema overheard Sabrene say to Verlain, "Find the body,"

before she passed out.

***

An intense white light hurt Akeema's eyes. It washed out the world.

Her attempt to shut her eyes was stopped by some kind of device strapped around her head. It locked her eyelids open. She wanted to reach up and rip the device away, but she couldn't move.

Her arms were bound in a type of bulky straitjacket laced with odd electrical attachments Akeema didn't recognize. Shackles were fastened tight around her ankles and attached to thick chains bolted to the smooth white floor. Her legs kicked and tugged at the heavy chains. It was useless.

Akeema concentrated on the chains, trying to tune them off. The result was a migraine the size of a bolder. It hardened inside her brain.

"You've ingested a tuning blocker," the pink bitch's voice echoed from beyond the white light.

And then Akeema realized. "Our food," Akeema gasped. "You put it in our food."

"A precaution. You're not strong enough to fight it," the voice continued. The lights dimmed a few levels. Sabrene walked into focus wearing protective goggles. "I can change that, Akeema. I can be very good to you. I can train you to be the most empowered Kaijen there has ever been. One that can crush Hiroshi Martel like a Chibakian cockroach. I know that's what you want more than anything."

"And in exchange I get to be your slave?" Akeema said.

"We would be allies. Equals," Sabrene said. "Or do you no longer believe in species equality?"

"I don't think that word means what you think it means," Akeema said. "Especially after I watched you murder an entire community of people who were practicing the very virtues you claim to uphold."

Sabrene groaned. "You mean the insurrectionists. That's what they were. All the major newsfeeds classified them as such."

"Outlets that cater to you."

"Because we're the good side," Sabrene said. "You were one of us. You could be again. Link with me. Give me what I want and you will be forgiven."

"Is this the same shitty deal you offered Jaxon? No wonder he tried to kill you." The room's white light brightened, filling Akeema's retinas with a punishing ache.

"Prolonged exposure will cook your corneas," Sabrene said.

Akeema's jaw clenched, her teeth grinding so hard that if there were coal in her mouth she'd have spit out diamonds. Her tears dried instantly on her cheek. "Jaxon died standing up to you. I don't mind joining him."

"Let's not talk about that ungrateful scrote. He wasn't capable of intelligent thought. Not like you. But you were tricked. You're the victim here, Akeema. Don't let some male drag you down when you have the potential to be so much more."

"I thought wanting to be more was against the Kaijen code," Akeema struggled to say as the ache in her eyes inflated. She began to moan softly, the stinging pangs surging through her skull like barbed tentacles. Sabrene dimmed the light to a tolerable level. Akeema exhaled with an almost euphoric relief.

"Don't be that way, Akeema. We are superior beings. We can talk honestly. When Jaxon Troy linked with you it was by force, wasn't it?"

Akeema coughed out a hard laugh that made snot bubble out of her nose and dribble down her lips. "I volunteered. Because I wanted to know the truth."

"Lie," Sabrene accused. She pressed a button on a remote that sent an electrical charge through Akeema's straitjacket; it acted as a body-sized taser. Akeema fell to her knees in agony. Sabrene said, "You didn't give a damn about the truth. You wanted the power. I listened to the argument you had with Castor after you encountered Martel. I know exactly what kind of woman you are."

"Takes one to know one," Akeema said. Sabrene dimmed the lights to a normal setting and lifted her goggles. She came to Akeema and cleaned the pale woman's messy face with a loose strip of her sari. Akeema wanted to bite Sabrene's fingers, but decided against it.

"What do you know about my people?" Sabrene asked.

"You're an Iskaran, like Sil Dasmis."

Sabrene sneered at the mention of his name. "On Pyralis, women control every aspect of our society. We run the government. We paved the roads. We built the infrastructure. We are the engineers. The intellectuals. The teachers. The soldiers. And do you know what the role of the males were?" Sabrene leaned in closer to speak into Akeema's ear. "To breed. That's all. We fed them. We provided for them. Protected them. We kept them safe. And all they had to do was remain docile and make children."

"Did they have a choice?" Akeema asked.

"It was their *duty*," Sabrene asserted. "Choice was irrelevant. They were happy in their role. Only one in one thousand Iskaran children born are male, so the loss of even one could impact the genetic diversity of an entire generation." Sabrene stood to her full height and breathed a heavy sigh. "Then Sil Dasmis had to go and abandon his role. He discovered a new world plentiful with lifesaving medicine that made him famous throughout the known worlds. Then all of a sudden our males were no longer happy with their role. They wanted to learn to read and go to school and be like the women." Sabrene's words dripped with aggravated disdain. She pulled a small dropper from her sari and used it to moisten Akeema's dry eyes.

"Some of the men even went so far as to have back-alley vasectomies in protest," Sabrene continued. "Others had themselves castrated. Many died from infection. Our once thriving civilization slowly eroded into a wasteland as our birth rates cratered. We had to rely on cloning, but without enough genetic diversity my species is now on course to go extinct within the next hundred years. All because one male made a stupid selfish choice."

There was a sorrow in her voice that might have won a crumb of sympathy from Akeema, had it been someone else. She was distracted by the stink of ballast filling her nose. She focused her mind. Sil Dasmis was a sore spot for Sabrene. Akeema couldn't hurt the pink woman, but she could at least annoy her. "Sil Dasmis was a great man. A hero. An icon. My race owes everything to him. He brokered a historic treaty that helped save billions of lives."

Sabrene's face darkened. "At the expense of his own *species*," she snapped. "By the time I was a young woman, males were being integrated into primary schools. I had one in my class. He wanted to be my friend. I don't remember how, but the fool fell down and broke his nose and some of his teeth. I was blamed. They were going to sent me to a detention camp. The Kaijen saved me. They took me in and shuttled me away from Pyralis under religious exception." Her tone was quiet and fragile. Her lips quivered with emotion. Tears wet her eyes.

Akeema couldn't stop herself from laughing. "Am I supposed to feel *sorry* for you?" she said between inhaling gulps of air. "What happened to your people was *their* choice. They saddled that pony. Now they have to ride it all the way to their extinction."

"Oh, I agree," Sabrene said. There was an exaggerated sweetness in her voice that concealed her contempt. "That's the problem. Choice is always the problem. People in large groups don't know how to decide for themselves. Someone needs to take the burden of choice away from the masses so that those of us who know better can choose for them."

"You fucking hypocrite," Akeema spat. "You never believed in what the Kaijen stood for, you just used them as a way to enable your bigotry. You saw Olen and her people as evil cultists who broke away because they were practicing actual equality between males and females and it disgusted you. It's all just projection. *You're* the cultist. You're the *villain*." Saying it out loud made Akeema's stomach turn. "Oh God. We were on the same side. I was too blind to even see it."

Any emotion Sabrene had evaporated. She slid her goggles down over her eyes. The lights turned up to a near blinding level. "No, that's just the delusion that's been put in your head by Olen. She is the single greatest threat to the Kaijen for exactly this reason. Because she's made you question us. Her thoughts infected Martel and Jaxon, and now she's infected you. The only way the Kaijen can survive is if we all have one belief. One point of view. It's for the welfare of our people. It's how we fight discrimination and keep things fair."

"By restricting and controlling what people think and say and do for the good of the group." Akeema said, mockingly.

"Yes. So you understand."

"That sounds more like intolerance disguised as fairness. You wanted to kill Olen because you wanted to censor the information she was sharing."

"I was protecting the *truth*," Sabrene shouted. Another electrical charge shot waves of misery through Akeema's slim body. "We can't have rogue Kaijen running around linking with whoever they wish. We bestowed upon you an incredible gift. One that needs to be controlled. That's what started the great Kaijen War. Thousands of us. Dead. All that knowledge lost. I won't be responsible for a sequel to that madness just because a handful of idiots put their so-called freedom above the safety of our society."

"Oh, so, it's better to kill a handful of innocents to save thousands? That's how you justify your tyranny?"

Sabrene's jaw tightened hard enough her teeth clicked. "Why are you so concerned about those people? A day ago you didn't even know they existed. Do you even know their names?"

"Shacora," Akeema began. "Dasia. Thekla. Rez. Kya. Khadime. Baalbek. Najia. Qadeerah. Boslau. Tabacchi. Behrens. Those were just some of their names. I remember them all. Their faces. The way they laughed. The way they ate their food. Their scents. Everything. I hear their screaming when you slaughtered them as clearly as I hear my own voice."

Sabrene waved her hand dismissively with an annoyed grunt. "You expect me to feel sympathy for those xenophobic traitors? How I handled them was a service. And better than they deserved."

"Even Olen's unborn son?"

"That one most of all," Sabrene said. "I've seen a vision of the tragedy that is to come. Killing that parasite surely saved the countless lives it would have taken had it been born."

"Oh. You see visions now?"

"I saw Olen. She was turning hundreds, thousands of minions against the Kaijen. I saw a war that would cause untold deaths. If killing a small few is the price of maintaining peace then I would call that a bargain."

Akeema's eyesight worsened. Sabrene appeared in front of her like a pink-skinned blue-haired angel; Akeema imagined wings made from flared light spreading out of the tall woman's back. Akeema staggered to her feet in a futile attempt to face Sabrene even though she'd need a decent step ladder to do so.

"Here's the deal," Akeema said. "I'll give you what you want. I'll link with you. But first, you have to link with me. Share your power with me. Then I'll tell you how to find Olen."

Sabrene paused. And then, she chortled. A thin smile curling her lips. "You first."

"No," Akeema said. "You want to buy my loyalty? That's the price. Share all of your power with me and then we'll talk. But you won't, will you?"

"I'll consider your request. But only if you swear your allegiance to me and kneel."

"The only reason to kneel is so that one can be decapitated," Akeema said. "No matter what you do to me you'll never silence my voice."

"Interesting choice of words. The Kaijen do believe in the rule of many voices. I think it's time you heard them." Sabrene backed away and faded into the light.

In her place, figures appeared. They surrounded Akeema.

Sabrene's Kaijen students. More than a dozen. They wore protective goggles and held electrified batons. Castor wasn't among them. Small mercies.

The group took turns shocking Akeema while yelling obscenities and spitting on her. *Traitor!* one voice yelled, then a shock.

Oppressor! another voice screamed, followed by another shock.

Abuser! Shock.

Repent bigot! Three shocks.

Xenophobic hatemonger! Two shocks.

Elitist! Materialist! One shock.

Shame! Four shocks.

The repeated electrical jolts from the batons caused Akeema's ears to ring. Her nose bled. Her cybernetic spine absorbed the heat, the nerve endings spasming in scorching pain.

If she angled her head and twisted her neck at just the right moment, she could trick one of them into shocking her in the face. That might kill her. That was the state of mind she'd been dragged into, where she welcomed suicide. It meant they'd won. Her sense of shame had never been greater. The torrent of voices blurred and her body went numb from the stinging shocks.

Akeema's mind prepared to pass out when a dark shape appeared in front of her, the light curving round it. Out of focus, the figure sprouted arms. Hands reached out and touched Akeema's glowing red face.

"Hold on," Jaxon whispered. She could see him now, dripping wet, as if he were directly underneath a running spigot. She could feel his cold breath on her skin and he smelled like the ocean. "Don't let them beat you. Fight. You have to fight. Don't give in. I'm coming for you."

The image faded into mist.

The sensation felt similar to when she'd been inside Olen's memory. It could have been an illusion. She chose to believe it was really him. It had to be. So she would endure.

Her torture lasted for several more minutes. Or hours. Akeema lost all sense of time. After a while the throats of the students grew dry and horse from yelling, their arms aching and tired from wielding the heavy batons. Akeema curled up in a pile on the floor. She appeared catatonic.

The lights dimmed. Sabrene knelt down to the beaten woman lying in a pool of her own blood and stinking urine. "Admit you were wrong to question us," Sabrene's voice boomed in the silent room. "Apologize and the pain will stop."

Akeema replied with a cold hard stare of defiance. She wouldn't yield.

Sabrene signaled the mob of Kaijen students to continue Akeema's reeducation. Their batons went up above their heads in a striking position when Sabrene's handheld chirped. She signaled the students to hold and thumbed open her handheld to answer the call. "Did you find his body?"

"No," Verlaina's voice said over the handheld's tinny speaker. "I found tracks. He survived."

The room erupted with a loud, horrible sound that echoed in everyone's ears. Akeema thought it was Sabrene screaming. It took Akeema a moment to realize the sound was coming from her.

She was laughing.

Chapter Twenty-Two: Jaxon

Jaxon inhaled. Water choked his throat and shot up his nose, stinging his nasal passages. He was drowning. He'd never bothered to learn how to swim. Only now did it seem like a massive oversight on his part.

The waterfall had thrown him deep into the current of a river. The waves refused to let him go, the surface getting farther away from him as he sank. His legs kicked and his arms flailed in a panic. His mind raced. Jaxon reached out with his hands, his mind, willing himself to the surface.

A white light bloomed around him.

The water in his eyes and ears vanished and Jaxon found himself inside of a strange white room.

In the center, a woman was being attacked. He couldn't make out her face, but the bright red hair was a dead giveaway. Akeema was being beaten. Jaxon reached out to touch her. He couldn't. He tried to say something, to tell her to hold on. He couldn't hear his own words. He wanted the moment to last longer, but the lack of oxygen to his brain pulled him back into the water.

When Jaxon's eyes focused, the surface of the water rushed up at him. He burst through it and landed slumped on the muddy soil of the river bank. He vomited water. He'd never swam before, but he'd been given the memories of someone who had. He'd reached into those memories and his muscles took over.

Jaxon rolled onto his back, sucking in the cold night air as he looked up at the sky. It was lit up by the planet's sparkling rings streaking through it like a stripe of stars, similar to moonlight, except for a dome-shaped patch of black created by the planet's shadow creeping in from the East. It was beautiful. He sat up and looked around. There was no sight of the cathedral's spire above the trees. The current had carried him further than he realized. The height of the waterfall was too tall to scale. There was no way he could've survived the fall.

But he had.

It frightened him.

Jaxon's left arm hurt. He'd hit a rock on the way down. It bled, but he could still move it without much pain. Fatigue had set in. It wasn't a surprise. He'd used his new tuning powers on pure reflex. It saved his life, but it drained him almost to immobility. He was hungry and the water tasted like prunes. Staying put wasn't going to solve anything.

He felt for his handheld and remembered he'd lost it in the conflict. *The plan*, he thought. The one he'd made with Betty. Jaxon pulled off his left boot and dug into his wet sock. He found the small transmitter he'd hidden. It wouldn't activate. The water may have killed it.

Jaxon rose to his feet, dizzy. He stumbled into the surrounding yellow forest. It was a concert of strange animal sounds and insects making their nighttime noises. He shook the water out of the transmitter and blew on it hard, airing it out as best he could before activating it. Static. He tried again. More static. This continued for several minutes.

"Who is this?" Yoko's distorted voice said over the transmitter.

"I need help," Jaxon said with what little energy he had left.

"Hoo-mon? How did you get this frequency?"

"Betty." There was a pause. "I am going to have a strongly worded conversation with my mecha once we are safely away from this place." Yoko said.

Jaxon imagined her scolding Betty for giving him one of their personal communicators. "Please. I need your help." The stinging pain of his injuries made talking difficult.

"Not my problem hoo-mon. Your cultists offered to pay off my bounty plus twenty thousand cubits if I left the system immediately. The casinos on Giannis are calling my name."

"They tried to kill me. I'm hurt. If you don't help me, I'm going to die." A pause.

"I already risked saving you once, hoo-mon. Remember? We're even. I owe you nothing."

"I saved you twice. First from Uthay's thugs on Giannis then again on Montanari, so technically you still owe me one."

"No," Yoko said. "Giannis shouldn't count, that was mostly your fault. Besides, I saved you when you were dying from a heart attack on my ship, remember? I gave you those gravity meds. Then we saved you after the prison ship. You'd be dead twice over if not for me."

"Betty gave me those meds and she restarted my heart."

"On *my* order."

"But technically she saved me, not you."

"Yeah, well, me and her are a packaged deal, hoo-mon. I'm already in orbit and I'm not coming back down there to save you. I've never risked my ship or my money for anyone, and I'm certainly not about to break that habit for you." The communicator screeched and cut out.

Jaxon tried to call her back. It was dead. "Shit."

He picked a direction. Jaxon trudged through the forest of satin trees and golden leaves, but he was wet and cold and the ground was uneven. The trek sapped away his energy, but he persevered. He didn't know where he was going or how far it was, only that if he stopped, he wouldn't be able to get going again.

Something up in the trees moved.

Jaxon caught glimpses of a shape out of the corner of his eye. It was tracking him. It wasn't an animal. Verlain dropped down behind him, an extended crossglaive in each hand. Both weapons had a curved scimitar-style blade that lit up the darkness like torches. The harsh light cast ugly shadows on her scowling face.

"Found you," she said, smirking.

Jaxon pushed himself to evade the glowing blades swinging at him. Her blades sliced clean through trees. They toppled over. Jaxon narrowly dodged them. The small Tzipkan leapt over the trees and pressed her attack.

"We don't have to do this," Jaxon said, talking fast enough his words blended together. "I'm no threat to you."

"Then you will die quickly," she said.

Jaxon ducked around more trees. Her movements were nimble and acrobatic as her twin blades sliced the trees down, creating a small clearing of stumps.

Every direction Jaxon fled, she appeared in front of him. One of her kicks found Jaxon's chest and his back hit the dirt. The thin woman lunged at him, her burning hot blades aimed to strike the killing blow. Jaxon's hands shot up in front of him in defense. On fear and pure instinct, he tuned a burst of energy that yanked the woman backwards and sent her crashing into a tree.

It staggered her, but she recovered quickly. "Nice trick," she said, then spit blood.

"There's more where that came from," Jaxon said. She wasn't convinced. Jaxon attempted to repeat his miracle. Nothing happened. Verlain rushed at him with a ferocity he'd never seen outside of a wild animal.

Again he tried to tune. Again nothing happened.

"Shit!" Jaxon said. Then she was on him.

This time, something was different.

Time slowed down for Jaxon. Leaves fell down in slow motion. Verlain's attacks came with a lag, allowing Jaxon to avoid her energy swords. This delay couldn't last forever. One of her swords burned Jaxon's arm and jolted time back to normal speed.

He cried out and crumpled to the ground, clutching his bleeding scorched flesh. He crawled, trying to back out of Verlain's kill zone. She came too fast. Jaxon tossed a handful of dirt at her face. She deflected. Nothing he could do could stop her advance.

Neither of them had heard the roar of the engine pods approaching. Floodlights from overhead blinded them both.

The nose of the *Saragos* lowered down from the sky, its main gun turrets spinning, then firing. The muzzle flashes were large bulbs of flame that spotted Jaxon's vision. The high impact rounds shredded Verlain's body in a spray of red mist and chunks of flesh that painted the ground crimson.

Jaxon heaved gulps of oxygen, exhausted from the fight and the trial and error of tuning. The ship's floodlights swiveled and found him.

Yoko's voiced boomed over a loudspeaker, "This means *you* owe *me* one, hoo-mon!"

***

The *Saragos* hung above the planet in high orbit under thrust gravity.

Yoko deactivated the ship's transponder, giving them a relative blanket of invisibility. Jaxon sat in the galley while Betty treated his injuries. Yoko was busy playing with Verlain's twin crossglaive swords. She'd taken them as trophies, swinging the energy blades around like toys.

"I'm keeping these," Yoko said with a gleeful smile.

Betty stared at her. Jaxon interpreted it as disapproval. "Yoko," Betty began, "there is a seventy-nine percent chance you will unintentionally kill yourself if you continue to handle those weapons —" Yoko lost her grip on one of the swords mid-swing and dropped it. The blade sheared off a corner of the metal dining table Jaxon and Betty were sitting at before the hilt slapped the floor and deactivated.

"Ninety-seven percent," Betty reported.

Yoko's face scrunched. She collapsed the other sword and carefully placed the hilt on the cut table. "Guns are better anyway," she snorted.

"Thank you for saving me," Jaxon said.

"It's becoming an unprofitable habit," she frowned.

"Do I have Betty to thank for changing your mind?"

"No," Betty said. "Yoko decided on her own—"

"Because I am a fool," Yoko cut in. "Why would your own people try to kill you? I thought all you religious fanatics stuck together?"

Jaxon turned to face Betty. "Did you get it?"

"Get what?" Yoko asked, her caterpillars hiked in confusion. On a display, Betty pulled up a video feed of Jaxon and Sabrene's conversation. Yoko crossed her arms. "What is this?"

"A confession," Jaxon said. "Betty helped me rig my handheld to stream a recording to the *Saragos*. I gambled Sabrene would be arrogant enough to confess her crimes to me." Jaxon watched the video in its entirety to make sure the audio was clear.

"Wait, she *skinned* a Thurlbii?" Yoko said while crinkling her nose. "Like, with her bare hands? What did she do with the rest of it? Did... did she *eat* it?"

"I didn't ask," Jaxon said.

"Well, I would have," Yoko said, then tilted her head and nodded. "I bet she did. It's going to take hours until I can drink that image out of my head. What are you planning to do with this recording?"

Jaxon didn't answer. He'd already proceeded to post it publicly over the wireless network where trillions of people across the known worlds would see it.

Yoko tensed with anger. "They're going to trace that to me!"

"I encrypted the transmission," Betty said. "It will not lead back to us."

"The cultists will know," Yoko said. "Now I'll have them *and* Uthay on my ass."

"I'll take care of the Kaijen," Jaxon said.

Yoko's hands grabbed her hips. "Oh? How exactly? That little Tzipkan tramp with the stupid hair almost cut you in half. How do you plan to take on a whole army of angry sexless cultists all by yourself? As well as rescue your friends? How does that not end with you getting all kinds of dead?"

Jaxon paused, then sighed. "You're right. I can't do it alone."

"I'm always right, hoo-mon," she added. "It's about time you realized that."

Jaxon began to send a transmission request. He took a moment to think, trying to focus his mind on the information Sabrene had nearly killed him for. The numbers revealed themselves in his head like decoded hieroglyphs. He sent the connection request.

Yoko's eyes probed Jaxon, her thick eyebrows shooting up her wide forehead when she put the pieces together. "Oh. I see. You're going to get the tattooed hoo-mon to do your dirty work."

"Does that make me a bad person?"

"Hell no. It's brilliant. Getting two enemies to kill each other? I didn't think you had it in you, hoo-mon. But he is a crazy one. I'd trust him about as far as I could throw him."

"I have his memories in my head. He'll do this because he has to. Neither of us has a choice."

Betty stepped away for a moment and returned with Jaxon's rocket boots. "Jaxon. I have repaired these for you."

Yoko's eyeballs almost bugged out of their sockets. "You *what*? Not for free you didn't. That will be two hundred cubits, hoo-mon."

Jaxon slipped the boots on. They looked even better than before. "Thank you, Betty," he said, then hugged her. Betty just stood there awkwardly until Yoko separated them.

"Hey, hey, hey, she's not that kind of girl, hoo-mon," Yoko said. Jaxon laughed. Yoko's protectiveness of her mecha was amusing as much as it was endearing. He couldn't blame her. Betty was unlike any mecha he'd ever encountered. She wasn't an object. She was a person. He'd be dead twice over if she were just another machine. He owed her as much as he owed Yoko.

Twenty minutes passed before Jaxon's transmission request was accepted. Martel's face appeared on the video screen. The estimated delay was around thirty seconds. That meant Jaxon would have time to carefully choose his words.

"Uh... hi," Jaxon said. Pause.

"If you're calling me, you must really be desperate," Martel said. "I've seen your exposé video. It's all over the wireless. They're just going to bury it, you know. Flushed down the memory hole."

"Sabrene has Castor and Akeema. You're going to help me get them back." Pause.

"What are you offering?" Martel replied.

"This is your fault!" Jaxon screamed at the small rectangular screen. "I'm in this shit because of you! Did you know they tapped our handhelds?" Pause. Martel's expression shifted.

"Of course I knew. How do you think I was able to gather so much intel on the Kaijen? Or on you?"

Jaxon slammed his palm on the table. "You should have warned us!" Pause.

Martel rolled his eyes. "Yeah, because you would've listened to me, right? You would've believed the crazy xenophobic speciesist rapist terrorist who killed your beloved mentor, right?" His point was made.

"Fine," Jaxon relented. "You wanted me to understand your perspective? Well now I do. You want payback? You want to take down the Kaijen? Burn it all to the ground? Well, that makes two of us. Are you interested or not?"

***

Three hours passed before the *Jezebel* dropped out of slipstream. Its braking burn lasted for another hour and change before it was able to rendezvous with the *Saragos* beyond the planet's rings. The *Jezebel*'s docking bridge accordioned out of the ship and hugged the *Saragos*'s external airlock with a secure seal.

Martel crossed the docking bridge and entered the ship. Yoko greeted him, wielding handguns akimbo aimed at his face. Jaxon stood next to her, close enough to smell the alcohol on her breath. His hand hovered near one of Verlain's crossglaive hilts hanging from his belt. Nervousness tingled his fingertips.

"Such a warm welcome," Martel smirked.

"You threw me off a building," Yoko said, staring at him down the sights of her guns.

Martel's smirk broadened. "You tried to kill me first, sweetheart. Jaxon, control your woman."

Two quick steps and Yoko had both gun barrels pressed against Martel's cheek. "From this distance I can't miss."

Martel didn't flinch. "You are adorable."

Jaxon gently pulled Yoko back. "Enough. And Yoko's not my woman. She's my friend." Yoko's gaze shifted to Jaxon, his words having softened her. She slid her weapons back into their holsters. "We're not here to fight," Jaxon went on. "We're here to make nice and shake hands. We need to form an alliance."

Martel chuckled. "See?" he said over his shoulder. "Didn't I tell you he would be on our side?"

Jaxon looked past him and saw Olen crossing the docking bridge, the foot of her cane clicking against the metal decking as she shuffled onto the ship. Her gravity harness sagged and looked too large for her frail body. Her skin was dry and cracked like an old oil painting.

In Jaxon's vision she'd been young and beautiful. Now she could pass for the grandmother of that woman. Her serious eyes penetrated deep into his and a meek smile split her withered face.

"It's always so strange," Olen said in her raspy voice, "meeting someone you've seen only in your dreams."

"Olen," Jaxon stammered. "You're not what I expected. Sabrene said you were—"

"An evil galactic bigot?"

Jaxon let out a quiet laugh. "More or less."

Olen sat on a bench molded into the wall with a heavy groan. She didn't have the strength to stand for long periods. "That's what the Kaijen do. Bigot. Speciesist. Obstructionist. These are words they use to discredit us. To associate those who oppose them with words and groups that already have a bad smell. They accuse others of what they are guilty of."

Jaxon sat on a bench opposite her. "You mean you don't do that too? You're just perfect?"

"Hardly," she exhaled. "I wear my flaws on my body. I believed, foolishly, that if I could just present a good argument, I could change the Kaijen culture with words. But the elders would just change the meaning of the words, and in doing so they manipulate those of us who must use the words."

"I don't understand," Jaxon said.

"You're not supposed to," Olen said. "That's the point. Words are the bludgeon they use to maintain control. The Kaijen don't care about right or wrong. Only power. I realized this too late and it got everyone I cared about slaughtered."

Jaxon leaned forward. He wanted to get a closer look at the woman, to examine this person whose legend was almost mythical. She seemed harmless.

"Why did this all happen?" Jaxon asked.

"You saw my memories, didn't you?"

"But why would the elders go so far as to have us all sterilized? Sexual relationships were already forbidden. Why punish us in this way?"

Olen managed a labored sigh. "It's another form of maintaining control. The ability to destroy something, to kill something, is power. They've convinced themselves they're doing it for the welfare of the Kaijen, but that excuse has always been the alibi of tyrants. It's just another form of linguistic thuggery the elders have mastered."

"I don't care about ideological dogma," Jaxon said, cupping his hands. "Castor and Akeema are all that matter. But Sabrene... she's way too powerful for me to take down by myself. Tell me you can beat her."

Olen cocked her head, considering his words. "In my prime? I'd destroy her," she said, then tried to stretch her arthritic fingers. Her face twisted in discomfort "But now? I'd need a lot of help."

"That's where I come in," Martel said to Jaxon. "I can take Sabrene out. But what do you have to bring to the table? If we go after her she will be aiming for our necks. You're not prepared to defend yourself. And she will have no problem using her students as shields. Are you capable of taking their lives?"

"No," Jaxon said. "What if they're like me? Technically, the students are innocent. Maybe there's a chance we could change their minds. If they knew the truth, they might join our side."

Thunderous laughter crackled from Martel's mouth. "Are you serious? He's serious. Jaxon, I had to force a link with you because talking didn't do shit."

"You didn't exactly do a great job convincing me with your words."

"It doesn't matter," Martel said. "They'll use your words but not your dictionary. Logic and reason doesn't work with them. The Kaijen conditioning is too ingrained. They see themselves as angels and people like us as demons. Angels don't try to make peace with demons. They slay them."

Jaxon shifted in his seat. "And what's your solution?"

"There are no solutions, only trade-offs," Martel said.

"So, we should slay them first? How does that make you any different from them? We can't give up on the novice Kaijen." Jaxon's passion bled through his words. "We just need to get through to some of them. If there's the smallest chance I can change even one mind I could never bring myself to murder any of them. I'd rather die trying."

Martel flashed with anger. "Then you're just a sheep begging the wolf to eat you last."

"I'm not a sheep. I'm a man. Just one man."

"We could be an army."

"Three people aren't an army," Jaxon said. "The recording I made of Sabrene is out there. The public will see it. The news service will have to report on it."

Olen cleared phlegm from her throat. "The news service is a nest of liars and smear merchants. They will say anything to protect the Kaijen. Your exposé will be labeled a hoax and anyone who says differently will be censored. There's only one way to stop the Kaijen for good."

"You mean we have to kill them," Jaxon said bluntly.

"There's an old saying among our people," Martel said. "Evil triumphs when good men do nothing."

His words weighed on Jaxon. He didn't want to kill anyone. Even when he fought Sabrene, that was in self-defense. He wanted her to surrender, to face a trial. If what Olen had said was true, a trial wouldn't have meant justice. And Sabrene was far too powerful to be kept imprisoned forever.

"What's a scrote?" Jaxon asked without thinking.

Olen winced. "It's Iskaran slang. A derogatory term for males who are viewed as useless and insignificant. It's one of Sabrene's favorite go-to insults."

"Oh," Jaxon said. It shouldn't have bothered him so much. Sabrene wasn't exactly a paragon of respect or nobility. It bothered him all the same. Because maybe, he worried, there might be some truth there.

Martel crossed his arms. "So. What's it going to be?"

"We're not friends," Jaxon said. "We're barely allies. But once Akeema and Castor are both free and alive, I will help you to stop the Kaijen."

"To kill them," Martel affirmed. "You'll help us to kill them. I want to hear you say it. Speak the words."

"If I have to, then yes. But only if there's no other way."

"How are your tuning skills?" Olen asked. "By the looks of that shoulder it would seem that your technique is still amateur."

"They could be better," Jaxon admitted.

"Come here, I can show you," Olen said, her twisted hands reaching out to link with Jaxon. He backed away.

"No. Absolutely not. No way am I letting either of you in my head again."

"We're only as strong as our weakest link," Martel said. "That's you. Refusing our help puts us all in danger."

"He has a point hoo-mon," Yoko chimed in. "Your fighting skills are weak and pathetic. What's the big deal? Just do your little psychic link ritual and be done with it. Stop being a baby."

"You were right," Olen said to Martel. "She is adorable, isn't she?"

"You don't understand," Jaxon said to Yoko. "The first time I linked it nearly killed me. The second time I linked I tuned and had a seizure. There's no telling what another link will do to my brain."

"So you're saying your hoo-mon friends aren't worth the risk of your own personal safety?" Yoko said. "I didn't think you'd be such a hypocrite."

Her words stung. "That's not what I'm saying—"

"The annoying red haired one was ready to stab me in my throat if I didn't agree to rescue you from that prison ship. And the one with the metal hand? I watched the wind nearly sweep him away to his death when he repelled down to that transport to get you. You almost died on Giannis. You almost got your ass cut in half down on that planet if not for my fantastic aiming."

Jaxon frowned. "Are you going to get to the point or just take the long way around?"

"The point is, you can't defend yourself," Yoko said. "You're noble and you're brave, which are two horrible, horrible traits to have. Unless you possess the power to back them up. This old woman is offering you that power. But you hesitate. Why won't you just take it?"

"I never *wanted* power."

Yoko scoffed. "Try charging head first into a battle without it and see how well that works out for you." Jaxon pondered. The truth was always the hardest thing to hear. He thought back to his fight with Sabrene. She'd beaten him without so much as messing her hair.

"Are you willing to die to save them?" Yoko asked.

"Without question," Jaxon said.

"No one writes stories about the man with the biggest stick up his ass," Yoko said. "Go let the old woman put her hands on you."

Jaxon hesitated. The fear of linking continued to have a stranglehold over him. Olen stood up, meeting him half way, her arms held open. Jaxon knelt, the decking hard against his knees. Olen joined him and placed her hands on his head. Their foreheads touched. He stared into her tired eyes.

"I'm afraid," Jaxon said.

"That's good," Olen said. "That lets me know I'm probably not making the wrong choice here."

His eyes lowered in shame. "I'm not the right person for this. I'm not ready."

Olen's hands slid down to touch his face, bringing his eyes to meet hers again. She managed a wrinkled smile. "It's not that you fear the problem being in your hands. It's that you fear your hands are weak. They're not. That's what I believe. Try not to prove me wrong, okay?" Her hands returned to the sides of his head.

A brief moment of silence passed.

Jaxon's scalp began to tingle. His eyes went heavy and slid closed followed by the itching sensation of spiders crawled around inside his skull. He expected it to hurt, like it always had before.

They linked.

The pain never arrived.

Chapter Twenty-Three: Castor

Night reigned on the far side of Terezakis. Darkness consumed the Kaijen cathedral. The students had retired to the rooms to sleep hours ago. Castor was given guest quarters. He'd been forbidden to bunk with the female students and ordered to stay in his room until he was called for.

He lay in the dark on his pillowy mattress, unable to sleep. When his eyes closed, he saw Akeema's beaten and blooded face waiting for him.

Castor stared at the stone ceiling. He imagined Jaxon's waterlogged corpse rotting under the planet's ring light, a spiked lump forming in his chest. He tried to tell himself it was sorrow. It was guilt. He'd delivered his brother to his death and threw his sister to the wolves, her dried blood staining his mechanical hand. The ultimate symbol of his betrayal. The lump in his chest grew. It was as large as a cat. He flipped open his handheld looking for a distraction. Harsh light from its screen illuminated the dark room. He searched for current events and scrolled past a string of stories being discussed from all the various known worlds. He'd thumbed past countless stories about vapid celebrities or dull superficial topics when he found something that made every nerve in his body spark.

A controversial video circulated among the heavily trafficked social feeds. Based on stills and the description of the video, he could tell it was about Jaxon and Sabrene.

His heart skipped a beat.

He tried to watch the video. Paths to the original posting had all been deleted, but once something is posted to the wireless it exists forever. Someone, likely several someones, had copied and reposted the video. A few million people would see it before it was taken down. And then, another rebel would repost it and the process would repeat itself into perpetuity.

Castor refreshed the forums every few seconds, waiting for a new path to be posted. When it was, he pressed his flesh thumb onto the link hard enough he worried his handheld's screen would crack. The forbidden video was filmed at a low Dutch angle. Watching it was like seeing a piece of himself die in a fire.

Sabrene's words stabbed at his ears and his heart simultaneously and without quarter. He listened to her confession, about how she'd sent Jaxon to die on Giannis, how she butchered Olen and her followers, who weren't terrorists. She admitted to breaking the Kaijen code for her own selfish reasons.

He'd heard this straight from her own lips, and still his brain didn't want to believe it. He couldn't. Because if he did, it meant he'd been complicit. It meant he'd betrayed his friends and himself, for a lie. The devastation of that reality was too much for him to bear.

The part of the video that upset him the most was what it didn't show. The recording had cut out long before Castor had taken his fists to Akeema. He'd been spared the justice of being exposed to the known universe as being one of the monsters. The guilt sat on his shoulders like an ever-expanding weight. It threatened to crush him. He wanted it to. He welcomed it.

Castor watched the video one more time before the path was deleted. He needed to know what people were saying about it. How the official authoritative outlets were covering the information. The answer shocked him.

They weren't.

The majority of the Protectorate-approved newsfeeds were ignoring the video, and the ones that acknowledged its existence had dismissed the recording as a doctored hoax cooked up by radical anti-Kaijen extremists. Akeema had once shown him how to access the underground feeds. They were popular with the independent worlds, outlets he'd be convinced catered only to crazies and fringe conspiracy theorists.

Castor stumbled across a live broadcast from Nyala Gley, an independent journalist. She was a species Castor didn't recognize who could almost pass for human if not for her bright peach skin and vertical eye slits. Her dark hair was mostly hidden underneath a black knit hat and her clothes fit loose on her thin frame. She appeared to be broadcasting from a makeshift set that could easily be located in someone's basement or garage.

"We haven't been able to verify the source of the video," Nyala said in her nasal bleat of a voice. "But the speed at which this information is being buried is like nothing I've ever seen before. We've identified the Iskaran female in the video as Sabrene Efiran, a member of the Kaijen religion. A high-ranking priestess it seems."

Nyala quickly scrolled through information on a larger version of a handheld. "If that name sounds familiar this is the same person who met with the disgraced former Prime Minister Karoi of the planet Herekino shortly before he was impeached for unsubstantiated accusations of sexual misconduct. Karoi was publicly against allowing a Kaijen temple to be built on Herekino, but his replacement Prime Minister Amalric approved the construction as one of her first acts as Prime Minister—"

The feed died.

Posted comments from users continued to drip down the screen's side scroll; mostly people arguing about the validity of the video or how attractive Nyala was. Minutes passed and the broadcast came alive again.

"We're back. Apologies to my viewers," Nyala said. "My servers are being attacked. Someone really doesn't want anyone talking about this story. I'll try to keep the signal going as long as I can, but I have never seen this level of censorship in all my years of—"

The transmission died a second time. And it stayed dead.

Castor searched for another independent outlet. They were all down. Any media service not approved of by the Protectorate was silenced.

Only now did the official media outlets begin to talk about the video. Their focus was on Jaxon. By this point, they'd obtained footage of him on Montanari and used a particularly unflattering still image of him holding Akeema's rocket launcher to present Jaxon as a murderer, a terrorist, and a hater of non-humans.

Castor tuned into a Protectorate verified feed. Two commentators were sat in their comfy chairs in a professional looking studio in their immaculately applied makeup. They were telling the known universe that Jaxon came to Montanari to slaughter non-humans. That he illegally obtained the rocket launcher and used it to kill eighteen people, including six children. That he'd derailed the maglev train and killed another sixty people while doing so. This fiction was conveyed to the viewing public through poorly rendered animated re-creations that showed a sinister cartoon version of Jaxon zipping around Montanari in his rocket boots blowing up parts of the city.

"Vile! Absolutely disgusting!" the male commentator yelled into the camera with over exaggerated bluster. He was a heavy-set alien with a beard and horns for ears. His face was awash with manufactured outrage. "This monster crossed planetary sectors to obtain an explosive weapon to kill innocents! But what else should we have expected from a backwards planet like Montanari where everyone is allowed to openly carry a deadly weapon!"

Castor read the never-ending stream of comments submitted by viewers all across the Protectorate worlds that appeared under the broadcast, all of which agreed with the belligerent commentator. Most of the viewer comments were calling for Jaxon's death.

"I agree," the reporter's female co-anchor yelled in a high-pitched voice. She was from another species Castor hadn't seen before with a long neck, a fleshy beak, and a hooked nose. She was never not shouting. "The booster boots used to carry out these atrocities were made by Hujiwana Drives, one of the largest manufacturers of consumer technologies throughout the known worlds. Their spokesperson has condemned the attack and demanded that the Protectorate annex Montanari and impose weapon restrictions on them to prevent another massacre like this from ever happening again!"

Their animated recreation went on to depict Jaxon taking control of the prison transport with the support of the prisoners, then crashing it on Briar in a deliberate attempt to kill a school full of children. The same children Jaxon almost died to protect.

Every single word these people reported was utter bullshit. Castor knew this only because he'd actually been there. He wondered, had he not witnessed it first hand, would he have believed their bullshit? *How can they get away with just lying like this?* he thought, infuriated.

That was why the major news services waited until after the

independent outlets were suppressed before doing their reporting. That way, there was no one to question their version of the truth. It was masterful how confident they were in their lies. Either they were convinced their reporting was accurate or they simply didn't care. And with Jaxon dead and Akeema in custody, there was no one to say otherwise.

No one, except for Castor.

On the video, Sabrene revealed the secret that all of the Kaijen's handhelds were monitored, including his. He crushed the device inside the grip of his vetronium fingers and palm, the pieces spilling quietly onto the carpeted floor. A little puff of smoke came from the ruptured power cell.

Castor opened the room's door and crept out into the dark corridor without making a sound.

The windows were positioned high on the walls, the planet's ring light casting harsh shadows through them. The cathedral was a large hollow building, but beyond its towers it only had two main levels and a handful of rooms. If he were fast and careful and a little lucky, he could figure out where Akeema was being held and with a little more luck get her away from this place before anyone had realized they were gone, and hoped she'd forgive him.

There wasn't a plan beyond that.

Everyone inside of the cathedral was likely asleep, but Terezakis had a nineteen-hour daily rotation. The sun would be rising within the hour. Castor had until then to escape the cathedral with Akeema, or they never would.

He snaked his way down the stone hallways and found his way to the grand stairwell. On the second level, he wandered the corridors until he heard voices. Two novice Kaijen were talking. Castor was still too far away to make out their conversation. Artificial light from one of the branching corridors splashed into the connecting dark corridor Castor approached from. The voices got louder and clearer.

"She's a tough one," a husky female voice said. "I went at her for over an hour and she never begged for mercy. Not once. It was kind of impressive."

"It's the hair," said a different woman with a squeakier voice.

"Scarlet haired aliens thrive on pain. It's the evil in them."

Castor peaked his head around the lit corridor and saw the two women standing guard. Husky Voice was youngish with a thick muscular frame. She had the familiar neck gills and dull pink skin of a Herekin. Her eyes were locked on her handheld, her thumb constantly scrolling through whatever she was looking at. Squeaky Voice was a Batelaan. Her bio-luminescent skin allowed Castor to see inky clouds of glowing blue fluid pulsing and dancing just beneath her exposed skin.

"I think I can break her," Squeaky Voice said. She was holding a stun baton that looked like a cattle prod. "Give me ten minutes alone with her. She'll break." The churning fluid under her skin appeared to speed up or slow down depending on her inflections.

"Have you seen what the other human did? The one who tried to rape the priestess?" the husky Herekin asked, never looking up from her handheld. "He's a murderer. He massacred over two hundred innocent people before coming here to kill all of us."

"I heard it was over three hundred?" Squeaky Voice said. "They said he specifically targeted women and children. At least twenty pregnant women were killed."

"Fucking monster," Husky Voice said.

"At least we know he's dead."

"I wouldn't be so certain. Verlain hasn't been answering her handheld. It's been hours since her last check-in."

"You think he killed her?" the squeaky Batelaan said, feigning shock.

"Here's hoping," the husky Herekin chortled. "I never liked that bitch. If she's dead that means we might get the chance to kill that evil speciesist ourselves. I'd really make him suffer."

"I guess we'll just have to settle for the red-haired witch," the squeaky Batelaan said. She sparked her stun baton. "I'll shock the hatred right out of that traitor. She deserves everything she gets." The luminous blue fluid under her skin slushed around in excited waves.

"Just don't kill her," Husky Voice said.

The Batelaan shrugged and raised a sinister eyebrow. "Hey, accidents happen." She disappeared into the room where Castor assumed Akeema was being held.

Alone, the beefy Herekin woman continued to stare down at her handheld. Castor pressed his back into the wall to the point he thought he might phase through it. Slowly, silently, he inched towards the Herekin. Her stun baton hung from her waist. Without his crossglaive, he was vulnerable. If she were too fast or if he were too slow or too far away, they would sound the alarm and he would be killed.

Castor slinked closer to the stocky Herekin. She'd been so entranced by the images on her handheld she hadn't noticed Castor's advance until he was almost a body's length away from her.

She saw him and her eyes widened, her hand jumping at the handle of her baton faster than a cobra strike. Castor closed the gap between them in two quick steps, too fast for the woman to activate the baton. He balled his mechanical hand into a fist and buried it deep into her nose. He heard the crushing of bones as his fist drove them into the soft tissue inside her skull. Her face concaved, like she'd been struck with a thick mallet. Thin blood fountained out of the indent. Castor had hit her with enough force to drive the back of her head into the stone wall, fracturing it. Her body slid to the floor, leaving a streak of blood in its wake. Her smashed nose made a sick gurgling sound as she struggled to breathe. She slumped over, twitching for a moment, then went quiet and still.

Castor froze in place. His fist remained cocked, his metal knuckles slick with watery blood. It dripped down his arm and onto the floor from his elbow. Blood spotted his face and clothes. The impact of what he'd done staggered him. Killing her wasn't his intention. He just wanted to stop her.

He had. Permanently.

Castor stood over her lifeless corpse. It reminded him of Martel, how he'd cut down Saveon. Castor hadn't thought of her much since the monastery massacre. They weren't close, but they were friends. Comrades. And now Castor had joined the ranks of the man who'd killed her. The lump in his chest blossomed into a bubble of vomit that he could taste at the back of his throat. He held it back. Every second he wasted feeling sorry for himself was another second Akeema was being tortured.

He searched the woman's dead body hoping to find a crossglaive. She only had the baton. It would have to be enough.

Castor entered the sweltering white room. The stink of urine, feces and ballast overwhelmed his nostrils and stung his eyes. The lights inside were bright, but not blinding. Clusters of tiny stars pinpricked his vision. When they focused, he saw the Batelaan woman. She faced away from him, her blue fluids stirring excitedly under her skin as she shocked Akeema with her baton. The alien woman's lips were curled in a pompous grin. She was enjoying herself.

Akeema looked like death.

Her hair was a frazzled greasy mess. Bruises and welts scattered her body. Her eyes were tired and bloodshot. The apparatus strapped to her head preventing her from closing them was smeared with red. She seemed comatose. Castor feared he'd been too late.

Then her eyes darted to him. Her anger was still there, shining through her pain, having simmered to a boil. The Batelaan followed Akeema's eye-line. She turned and saw him. Castor stabbed at her with his baton. She moved fast, dodged, and countered. She drove her baton into his ribs, sending razors of electricity surging through his body. His muscles seized for a brief moment. He overcame it and grabbed the baton's shaft with his mechanical hand, crushing it.

They grappled.

Castor was larger, but she was nimble and skilled. She climbed Castor like a stepladder, wrapping her legs around his neck with her crotch in his face. She shifted her weight and they toppled to the warm floor with a hard thud. Her thighs squeezed Castor's throat tight, choking him.

Unfortunately for the Batelaan, Akeema was close enough to hook her ankle chains around the woman's neck in a similar fashion. Castor grabbed the Batelaan's leg with his vetronium hand and squeezed until she cried out. Her grip loosened with a stifled scream.

Castor coughed in the room's stale humid air. His face flushed, sweat beading his skin. He was defenseless, worried the Batelaan would break free of Akeema's grip and come at him again.

Akeema made sure that didn't happen.

The Batelaan was locked tight in her death grip. Akeema had no intention of letting her go. Not for anything. The alien woman clawed at the chains strangling her.

Castor heard the woman's neck snap with a violent crunch.

Even after her sloshing blue fluids lay calm and restless, Akeema didn't stop choking her. She stared into the alien woman's dead eyes until she was sure. A soundless moment passed, and something like terror, or perhaps a pang of regret, stirred in Akeema's irises. It mixed with her tears. Her heart looked to be ticking at her chest. She seemed entranced by the Batelaan's hollow expression.

Castor moved for Akeema, reaching for her with his mechanical hand. She flinched.

"It's alright," Castor said in a gentle tone. "I'm with you. I'm here for you. I'm here to help. Be mad at me later."

Akeema's chest expanded and contracted so fast Castor wasn't sure she'd heard him over her own breathing. There was a disturbed, feral smolder to her that unsettled him. The eyes staring back at him didn't belong to his sister. These were the eyes of a vengeful god capable of glassing the entire planet with a wrathful glare.

Castor removed the device pinning her eyes open. She closed them for a long moment. He undid her straitjacket and freed her arms.

Then he held her.

"I fucked up," Castor said. He wiped the muck from her face. "I should have listened to you."

"You hit me," Akeema said. Her throat was dry and hoarse.

"I… I killed someone."

"Then I guess that makes two of us. Is Jaxon with you?"

"Jaxon's dead, remember?" Castor said. He went to work on breaking Akeema's ankle chains with his mechanical hand.

"No," Akeema muttered. "I saw him. He's alive." Castor bent the ankle chains until they snapped off. Akeema kicked them away.

"If he isn't dead, he soon will be once the Protectorate finds him," Castor said. "His face is all over the news outlets."

"Then our plan worked," Akeema said. Her legs trembled as she stood. She bent over and grabbed the one working baton Castor had stolen. He held on to her so she wouldn't fall over.

"He published a video of Sabrene confessing to her crimes, but it's already been removed," Castor said. "Now everyone thinks Jaxon's a murderer and a terrorist. They'll be saying the same about us."

"Then let's not disappoint them," Akeema said.

She limped towards the door like a toddler learning to walk. Castor tried to guide her. She shrugged him away, insisting on moving under her own power. She took her baton to the room's floodlights and destroyed them, drenching her and Castor in darkness with only brief flashes from the shattered bulbs that sparked intermittently.

They entered the corridor, greeted by dim light. Castor stepped in a pool of runny blood from the alien woman he'd killed. Akeema glanced at the corpse, then at Castor, then stepped over the dead woman like discarded trash.

"We need weapons," Akeema whispered.

"We're in no position to fight," Castor said. "We have to run."

"Not before we burn this entire place to the fucking ground," Akeema said. "And everyone in it." Her words glowed with rage.

"I don't disagree, but you can barely stand. How are your eyes?"

"I can see just fine—" she said before stumbling into a wall. Again, Castor tried to help her. Again, she refused.

"Then what? Where would we go?" Castor said. "The drunken pilot left hours ago. We don't know anything about this planet."

"We can worry about that after," she said as her knees threatened to give way beneath her. Castor made a third attempt to help her.

This time she let him.

They moved through the cathedral together. Gradually, the dark hallways began to brighten. The sun was rising, and with it, their chances of being discovered. They made their way down the grand staircase, their footsteps making a cacophony of echoes that might as well have been church bells.

"They drugged me with a tuning blocker," Akeema said, her balance getting away from her.

"I'll carry you."

"I can make it."

They reached the extravagant main hall. Akeema made it

halfway across the hall before her knees failed her and she spilled onto the floor. Castor brought her to the hall's water fountain and forced her to drink. She struggled to keep her strained eyes open. Castor started to pick Akeema up and throw her over his shoulder when all of the hall's lights turned on at once.

A stampede of footsteps approached from all directions.

In seconds they were surrounded. More than a dozen crossglaive blades were drawn, raising the hall's temperature by several degrees. The glowing energy swords were angled to lance Castor and Akeema in an instant.

"I'm disappointed in you, Castor," Sabrene said. She emerged from the crowd, her imposing height dwarfing all of her students. Castor set Akeema down and drew his stun baton, ready to defend her to the death. "Oh, please," Sabrene scoffed. "You look ridiculous, child. I had such plans for you. Where did your devotion and loyalty go? I thought you believed in what we stood for?"

"I did," Castor said. "And then I saw Jaxon's video. You're a liar and a murderer and the proof is out there for everyone to see."

Sabrene's lips formed a thin smile. It felt like a threat. "Our algorithms flag any unfavorable information about the Kaijen as hate propaganda. It's already been removed. Anyone who talks about it is automatically censored. You've lost. You're all alone."

Castor tensed. He believed her, which meant they were fucked. He could drop the baton and beg for mercy. That didn't appeal to him. If it was his time to die, then it was better to do it standing instead of kneeling.

"Do you really think you can take us all on and win?" Sabrene asked.

"No," Castor chuckled. "But I might take a few of you with me." Sabrene's faced twisted in anger. Castor was convinced his defiance had rankled her more than an insult or an idle threat ever could have.

"Kill him," Sabrene ordered her students. "Take revenge for the two of your sisters he killed. Then bring me his head."

They all closed in on Castor like a tightening noose. Dozens of pairs of eyes in dozens of different shades and hues and sizes locked on to him, ready to kill. Their crossglaive swords were held high and primed to strike.

Castor welcomed them.

And then, something incredible happened.

Castor's blood throbbed loud in his ears too loud to hear the approaching roar outside of the cathedral. A ship's engine pods. Their growl vibrated the cathedral's windows as floodlights shined through them.

Half a second later, the beautiful stained glass tapestries were shredded by thunderous rapid gunfire. High velocity rounds tore through the crowd of sword wielding Kaijen in a storm of bullets and blood.

Chapter Twenty-Four: Yoko

The *Jezebel* had disembarked more than an hour ago. It had taken the old Asabi woman with it. Yoko was strapped in her pilot's chair putting the *Saragos* on approach for Terezakis from the cover of its rings, their bright shimmer hiding the ship's vector from anyone on the surface who might be watching for them.

On her screens, the planet's ring belt looked like a tidal wave of shimmering diamonds the size of small cities. She guided her ship through the floating chunks of rock, the gimbaled decks creaking and bucking as she threaded the tight cluster of smaller building-sized rocks that hovered between the larger chunks. Yoko promptly ignored the legion of proximity alarms yelling at her every few seconds. Even after she'd turned the alarms off, Yoko could still hear them going off in her head. It wasn't the thought of rocks denting her beautiful ship that worried her. It was the creeping realization that maybe she was beginning to regret her decision.

"Betty," she said, "I am beginning to regret my decision."

Betty's eyes blinked. She ran a few quick calculations on her co-pilot's console. "I have confirmed you have chosen the best course to mask our waste heat and minimize our detection."

"No Betty, I mean agreeing to help the hoo-mons. It's too risky. We could die. Or worse, the ship could get damaged. It's not worth it."

Betty turned to her. "But Yoko, it is the right thing to do."

Yoko rolled her eyes, exaggerating the gesture. "And when has doing the right thing *ever* been the right thing for *me*? This isn't even profitable! Those goofy robed cultists paid me a lot of cubits to abandon the hoo-mons. You think they're *not* going to renege on our deal and want a refund once they realized we've betrayed them? They'll probably take me to claims court. You know judges don't like me." Yoko tried to imagine a scenario where she could come out of this ordeal with the money she'd been promised. When she couldn't, it just made her angrier. "Foosha this! I'm getting us out of here."

Yoko began to adjust the ship's heading away from the planet.

Betty reached over and placed her hand on Yoko's, stopping her. "It is the right thing to do," Betty said.

Yoko stared deep into the glowing emerald irises that were Betty's photoreceptors. She couldn't detect any visible emotion there, yet she could feel Betty's empathy even though she knew in her bones how insane that was. She'd reprogrammed Betty. She knew all the incredible things her mecha was capable of. Emotion wasn't one of them. With the ship's proximity alarms off, Yoko didn't realize a small chunk of space rock had wandered into the ship's path. It scraped the hull with a nasty shriek that sounded expensive.

"Foosha," Yoko muttered. She refocused her attention on maintaining her flight path. "You're going to fix that," she said to Betty, who responded with blinks.

In Yoko's armrest holder sat a secured cup of bourbon next to a small bowl containing two live bokah. She'd been too stressed to eat them earlier. Yoko thumbed open the bowl's tethered lid, plucked one of the squirming creatures out of its flavoring broth, and tossed it into her mouth. It poked around at her teeth and cheeks until it wiggled down her throat the way she liked, then chased it with a gulp of the bourbon. Her stress melted away like butter on a skillet.

The cockpit door slid open and Jaxon entered. He'd collapsed after Olen linked with him, but didn't pass out. He'd spent the last half an hour or so resting. His disheveled hungover-look told Yoko he hadn't fully recovered.

Jaxon rubbed the back of his head. "What was that noise?"

"You look terrible," she said, ignoring his question.

"My head feels like someone stuffed it full of razor blades and shook it around for a few hours, but I'll be fine by the time we get there." Yoko grunted her response. Jaxon started to say something, but the words froze in his throat. His hand moved to rub the back of his neck while he searched for his words. "I... I wanted you to know that I really appreciate your help."

"Well, I *am* being compensated," Yoko said.

"Yeah, Martel told me. It would be out of character for you to do anything purely out of the kindness of your heart."

"Right," she nodded.

Jaxon's posture shifted. "But you still could have said no. I'm glad you didn't. I wouldn't have made it this far without you."

His words softened Yoko's smugness. She looked back over her shoulder, seeing the raw sincerity in his brown eyes. She had to look away to focus on her flying. "You're a revolutionary now. Your newfound disrespect for religious orthodoxy appeals to me. It's an acceptable risk."

Jaxon's face lit with surprise. He paused for a heartbeat. "We could have just as easily used Martel's ship instead."

"I don't trust him," Yoko whispered.

"But you trust me?"

Yoko snorted. "You flatter yourself, hoo-mon. I suppose that is to be expected, given you are now a notorious mass murderer."

Jaxon's eyes widened and his jaw went slack. It was the exact response Yoko had aimed for. "What are you talking about?" Jaxon said.

"Betty, tell the hoo-mon how many innocent civilians he has viciously killed."

"Yes Yoko," Betty said, then checked a newsfeed on one of her screens. "The death toll of the Montanari attack has been revised up to three thousand casualties."

Jaxon's eyes ballooned even wider. He checked the newsfeeds for himself, scrolling through dozens of media posts about the incident on Montanari. Yoko had already seen multiple images of Jaxon holding Akeema's rocket launcher.

"This is bullshit," Jaxon said, his voice a mix of anger and disbelief. "No one was killed. I didn't... I didn't do this!"

"Well, I know that," Yoko said, doing her best to stifle her amusement. "I'm just shocked at how ridiculous that death toll is. They didn't even try to make it sound even remotely realistic." Jaxon continued his frantic scroll through the feeds in a desperate attempt to find something, anything that had reported some semblance of the truth.

"Where's my video? No one's even talking about Sabrene's confession. I can't find it anywhere."

"They scrubbed it," Martel's called out from the galley. Yoko could see him on a small closed circuit security screen. "I warned you. You're not the first person to try and expose the Kaijen. Now they're busy controlling the narrative and making certain that everyone thinks *you're* the villain. All shaming and no forgiveness."

On the small screen, Yoko watched Martel make himself a drink. Over the comm system she said, "Are you drinking my booze?"

Martel flipped open his handheld and flicked his finger. Yoko received a transaction of seven hundred cubits.

"It's my booze now," Martel said, then drank his bulb of whiskey in one gulp. Then he swigged from the bottle. It was his, after all. He'd paid her enough money to buy two bottles. Martel returned his cup and the bottle to the secured pantry cabinet he'd gotten them from.

Jaxon hadn't stopped scrolling through the newsfeeds. His lips were pursed and his breathing had gotten fast and heavy. Yoko noticed her instruments had begun to move by themselves. The chairs shook and the walls groaned as the ship's hull began to warp. "Hey, hey, hey, hey, hey!" Yoko yelled at Jaxon, snapping him out of his anger. "No using your freaky magic powers on my ship. Get a grip."

"Listen to her," Martel said as he entered the cockpit and strapped himself into a harness on the passenger's couch. "Save it for Sabrene. Now strap yourself in." Jaxon tore himself away from the newsfeeds and buckled himself into the passenger's couch next to Martel. Turbulence slapped the *Saragos* as it reentered the planet's upper atmosphere, bathing the ship in fire.

It gave Yoko time to reflect. It bothered her, seeing the anguish and distress in the hoo-mon's young dark face. It unsettled her. She wasn't sure why. She'd started to get used to his kind smile and his unreasonable optimism. He didn't wear sadness well. "Did you really expect the government-controlled propaganda outlets to do fair and honest reporting?" The turbulence vibrated her body, making her voice hard to hear.

"I never had a reason to question the newsfeeds until now," Jaxon said, sullen. "I just don't understand it. The video is real. It's the truth. Why would the news outlets *lie*?"

Yoko snorted a laugh. "It is impressive how naive you are, hoo-mon. Truly. The news service has told more lies than there are stars in the sky. If a news story doesn't make the Protectorate look good or the independent worlds look bad then they simply ignore it." The planet's gravity pulled at Yoko. The ship's gimbals readjusted to their "train car" position.

"Listen to her," Martel said. "Whoever controls the media controls the message. If you can control the message, you can control the people. The media outlets are in bed with the Kaijen."

"But there have to be people who see through the lies," Jaxon said. "People who value the truth. Who value their freedom."

"Most people are free to do exactly what they are told," Yoko said as turbulence rattled the ship harder. "It was like that on my planet. They specialize in making the destruction of culture and economy look like progress."

"You keep talking like that and we're going to end up being best friends," Martel chuckled.

"It's funny how much people can have in common when they're not trying to kill each other," Yoko said. The turbulence smoothed out. The *Saragos* sailed through the sky just as the sun crested the horizon. Martel unstrapped himself from his couch and removed his gravity harness. Jaxon copied him. Martel left the cockpit and headed for the loading bay. Jaxon hung back.

"This plan of yours doesn't seem very smart," she said.

"We just need you to get in close enough for us to reach the cathedral on foot, then take off. Don't risk your ship."

"Oh, if you can count on anything it's that," Yoko assured him. "I just don't get why the old woman isn't going with you. Isn't she supposed to be some kind of super powerful witch or something?"

"She used to be," Jaxon said with melancholy. "She's not a fighter anymore. I think Martel sees her as being more valuable as a symbol. I imagine she'll be more useful in the battles to come as a leader and folk hero instead of a martyr. Besides, if everything goes the way we hope it will we shouldn't need her help. We're going in to rescue Akeema and Castor, not to take on an army of Kaijen."

"Does the tattooed hoo-mon know that?" Yoko asked in a way that sounded rhetorical.

"Jaxon," Betty said. "You may require these." She handed him a pair of her welding goggles.

Jaxon accepted them graciously. "Thank you. In case something goes wrong I just want you both to know this has been the best ship I've ever flown on."

"Be sure to leave a positive customer review," Yoko said. "Just don't use your real name." Jaxon smiled, but it didn't quite reach his eyes. Yoko wasn't sure if it was fatigue from linking or the newsfeeds still affecting him, or the anxiety from what he was about to do, or all of it.

"Be honest with me," Jaxon said. "Do you really think we can win this?"

A smile curled Yoko's lips, remembering. "It's not about who wins. It's about who loses the least. You just watch your ass down there, hoo-mon. You still owe me one. I can't collect if you're dead."

He nodded.

Then he was gone.

On a navigational display, the cathedral appeared. They were less than five minutes away. Yoko flew the ship in low just above the treetops, reducing the chances of tripping any detection systems until it was too late. If the Kaijen had any kind of hidden surface-to-air missile batteries tucked away somewhere in the area she wouldn't have time to evade.

On a different display, Yoko saw a live security feed of Jaxon and Martel in the cargo bay waiting to receive her go signal. Yoko's hand reached to turn on the ship's thermal scanners, but Betty had predicted the action and turned them on.

Yoko beamed with pride. "Did you know I was about to do that?"

"Yoko, you programmed me to anticipate your needs," Betty said.

"Remind me never to play cards with you," Yoko said. "Focus the thermal laser. Let's see if we can't find our missing hoo-mons." A thermal image of the cathedral appeared on Yoko's screen. The structure rotated ever so slightly as the ship rushed towards it, still several kilometers away.

A series of glowing amber blocks lit up the display; body heat from the beings scattered throughout the building. One amber blob glowed brighter than the others, and it was moving.

As the *Saragos* tracked closer to the cathedral, the thermal imaging became clearer. The bright amber blob wasn't one being, but two, moving together down what could only be stairs. Nearby in another part of the building, a mass of bodies were converging on the two blobs. And a few moments later, the blobs were surrounded in the main hall.

"Foosha," Yoko said. She tried to patch the feed into Jaxon's handheld. She received a connection error, then remembered he didn't have a handheld anymore. She patched the feed to Martel's handheld instead.

"Are you seeing this?" Yoko asked them over the ship's internal comms system. On the security feed display, Yoko watched Jaxon and Martel looking at the handheld.

"That's them," Jaxon announced. "It has to be." On the thermal display, the group of glowing blobs surrounding the Akeema and Castor blobs began to glow even brighter. It resembled a circle of orange and white candles.

"Those are crossglaive blades," Martel said fast. "They're going to kill them. We won't reach them in time."

Yoko skipped thinking and reacted.

Two taps, and the ship's forward point-defense gun turrets pushed out of the hull. Yoko fed more fuel to the engine pods. The acceleration pinned her to her seat as the *Saragos* bucked from the boost of speed. "Get ready, we're going in hot!" Yoko said over the comms. Betty's programming prevented her from intentionally harming organic lifeforms, even if Yoko was under direct threat of death. An antiquated holdover of the Mecha War. Yoko took control of the gun turrets and transferred flight control to Betty. "You fly, I'll shoot."

Yoko lowered the loading ramp in the cargo bay. On the display she watched the rushing wind whip around Jaxon and Martel as they waited for their opportunity to jump out. The *Saragos* was seconds from reaching the cathedral when Betty threw the engine pods into reverse in a hard-braking maneuver.

At their current distance, the thermal imaging was in high resolution. Betty put the ship into a hover just outside of the cathedral's western wall, the RCS thrusters having blasted a cloud of dust from the building's facade. Yoko targeted the crowd wielding the energy swords and opened fire.

The jackhammering sound of the gun turrets spitting hot metal rippled through the ship. Heat from her tracer rounds strobed on the thermal display, overwhelming it into whiteout. Yoko halted her gunfire long enough for the display to re-adjust.

It gave Jaxon an opening to swoop into the building on his rocket boots through the large shout-out windows. Martel jumped through a separate window after him. Missed rounds chewed away at the exterior stone and thick interior support columns, whipping up a fog of dust. Yoko's display showed the four hoo-mons regroup. After a moment they formed a defensive line.

Many of the glowing amber figures Yoko had shot weren't moving, their heat signatures cooling off. The ones she hadn't killed had taken cover behind the building's pockmarked support columns.

All except for the tallest figure, Sabrene.

There were more than a dozen glowing amber figures in other parts of the cathedral moving to converge on the main hall. The hoo-mons were about to be overwhelmed.

Yoko fired off more high impact rounds at the swarm of enemy Kaijen. To her disbelief, the bullets intended for the tall pink woman curved around her. On the infrared monitor, Yoko watched the woman's hand reach up towards the *Saragos* and the ship jerked, like they'd hit something. The hull whined and alarms blared.

That bitch is using her mind powers. That's cheating!

On the infrared, Yoko saw the hoo-mons attack Sabrene, disrupting the tall woman's telekinetic hold on the ship. The *Saragos* swayed with a grunt. One of the forward engine pods crashed into the cathedral, punching a chunk of stone off of the building. Betty regained control, using the RCS thrusters to stabilize the ship's hover.

Yoko noticed something on the infrared. Two glowing amber figures on a terrace high above the *Saragos*. The two Kaijen warriors leapt down and landed on the ship and their energy swords began cutting into the hull.

"Switch over!" Yoko barked. Betty gave her back flight control and Yoko wrenched the controls to port, forcing the ship to tilt sideways a full 90 degrees. The gimbals weren't designed to rotate laterally and stayed locked in place.

On external cameras, Yoko watched the Kaijen idiots attacking her ship holding on for their lives. One woman lost her footing and fell. She impacted the ground, bursting open like a garbage bag filled with chunky red vegetable soup.

Yoko switched to an alternate view of the hull. From this angle, she saw the one remaining Kaijen's feet dangling as she held on. Hanging from one hand, she used the crossglaive in her other hand to slice her way into the ship.

"Yoko, we have been boarded," Betty said. Yoko groaned. Her blood had pooled to one side of her body and disoriented her. She leveled the ship and the pressure inside her head relieved itself, but left her dizzy.

"Foosha," Yoko growled and turned to Betty. "Seal the cockpit."

Betty nodded, but it was already too late.

The intruder, a young bald Velibor girl with an angelic sweet face and slick pale geometric skin, had slashed the cockpit door open with her crossglaive. The girl barged in and saw Yoko and Betty. Her eyes dilated with surprise, as if she'd been expecting to find fanged monsters or undead ghouls instead of a Kish and her mecha.

The girl focused on Betty for half a second, given she was the target closest to the cockpit door. Satisfied she wasn't a threat, the girl's silvery eyes shifted to Yoko, having identified the real threat.

Yoko was strapped tight in her chair's harness. She couldn't pivot to defend herself. Terror shot through Yoko's spine as the Velibor girl raised her blazing crossglaive blade and moved to lance Yoko with a killing blow.

Betty stepped between them, and the blade melted through her.

"Betty!" Yoko screamed as the energy sword bored into Betty's chest and out through her back with a puff of heat and smoke, the blade's tip stopping just short of killing Yoko. "No! Stop!" Yoko cried. She clawed at the release catch for her harness straps in a panic.

The Velibor girl tried to pull her crossglaive free of Betty's mechanical frame, but Betty had clamped her hands around the girl's wrist, locking her in place to ensure she couldn't immediately harm Yoko. Even when the flaming hot sword began to set fire to her internal systems, Betty wouldn't let the Kaijen girl go. She was sacrificing herself to protect her owner, just as Yoko had programmed her to do. It seemed cruel now. Her fear for her own life shifted to her friend's.

Yoko cut her fingers escaping the safety harness of her pilot's chair and extended her right arm. With a flick of her wrist, she activated the apparatus attached to her arm underneath her jacket and a small pistol slid into her palm. The scary Velibor girl's eyes enlarged, her mouth agape when Yoko squared the gun's dwarfish barrel at her.

With her free hand, the terrified Kaijen girl made a desperate grab at Yoko. The gun let out a cute little pop sound that betrayed its deadliness. A tiny high impact bullet blew the young girl's hand apart, then the bullet continued forward, punching a larger hole through her pitted forehead and blowing the back of her skull to pieces. Little chunks of bone and tissue painted the cockpit ceiling and walls behind her.

The girl's body fell back onto the decking, taking Betty with it. The still active crossglaive continued to melt Betty's chassis into slag; her internal fluids sizzled and popped under the intense heat and the acrid smell of burning oil and synthetic flesh filled the small space.

Yoko wanted to stop it. She hoped that, if she acted quickly enough, there might still be a chance to save her friend. She stopped herself. The ship was vulnerable. If another *baizuo* Kaijen had decided to board the ship, or several *baizuo* Kaijen, she wouldn't be able to fight them off by herself. Then they'd both be dead, and Betty's sacrifice would have been for nothing.

So she chose.

Yoko grabbed the controls and flew the *Saragos* away into the horizon.

Chapter Twenty-Five: Jaxon

"Get ready, we're going in hot!" Yoko's voice boomed over the cargo bay's speakers.

Jaxon's heart beat faster than bird wings. His adrenaline pumped high enough he worried a blood vessel would burst. Jaxon gripped a handhold bolted to wall as the ship rocketed faster with a sudden burst of speed that nearly knocked him over. He glanced over at Martel. The bald man looked almost bored.

The cargo bay ramp lowered and a gust of wind barreled in. The golden treetops beyond the ramp rushed below this ship so quickly it looked like a yellow road. The *Saragos* accelerated faster. Ahead of them, the tiny image of the cathedral stood ominous in the distance. It slowly enlarged the closer the *Saragos* got to it.

"Are you ready?" Martel said over the churning wind.

"Yeah," Jaxon said.

"You don't look ready," Martel said.

Jaxon's stomach bubbled. He wished he had remembered to use the toilet before now.

"I'm scared," Jaxon said, almost too quiet for Martel to hear.

Martel clapped his hand on Jaxon's shoulder. "I'll keep you alive."

"It's not me I'm worried about," Jaxon said. "We're going to kill a lot of people just because they don't know any better. Castor and Akeema could already be dead."

"That's why we're doing this," Martel said. "To stop others from falling into the same trap."

"You think you're going to die," Jaxon said. Martel's head bent in confusion. "You drank," Jaxon continued. "You promised yourself you wouldn't do that. Not unless—"

"I'm going to live," Martel said. "I'm going to try. And if I don't? Make sure you do. Don't be a hero. Follow my lead. Protect my back. Don't lose your crossglaive. And for fucks sake, don't show these people mercy."

"Right," Jaxon swallowed. "Easy peasy squishy lemon."

Martel gave him an odd, perplexed look, then slapped him on the back. "Exactly," he said with a chuckle.

Jaxon's hands shook like a snake's rattle. Tremors spread to his legs. It got worse as the ever-enlarging cathedral came up at him like an oncoming train. He felt the vibration of the ship's engine pods rotate before the *Saragos* braked hard. They came to an abrupt stop outside the cathedral's walls, the sudden change in momentum almost launching Jaxon forward out of the hangar bay like a human-shaped torpedo. Had he not been clutching a handhold he might have been flung into the stone siding. RCS thrusters put them into a hover and the ship's point-defense gun turrets roared to life.

Jaxon covered his ears. The rounds punched softball-sized holes into the cathedral's walls and turned dozens of windows into raining shards. Clouds of pulverized stone spat dust into the air. Jaxon covered his mouth and nose and tried not to breathe it in.

When the shooting stopped, Jaxon's ears rang for the next few seconds and nausea clouded his senses. The ship maneuvered to put the cargo ramp as close to the building as it could without crashing into it.

Jaxon peered down at the blown-out windows. Through the haze of dust, he saw into the main hall. The novice Kaijen that hadn't been killed had taken cover behind the hall's numerous stone support columns, the high impact rounds having eaten huge chunks out of them.

Sabrene didn't hide. She stood her ground, her unmistakable pink skin and statuesque figure unmovable and defiant as the onslaught of bullets streaked around her. Jaxon's focus darted to Akeema splayed out on the floor near the grand water fountain and half conscious. Castor guarded her from the horde of Kaijen swinging what looked like a club.

Jaxon didn't wait for anyone's permission. Two taps on his wrist controller and his rocket boots lifted him out of the ship's cargo bay and lowered him into the danger zone. The morning sun at his back, he floated down into the cathedral's main hall and landed next to his friends. He drew his salvaged crossglaive hilt, its extended blade a glowing strip of flame.

Sabrene's face curdled, recognizing whose blade Jaxon was wielding and its implications. Her face went tight with anger as she deflected the barrage of munitions coming from the *Saragos*. It stopped her from unleashing her wrath on Jaxon, the continuous gunfire from the *Saragos* having kept her young soldiers pinned down. Castor dragged Akeema by her arms around to the opposite side of the water fountain to cover. "She needs help," he shouted over the deafening gunfire.

Jaxon came to his brother, ducking to avoid the tracers whizzing by overhead. Only now did Jaxon see the state of Akeema, covered in bruises and her eyes red and swollen. She looked dehydrated with thin black burn scars scattered across her skin. She stank like a public toilet. "What happened to her?" Jaxon said, outraged.

Castor couldn't hide his emotions, overwhelmed to see his brother was still alive. His face smoothed when Martel jumped down through the broken window, using his tuning powers to cushion his landing. He formed up next to Jaxon.

"She's been drugged with a tuning blocker," Castor yelled over the barrage of weapons fire, his suspicious glare fixed on Martel. "The fuck? Are you two best buddies now?"

"We don't have time for that petty shit," Martel said and pulled an injection needle from his inner pocket. He tossed it to Castor. "Give her that, it'll counteract the blocker and give her a boost. Do it quickly."

Castor scowled. He looked to Jaxon. The expression of concern and fear on Castor's face appeared louder than the *Saragos's* wailing guns.

"Do it," Jaxon urged him. Castor obeyed.

Akeema's eyes shot open and she inhaled deeply, like a resurrection. She sat up fast as if she'd just woken up from an adrenaline-fueled nightmare. Her eyes found Jaxon and stared in disbelief. Jaxon and Castor took an arm each and pulled Akeema to her feet.

The novice Kaijen came out from behind their support columns as reinforcements arrived from multiple entry points. Akeema looked to her two brothers, then at Martel with scorn, then returned to

Jaxon. Without a word, she expressed a hint of understanding. Her head snapped to a crossglaive dropped by one of the Kaijen warriors cut to pieces by the guns.

Tuning, Akeema held out her hand and the crossglaive hilt slung itself into her palm as if it had always belonged there. Vengeance radiated from her like heat from a fire. Jaxon handed Castor a crossglaive hilt, the other half of the pair he'd taken from Verlain. The four of them formed a defensive line and held their crossglaive blades in combat stances.

Over their heads, rounds from the *Saragos's* chattering guns continued their suppressing fire, destroying windows and support columns and keeping the small army of Kaijen from attacking. Only, Jaxon noticed the shots were missing Sabrene, her large pink hand extended out, reaching out with her powers and grabbed the *Saragos* in a telekinetic grip.

"Yoko," Jaxon said to no one. He moved towards Sabrene, but Martel stopped him. A small knife appeared in his hand and he threw it, guiding the blade with his tuning ability. He aimed for Sabrene's head. She shifted her focus and the blade froze in midair a nail's length from piercing her forehead. The act forced Sabrene to break her hold on the *Saragos* and the ship swayed, crashing into the cathedral's exterior like a wrecking ball. The impact vibrated the entire building, causing the already damaged support columns to shed chunks of stone.

The *Saragos* recovered, its RCS thrusters blowing gusts of warm air and dust through the destroyed windows.

Gravity brought the floating knife to the floor, joining the collection of debris, bodies, and blood. "This attack officially makes you all terrorists and failed assassins," Sabrene said.

"You're a mass murderer and now the whole galaxy knows it!" Jaxon yelled. He didn't sound nearly as intimidating as he'd expected.

A frown creased Sabrene's face. "I only regret not having added you to my number. The universe won't miss another speciesist."

"I don't think that word means what you think it means," Martel said. With the ship's guns silent, Sabrene's army of young Kaijen found their courage. They slinked from behind their hiding spots and gathered behind Sabrene, numbering close to thirty strong.

Sabrene forced a laugh. "Oh? I see four armed humans threatening a group of non-humans," she said, mostly to her group of young loyal soldiers. "These human speciesists are here to kill us because we're different. They hate our diversity."

Akeema stepped forward, her rage bleeding through in the redness of her face. "You tortured me, for *hours*, you evil pink bitch." Her words came out harsh and guttural.

"You see?" Sabrene gestured to her flock. "They hate us because of the color of our skin."

"No, you pink bitch," Akeema shouted over her. "We hate you because you're a liar and a self-righteous murderer."

Sabrene ignored her and spoke only to her flock of young shell-shocked soldiers. "There is no reasoning with these bigoted fanatics. They do not see us non-humans as people. They hate our very existence and seek to destroy us just like your dead sisters around you." Slowly, the army of frazzled Kaijen raised their crossglaive blades, ready to strike flesh. "These evildoers leave us no choice but to slay them, or they will slay us! Show no mercy. It was not we who chose violence, *they* did."

"You're goddamn right," Martel said.

And the battle was on.

The horde of women warriors came at the four humans in a rush of stomping feet and war cries. Sabrene hung back, letting the pawns go first. Jaxon found himself in the thick of the swarm, fighting for his life. Heat radiated from the blades like torchlight. It made him sweat. Time slowed for him like it had in the yellow forest. He could see each of the Kaijen's faces; a wide assortment of alien females awash with mixtures of fear, anger, and steely resolve. These women were confident that Jaxon and his team were the enemy, and that running them through with a super-heated energy sword was justice. It broke his heart that he had to hurt these people.

Admittedly, Jaxon knew he'd never been a great fighter. He trained as hard as his peers, but the skills never solidified in his mind or his muscles. Linking with Olen had changed that. Accessing her memories, her skills, wasn't something he could do on command. It was a reflex. An impulse. A storm of energy swords swung at him from all directions. He trusted his body and let instinct guide him.

A green skinned Chibak was nearest, her blade aiming to slash his torso. The way to kill her in a single blow flashed in Jaxon's mind, as well as how to disable her, but with greater risk to himself. He chose to take her hand instead of her life. The Chibak girl shrieked, her stump spurting a sparkle of crimson all over Jaxon's clothes.

Another Kaijen, this one a brown and white Misakian, moved to attack his flank. He dodged her blade's thrust, and brought his own blade down on her right leg, slicing it clean off. The coppery stink of blood and scorched flesh peppered the air. The next attack he parried, then slashed. Duck. Roll. Slash. Parry. Slash. The gruesome ballet continued with a few more Kaijen warriors before their desire to not be gored overrode their desire to attack and they hesitated. This gave Jaxon a moment to breathe. He looked to the shattered windows.

Something had happened to the *Saragos*.

The rickety ship had turned and lurched away, leaving a trail of smoke as it left his view. Jaxon's fears turned to Yoko. If she was able to retreat it meant she was likely okay. If she wasn't... he shoved that thought to the back of his mind and focused on what he could control.

Castor was near him. He'd adopted the same sense of restraint Jaxon had, opting to beat back or disable his attackers rather than execute them.

Akeema was not having any of that shit. Every Kaijen who entered the range of Akeema's crossglaive was killed. Whatever they had done to her in that light room from Jaxon's vision, Akeema was giving it back to them in spades. She didn't wait for them to attack her. She aggressively went after any Kaijen in her blade's reach. She was a brutal predator and she was collecting scalps.

Martel was laser focused. He left a string of severed limbs in his wake as he slashed his way towards Sabrene. His crossglaive scraped and sparked against the blades of the novice Kaijen protecting her. Martel blunted their assaults and cut them down with crude efficiency. At the end of the line of disposable young warriors was Sabrene, waiting. That familiar creepy smile of hers hung on her lips. Martel was an expert duelist; young, aggressive, and hungry for retribution. Jaxon had witnessed him defeat his mentor Priestess Nisame, the strongest being he'd ever known, in just a few moves.

His match with Sabrene wasn't as easy. Where Nisame was betrayed by hubris, Sabrene let Martel lead their battle. She countered every move he made with smooth, measured skill. It was a game to her. As if she'd been a dancer with weights attached to her legs, and now those weights had finally come off.

For the first time, Jaxon saw Martel sweat.

He moved faster than Jaxon's eyes could track, trying his best to lance Sabrene and failing.

It pleased her. Martel's thrusts slowed as he ran out of steam. She'd worn him out, waiting for the moment to strike. She could afford to. He couldn't. Martel was outclassed, and Jaxon suspected he knew as much.

A quick boost from his rocket boots and Jaxon could be at Martel's side in seconds.

The only thing stopping him were the writhing novice Kaijen on the floor, bleeding out. Their haunting moans and cries of pain chilled him. The women he'd dismembered would be dead soon if left untreated. There were an almost equal number of Kaijen warriors still standing, still a threat. The intact Kaijen grouped together, their faces a collage of terror and caution.

Castor stood by Jaxon, ready to face the group together. Akeema had just finished lancing a stray Kaijen outside of the group. She moved to vault into the group head-long. Jaxon blocked her path.

"Wait," he pleaded, then collapsed his crossglaive. "This is your one and only chance," Jaxon said to the surviving Kaijen. Their fear of death was palpable. "Take your wounded and leave immediately or you will all die where you stand." Akeema hadn't heard a word Jaxon said. She tried to push past him, but he held her back.

"Get the fuck out of my way," Akeema snarled.

"We're not monsters," Jaxon said. "I'm giving them a chance to retreat."

"They don't *deserve* a chance!" Akeema said, her hands and the hilt of her crossglaive dripping with blood.

Jaxon returned his attention to the novice Kaijen, some of them shaking to the point their crossglaive blades wobbled. "No one else has to die here. Take my offer and live before it's too late."

One of the Kaijen warriors, a Sidonan with light plum colored skin, spoke for the group. "You're the butcher of Montanari. We can't trust you. You'll just kill us."

Jaxon's face twisted, and it wasn't from the copper stink of blood or seared flesh stinging his nostrils. He was angry. He wanted to argue, to tell them all about how they'd been manipulated by Sabrene and the newsfeeds, but Jaxon knew, instantly, how futile that would be and how they'd just get themselves all killed. Telling the shell shocked young soldiers the truth wasn't going to save them from the slaughter.

In that moment, saving the lives of his enemies meant more to him than his reputation. If being a monster kept these women from meeting their end at the tip of Akeema's crossglaive, then a monster he would be.

"That's right," Jaxon said with a false confidence he prayed the group couldn't see through. "I *am* a butcher. A killer. None of you can beat me in a fight. If you try, I will kill you all, slowly, agonizingly, and without quarter." A wave of dread choked the naive gang of Kaijen. "But I'm trying to change. Killing you would be a waste of my time. So I am giving you the opportunity to take your wounded sisters and leave in that skiff parked outside, or you can make this your last day among the living."

The Kaijen hesitated. Jaxon could see them working over his offer in their heads, their eyes scanning and darting around at the carnage of bodies and limbs and pools of blood they were all standing in.

Then the Sidonan woman collapsed her crossglaive. She ripped off a strip of her tunic and knelt down to one of the maimed Kaijen warriors, wrapping a tourniquet around the bleeding woman's stump. The other standing Kaijen did the same, dropping their energy swords and helping their wounded comrades.

Jaxon, Akeema, and Castor stood by as the surviving Kaijen made their way down the hall's long entrance and exited through the cathedral's tall heavy doors, leaving a trail of multicolored blood behind them.

"You shouldn't have done that," Akeema said. "They could come back with reinforcements."

"They were just kids," Jaxon said. "Young and stupid kids who believed what they'd been told."

And then, with the clarity of someone who'd been deceived, Akeema understood. The burning rage and anger she'd been harboring like an open wound appeared to have scarred over and faded. The meanness and tension in her face relaxed. She exhaled like she'd been holding her breath. "Okay," she nodded.

"There's still one more," Castor said, drawing their attention to Sabrene battling Martel at the far side of the main hall.

From where he stood, Jaxon could tell Martel was losing. Sabrene continued to play with him, anticipating each of his moves like she'd already seen it happen. Martel's face was slick with sweat, each of his thrusts slower and weaker than the last.

"We have to help him," Jaxon said. Castor and Akeema exchanged looks. They weren't going to move. "We need him," Jaxon insisted. "We can't take Sabrene down without him. Without all of us, working together, as a team." His brother and sister weren't convinced.

Martel had gotten desperate. He resorted to cheap shots and frantic thrusts. Sabrene swirled her crossglaive and lunged at him, which he parried, creating an opening to run Sabrene through.

A trap. And he'd fallen into it.

With both hands on his crossglaive he stabbed at Sabrene's midsection, and missed. Sabrene swung her crossglaive in a blind upthrust behind her back meant to cut off Martel's arms. He released his left hand's grip on his crossglaive to avoid the dismemberment, but in doing so opened up his torso for attack and Sabrene's superheated blade slashed Martel's chest. He cried out, his voice echoing through the hall. The blade burned through his vest and into his skin. He lost his crossglaive and stumbled backward, his clothes having caught fire. Martel screamed in agony, working in a panicked frenzy to remove his vest, a glowing cargonite plate tucked inside of it hot enough to melt. It saved his life.

At least, for the moment.

Martel was in immense pain and completely defenseless. Sabrene's snake-like smile widened as she stalked after him, her blade angled for the killing blow. It came at him and Martel tuned, stopping the blade from slicing into his skull, but he was drained and couldn't keep the blazing metal at bay for long.

Two taps and Jaxon's rocket boots carried him across the large hall. His crossglaive intercepted Sabrene's blade just before Martel's tuning forced him to collapse in exhaustion. Jaxon and Sabrene's crossglaive blades grated against each other, spitting sparks that shot out like fireflies.

"Fools," Sabrene taunted. "I trained with Olen for *years*. You think I don't know all of her moves?" She swung and Jaxon ducked, narrowly avoiding a decapitation. Sabrene's height gave her too much reach.

Two taps and Jaxon's rocket boots hovered, putting him at Sabrene's eye level while they clashed swords. He read her expression as less amusement and more disgust. Hate. It came off of her like a bad smell.

Their blades locked and Sabrene's fist shot out at Jaxon like a thrown punch. She didn't hit him, but a shockwave of tuning energy did, like a brick wall. The blast threw him back and his vision streaked. A moment of chaos before his body ricocheted off a damaged stone column, pain rippling through this abdomen. Jaxon crumpled to the floor in a heap, the bodies of the fallen Kaijen cushioning the impact. Their blood smeared him.

Oxygen evacuated his lungs and they stalled, his muscles feeling like broken glass. Castor and Akeema leapt in to stop Sabrene from pressing her attack. Castor came at her from behind while Akeema went at her straight on. Sabrene's smile never left her lips. She was having too much fun. Her crossglaive whipped through the air like a propeller blade, keeping her attackers on the defensive.

Sabrene's long slender leg shot out and kicked Akeema in the stomach, putting her down. Sabrene swiveled and hit Castor with a tuning punch that catapulted him halfway across the hall. The tuning drained her, perhaps more than she'd expected.

Martel pulled himself to his feet. He bit back the pain of his scorched chest and recovered his crossglaive. Martel limped towards Sabrene, his back hunched and his confidence cut in half.

"It's a shame, really," Sabrene said slightly out of breath. "It's so rare that I get to practice my skills on an equal. Too bad that's not you."

"I'll take that as a compliment," Martel stammered, unable to hide the stress on his body.

"I wouldn't," Sabrene snarked. "There are four of you and you haven't even managed to mess my hair. I expected more from the disciples of Olen. You're little more than an interference. You're nothing."

"Show of hands," Martel said. "Which of us hasn't killed an unborn child in its mother's womb?" Martel raised his hand. Jaxon raised his. Akeema and Castor, who were still tender and bruised from their fight, raised theirs. "You see, you're not a nice person," Martel said. "You're a faker. You pretend and you manipulate and you use others to achieve power only for yourself under the guise of equality. You're a lunatic who's deluded herself into thinking she's morally superior to everybody else. You're just another tyrant."

Sabrene paused, considering his words. "That's exactly how I see you."

Martel began to levitate, and not of his own doing. The time they'd spent talking, Sabrene used to recharge. His body twisted and jerked against the unseen tuning energy constraining him.

Crushing him.

Jaxon could see what he had to do. He just had to find within himself the strength to do it. He forced himself to stand. His boots and wrist controller were busted. Sabrene stood several meters away, her back to him. He inhaled a deep breath and focused on the extraordinary feat he needed to achieve.

Then he took a literal leap of faith.

Jaxon launched himself across the room, his tuning power extending his jump further and higher than a normal human was capable of. He landed on Sabrene's back and straddled her. He hooked his right arm around her throat, choking her. Martel was released from Sabrene's telekinetic grip and he crashed to the bloody floor while sucking in air.

Sabrene struggled to shake Jaxon off of her or dislodge his choke hold. She failed. Her crossglaive stabbed at him, but it was too dangerous for both of them. Martel struck at Sabrene with his crossglaive, not expecting to land a hit, but to keep her distracted. If her focus was on him, it wasn't on Jaxon. He just had to wait her out and soon she'd die.

Akeema and Castor staggered to their feet and, much to Jaxon's surprise, backed up Martel.

And still Sabrene was able to fight off all three attackers, but the lack of oxygen drained her at an alarming rate. She backed away from the trio, her bright pink face turning dark blue. Her eyes started to bulge. She was drooling and gagging, desperate for air.

She dropped her crossglaive and knelt.

Her hands reached behind her head, onto Jaxon's. He never expected her to initiate a link.

Jaxon's world ended.

The space inside the cathedral's main hall washed away and Jaxon fell into darkness. A flash of images came rushing at him like the blinding headlights of a speeding train. He saw running. Killing. Something breaking. A kiss. Yelling. An explosion in space. Crying. Manic laughter. Red tentacles reaching out.

The connection ended.

Jaxon's mind returned to the cathedral's main hall. Only now, his brain was on fire. The experience was too intense of a shock to his system. His eyes clouded and rolled back into his head. His body seized and his grip on Sabrene's neck was gone, freeing her.

Chapter Twenty-Six: Akeema

Sabrene's kick had left Akeema's stomach empty and knotted like the rest of her beaten body. She swallowed her pain and watched with morbid jealousy as Jaxon slowly strangled the life out of the gangly pink bitch. The lack of oxygen turned her long smug face a lovely shade of blue. It filled Akeema with such a potent thrill of pleasure it bordered on being sexual.

Akeema's pleasure shifted to horror when Sabrene's large hands grabbed Jaxon's head. Their link only lasted a brief moment, two or three seconds, but the effects were immediate. Sabrene's body bent forward at the waist in a violent bow, flipping Jaxon off of her. She slammed Akeema's little brother onto the blood-slick floor with enough force to fracture the stone upon impact. Jaxon writhed and convulsed violently, as if he were being electrocuted. He curled up into a ball and went still. Akeema's chest tightened. She feared, this time, he may actually die.

Sabrene initiated the linked just to break free of his choke hold. Akeema had to give the bitch points for creativity.

"Jaxon!" Martel yelled. He shuffled to the younger man's side to revive him. "Can you hear me? Get up!"

Akeema questioned his sincerity. Seeing Martel as an ally made her skin crawl in at least eight different directions. She set the thought aside and focused on her hatred for Sabrene. The tall pink woman fell to her knees, hacking and coughing in air. Her pink hue had overtaken the oxygen deprived blue, but she was still unarmed. An opportunity.

Akeema barreled towards Sabrene with her crossglaive, but her aching and bruised body couldn't carry her fast enough. The crunch of pulverized sandstone under her feet announced her approach. It was all the early warning Sabrene needed; her eyes tracked Akeema coming. Her reaction was slow, but not slow enough.

Sabrene's long thin frame bent contortionist-style away from

Akeema's thrusting crossglaive, just barely dodging the blade, the tip slicing through a loose article of Sabrene's sari. The pink bitch was still weak and vulnerable. One good strike would end this. Akeema's ferocity blinded her, too determined to cut down the Iskaran. It caused her to underestimate the pink woman to where Akeema couldn't see what Sabrene was really doing.

Sabrene pulled at her sari where Akeema had cut it, ripping a strip of fabric free and twisted it into a thin rope. Akeema lunged and Sabrene hooked the fabric around the smaller woman's wrist like a handcuff. In one move she'd stolen Akeema's crossglaive from her. The blade flipped around and its searing hot tip was on course with Akeema's face, feeling the heat of death on her skin.

The blade froze, stopping just short of killing her.

Castor had grabbed the blade at its midpoint with his mechanical hand, saving her. His vetronium hand quickly absorbed the energy sword's heat and glowed amber. He bellowed a terrifying roar; the boiling metal having singed the living tissue connecting it to the rest of his body. Sabrene attempted to wrench the blade free, but he held on despite the pain. Castor's mechanical wrist twisted and the sword's blade snapped in two.

Sabrene's broken half of the crossglaive continued to emit heat and she drove it deep into Castor's gut.

A strange high-pitched scream escaped his throat. Then Akeema realized, it was actually *her* that had screamed. Castor cringed and pushed himself away, the broken blade leaving his body. Blood dumped out of the charred gash. It was bad. He tried to say something. The words never came. His knees buckled and he doubled over.

"Castor!" Akeema wailed. He didn't respond.

Sabrene stared down at her, a sick grin wrinkling her mouth. The broken crossglaive in her hand was cooling down, but still hot and steaming from Castor's blood. It filled the air with the stink of rust. The jagged metal came at her, angling to impale Akeema through her crooked nose. Once more her face avoided further disfigurement. Something, like a ghost, hugged her body, yanking her away from Sabrene's killing strike and across the messy stone floor.

It was Martel. The man who'd crippled her, who she'd vowed to kill, had tuned her out of death's jaws.

Sabrene stabbed down at Akeema. The ghostly hug jerked her away from the blade. Another strike followed another jerk, each tuning pull having drained Martel's energy. Sabrene's thrusts were relentless, each strike getting closer to landing a killing blow. Displaced air from Sabrene's strikes slapped Akeema's face.

The pink woman's attention shifted to Martel. She chucked her broken crossglaive at him javelin-style and the blade caught his arm, taking a chunk of flesh with it. Sabrene tuned the broken sword, whipping it around like a mace targeted at his neck. Martel bent backwards at the knees, ducking the twirling half-sword. It came around for another pass and his hand shot up into its path. Akeema expected the blade to lop it off at the wrist, instead he caught the hilt.

"Enough," Jaxon said, having covered somewhat. The forced link left his posture rigid. His knees trembled to the point a strong breeze might've tipped him over, but there was a confidence in his voice she hadn't heard before. The timid fear hiding behind her brother's eyes had been replaced with a steely resolve. Something about it unsettled her. "This has to stop."

"It will stop," Sabrene said, "once I've ended this insurrection by murdering you all. That's how this will end. You must see that."

"You have no idea how catastrophic of a mistake you made by linking with me," Jaxon said.

"Child," Sabrene's creepy smile said. "I gave you nothing. Only the bare minimum to establish the link."

"There's always some bleed-through," Jaxon said, mockingly. "A taste was all I needed. I know how you think now. What you fear. You're not better than us."

Her smile smoothed and the corners of her mouth sank. "But I *am*. I'm fucking better than you. *Much* better. Compared to me you're *garbage*. I'm the best of all the Kaijen." She spat the words. "*You're* the villains here. When I kill you and Olen I will have saved the known worlds from having to suffer your oppression."

"Believing you are the hero does not make you the hero," Akeema said as she lay helpless on the sticky floor.

Sabrene gestured to the bodies and severed limbs strewn around them. "Do heroes murder innocent women?"

"You're one to talk," Martel said. "At least these women were given the chance to defend themselves."

"What's done is done," Jaxon said. "What we do going forward is what matters. We can settle our differences with words, not violence." He tossed his broken crossglaive hilt away. His palms were open, showing how defenseless he was. "I don't think you're evil," Jaxon continued as he approached Sabrene. "It's not your fault. You were raised to believe certain things that warped your sense of morality, to see everyone around you as an oppressor. But that can change. *You* can change. You can end the bloodshed right now. We can work together to find a peaceful resolution."

Sabrene paused. Her shoulders loosened and the malice in her eyes appeared to dissipate and settle.

The thought of Jaxon reaching the murderous pink woman with words perplexed Akeema. It wasn't an option she'd have ever considered. Akeema held her breath. Her heart ticked in her chest like a klaxon. She found Castor lying among the debris, blood pooling underneath him.

If Sabrene conceded, Akeema wondered if there was still a chance he could be saved. Not that she thought it would happen. Sabrene confirmed her suspicions and squared her shoulders. "Did you offer Verlain the same peaceful resolution?" Jaxon's approach halted. "I loved her like my own kin," Sabrene said with a sting of fury. An abandoned crossglaive hilt flew into Sabrene's hand like lightning, its blade extending at the same time. "Heroes don't negotiate with speciesists," Sabrene said with the kind of smug arrogance that takes real practice and dedication to cultivate. "I'll make you a deal. I'll consider your offer if you can stop me from killing you."

She sprinted, her long legs reaching Jaxon in three quick strides. Her crossglaive swung for a fatal blow.

Then she stopped dead in her tracks.

No, not stopped. Not completely. Slowed down.

Jaxon was tuning. The strain on his mind and body had to be immense. He manifested a near-invisible barrier, a shimmer, that kept Sabrene from advancing, but it wasn't holding. She was moving through the barrier, but in slow motion. Jaxon's face warped in agony as he fought to keep her at bay. Sabrene pushed forward like an unstoppable force, picking up speed.

Martel brought his burned and wounded body next to Jaxon and tuned with him. Their powers combined and strengthen the shimmer barrier, growing and expanding.

And yet still, Sabrene advanced.

The tip of her crossglaive inched forward and pierced the veil of the tuning barrier; the sword's metal warped and melted away like an icicle in an inferno. She dropped it and switched to using her own tuning powers to push back against the barrier, the soles of Jaxon and Martel's boots sliding back against the blood-stained floor. Their attempt to hold the line was failing. Sabrene's power was overwhelming. The prolonged attempt to tune her back was killing the two men.

"Akeema!" Jaxon yelled over the noise and fury of the building energy. "Help us!"

Akeema scrambled. The pain of her spine stabbed sharper and brighter than the dozens of cuts and bruises she'd suffered over the last few hours. She stepped past Castor's body and joined the men, trying to force herself to tune with them.

Then nothing.

Tuning wasn't an exact science. Akeema hadn't had time to practice or experiment with her abilities since Jaxon linked with her on the *Saragos*. The only thing she'd learned in the brief sliver of time in between was emotion. Intense, horrible, torturous emotion. She'd locked it all away in the basement of her mind ever since she was a scared little girl with a dead mom. It was a place she vowed never to go again. Akeema dug down deep into the recesses of her mind and unlocked that memory, that old wound. It was like a cancer coming out of remission. A single image from her girlhood was all it took; the last time she saw her mother's face.

Akeema screamed. It was louder than a siren. Her lungs threatened to pop and take her larynx with them. A gargantuan wave of tuning power shot out of her and merged with Jaxon and Martel's, forming an umbrella of energy in front of them. The effect on her mind and body was punishing. The sharp buzz of tinnitus rang in her ears and her intestines felt as though they'd been tied tight around her kidneys. Her breasts ached like they were being sand blasted. Akeema, Jaxon, and Martel, as one, focused their telekinetic powers on Sabrene and the barrier of energy grew into a transparent ever-expanding wall of light.

And, even still, Sabrene's advance continued. She would not be defeated.

The longer this spectacle dragged on the more drained Akeema became. Her bones were weights inside her body. Her skin burned. Whatever amount of power the trio were throwing at her, Sabrene was throwing it back doubled. Veins all over the pink woman's body enlarged like worms under her skin; her nose bled and her eyes enlarged and hemorrhaged red.

In a way Akeema didn't understand, Sabrene took the bubble of built up telekinetic energy and shot it back at the trio with a thunderous clap. It ended in a colossal explosion that shockwaved out in all directions. The hall's grand water fountain disintegrated. Large spider cracks formed in the stone support columns and the ceiling and the walls, further compromising the structural integrity of the entire cathedral. The entire building shifted, threatening to buckle and crash down around them.

The concussive force of the blast sent everyone pinwheeling through the air like ragdolls. The hall fell silent. Only the rustling sound of loose stone in the crumbling ceiling and the fractured walls interrupted the quiet. Akeema remained conscious, but her body refused to move. Her muscle fibers tingled, right down to her nerve endings. Her limbs wouldn't respond. Jaxon and Martel weren't moving either, their eyes shut. Possibly alive, maybe dead. The only person who'd recovered from the melee was Sabrene. She was exhausted and fatigued, but she was the only one left standing.

Akeema's crossglaive hilt was within her reach. She attempted to tune it to her hand, but the weapon stayed put. She regained mobility of her hand and clawed at the weapon. Sabrene brought her foot down on Akeema's arm and her radius snapped. The pain was dull at first, then shot up her arm and spread through her abdomen. Akeema didn't have the will to scream. Her teeth clenched and she squeezed out tears.

Sabrene took the crossglaive, its extended blade vibrating with deadly intensity. The pink woman towered over her. Akeema imagined she was an insect just before it met the heel of a boot.

"Now," Sabrene said. "Where were we?" She raised her foot as high as she could, ready to stomp Akeema's throat.

"Don't!" a woman's raspy voice shouted. It came from across the hall, near the entrance. Sabrene turned towards it, and her entire demeanor changed. "Please," Olen said. She looked so much different than she had in the memories Akeema had been given. The old woman's feet dragged across the filthy marble floor in long scratchy strokes.

Sabrene's expression was curious, as if she were seeing a long-lost friend or a dead relative. Tears streaked her cheeks. "That was smart of you," Sabrene said, her voice cracking. "Sending your pawns in first. But did they drain me enough for you to beat me?"

"I'm not here to fight you," Olen said. Her smokers voice reverberated like an instrument. "I'm here to talk."

Sabrene spit a harsh laugh that didn't reach her eyes. "Would you believe me if I said I missed you?"

"I would. We were sisters. We loved each other. Which is why your betrayal cut so deep."

Sabrene flashed with a fury that almost leapt out of her face and across the room. She poked her long thin finger at the old silver-haired woman. "No, *you* betrayed *us*! The Kaijen gave you everything you could have ever wanted! We were your family! You were happy!"

"I wasn't. Because I wasn't free. I wanted the ability to choose. I wanted a family of my own."

"I, I, I," Sabrene mocked. "That's all you ever cared about. What about *us*? We were your people and you abandoned us. You always wanted more. You were always so selfish. And now your authoritarian revolution has finally died at my hands." She held the tip of her flaming crossglaive near Akeema's neck close enough to singe her pale skin.

Olen pulled the album from her clothes. "I'll destroy it," she said. Sabrene withdrew her crossglaive. Akeema had been holding her breath again. She exhaled.

"It's not too late for you," Sabrene said with forced sincerity.

"Return to us. Admit you were wrong and beg for our forgiveness and I promise that all will be forgiven."

Olen's eyes went flat. "You killed my son."

"No, you killed that parasite of yours the moment you chose to conceive it," Sabrene said. "I freed you from the tyranny of motherhood. You're welcome."

"That wasn't your choice to make!"

"You made it my choice when you betrayed your code," Sabrene said. "You thought you could just pick and choose which rules to follow with no consequences? Unlike you, I take my oath to preserve the Kaijen way seriously. Your movement fractured our society and risked civil war. If killing your bastard stopped just one loyal Kaijen from dying then I was right to do it."

Olen gestured to the hell of bodies littering the hall. "What do you call this?"

"This was the doing of your cultists," Sabrene said through her thin smile. It betrayed her tears. "Didn't you ever wonder why I turned on you? I saw this coming. You weren't the only one who saw glimpses of events before they happen. The day you linked with me I saw into your mind. The sea of red. I saw a cataclysmic event coming that would extinguish entire worlds. You were at the center of it."

"I saw that same vision. The war is coming, no matter what either of us does. But billions will be saved because of what I'm doing right in this very moment. Everyone in this room has a role to play in that outcome, even you."

Sabrene twitched, as if she suspected she were being tricked. "Even Akeema here?" she said. The cold dirty heel of Sabrene's shoe pressed against Akeema's neck, little fragments of dirt and shards of glass stuck to the shoe's underside cut into her skin. "Is this one vital to your *vision*?"

"Extremely," Olen said. Sabrene's foot choked Akeema, but her mind was caught on the old woman's words and their meaning.

Sabrene held out her empty palm. "If that were true then you would gladly trade her life for the album, wouldn't you?"

Olen inhaled, long and deep. Her eyes closed and her head shook. "We could have resolved our issues without violence. We could have reached a compromise."

"You can't compromise with a fire while it's burning you," Sabrene said, her voice thick with venom. Her outstretch palm morphed into a cupping motion and Olen shuddered. Sabrene was tuning.

Olen groaned, resisting. Pain gripped her. "Don't—" she grunted before her torso constricted in on itself.

"You kill it or it kills you," Sabrene continued as she squeezed the old woman's chest. Olen stopped fighting it. Or maybe she couldn't. Her head flung back and her face twisted in agony. The pressure of the telekinetic embrace increased. Sabrene closed her hand into a fist and all of the old woman's ribs shattered, her abdomen caving in like a crushed beer can.

Olen coughed blood and crumpled in a broken heap. The album fell from the defeated woman's hand and landed in a puddle of someone's sticky blood.

"I used to envy you so very much," Sabrene said with a tint of sorrow. "Now look at you. I've made you nothing more than a weak pathetic old fool. How small you've become."

Sabrene opened her fist. The album hovered up off the floor like a magic spell. She flicked her wrist and the album knifed its way towards her, then curved around the pink monster and sped past her. Confused, she swiveled to track the object, as did Akeema.

It went to Jaxon.

He'd stood up and the album slapped itself into his open palm like a baseball into a catcher's mitt. In his hand, the strange ethereal creepy as fuck little artifact vibrated with unreal energy. He'd activated it. Or it had activated him. Jaxon's eyes glowed. They were opaque red orbs that pulsed in unison with the album, as if it were possessing him.

Sabrene was afraid. "Give that to me," she growled like an impotent child whose parent wouldn't give her back her favorite toy.

Jaxon didn't react. Either he couldn't hear her or he simply didn't care. In his hand, the album opened up like a blossoming flower.

"Stop!" Sabrene mewed. She tried to tune the album out of his hand. Nothing happened. "You have no idea how dangerous it is. You'll destroy the entire planet!"

Jaxon continued not hearing her, entranced. His head looked

around from side to side, curious, as if he were tracking a slow-moving fly that wasn't there, or just something Akeema couldn't see. The album had taken him over. He was under its spell. Sabrene forgot about the woman under her foot and the pressure on Akeema's throat vanished, letting her breathe again.

"Give it to me!" Sabrene snapped. She sprinted towards Jaxon. He stood there, completely unaware of the tall woman charging at him.

Jaxon's wandering head suddenly locked into place, his blank eyes staring straight forward at Sabrene's long bony fingers reaching out for the album, then grabbing hold of it.

Something ignited, and Sabrene began screaming.

A red flame that wasn't a flame started at her hand and raced up her sari's sleeve. In less time than it took to blink, Sabrene was engulfed in fire.

Chapter Twenty-Seven: Jaxon

"I'll consider your offer if you can stop me from killing you," Sabrene said, then moved to impale Jaxon with her burning crossglaive.

Her speed was terrifying. It triggered Jaxon's fight or flight response. The energy rose up in him like the prelude to a sneeze and expelled itself through his hands, staving off Sabrene's attack. The energy was transparent at first, then gained an opaque hue. The effect on his body was grueling. This form of tuning carried with it the trauma of a bodily violation.

A new surge of pain racked his flesh the moment Martel joined him. He cried out for Akeema's help, and then she too joined him.

In ways Jaxon felt more than understood, the three of them were connected mentally. Not like a link. A link was more of a hardline connection. This was closer to wireless fidelity, except less of a mental violation and more physical torture.

Their pain became his. The sting of Martel's seared chest and slashed arm became his. A wave of needles stinging his spine that had to come from Akeema. And something weird was going on with his nipples. His testicles were two swollen globes of infinite misery. That pain was his own.

In spite of it all, a sense of calm flooded Jaxon's mind. Sharing their individual tuning abilities caused a contrary blend of intense agony and what could be interpreted to be pleasure, all combined and focused on ending Sabrene. For a brief stretch of time, Jaxon thought it was working. A deafening roar escaped his throat and his lungs poked painfully into his ribs. He'd hoped Sabrene would back down before the act drained them of energy.

She wouldn't.

Sabrene's advance continued like a slow-moving bullet. There was no stopping her, no evading her. Sabrene met his gaze and her eyes bored into his as if she were a hungry demon eager to devour his soul. She was winning.

Like a flipped switch Jaxon's entire world stopped. Every atom of it came apart and blew up in his face. The energy bubble had burst. It threw him back, followed by a moment of weightlessness before his mind sank into the black. Time dilated.

When Jaxon recovered, he was light-headed and bone-weary. The room spun around him. His vision focused on Akeema lying defenseless on the stone floor, her arm broken and Sabrene's foot pressed against her neck. It should've registered to him as alarming. Instead, it all felt so familiar. Like seeing a clip from an old video he'd watched once years ago.

Olen had arrived, adding to his confusion. She was supposed to be on the *Jezebel* remotely accessing the cathedral's mainframe, not here putting herself in the fray. She'd distracted Sabrene. Jaxon could hear their voices, but their words sounded like clicks and gibberish. His subdermal translators had dislodged themselves during the conflict. He rubbed his temples and jabbed his palms into his ears like a plunger unclogging a sink until he heard a pop. The devices under his skin slid back into place.

"You can't compromise with a fire while it's burning you," Sabrene said, followed by a stifled, "Don't—" from Olen as the life squeezed out of her. "You kill it or it kills you," Sabrene said, then used her tuning power to pulverize Olen's abdomen.

He'd inherited Martel's feelings for her. Watching the old woman's body crumple to the floor was like watching Jaxon's own mother being killed in front of him. It also triggered something in his base memory, something buried deep that'd been wrenched open.

He'd seen this before.

The crumbling pillars. Akeema's position on the floor. Sabrene's outstretched hand. Olen's injury. The way the album rolled out of her twitching hand and came to rest atop the debris of the battle. Deja vu all over again, again.

Jaxon accessed the memories tied to that image. In his mind, he saw what would come next. Sabrene would bring the album to her hand, and then she would kill them. First would be Akeema, her throat crushed. Then Martel, stabbed through the head. Then Castor, who was still alive, would bleed out. Then she would tune Jaxon's head, crushing it like a watermelon. It was the same feeling as when he'd seen Martel's attack on the monastery. He knew it would come true.

Fear forced his reaction.

This vision will not come true.

The young man extended his hand palm up, as if he were trying to stop an oncoming vehicle. Every cell in his body seized and stretched like a trillion elastic bands made of flesh and blood. Each time he tuned it hurt him, like tearing open the stitches of a healing wound. His mind reached out and snatched the album at the same moment Sabrene had. Her skills were far more advanced than his, but she'd allowed herself to slack. People who were convinced they'd already won rarely pushed themselves harder than those who feared their impending death via crushed skull. The album represented all of their lives. He clung to it as such. The album sailed past Sabrene and landed in his grip. Stunned disbelief and betrayal registered on her long pink face, as if the object were a beloved dog running to greet a stranger instead of its rightful owner. Before Jaxon could decide what to do with the object, it decided for him. The album burned his palm like a lump of hot coal.

An instant of pain, and he'd been transported back inside the dark space, into the weird black void.

He panicked. While his mind was here, his body remained back in the cathedral, at Sabrene's mercy. She could be carving him up like a turkey and he wondered if he'd be able to feel it. His instinct was to let go of the album. It wouldn't let him. It had taken him over.

Something drew Jaxon's attention up at the sheet of black above him. Pinpricks of red light blossomed across the darkness like confetti. Jaxon searched for a pattern until he found one. He found several. The lights elongated like tentacles into lines, into branches. They reached out, making connections among each other. The amaranth vines pulsed electric like thousands of individual beacons, their rhythm resembling a heartbeat. As if they were alive. The album pulsed in unison. Jaxon could almost understand what it meant, the knowledge dangling on the edge of his mind like a massive logogram seconds away from translating itself.

The album jerked in his hand, forcing Jaxon's consciousness back to the present like waking from a dream. Back inside the cathedral's main hall, his vision was strange and warped. He registered Sabrene. She was charging at him, yelling and threatening, her scary pink hand lunging for the album. Knowing what she was capable of, he feared what terrible thing she'd do if he let her have it.

There was no more trying to talk. No more negotiation. Jaxon couldn't see past his fear of her. A single image sparked in his mind. Sparked, being the primary thought. The album blistered with heat in his palm. Sabrene laid her pink hand on it, and then she was screaming.

Fire consumed her.

Her sari and blue hair became a blur of smoke and flame. Her arms flailed helplessly as the roaring flames drowned out her voice. As this happened, she was tuning. Like a blind gunman, her powers lashed out in random directions, damaging or destroying anything in her vicinity.

In particular, the hall's floor-to-ceiling support pillars.

The building vibrated and shifted the way it would under a massive earthquake and the compromised stone pillars began to give. Sabrene stumbled into one of them, the force of her tuning powers collapsing it. Half of the pillar fell on top of her, starting a cascade of falling blocks of jagged rock and cargonite rebar. The ceiling and everything above it collapsed in on itself.

"Run! Everybody out!" Jaxon yelled. He looked down at the album still clutched in his hand. It had cooled and blackened like a spent match. He shoved it inside his pocket and ran to Akeema. She climbed to her feet, but her legs were debating whether or not they were going to buckle. Martel had already recovered and scooped Olen's broken body into his arms. He sprinted for the cathedral's large entry doors with her.

Jaxon helped Akeema navigate around the chunks of collapsing ceiling and pillars. They reached Castor, still lying face down and motionless.

"His he alive?" Akeema asked, her words barbed with anxiety.

Jaxon rolled Castor onto his back, his bionic hand pressed over his stab wound. The heated metal had partially cauterized it. Castor wouldn't wake, but his eyelids fluttered. Jaxon hooked the man's fleshy arm over his shoulder and carried him. Akeema moved under her own power, her legs still threatening to fold underneath her. They didn't. She cleared a path for them using her unbroken arm to tune away the heavy debris raining down on them. Her broken arm hung lifeless and mangled at her side, the snapped bone poking around underneath her bruised skin.

The five of them shuffled out of the cathedral as it disintegrated around them.

Martel and Olen escaped the cathedral first. Akeema, Castor, and Jaxon stumbled through the tall double doors just as a plume of dust and smoke shot out of the main entrance like gases from a fired gun.

They retreated a safe distance and watched the decadent building's two smaller towers collapse under their own weight, bringing down much of the entire structure. The main third tower tilted backwards in slow motion. It whined like a massive falling tree, tumbled a while, and crashed against the protruding rocks of the waterfall several hundred meters below. In minutes the cathedral had been reduced to rubble with only a few stray pillars sticking out of the ruins like jagged spikes.

Martel was preoccupied with Olen. She was alive, but barely. Her abdomen resembled a deflated balloon, her breathing shallow and labored. The *Jezebel* sat parked nearby where Olen had left it.

Martel used a small wrist communicator to summon his mecha. "Sel, Olen has suffered severe internal damage," Martel said into the device, tripping over his words. "Prep a medical pod for emergency stabilization."

Akeema ignored her broken arm and examined Castor. He remained unresponsive. "He's lost a lot of blood. If he doesn't get surgery he'll die."

"The closest safe planet has to be at least four hours away," Jaxon said.

"I have a spare medical pod on my ship," Martel said. "If my mecha can get him stabilized I have surgical mechas who can treat him at my base."

Akeema flashed red. "He's not going *anywhere* with you," she snapped.

"Then he'll die," Martel said flatly. "I saved you back there, remember? I thought we were friends now."

"If Castor dies our deal is off," Jaxon said.

"Then let me take him," Martel said. Akeema shot Jaxon a dirty look. He pretended not to notice and examined her broken arm. "I can fix that too," Martel said. Akeema's face reddened even more.

"Akeema, we don't have time," Jaxon said, anticipating her objection. "Hate Martel all you want, but let him heal you. I'm not asking you to forget what he did. But please. For Castor."

Akeema held on to her rage for longer than a heartbeat. Then her eyes softened. "I don't like this."

"I'm not asking you to," Jaxon said. Akeema considered, then nodded.

"Sel, prepare two pods," Martel said into his wrist communicator. "And bring an arm brace. Hurry."

The *Jezebel's* boarding ramp lowered. Martel's mecha arrived with two floating med pods in tow. Martel helped his mecha place Olen into the nearest pod. She wheezed, blood caking her lips and chin. Martel kissed her forehead before the pod sealed hermetically, freezing her in stasis.

Jaxon and Martel helped load Castor into the second pod. The mecha placed a mesh arm brace on Akeema that resembled an old opera glove with the fingers cut off; it shrank around her arm and set the snapped bone into place. She winced. Jaxon squeezed Castor's organic hand before Akeema placed her hand over top of theirs. Then the pod sealed, placing Castor in a stasis coma.

"Promise me he'll survive," Jaxon said. "I want your word."

"You have it," Martel said as his mecha treated his wounded arm and chest with sheets of healing mesh.

"We can't trust his word," Akeema snarled.

"I could have let Sabrene stab you in the face, but I didn't," Martel said. "And don't think I didn't notice how you and Castor sat back while I fought her. But I'm willing to set aside our grudges. Like it or not, Red, we're on the same team now. And your hands are just as bloody as mine. Bloodier, now."

Akeema glared, but held her tongue. Jaxon recognized the look, when her mind worked on a problem and couldn't find a better solution. "You're going to save him," she said. It sounded like a threat. It likely was.

Martel responded with a tilt of his chin. He signaled his mecha to ferry the pods aboard his ship. "Thank you for trusting me."

Jaxon waited until the pods were secured before he hugged Akeema, mindful not to disturb her healing arm. She still smelled awful. He didn't dare tell her. "Watch after him. I'll see you when I can." He broke away from them, heading into the surrounding forest.

"Where are you going?" Akeema called after him.

He pointed to a wisp of black smoke rising above the tree tops. "Yoko's ship was damaged. I have to make sure she's alright."

Akeema scowled. "Why? She doesn't like humans. She doesn't care about us. She's not our problem."

Jaxon stopped to face his sister. "She risked her life to save ours. We owe her. I owe her."

"Wait," Martel said and ran into his ship for a moment. He came back and jogged to Jaxon, handing him a custom handheld. "Take this. It should help."

Jaxon accepted the gift. He glanced over its default profile. "This account has over two million cubits in it. Where did this money come from?"

"Where do you think? I stole it," Martel said. "I back-doored my way into one of the Kaijen's private expense accounts. They've been unknowingly funding my entire operation."

"So what about me?" Akeema said. "Where do I go?"

"You're free to come with me," Jaxon said.

"I'm not leaving Castor alone with this narcissistic psychopath."

"You're right, he'll want to see a familiar face when he wakes up," Jaxon said. "You should be there when that happens."

"You know she's going to try and kill me, right?" Martel said.

"Oh, I'm not just going to *try*," Akeema said.

"You're not going to do *anything*," Jaxon said with an assertiveness that surprised himself as much as it had the others. "We just declared war on the Kaijen. They're going to come after us. If we can't work together as allies we're doomed. You don't have to like each other but you will protect and defend each other. Yeah?"

His words shocked Akeema, but she didn't protest. Martel appeared to stand just a bit taller than he had a moment prior. "So…

you're the leader now?"

The question blindsided Jaxon. "What? No. No. I'm no leader. I'm just the only level-headed one here. All I want is for us to work together."

"No. It's more than that," Martel said. "You've changed, Jaxon Troy. What did the album do to you? What did it show you? What did you see?"

Jaxon hadn't had time to process what happened. A million different thoughts swam through his mind and clouded his thinking like smoke. "I don't know. It showed me stars. Stars that turned into vines or tentacles. They were all connected somehow. I don't know what it means and I don't care."

Martel held out his palm. "Then you won't mind giving it to me."

Jaxon tossed Martel the charred black album. "It's all yours."

Akeema hugged him this time. "Come back to us," she whispered, then kissed his cheek.

Martel gave him a nod before heading back towards the *Jezebel*. Akeema joined him, reluctantly. They locked eyes. It was all over their faces; they were absolutely going to try to kill each other.

The boarding ramp retracted and cycled closed. A warm gust of air preceded the black ship as its RCS thrusters lifted it up and the *Jezebel* shot off into the golden sky.

***

With his rocket boots out of commission, it took Jaxon the better part of an hour to trek his way through the yellow forest. He regretted not asking Martel for a lift.

Jaxon found the *Saragos* parked in a small clearing, its forward starboard engine pod bleeding smoke. The familiar sizzle of a sparking arc welder carried on the air. Yoko was on top of the ship welding a hole shut in the hull. She wore protective goggles like the ones Betty had given him. She noticed Jaxon and stopped.

He called up to her, "Are you alright?" Yoko flipped her goggles up, wearing the lenses on her forehead. Her thick eyebrows almost appeared to hold them in place. Then she hesitated. She was upset.

She'd been crying.

"There's a hole in my ship," Yoko said. "There's. A. *Hole*. In. My. *Ship!*"

"I'm sorry," Jaxon said. It was all he could think to say.

"Sorry doesn't make it better, hoo-mon. Deck three's gimbals are foosha'd so that's ten thousand cubits down the toilet. If something goes wrong during flight, I don't know what..." Yoko trailed off, but didn't appear to realize it. She wore her grief like a mask.

Yoko pressed a button on her handheld. The loading ramp lowered, its gears creaking and groaning. Jaxon entered the ship and stopped outside of the room housing the gravcouches. The corridor's lights were low and flickering, signs of a bad power conduit somewhere. That's where he found Yoko. She'd entered the ship through a service hatch wearing a repair vest and a belt full of tools that weighed down her tiny frame. A jagged hole had been cut into the corridor's ceiling, the scorch marks obviously made by a crossglaive. She'd welded a sheet of cargonite over the holes in the two sides of the outer hull and was preparing sheets for the two additional holes made in the inner hull.

Her hair was a tangled mess. Streaks of dried tears marked her cheeks. Only then did it occur to him to ask, "Where's Betty?"

New tears traced lines over top the dried ones. Yoko looked away and sleeved her tears, trying her best to conceal her emotions. "She, um, she's dead," Yoko said to the wall. "One of those bitches cut her way into the ship and..." She wouldn't face him. Her gaze remained on the wall and lowered, as if she were talking to an invisible dog. "Betty's chassis was completely destroyed. She's... she's gone."

"What about her memory core?" Jaxon asked. Yoko's gaze finally found his. The grief in her smoky eyes was unbearable.

"I pulled it," she said, showing him a small spherical device tucked in her pocket the size of a golf ball. "Her cortical shield was cracked. I'm pretty sure her core was damaged. I won't know how bad until I get it to a coder." Her fist closed around the neuroplastic ball. Manufacturers designed all post-war mecha data cores with encryption that prohibited a mecha's memory from being uploaded or copied. Data could be updated and overwritten, but it couldn't be transferred. If a mecha's data core was corrupted or destroyed, that mecha died. A form of digital mortality.

"This is my fault," Jaxon said. He meant it as an apology. "If she can be restored I'll do everything I can to make that happen."

"Don't worry about it," Yoko said dismissively, forcing herself to smile. "It doesn't matter," she shrugged. "It's not like she was real. She was a machine. I programmed her to protect me. Even at the cost of her own life. She did what she was supposed to do. That's great. I should be happy she's dead and not me." She wasn't trying to convince Jaxon.

"But she was your friend," he said softly.

Yoko shook her head. The sudden sharp motion caused her tears to zigzag across her face in the planet's reduced gravity. "No. She was a mecha. It doesn't count if the person doesn't have a choice."

"She was still your friend."

Her words stuck in her throat; her caterpillars bunched high up her wide forehead. Yoko's eyes narrowed as the dam behind them broke. Tears came down in a flood. All Jaxon could think to do was hold her. His arms reached out and coiled around her. She resisted him.

At first.

Her body went slack and his embrace was the only thing keeping her from spilling onto the decking. She buried her face deep into his chest and let out a muffled wail that rattled him. It should have. He was responsible.

Minutes passed. Yoko calmed and everything went quiet. Jaxon started to release his hold on her. She wouldn't let him. Her grip was strong and firm, like when he'd caught her. It made Jaxon feel uncomfortable and awkward, but he didn't let go. Neither did she.

***

It took the two of them several hours to get the *Saragos* ready for dustoff. In the cockpit, Jaxon found the dead Velibor girl . The mess that had been her brains were scattered all over the decking in a pattern that wouldn't seem out of place in some overly pretentious art museum. A huge burn mark in the decking told him where Betty's chassis had melted. He stripped the dead body of its clothes and transported the young woman's corpse to the waste recycler where it would be broken down and turned into reusable material, most likely water.

Jaxon didn't know this woman's name. He'd never met her, but he considered her death to be on his hands. He didn't blame her for what she'd done. Her only crime was blindly believing what she'd been told and giving her life for a lie. He salvaged her crossglaive and would make it his own. He took time to repair his rocket boots by swapping out their repulsorlift motivators. He used them to reach the ship's damaged engine pod, accessing the external maintenance hatch and fixing what he could. With Yoko's welding torch he fixed loose hull panels until his arms and shoulders ached.

In the distance, a low hanging mist bullied its way into the yellow forest; the prelude to a storm moving in from the ocean. Jaxon cleaned up the mess in the cockpit to the point where he could barely tell someone had been killed in it.

When Yoko appeared, she'd washed her face and tidied up her French twist hairstyle. Any trace of emotion or bereavement she had, she'd buried deep inside herself and smoothed it over with reinforced concrete. She slipped into her gravity harness and took her pilot's chair, actively ignoring the melted grating where Betty had died. Yoko ran pre-flight checks and a series of chimes told her the ship was more or less ready to fly, but there were half a dozen warning lights that told her several critical components needed to be serviced. She ignored them and spun up the reactor. Jaxon shouldered on his gravity harness and sat next to her in the co-pilot's chair.

"You know how to pilot now?" Yoko asked without looking away from her monitors.

"Olen did," Jaxon said. "So now I do. That's kind of how having someone else's memories stuffed inside your head works."

Yoko reached for a cup of bourbon left sitting since before the attack. She brought the rim to her lips, held it for a moment, then set the cup back down. "I want to leave this cursed planet. My ship needs maintenance. There's a mechanic on Giannis I trust."

Jaxon accessed the ship's navigational array and calculated a course for the neon planet. Yoko double checked the numbers. She didn't change them. "I take it your people abandon you, huh hoo-mon?"

"I was kind of thinking you were my people."

Yoko went still. She sat there, stiff as a statue for a heartbeat, letting the ship idle. Rain sizzled down, pinging the hull like an infinite stack of needles. After three, maybe four breaths, Yoko fed power to the engine pods and the *Saragos* shuttered. Jaxon gripped his handrest, fearing the ship would come apart. Then it stabilized and hovered above the yellow forest, harsh raindrops pummeling it.

The *Saragos* raced towards the stars. The planet's gravity fell away and the ship's gimbals hissed as they shifted, aside from the broken ones on deck three. The ship accelerated into the black and they left the death and misery and heartbreak of Terezakis behind.

Jaxon shut his eyes and relaxed, secure in the knowledge that despite it all, despite the horribleness that had occurred and all the blood that had been spilled, at least he knew with absolute certainty that Sabrene was dead.

Chapter Twenty-Eight: Sabrene

Eleven years into her girlhood and brimming with raw ambition, Sabrene Efiran lived on Pyralis, the planet settled by the Iskarans. It was a hot, muggy world with binary suns; volcanic deposits in its atmosphere made sure the moon-sized planet never saw winter. From orbit, it resembled a rotten orange.

Chartia was the largest of the planet's four continents. Its capitol city, Takora Province, was a large shantytown and agricultural hub home to more than 600 thousand people. Sabrene was third generation Takoran, her family having immigrated to the region after the cultural revolution that granted Iskaran males equal rights under the law. Sabrene loved the city. It bordered a rain forest of trees with ivory stocks, wide spiraled crowns and chunky marigold leaves. They grew in a variety of fractal patterns that appeared to be more designed than grown.

It was also where the planet's dragons lived.

The Pyralian wyverns were once massive bloodthirsty beasts as large as a starship that hunted the Iskarans for sport. Time and evolution reduced them to the size of elephants. They walked on four stumpy legs, had thick elongated necks, and bat-like wings too vestigial to grant them flight. Their tales were barbed and capable of impaling a careless Iskaran that didn't respect the creature's space.

With the childish innocence of a young girl, Sabrene worshiped these animals. She felt a deep a reverence and mild kinship with the winged beasts and often dreamt of being one in its prime, soaring through the humid air and singeing her prey with her fire breath. It was all so romantic in her imagination.

This was the year Sabrene signed up to participate in the annual wyvern hunt; a sacred tradition requiring Iskaran youths to work together to hunt and capture one of the wild flightless beasts. Its organic kerosene would be harvested and used in their annual community celebration, then the beasts would be released back into the wild to repeat the process the following year. The tradition wasn't without danger, having resulted in numerous injuries and even a few deaths in the past, but successful completion brought a national mark of bravery and accomplishment to the participant's families.

Sabrene's mother, Abrus, never cared for the ritual. She was a brash, stern woman who'd expressed her disapproval of Sabrene participating because of her youth and inexperience. Sabrene was small for her age and hadn't had her blood yet. Her growth spurt was at least another rotation away.

Her mother reminded her of this constantly, making a point to criticized Sabrene's lack of speed and strength. How could her weak daughter ever hope to subdue the massive creature with her squat height and pathetic waifish body? "I won't give you permission to bring disrespect to my name," she told the small pink girl.

Sabrene feared this woman. She was slender with a long face and tall, even for an Iskaran. Her blue-white larimar skin marked her as a descendant of the revered Ona-Eyal warrior caste from a time when Iskarans hadn't known peace among the tribes. All of Sabrene's sisters had the skin of their mother.

All but her.

Sabrene stood out as the sole pink member of her family, a trait she'd inherited from her donor. It was a shame Sabrene wore like a scar, something her cruel sisters wouldn't let her forget. It remained a blemish her mother couldn't see past. Sabrene wouldn't be permitted to participate in the hunt with her mother's permission, which she refused to give. The pink girl hadn't inherited her mother's warrior skin, but she had adopted the woman's stubbornness and cunning.

The pink girl accessed her mother's handheld and sent the permission conformation to the gaming officials. She gambled that completing the hunt would win her mother's smile. Because, in her heart, she believed a mother's love was something to be won, not given.

Sabrene's home was a single level stucco building with an oval roof in one of Takora's densest sprawls. Its gray-blue walls and cobblestone walkways were the color of the local clay. The doors and ceilings were overly tall to accommodate the average female

Iskaran's height. Sabrene shared a small room with four of her sisters.

This was one of the rare days she had the space to herself. She crimped her shoulder-length neon blue hair in the popular style of the time, put on her best boots, and snuck out while her mother was busy weaving nets for the local fishers. Sabrene caught a tram to the staging area, arriving in a thick patch of forest populated by odd geometrically patterned trees and leaves. Lush bronze-scarlet foliage covered the forest floor. It all worked together to create an ecosystem where thousands of wild animals and millions of insect species could flourish. It was the only part of the planet where the oppressive heat prevented the wyverns from dying out completely.

Sabrene checked in with the commission representatives and showed them her forged permission waiver on her handheld. They barely gave it a glance. Her deception had worked. Sabrene's confidence in herself was never higher than in this moment. Her smile couldn't have been wider. An official with long green hair assigned her to a team. Sabrene was introduced to a group of girls much older than she was. It was thrilling to her, being in the company of mature peers.

Then she tensed when she recognized one of her teammates was a male.

This was the first year Iskaran males were allowed to participate in public functions. The sight of an unaccompanied male out in public soured Sabrene's smile and twisted her stomach. He was a round faced child with the golden and teal skin of the laborer caste. He was three years older than she was, but mirrored her in size and body type. Once she had her growth spurt, she would be almost twice his size, but for now they could be different shades of the same person.

The boy greeted her with a folded hand gesture.

"Hello," the little scrote had said to her. His voice was high pitched and his lips were curled up in a kind smile Sabrene didn't interpret as friendly. "My name is Sabrin. What's yours?"

Sabrene's disgust reached her throat. It was an insult, a humiliation, being talked to by a male in a public place. Even his name, the male variation of her own, she'd taken as an offense. He stood close enough to smell his breath, the slightly tart scent of Boam fruit filling her nostrils. It made her sick. She didn't respond to his question, fearful of how harshly the older girls would judge her. When she looked to them for confirmation, Sabrene realized none of them noticed. They didn't appear to care. Their indifference just made her angrier. *There used to be rules. There used to be etiquette. People used to know their place.*

The boy held his innocent smile for a stretch of time just short of infinity but couldn't have been more than a few seconds before the boy's face darkened and his meek smile faded. He'd figured out his greeting wasn't welcomed. He wasn't disappointed. He was afraid.

Good, Sabrene thought. It empowered her.

The child took a step back, bowed, then returned to his position. And that should have been the end of it. If he had disappeared or dropped dead, it would have.

Sabrene's mother had taught her that there was no such thing as forgiveness. Her mother held on to grudges as if their value would increase with time. The group's instructor, an old Iskaran woman thick around the belly, recited the hunt's rules and protocols. Sabrene didn't hear any of it. Her brief encounter with the child had thrown her emotions into chaos. She couldn't think. Couldn't focus. All she could feel was a bitter taste in the back of her throat, like copper coins. She wanted to vomit.

She and her teammates road a buggy deep into the province's thick rain forest to the cave entrance of a wyvern's den. There, they were given light armor which included a breast plate, a helmet marked with tribal engravings, and a thin metal shield. Each were handed a long wooden lance tipped with a taser to stun the beast into submission.

The instructor released a cannister of pheromones into the air to coax the wyvern out of its lair. Soon the ground rumbled and the creature emerged, hobbling into the warm binary sunlight. The older girls worked together in an almost practiced way to corral the beast. Sabrene followed their lead, but her concentration was split. The boy. The wyvern's angry jaws parted and it spit fire. Their shields deflected the sputter of flames, including the boy's. It annoyed her.

The beast wailed and growled as their taser spears shocked its thick keratinous skin. The beast snarled and hissed in pain; it sounded like an unlit blowtorch. A few more shocks and the wyvern collapsed in a huff. All there was left to do was to extract its kerosene.

The boy volunteered.

He had the extractor, a rifle-like device tipped with a long over-sized hypodermic needle strong enough to puncture the wyvern's thick scales. Sabrene's mind exploded with rage. *I should be the one. This should be my victory.* Before she'd been aware of it, Sabrene had dropped her taser and her hands were on the barrel of the extractor.

"You don't deserve it!" she shrieked. "You don't belong here! Why are you here?" She wrenched the extractor away from the boy and pushed him into a prickly bush. Thorns scratched his arms and he began to bawl, tears wetting his face. "If anyone deserves to do it it's *me*, you worthless scrote!" she said, shouting over his cries. Sabrene kicked the boy, much to the dismay of the other girls.

"What are you *doing*?" yelled a large nosed girl with curly violet hair. She withdrew her taser from the beast's skin and grabbed Sabrene's arm, stopping her attack. "Enough! You're hurting him!" large nose said, then knelt down to help the wounded boy, attempting to calm him.

The wyvern regained its strength and bucked hard against the remaining tasers shocking its body. It bucked again, higher this time, and stomped the ground. The tremor threw the other girls off balance with a few of them being knocked to the ground. With the threat of the tasers gone, the wyvern's deadly tail whipped around like a spiked mallet and two of the girls still standing caught its barbs in their unprotected legs. The girls screamed and writhed in the dirt, clutching their gored limbs.

Sabrene didn't notice them. Her vision had tunneled, her blood running hot and loud in her ears. Nothing existed beyond her hatred for this small, terrified boy.

The wyvern belched a raucous moan. Sabrene turned and found herself staring into its gaping mouth of sharp teeth, a little flame at the back of its throat like a fleshy candle.

Her blood chilled. A burst of emerald flame came at her before everything went black.

Sabrene's next memory picked up more than a week later, after she'd woken from her coma in a hospital. Her pink skin, now a beet red and blistered, was moist with healing agent. It ached like the worst sunburn imaginable. Every member of her group had died that day, except for her.

As luck would have it, her pink skin was indicative of a rare genetic trait among a small number of Iskarans. It made her unusually resistant to intense heat, at least for a time. Had she been exposed to the wyvern's flame a minute longer, she would've been immolated along with the rest of her team.

It was a thrill for her, to come so close to death and survive. That was until she learned where the genetic trait had come from. It was passed down through Iskaran males. Through her donor. For a small imperceivable moment, she'd wished the wyvern had killed her.

When questioned about what had happened, Sabrene told the adults the truth. That the boy had lost his nerve and provoked the wyvern with his childish crying. It was all his fault. And with no one left alive to refute her story, everyone believed her. Why wouldn't they? No shame was brought to her family. She was held up as a brave hero, the girl who'd been touched by dragon fire and lived.

The only thing that hurt worse than her singed skin was that she never did get to see her mother's smile.

***

Hours after the cathedral's collapse, night fell on Terezakis, clouds obscuring much of the planet's ring light.

Sabrene spent the day buried beneath rubble on the edge of death, hoping it would finally come. She detested herself for that. This was not the grand death befitting a being of her power and status. Of her prestige. At the hands of an inferior male. The reality of her defeat repulsed her; it bit into her pride with its poison.

The pillar that brought the whole cathedral toppling down around her had broken a meter from its base, creating a small arch. This was where Sabrene lay pinned, face down. Heavy debris pressed down on her like an unwanted lover. Every breath sucked fine dust into her sinuses and down her throat where it stung and scratched at her lungs. She couldn't move. Every time she tried, the debris punished her. Hunger seized her stomach and sapped her strength. The fire had burned away her clothes and all her hair, even her eyebrows. Her pink skin was now a deep tomato red, but not like how it'd been after the wyvern's fire touched her. This was far, far worse.

Sabrene's skin burned like an open wound. The constant overwhelming pain kept her awake. A storm of rage churned inside of her, mirroring the storm brewing outside.

She focused it into her tuning.

The debris vibrated and shifted, but the weight was too much for her. The crack and roll of thunder in the skies above echoed down into Sabrene's hell. Pounding rain dribbled its way to Sabrene's lips. The liquid was tart and gritty like wet sand in her mouth, but her body craved it. The rain quickly became a torrent and water began to pool.

In a few precious minutes, Sabrene would be drowning.

Her desire for death to end her suffering was eclipsed by the impending fact that if she didn't claw herself out of this grave it would be her tomb.

Tuning the tons of rock and twisted cargonite steel stacked on top of her was a feat only the most powerful of Kaijen could accomplish. Sabrene always believed herself to be one of those Kaijen. Her religion instilled in her the belief that all disciples were equal. It was a lie, of course. There would always be a Kaijen more powerful than the others.

Because there had to be.

There had to exist one special being who was the best and greatest of all Kaijen. Why couldn't it be her? *Who deserves that honor more than I do?*

The water rose quickly. It reached her mouth and nose, choking off her oxygen. Fear and adrenaline shot through Sabrene's blood and she lifted her head out of the bubbling puddle as much as she could.

Desperately, she inhaled her final breaths. She reached deep inside herself to trigger the process.

Sabrene conjured every bit of memory she could, every strong emotion, every incident, every image contained within her neurons to fuel her ability to tune herself free. The most powerful path had always been anger. The animus she harbored for her old friend Olen acted as a potent narcotic, bringing with it shards of emotional distress that cut her deeply. Nisame's death fed her rising fury, but only a bit.

Her mind shifted to Verlain, her right hand for the past three years. She was the closest thing Sabrene had to a best friend. Her respect and loyalty had been an invaluable asset. The loss of Verlain had left a hole in Sabrene's heart that couldn't be easily filled. Jaxon Troy had taken this from her. He'd brought dishonor to her sanctuary, gotten her students massacred, and snatched the album's power out from under her. The mental pain of that humiliation coupled with Verlain's death touched her in the most uncomfortably intimate way, as if she'd been turned out and violated like a common alley whore.

Sabrene held on to that pain and sharpened it into a weapon. Her head ached with the severity of having been struck, the pain throbbing inside her mind. She screamed her throat raw, but refused to stop tuning. The pain had become the God that superseded all Gods.

The pile of rocks pressing down on her trembled.

Sabrene remembered Jaxon's arm hooked around her throat. Him choking the life out of her with his dark degenerate hands, and how close to death she'd come. The rubble above her levitated, then shot up into the storming sky, disintegrating into an explosion of metal and stone pebbles. She coughed out the bitter rain water in her nose and mouth and huffed in air. She rolled onto her back and saw sky. She wanted to stand, but her legs were numb. They'd been crushed. She crawled.

Gravel and jagged pieces of rock cut and scraped her naked stomach and chest. Her legs bled. Her swollen red skin ached. It was debilitating, but she persisted. Smears of red were left in her wake as blood leaked from her fresh cuts before the rain diluted and swept them away. Sabrene didn't know where she was going, only that she had to go somewhere. It hurt to breathe. She wondered if her enemies were still in the area. If they were, she would be powerless to stop them.

Sabrene's arms began to cramp. She rolled onto her back again, letting the rain batter her bruised, naked body. She caught a flash of metal in the courtyard, a shimmer in the light of clapping thunder. The students who'd deserted her had taken the skiff and left Sabrene's shuttle. She dragged herself across the cathedral's muddy grounds, tiny pebbles and fine stone fragments poking at her arms and elbows and breasts. She kept going.

By the time Sabrene reached the vessel she could barely breathe. External scanners recognized her and the boarding ramp lowered. She dug her dirty fingers into the grating, lifting her long wet swollen body up the ramp and onto the decking.

In the ship's belly, she reached the compartment housing the medical pod. A pair of surgical arms extended out of the wall and placed her in the pod. It washed away the mud and dirt and the computer scanned her. Both of Sabrene's legs were fractured in several places, her lungs were scorched from smoke inhalation, and she'd suffered second degree burns all over her body. That one she'd already figured out for herself.

A third surgical arm revealed itself. It injected Sabrene with cocaine, a powerful painkiller and healing agent for Iskarans. Her legs were wrapped with bracing mesh while her cuts were treated with antiseptic. A breathing tube inserted itself down her throat and pumped oxygen to her damaged lungs, another violation she was forced to suffer.

A medical printer buzzed to life and crafted a respirator vest. The surgical arms sat her upright and placed the vest on her, its locking clamps fitting the device tightly around her torso. Little drills inside of the appliance punched through her breast plates and into her struggling lungs, pumping a steady flow of air into them.

The pod's diagnostic display made a shrill series of chirps that didn't sound promising. Sabrene craned her neck, bearing the pain to see the medical readout. It showed a virtual scan of her body. Her legs were blinking yellow. Sabrene didn't know what that meant. Fear stabbed. The medical printer spun up again and began to weave something new. Before Sabrene could figure it out, the third surgical arm injected her with sedatives and she blinked to sleep.

***

Alarms stirred Sabrene awake. She sat up in the pod and couldn't feel herself, the anesthetic having left her numb all over. Surgical arms dressed her in a medical gown, but she sensed something was wrong.

Her legs.

The diagnostic display spelled out the details in cold hard medical jargon. Her crushed legs had contracted an infection. There was a fifty-two percent chance that infection could spread to her heart. More than half. The computer made the choice to amputate, above the knee. The surgical arms attached her newly printed legs. They were as dull and artificial as one would expect them to look. The rage welled up in Sabrene like a pocket of methane. One spark and it would detonate. Shuffling feet let her know she wasn't alone in the ship.

"Priestess," a small quiet voice said. It was Novotna, one of her Sidonian students that had abandoned her during the battle. Novotna exhaled, relieved. "We feared you died in the collapse."

"Why did you leave me?" Sabrene said. Each word had an edge.

Novotna's face darkened. She took a moment to choose her words. "We... we were outmatched and went to call for help. It was clear the battle was lost. Many of us were injured so we decided—"

"You... *decided*?" Sabrene said. "Were you able to contact anyone?"

Novotna met her gaze. "No, priestess. The skiff's transceiver has a limited range so—"

"So no one knows what happened here. Besides us."

Novotna went stiff. Sabrene did a terrible job hiding her intent. There was a small shred of hope in Novotna's eyes, as if this could still somehow end well for her.

"Actually," Novotna stuttered, "there's a very good chance our signal did get through to the repeaters and we all—"

Sabrene killed her.

The young girl clawed at her neck, hard enough to break the skin. She struggled against the invisible force collapsing her throat in on itself. It wasn't instant. The young woman wasn't strong enough to fight back. After several minutes Novotna's limbs went limp and her body hung in place like a marionette, then crumbled to the grating.

Sabrene stood on her new legs. They were awkward and uneven, a poor substitute. Anger fueled her movement. She retrieved a spare crossglaive from a storage compartment and stumbled out of the ship. Her vest breathed cool air into her lungs. It was night and the streak of the planet's rings shown bright and elegant above. The ring light highlighted the skiff parked nearby. The mutineers were gathered outside the vessel, half of them wounded and missing limbs from the battle. They appeared starved and frightened, looking to Sabrene for guidance.

For forgiveness.

She greeted them with a smile, and for a moment, they were relieved.

Sabrene extended her crossglaive and their relief melted. Everything Sabrene wished she had done to Olen and Jaxon Troy, she did to them. Her crossglaive cut through the slow and wounded. The ones that ran, they got it the worst. They floated up off their feet while Sabrene sliced them to mush.

When the screaming ended, Sabrene returned to her shuttle, her gown smeared and spotted with different shades of blood. She accessed the shuttle's transmitter and prepared to send the elders a connection request, but first, she spent some time rehearsing her truth. How the xenophobic terrorists led by Olen had attacked her without provocation. How they slaughtered all her students, who were unarmed. How the violent human speciesists had leveled the cathedral with Sabrene inside before she had any chance to fight back. How she nobly and bravely pulled herself out of the rubble as the sole survivor of the massacre.

She would erase the truth and her lie would become the truth.

She knew that she would be believed. She always was.

Chapter Twenty-Nine: Akeema

Akeema had lost track of how long the *Jezebel* had been traveling at slipstream. She loathed every second of it down to her marrow. Being this close to Martel, breathing his air, receiving his aid, made Akeema want to throw up in her own mouth. A part of her considered stepping outside, but didn't want to give him the satisfaction.

They hadn't spoken a single word to each other since they'd left Terezakis. Martel confined himself to the cockpit while his mecha gave her antibiotics and a bone rebonding cocktail for her broken radius. Akeema squatted in the common area, eating Martel's food, and drinking his water. She found a package of freeze-dried cucumber sandwiches and what looked to be real sesame chicken breast, though it was more likely reconstituted from soy meat paste, but god if it didn't smell good. She bit into the hot meat and the pleasure it brought her only deepened her resentment.

The ship dropped out of slipstream and thrust gravity ended. Akeema floated down the deck ladder to the crew compartments and wandered, conscious of the fact Martel was probably monitoring her movements. Not that she cared. She found the crew head and locked herself inside, removing her gravity harness and placing it on a secured hook. She stored her soiled clothes in a cabinet and floated into the shower.

A transparent floor-to-ceiling tube lined with jets shot warm steam at her which condensed into water against her cool bruised skin. Fans forced the water down to keep it from floating free in the microgravity. It was a sensual, relaxing experience, the way she imagined what good sex felt like. Akeema finished and toweled off, catching sight of her pale naked self in a tall mirror. The floating woman in the reflection, she didn't recognize.

Her skin was a collage of welts, cuts, and wine purple bruises; the newer ones she'd suffered in the white room. They read like a map of her abuse. Akeema adjusted the mirror's hinges and viewed her backside where she found more bruises. They tracked all the way down to and including her ass. The surgical scars lining her spine remained the most repulsive part of it all. Pain doesn't happen in a vacuum.

Akeema braced herself against the sink, her grip tightening as a tremor rippled through her body. The mirror cracked. A terrible ache crept up the back of her head, forcing her eyes to slam shut. The tremor spread out around her to various objects in the small room, many of which began to warp and deform.

To calm herself, she focused on her father. He'd made her cherry cheesecake for her tenth birthday. It was the sweetest, creamiest thing she'd ever tasted. Her father's cooking had always shined a light on the darkness of her early childhood. It was a memory she cherished alongside her mother's face. The moving objects in the room fell still. Akeema returned the mirror to its original position and vowed never to look into it ever again.

Thrust gravity returned and pulled Akeema down to the floor.

She went to put her soiled clothes back on until she caught a whiff of them and her nose wrinkled, smelling the stink of piss and vomit and blood. She wondered why no one had told her. Given no other choice, Akeema was prepared to wear them when a hollow knock came from the door. Martel's mecha. Waiting for her outside of the head was a freshly printed change of clothes. They were cut and styled similar to what Martel wore; black with red highlights. They were her size, though the fit was a bit tight for her taste.

The laces on her boots were too long. She looped them around her ankles and fastened them. Her gravity harness hung a little loose and tugged on her sore hips. Akeema tied her red mess of hair up in a simple bun that, coupled with her clothes, made her look like an evil flight attendant. She climbed to the command deck and returned to the common area. There she found Martel lounging at the crew dining table, eating what smelled like chicken noodle soup. He pretended not to notice her. A second bowl of soup sat on the table next to him that included a pair of ripe avocados. Martel moved the magnetically secured bowl in front of the chair closest to her. Akeema resisted, then sat; the chairs were mounted on a sliding track bolted to the deck where they could be locked into place during high g maneuvers.

Akeema pretended not to enjoy the food even though it smelled wonderful and her hollow stomach begged to be filled. They ate in silence. Without the hazy aftereffects of torture or the adrenaline dump of combat flooding her veins, she could focus on the details of Martel's face. They didn't match the evil villain persona her memory had conjured. His face was square and young with long thick eyebrows and the beginnings of crow's feet around his wide dark eyes. His once bald head was now a shadow of blonde stubble. No longer did he represent the invincible monster she'd built him up to be. She could see now that he was just a man who was beatable.

Killable.

He looked up from his meal and met her gaze. "How's the chicken?" Martel asked with casual interest. "I prepared it myself."

"Dry," she lied.

He laughed, almost choking on his soup. "That's too bad. I have plenty more down in storage. I guess I'll have to eat it all by myself."

"I bet you're used to doing plenty of things all by yourself," Akeema said, then bit into an avocado. The mix of sugar and salt on her taste buds was divine. She swallowed and took a second bite.

Martel wiped his mouth. "How's the arm?"

"It still works," she said, wagging her injured arm still sheathed in its mesh brace. "Clean break. In a few days it'll be good as new."

He chuckled. "Too bad you can't say the same about your spine."

Akeema didn't remember standing, or slamming her spoon on the table; it bounced off and floated down to the floor in the one third of a g. The action made the mending bones in her wounded arm tingle. Clutched in her hand was her crossglaive hilt. She didn't know how it got there.

"It wasn't my intention to trigger you," Martel said, unconcerned by the threatening woman staring down at him. "I sincerely apologize for the pain and trauma I've caused you. It's important to me you know that. And I'm hoping that now, after all that's happened, all we've been through, we can start to—"

"You mother fucker," she said through her clenched jaw. "You think just because you helped us that somehow absolves you for trying to kill me?"

Martel leaned back in his chair, spreading his hands. "Sure it does," he said, spacing out each word. "I watched you. The way you handled those Kaijen? You weren't just defending yourself. You cut through those girls like someone bet you that you couldn't. You were ruthless. You enjoyed it."

Her blood froze in her veins. A lump formed in her throat that she couldn't swallow. Akeema recognized it as fear. Fear that maybe he wasn't entirely wrong. "They *hurt* me," Akeema said, her voice fragile and choppy. "They *beat* me. They *tortured* me. For *hours*. They had it *coming*."

Martel dropped his chin in a nod. "Oh, I agree," he said, a little smug smirk twisting his mouth that made his face even more punchable. "You know who else deserved it? Nisame. And I got my revenge. Just like you got yours."

I could kill him. If she was quick enough, she could end it all right here. Her thumb rested on her hilt's trigger. *It would be so easy. Just a little pressure and the blade would skewer him.*

Martel held her gaze, then shook his head, as if he'd read her mind. Her thumb eased off the trigger. She relaxed her shoulders.

"I'm not judging you for what you did," Martel said. "It doesn't mean you're a bad person. If anything, I respect you more for it. But you can't justify your own revenge without justifying mine too." His head leaned to one side. "Well, I guess you can, if you're a hypocrite."

"Then I'm a hypocrite," Akeema said, having lost her fire and conviction. "I don't care. I don't give a shit anymore. It doesn't matter if we did the same things for the same reasons. I can never, will never, forgive you for what you did to me."

"I'm willing to make amends."

"I won't settle for anything less than your death."

Martel stood, his palms braced against the table. He leaned in to face her, close enough she could smell the hot soup on his breath. "I'm not asking for your forgiveness. I'm demanding your cooperation. And I am doing it very nicely if I do say so myself."

"You're being ridiculous. You know that'll never happen."

"It already *has* happened," Martel said, raising his voice a few decibels. "We declared war on the Kaijen. Both of us. You're on my ship eating my food breathing my air under my care because we are allies now." Her crossglaive pulled its way out of her grip and landed in Martel's palm. "But your skills are still amateur," Martel said. He held the crossglaive hilt in his open palm. "Go on. Try and take it."

She reached out with her mind. The hilt wobbled side to side like a broken compass, but it wouldn't come to her. He was counter-tuning it. An ache grew in the front of Akeema's brain and her face reddened as she tuned harder. When the pounding in her skull became too much, she let it go. Akeema floated down into her seat while gasping for breath. Sweat beaded her brow and pooled there in the lower gravity.

"See?" Martel said, sounding annoyed. "Your tuning skills are dogshit. That's why it took three of us to kill Sabrene. That was easy compared to the elders. When the Kaijen come to kill us, we need to be at our strongest, and I'd rather not see you die instantly because you were too much of a chickenshit to accept my help. I need to train you, and you need to let me."

Realization hit her, sharp as a slap. "You want to link with me."

Martel sighed, his eyes rolling over. "Want is a strong word."

A harsh laugh crawled out of Akeema's throat. "I'd sooner shit in my own hand and clap before I ever let you do anything to me. I don't need you or your fucking training."

A painful smile creased Martel's lips. Anger danced behind his flat eyes. "Do you know what the two most common elements in the universe are? Hydrogen and stupidity. Can you guess which one you're full of right now?"

"How the hell did you manage to dodge a coat hanger for nine months?" Akeema said.

"Gracefully," Martel smiled.

Akeema pushed off the table, her chair sliding back on its track. She stood in a huff. "If someone does come to kill us my only hope is that I'll get to see you die first." She stalked off, her boots pounding the decking even in the reduced gravity.

"You could be a great warrior, Akeema," Martel called after her as she reached the deck ladder. "But you'll never be the greatest. Not without my help."

The lower half of Akeema's body disappeared down the deck ladder. "I'm leaving."

"Stop being an asshole about this."

"Leaving!"

"If you need to announce that you're leaving, you don't want to go, you just want attention," she heard Martel say before she reached the lower deck where his voice wouldn't carry.

Akeema found her way to the med bay where Olen and Castor's pods were. It was a chilly room with low lighting and stank like an old basement. The air recyclers hissed, needing to be serviced. She sat next to her older brother, her hand on the pod's frosted glass view window. He looked peaceful. She wondered what he might be dreaming about until, eventually, she was dreaming too.

***

The *Jezebel* was braking for Skerritt, a blue-gray shithole Akeema dreaded having to call home for the foreseeable future. The ship hit atmosphere and the gimbals shifted. The *Jezebel* dropped out of the storm clouds and cut its way through the ocean planet's torrential rainstorms. Their destination was a rusting skyscraper that stood out of the ocean like an ancient obelisk or a middle finger, depending on the mood. On its belly, the ship set down inside the old relic in a makeshift landing bay.

Bare-bones mechas with no clothes or skin greeted them and took custody of the med pods. Akeema followed them through the rotting building. Frigid ocean air blew through much of the structure; everything was damp and the ceilings leaked in places. Many places. The only clean and well-lit area in the whole place was the lab. Pristine surgical mechas operated on Castor and Olen inside of a sterile room with transparent walls.

Castor's procedure went smoothly. His broken ribs were repaired, his ruptured liver and destroyed kidneys having been replaced without incident. He would recover.

Olen wasn't so lucky. Akeema didn't understand the intricacies of Asabi physiology, but she assumed having your entire ribcage crushed wasn't a wound you could walk away from. The mecha surgeons repaired or replaced what organs they could, but the woman was geriatric and her cells were irradiated. They kept her comfortable and on life support, but her time was short.

Martel dealt with her prognosis by retreating to his work station. Despite his emotions being kept under heavy guard, Akeema could see he was hurting. He focused his attention on the frayed album, which looked like it'd been left in the oven too long. Martel placed the device on a scanning pad and threw an ungodly amount of tests at it, hoping for some kind of cure or magic wish he could pull from the object. His last hope to save the old woman rested in the album.

Akeema didn't care either way. She wouldn't allow herself to. Their truce didn't change her feelings, or the condition of her spine. Seeing Martel as a human being capable of grief and empathy for a dying old woman he couldn't save wasn't going to change that either. Nothing would.

Nothing ever would.

**

With Castor on the road to recovery, Akeema began to plan Martel's murder.

She spent two weeks watching him, studying his routine. When he slept. When he ate. When he shit. Like a stalker, she memorized every move he made inside the dreary tower. Her arm had healed and she was ready for combat.

Akeema found a spare crossglaive in what laughingly passed for the building's armory and printed herself new clothes that were form-fitting and allowed for greater mobility of movement.

Every midday, or what passed for midday on a planet with no sunshine, Martel would pass through one of the tower's corridors on his way to the makeshift gym. Akeema used holes in the corridor's walls and climbed to a small perch overlooking the passage where she wouldn't be seen. There, she waited for her moment to strike. Her legs were braced against the walls of the narrow corridor, ready to drop down and attack from above.

Time stretched.

After ten minutes Akeema's knees and the joints of her fingers began to ache. Martel was late. He was never late. He'd always been punctual to an obsessive degree. This should've tipped her off that she'd been made, but she held her position even as the sting of muscle fatigue began to set in.

An invisible force grabbed her leg and jerked her down. Akeema fell three meters and crashed to the damp carpeted floor in a heap. Martel stared down at her, his hands laced behind his back, his bald head having grown into a blonde crew cut.

He sighed. "I guess we had better get this out of the way." Akeema ignored her screaming joints and jumped to her feet, her crossglaive blade extended. Martel remained still.

"You're not even going to defend yourself?" Akeema said, annoyed he wasn't taking her seriously.

"If you lance me then I deserve to be lanced," Martel said.

Akeema didn't make the mistake of charging at him head-on. She waved the tip of her crossglaive around in front of Martel, goading him to dodge or flinch.

He didn't move.

She faked a lunge. His eyes rolled, bored.

Akeema went for a quick thrust. A flash, and the room spun around her. Hands grabbed her, slamming the pale woman onto her back. Martel stood over her, upside down from her view, holding her crossglaive. Akeema's right hand was clasped around nothing. She hadn't realized he'd taken her weapon. Martel collapsed the blade and tossed the hilt away.

"Come on, get up," he instructed her. "I'll show you what you did wrong. Which was everything."

Akeema was slow to stand, her legs shaking. Her clean new clothes were stained with damp patches where she fell. The anger came and she flung herself at Martel with a drunken flurry of punches and kicks. None of them connected. He blocked or sidestepped the blows, wearing her down. It was the maglev train all over again.

Frustration caused her to unintentionally throw a mild wave of tuning energy that staggered Martel, allowing her to land one clean slug to his face. Her knuckles cracked against his brass jaw. Blood trickled from the corner of his mouth. Her moment of pleasure was brief.

Faster than a rattlesnake, his fist came at her with the speed of a piston and too fast to avoid. His thick meaty fist smashed into her nose like a steel mallet.

Akeema's head snapped back, her eyes welling up from the sharp, throbbing sting. Her vision blurred. The wall collided with her back, the pain mushrooming throughout her face like a bomb. Her legs quit and she slid down to the floor, her nose congested with blood. Akeema coughed and hacked, fighting to take in oxygen.

Martel stood over her, sullen, waiting for her to recover.

"Are you alright?" Martel asked. His concern sounded genuine. Akeema wanted to curse at him, but it was taking everything she had not to burst into tears. She said nothing aside from the hiss she made when she touched the point of impact. Her head tilted back and she pinched her nose, releasing bolts of agony. Martel met her gaze and she let her wounded scowl speak for her.

"I didn't hit you at full force," Martel said. There was no pleasure in his words. "That was me *holding back*. That was me being gentle. And you still lost. And you will continue to lose. Because you have not been properly *trained*. Now, if you like losing we can keep doing this dance over and over again if humiliation and masochism is your kink. *Or*, you can stop acting like a spoiled child, grow the fuck up, swallow your pride, and accept my help."

The corridor fell silent. Only the distant howl of the churning storms outside and the echo of dripping water coming from somewhere.

Martel held out his hand.

Akeema sat there, the pain in her face still bright and fresh and palpable. Despite herself, she considered his offer. Deep down, it was what she wanted. To be better. The best. Undefeatable. She could fool him. Convince him she'd set aside her vendetta, let him teach her, build her up to be as powerful as he was. Then slit his throat. The image brought a visible smile to her lips, red on her teeth. Perhaps she could tolerate being around him until she'd drained him of all the knowledge he had to offer, then smile in his face as he choked on his own blood. It was a fantasy that could keep her going for ages.

Akeema reached out to Martel. He leaned in to take her hand. She slapped his palm away.

***

Akeema found a secluded room and sulked. In the hours after her humiliating loss, she still had trouble breathing through her bandaged nose. It was an odd feeling. There were no cuffs on her wrists. She wasn't in a cage. She was free to roam and go wherever she wanted, but she was a prisoner all the same.

In the lab, Castor remained comatose on his bio-bed. He'd lost weight, his high cheekbones appearing sunken and gaunt. Akeema sat next to him, holding his flesh hand. His veins were large and squishy and she could feel his blood pulsing through them. She wondered if linking with him would allow them to talk to each other inside Castor's mind the way she had with Jaxon on the *Saragos*.

Akeema put her hands on Castor's head.

"Don't," a small hoarse voice said, startling her. The old woman was conscious. "You'll hurt him. Linking with someone without their consent can be extremely dangerous."

"That didn't stop your psycho lapdog," Akeema said with dry snark.

"That was against my wishes. Hiroshi has a hard time dealing with his anger. It makes him... impulsive. You two have that in common."

Akeema hardened, her defensive wall going up. "You don't know anything about me."

"I know more about you than you think. Come here, Akeema. Let me see you."

Akeema hesitated. Her curiosity got her to move. She approached the Asabi woman whom she'd never officially met, but knew intimately.

Olen had to lay on her side, the bones in her back having been too badly broken. Her labored breathing taxed her whole body with every inhale. Olen stared at her with an appraising gaze.

"Hiroshi did that to you," Olen said, referring to Akeema's nose.

"You provoked him. Even though you knew you couldn't win."

"I could have beaten him," Akeema lied.

Olen managed a painful, knowing smirk. "Yes, certainly, but let's not talk about him. Ask me what you want to ask me."

Akeema hadn't realized how true the woman's statement was until she heard it spoken aloud. "Was I really that important to whatever it is you're trying to do? Or were you just blowing smoke up Sabrene's ass?"

Olen didn't get the idiom, but seemed to parse the context. "I don't lie, Akeema. I don't need to. I have the truth."

"What about Jaxon? I thought he was the special one. Are you saying I'm more important to your plan than he is?"

Olen experienced a brief coughing fit. Akeema wiped the woman's mouth and she said, "Your future is a river that will narrow, but deepen. When I accessed the album, it showed me what I believe to be events that haven't happened."

Akeema squinted. "You saw the future?"

Olen pursed her lips and exhaled. "A possible future. One of many different outcomes that can be altered for better or worse depending on the smallest of decisions by many individuals. But in order to set those events into motion it usually starts with one decision. Made by one person."

Akeema let out a skeptical laugh. "You mean me?"

"The success of what we need to accomplish hinges on more than just one person. It will require all of us to do our part."

Concern creased Akeema's face. "But how do you *know* that?"

"It's gotten me this far, hasn't it? The next crisis will depend on what you choose to do."

"What crisis? What's going to happen?"

Olen held out her palms. "It would be easier if I showed you."

Akeema leaned back. "You seem nice and all, but I don't trust you. You may not have told Martel to do what he did, but he did it because of you. For you. You're just as responsible for my pain as he is."

Olen frowned. It made the white-haired Asabi appear even more frail. "Hiroshi has taught me a lot about Earth history. Humans are a wild, untamed people. The story of your species is filled with tremendous turmoil and hope and… contradiction. You're—"

"We're intergalactic drug dealers," Akeema said dryly. "We're gullible and easily manipulated by our feelings. We weren't even smart enough to invent a Gravity Drive. We had to buy ours. There's nothing special about us. We just got lucky and had something all the other worlds wanted. Take that away from us and what are we? A planet-sized tourist attraction. Earth was a garden and we irradiated it." Akeema paused for a heartbeat, then her voice fell to just above a whisper. "Now I'll probably never get to see it again. Because I devoted my life to a religion that had me sterilized. I am alone. Just about everyone I've ever given a damn about is either dead or close to it. You say I'm special? I don't believe you."

Olen sighed. It pained her failing body. "Centuries ago on your world," her raspy voice began, "there was a human explorer, a conquistador, named Hernán Cortés. He sailed across Earth's great oceans on primitive sail boats and landed in the new world. There he found himself and his small band of soldiers besieged by a powerful empire. They were impossibly outnumbered. Victory seemed hopeless.

"Cortés should have turned around and gone back home. Instead, he ordered his men to burn all their ships so that retreat was no longer an option. You've burned your ships, Akeema. You're trapped in the new world and you're staring down an army that you are not equipped to defeat. Not all by yourself. But you are not alone. You have Jaxon. You have Castor. And, yes, as hard as it is to believe, you have Hiroshi."

Akeema coughed a laugh, turning her aching nose up at the notion. Olen reached her thin wrinkled fingers out and touched Akeema's arm. Her leathery skin felt warm and comforting.

Olen cleared the phlegm from her throat and swallowed. "I know you will never accept his help, but would you be willing to accept mine?"

Her words took a moment for Akeema to process. "You're too weak to link with me. The process would probably kill you."

The corners of the old woman's mouth curled into a heartbreaking smile. "I've already been killed, my dear. But I can decide how I spend my last moments. I can lay here and slowly fade away, or I can give you the gift that will save you. A gift you can pass on to Castor, and any others you find worthy."

Shame chilled Akeema. This was what she wanted, without having to go through Martel, but the cost didn't sit right with her. Akeema had seen what this woman had gone through, what she'd lost, but when she died, all of her power and knowledge would be passed on solely through Martel's twisted lens. Akeema owed it to the old woman to make sure that didn't happen.

At least, that's the bullshit excuse she told herself. Akeema couldn't face the fact that she'd just agreed to kill this woman. She pulled herself close to Olen, the old woman's bent copper thumbs brushing away the younger woman's tears.

"This isn't a sad moment," Olen assured her. "It's the beginning of your journey to becoming something greater." She placed her warm arthritic hands on Akeema's crown and pressed their foreheads together. Akeema's eyes closed, the familiar sensation of insects crawling inside the back of her skull beginning to envelope her mind.

They linked.

Only, it didn't feel right. Tingling shot down Akeema's spine like a bolt of lightning, followed by a swath of pain. She felt herself drifting, slipping away. Like being overtaken. She wanted it to stop, but there was nothing she could do to terminate the process.

Only after it was too late did she realize she'd made a terrible mistake.

Chapter Thirty: Yoko

The *Saragos* spent six days limping its way to Giannis. Slipstreaming through void space was dangerous enough, but even more so with a damaged ship. Yoko erred on the side of caution, refusing to push the *Saragos* too hard and making frequent stops out of fear the compromised hull might shake itself apart or veer into the void's edges to its destruction. At least then her problems would be over.

Yoko spent most of the week-long trip avoiding Jaxon.

She was embarrassed. Seeing his hoo-mon face reminded her of how vulnerable she'd allowed herself to be in front of him, as well as the friend she'd lost. It made her want to drink. Her bereavement wouldn't let her. She'd bought into her own lie, fooling herself into believing she was a perfect stunning and brave independent woman who didn't need anyone's help. It was an easy enough lie to believe when she had a programmable mecha protecting her from reality and doing most of the heavy lifting. That time had passed.

Being trapped on her ship with a person she barely knew, one with magical powers, her imagination flooded with horror scenarios. Had she been a poor judge of character? What if this hoo-mon decided he wanted to kill her? Or worse? With his devilish mind powers, how could she stop him? People always disappointed her. It was why she never trusted them.

She reminded herself how he'd saved her life on Montanari, a fact she couldn't ignore, but what if that made him feel entitled to her body? Males of every species tended to be violent unpredictable creatures at one point or another. The females too sometimes, to be fair, but she wasn't worried about *them* right now.

Yoko carried her sidearm at all times, loaded with high impact rounds. If he tried anything, she would explode his head.

Whenever they would meet in the galley to eat or discuss ship maintenance, Yoko's fears and mistrust of the hoo-mon hung in the air like a rotten stink. She dared not breathe it in. Yoko speculated about triggers that might set the hoo-mon off. She was, by her own estimate, the most attractive Kish female the universe would ever witness. If she wore something a little too sexually charged or that accentuated her curves a little too tightly, would that send the primitive hoo-mon into a blind sexual rage?

Yoko thumbed through her wardrobe looking for clothes that were looser or made her look frumpier to avoid any confusion or misinterpretation. It was a decision she immediately regretted considering in the first place.

Instead, she decided she wouldn't change a thing. She would continue to be herself and do as she pleased on her own ship, and if the hoo-mon stepped out of line for even a moment, she would murder him. The whole galaxy already thought he was a terrorist. They'd probably give her a medal, or at the very least a reward that would pay off her debts.

But the moment never came.

Yoko used the ship's internal cameras to watch the young man's every move, looking for the slightest infraction to fault him. Jaxon never gave her so much as a strange feeling to question his honor. She tasked him with doing all the dirty jobs. He drained the sewage lines. He cleaned the air filters. He serviced the waste reclamators. He even did her laundry. He did whatever she asked him to do without hesitation or innuendo. His talent as a mechanic was above par. It surprised her, which meant it also annoyed her.

As a test, Yoko slipped on a snug jumpsuit that didn't leave much to the imagination. She roamed the ship with the zipper pulled down below her bust where a wandering eye would see skin. Jaxon didn't ogle. He didn't sneak glances. His brown eyes didn't so much as wander below her neckline. He didn't say or do anything that excited her anger or made her feel uncomfortable. He was so well behaved she began to doubt he was even interested in females. Or maybe he just wasn't interested in her. She laughed at the notion. *Everyone breathing is interested in me,* she thought.

Her annoyance was amplified. The audacity of this hoo-mon. Not even having the dignity to give her a reason to kill him. It was insulting. How dare he,

Foosha.

She carried her frustration with the hoo-mon into her dreams. Yoko dreamed of him cutting through the lock of her quarters with his plasma sword. Him sneaking into her bed. His weight pressing down on her. She felt the warmth of his breath on her neck.

And then, she was falling.

In her dream, Yoko had been flung off the landing platform on Montanari, seconds away from becoming a smear of red blood and gray flesh. And then she wasn't. Because the hoo-mon had caught her. His arms wrapped around her and she was safe. Yoko's glassy eyes met his and there wasn't lust in them. It was something else. Something Yoko didn't recognize and it...

The dream ended and it never returned.

***

The neon lit surface of Giannis was twelve hours into its rainy eighteen-hour night. The *Saragos* parted the sky and floated down from the stormy clouds on an erratic vector. Its damaged RCS thrusters fired unevenly, threatening to capsize the ship. Warning alarms shrieked as the ship wobbled, seesawing like a falling leaf at the mercy of the wind. Yoko pretended not to panic. Jaxon sat next to her in the co-pilot's chair. He silenced the alarms, allowing her to focus. It took Yoko longer than she was comfortable with to compensate and even out her descent. She set the *Saragos* down hard on a starship repair platform east of the planet's main city.

The ship's damaged engine pod powered down and sounded like a bucket of ball bearings being thrown into an angry turbine. The landing platform retracted, pulling the *Saragos* inside of a hangar bay with a collapsible roof that was closed to keep out the constant rain.

Yoko rode the crew elevator down, the gears squeaking and groaning even worse than before. It stopped a meter short of touching the ground, the gears having seized and jammed. Yoko jumped down, her boots splashing onto the slick floor.

A gray woman in engineering coveralls greeted them.

Cinzia was a thirty-ish Kish woman with pompadour style hair crowned by a wild halo of dark curls; she was a slightly taller, slightly thicker version of Yoko. Her silver complexion was a noticeably darker shade than Yoko's, closer to gunmetal. Her coveralls were stained and torn and stank of sweat and engine grease. She wore her sleeves rolled up, showing off her intricate sleeve tattoos done in chrome ink.

"What have you done to my stunning and beautiful *Sara*?" Cinzia frowned, her voice a crisp flighty soprano.

"She's not yours, Cinzia. And she never will be. She's taken. Get over it," Yoko said like a teased younger sister.

"She feels like mine. I've replaced enough of her parts she might as well be." Cinzia's said. Her curious eyes scanned the crew elevator. "Where's my lovely Betty?" Hearing her name was enough to cripple Yoko. She tried to hide it, but Cinzia had good eyesight and even better intuition. She mimicked Yoko's somber eyes. "Foosha. How'd it happen?"

Yoko wanted to tell her everything. Just to get it all off her chest. It would've been a stupid impulsive move on her part and would've taken too much explaining. A short lie was always better than the long depressing truth. "Some dumb bitch tried to kill me and Betty jumped in the way," Yoko said with a sliver of pride. It wasn't even a lie.

The corners of Cinzia's mouth rose in sympathy, but her eyes remained sullen. "I'll miss her. But you're alright?"

"I will be," Yoko said.

The ship's boarding ramp lowered and Jaxon appeared, keeping his distance. In an attempt to hide his identity, he'd shaved his head bald and used a follicle stimulator to grow a short beard that made him appear older than he was. He looked ridiculous, but he was a wanted man. Looking silly was a small price to pay if it kept him anonymous.

Cinzia's sights locked on Jaxon, squinting at the brown hoo-mon. "Hey, isn't that the hoo-mon who's all over the newsfeeds?"

"What? No. Get your eyes checked," Yoko said. "You know how hoo-mons are. They all look alike." Cinzia kept staring. Yoko worried she could see right through his stupid disguise.

Instead, Cinzia nibbled her lower lip. "Is he... spoken for?" Yoko's thick caterpillars frowned. Cinzia shrugged. "What? You know I can't lay off the dark ones."

Yoko's eyes flattened. "I'm here to get my ship fixed, not to get you laid. Though it's clear how much you desperately need it."

Cinzia snorted. "Speak for yourself," she shot back, then gestured at Yoko's ample cleavage. "Ma'am, this is a repair garage, not a titty bar. Take those down to the red strip district and maybe you'll earn enough cubits to pay me for these repairs."

Yoko rolled her eyes and zipped up her flight suit, her hands finding her hips. Cinzia smirked, pleased with herself. She pulled up her diagnostic tablet which resembled an over-sized handheld. Sensors embedded in the hangar's walls scanned the *Saragos* stem to stern, identifying the ship's problem areas. There were more than Yoko had expected. A lot more.

"How bad?" Yoko said, not wanting to know the real answer.

Cinzia sighed. "If she were an animal, I would have her put down." Her fingers flicked and swiped through the long list of tabs on her screen. "We're talking at least seventy thousand cubits worth of work."

Yoko's stomach dropped. "Do I look like I have that kind of money? What about... what about a discount?"

Cinzia grimaced. "What's a *disc count*?"

"It is a hoo-mon word. It means you do the required work, but charge me less money for your labor."

Cinzia paused, her nose wrinkled with confusion. "That's stupid. Why would anyone do good work for less money?"

Yoko shrugged. "I don't get it either. It was worth a try. How much time is this going to take?"

"I have six other ships queued. It's going to be at least a week."

The sick feeling in Yoko's gut worsened. "I don't have a week, Cinzia. Can't you bump me up? I thought we were friends? This isn't friendly behavior."

"We're only friends when you need something," Cinzia teased. "If you want me to move you up and get the work done faster it won't be cheap. Eighty-five thousand cubits and I can get her done in six hours."

Yoko rolled her eyes, throwing her head back with a groan like a spoiled child.

"However," Cinzia went on, "I may be willing to reconsider your *disc count* if you give me an hour alone with your hoo-mon." She lowered her chin seductively, looking past Yoko at Jaxon

"I'm not for sale," Jaxon called back from the loading ramp.

Yoko hadn't realized he'd been listening in. She rubbed her chin. "How big of a discount?"

"I could do twenty percent," Cinzia said. "Thirty percent if he makes me—"

"Not for sale," Jaxon repeated.

"Oh, come on hoo-mon!" Yoko shouted over her shoulder. "We're talking thirty percent here!" Yoko's handheld chimed. She flipped it open and found a recent transfer of 100,000 cubits added to her balance from an anonymous account. She deduced pretty quickly where it had come from. Where Jaxon had gotten that amount of capital and why he hadn't given it to her sooner were questions for another time.

Yoko transferred 85,000 cubits to Cinzia and her handheld chimed with the received payment. Cinzia whistled, her eyes having ballooned. "What happened to not having the money?" Yoko opened her mouth to speak. Cinzia didn't let her. "See? This is just like you light-skins. Always trying to swindle us dark-skins with lies." Her tone was mocking, but with a sliver of seriousness.

Yoko glared, her arms crossed. "It's not like that and you know it. I salvaged Betty's memory core," she said, showing Betty's neuroplastic ball to Cinzia. "It's probably damaged, so it won't be cheap to fix."

Cinzia scratched her neck. "That's for sure. Finding a compatible chassis that isn't a piece of shit is going to be expensive."

Yoko spread her hands. "So you see my problem."

On her tablet, Cinzia pulled up a different screen, her nimble gray fingers working the device like a musical instrument. She flicked her finger, transferring an information packet to Yoko's handheld.

"That's an appointment for a friend of mine. They deal in hard to find hard to fix tech. If anyone can help you, they can."

Yoko bowed her head, and with a pang of hesitation she said, "Thank you."

Cinzia nearly fainted with shock. "Wait, say that again, I want to record it. No one will believe me if I don't have proof."

Yoko stuck her middle and index fingers in the air, a visual Kish expletive. Cinzia giggled, then signaled her crew of mecha mechanics, around forty with work gear, to go to work on the *Saragos.*

Yoko met with Jaxon near the loading ramp. "Where did you get that money? Was it stolen?"

"Liberated," Jaxon said. "A gift. From Martel."

"That tracks," she said. "I have to go. If you stay here, I cannot guarantee you will remain unmolested by Cinzia."

"I have someplace to go, too," Jaxon said.

Yoko cocked her head. "Is that smart? You being a wanted terrorist and all?"

"I have it covered. Look." Jaxon slipped on a pair of sunglasses. "See? I'm invisible."

Yoko cocked her neck with a blank stare. "There's no sunlight on this planet. You look foolish."

"Oh, like this is the most foolish thing you've ever seen someone wear on this planet."

Yoko tilted her head to ponder. He wasn't wrong. "Fine, hoo-mon. But if you get caught, don't expect me to come rescue you. I am not in the rescuing business." Jaxon smiled. Much to Yoko's surprise, it made her relax.

Jaxon handed her his crossglaive hilt. She recognized it as the one that killed Betty. It darkened her mood.

"In case you run into trouble," he said.

"I don't need that," she said, taking it as an insult. "Just because I can't take my weapons doesn't mean I'm harmless. I may be small but I have teeth."

Jaxon closed her palm around the crossglaive hilt. "This bites just a little bit harder than teeth."

***

The blackened sky pissed on the neon lit city harder than usual. The transportation union's strike had ended and traffic was unbearable. Yoko caught a taxi to a small shop hidden in the side of an alley, a place that would've been impossible to find without a map and a spirit guide.

Entering the shop was like walking into an ice box. Cooling units were on full blast to counter the heat radiating from a wide array of overclocked tech that populated the shop. Server towers that could pass for makeshift nuclear bombs hummed in symphonic union in a perpetual countdown.

Yoko zipped her jumpsuit up to her neck, the chilly air waging war on her chest. Her nose stung, catching a subtle whiff of ozone and morning breath that emanated from the shop's owner. The strong smell made breathing difficult. She would just have to bear it.

Cinzia's friend was an Erwei, a genderless species of centipods over two meters tall and in the shape of a giant hand with ten finger-legs. Erwei didn't have eyes or ears. They relied on their hyper perceptive skin to sense and transmit vibrations in a sort of intricate echo location system Yoko didn't fully understand. Their aposematic skin changed color to reflect their moods, triggering the primitive threat perception part of Yoko's brain to be afraid. It made her silver skin crawl.

Yoko's subdermal translators weren't designed to process Erwei communication. The Erwei were not a stupid race. They made up an unusually large portion of engineers and tech designers throughout the known worlds. The shop owner had programmed a mecha to act as their personal translator; an outdated combat model with a broad chest and thick limbs that must have doubled as the shop's security guard. The mecha was skinless and modeled after a species with a cranial structure Yoko wasn't familiar with.

"Hi," Yoko waved, nervous. "Cinzia said you could help me?" She pulled a padded container from her shoulder sack containing Betty's memory core and handed the shiny ball to one of the shop owner's creepy tentacled hand-feet. The flexible tentacle placed the core on a work table. Data lasers interfaced with the device and linked it to the main computer. A rainbow of vibrant unsettling colors washed over the shop owner's moist slimy skin as they analyzed the memory core.

"There is damage," the mecha's monotone voice spoke,

interpreting for the shop owner. "But there is luck. Only twenty-three percent of memory partition corrupted. I can fix. There will be errors. But salvageable. There will be difficulty finding compatible chassis. This model no longer in production."

Yoko exhaled a long, annoyed groan. She didn't realize she'd been holding her breath. Not because of the smell, which had only grown more pungent in this short time, but because she'd been bracing herself for the worst. *It's fried. She's never coming back. The best friend you ever had is dead and it's all your fault,* but in a series of weird vibrations.

Instead, she'd been gifted a measure of hope. "Find me a compatible model and I'll pay you a finder's fee," Yoko said so fast it sounded like one big word.

The shop owner's hand-feet worked several different custom touch pads ergonomically attuned for Erwei physiology. "Found a seller with a compatible chassis on Herekino," the mecha spoke, then craned a monitor so Yoko could see the details.

The mecha was a male model. Yoko shook her head. "No, that won't do. Betty was coded as female. I want her back the way she was. I need a lady model."

The shop owner did some more searching. An endless series of mechas flashed by on the display screen too quick for Yoko to focus on each one. Soon, the display settled on a mecha similar to Betty's model, but different. She was a taller variant with black hair, an angular face and a significantly reduced bust size. An annotation listed her ethnicity as Swedish. Yoko didn't know what that meant.

"That one," Yoko pointed. "How much for that one?"

"Twenty thousand cubits." It was a good price. Too good of a price.

"Condition?"

"Acceptable."

Foosha. That usually meant the displayed picture wouldn't look anything like the actual item and was just as likely to be in far worse condition than advertised. Yoko's caterpillars raised. "Where?"

"Chicaul Station." Yoko didn't recognize that station, and she knew all of them. Reading her confusion, the mecha continued, "It is a trading outpost. Beyond the catapult."

"Foosha!" Yoko muttered. Her face knotted and her chest went tight. Yoko despised the worlds beyond the catapult. They were a mishmash of barren and lawless realms filled with thieves, slavers, and savages. Yoko swore on the grave of her dead cats that she'd never go back to that awful wretched shit stain of space. She wasn't going to break that vow. Not even for Betty. "There has to be another model somewhere local."

"We have searched. There is none."

Yoko's caterpillars frowned, her anxiety settling in her jaw. There was no justification in the universe that could make this sketchy chassis worth the time, money, and danger she would be facing to secure it. *No. No. There must be another way.* It would be easier to just buy a new mecha and program it as best she could to Betty's specifications and hope for the best. She could do that. It would probably pacify her.

For a little while.

Then she'd have to face the facts. The new Betty wouldn't be her Betty. She'd have to come to terms with the knowledge that the only thing stopping her from getting her friend back was her cowardice.

Yoko pinched the bridge of her nose and let out a long breath from her chilly lungs that rattled her throat. Her eyes shut tight enough to hurt. Her head shook, willing herself to make the easy choice. But the moment passed, and she knew it was pointless. She'd already made her decision the moment there was no other choice to make. It was inevitable, fighting it was futile.

She opened her eyes and said, "Place a reserve order."

***

Rain drenched the city.

Traffic was at a standstill. Yoko wasn't about to pay to sit in an idling taxi for the next few hours. She walked, the rain matting her slick hair to her skin. She cursed herself for not wearing a hat. Compared to the smelly stifling tech shop, the cool air and light drizzle was a welcomed relief.

The ambient sounds of the city faded and the trickling rainfall became white noise. Yoko's mind spun in all directions. She attempted to calculate the logistics of her upcoming journey. It made her want to cry. Traveling beyond the catapult and back would take several weeks if not an entire month to complete. Worst of all, it wouldn't be cheap.

The last time she'd gone beyond the catapult, which had been the first time, the trip had taken six agonizing weeks. The threat of being attacked by pirates or running out of fuel pellets had been a daily concern. She'd lost seven kilos in water weight from the stress. The only reason Yoko could bear it was because Betty had taken care of her. Now she'd be flying alone for the first time since her father's death. The thought of making the trip by herself coupled with the rain soaking her skin made Yoko feel like she was drowning. Mentally preparing herself for her upcoming voyage distracted her. She hadn't noticed she was being followed.

Two thick well-dressed Tzipkan assholes stood in front of her shoulder to shoulder, blocking her path. Yoko turned and found two more Tzipkan goons flanking her. She turned again and bumped into two more behind her. Uthay's thugs. The same ones she'd encountered in the back alley of Decadence, the limbs Jaxon took from them replaced with gaudy cybernetic upgrades. Yoko scanned for a door, an alley, somewhere to escape to. The goons waited until she'd passed a stretch of brick wall before they cornered her.

Yoko's hand snaked inside of her shoulder sack, finding Jaxon's crossglaive hilt. She was prepared to cut her way through them, or die in the attempt. Whichever came first.

One of the thugs patted the air, signaling her to calm down. "We're not here to hurt you," he said in a deep booming voice. "The boss just wants to talk." His partner held a handheld with an open connection to Uthay, who was someplace dry and smoking a cigar.

"I paid your outrageous debt, Uthay," Yoko shouted over the rain. "In full. I never pay anything in full."

"And I appreciate that," Uthay nodded with a false smile, his voice tiny and sharp on the handheld. He was hard to hear over the downpour. His cigar smoke clouded the screen. "I have a business proposition."

Yoko's eyebrows climbed up her forehead. He was playing nice. Which meant her life wasn't in immediate danger. Her heart relaxed a bit, but not by much. "I'm listening."

"The human who interfered in our negotiation. People are looking for him. People with very deep pockets."

That explains it, she thought. The thugs hadn't slipped a shroud over her head or shoved her in the trunk of a car or beaten her because they wanted Jaxon. "Who are these people? What do they want with him?"

"Don't know. Don't much care," Uthay said, breathing smoke. "But they're offering five million cubits for his whereabouts. Help me find him and you'll get a nice kickback."

"A bounty that big I would have heard about."

"It's off the books. Private party. All very under the table," Uthay said. His viridian eyes looked like tiny green marbles on the handheld.

"If I knew where the hoo-mon was why wouldn't I just cash him in myself?" Yoko said.

"Have you seen the newsfeeds? He's a mass murderer. You can't take him alone. And I'd hate to see you lose your pretty little silver head."

Yoko's eyes narrowed to slits. "What would be my cut? And I better like what I hear."

"Given you paid back your debt to me so promptly," he said, really pouring in the sarcasm, "I'm feeling generous. A million cubits. How's that sound?"

Yoko's jaw hung open. She immediately began to spend the money in her head. She could custom build Betty a new chassis. She could afford special upgrades to the *Saragos.* Bigger, better gun turrets. A missile battery. Maybe even a concealed magnetic accelerator cannon. Yoko fantasized about turning the *Saragos* into a gunship, even though it was a little too small for that. One million cubits was a lot of money...

Too much money. *No way would he give that much up.* Either the bounty was higher than he was saying or he'd ordered his goons to kill her the moment she complied. Yoko convinced herself that was the reason she was turning down Uthay's offer.

"He paid me to take him to an ugly rock called Terezakis," Yoko said. "I last saw him boarding another ship. A hoo-mon gunship.

Start there."

Uthay groaned. "That's not helpful."

"It's all I got. But I'll tell you what. If I find him, you'll be the first one I call. Trust me." Yoko attempted to squeak past the thugs. They didn't let her.

"I would," Uthay said. "If you were trustworthy. I feel like you're not being completely honest with me, Yoko. Are you *protecting* this human?"

Yoko scoffed. "Have you ever known me to protect anyone other than myself? Especially not when there's this much profit to be made. I'm insulted, frankly."

Uthay puffed on his cigar, considering. His head tilted to one side, then nodded. "You have a point. That would be wildly out of character for you. I've always admired your capacity for selfish greed. Makes you easy to predict. You will let me know if you see him, yeah?"

"First thing," she said with a thin smile.

"That would be the smart move. But if I find out you're lying to me—"

"I am an honorable Kish woman. We don't lie." The moment stretched. The sound of rain. Uthay signaled his men to let her pass. Yoko squeezed her way through the thugs and scampered off with a confidence she hadn't felt in ages. Standing still for so long, the rain had soaked into her jumpsuit and made her feel heavier and cold. She despised the cold.

Shivering, she waited until she was out the thug's sight before flicking open her handheld. She sent a connection request to Jaxon. He accepted and his face appeared on the screen. Wherever he was, it was bright and indoors and more importantly, dry.

"Hoo-mon, you don't owe me one anymore," Yoko said with a sly smirk. "Now you owe me two."

Chapter Thirty-One: Jaxon

He'd left Yoko at the repair dock more than an hour ago, his repaired rocket boots having carried him through the rainy sky. Jaxon landed on the spot where he'd stepped off the rail train at the beginning of this journey. He walked the wet streets and sloshed through puddles, convincing himself he wasn't looking for Sherae. When he didn't find her, he started asking the other streetwalkers in the area if they knew her.

One of them, a pear shaped Velibor woman with a wide toothy smile holding an over-sized umbrella, recognized the name. She chatted Jaxon up before offering to reveal Sherae's usual haunt. For a fee. He paid her double.

A short flight across the night's sky and Jaxon landed at a small beach-side tavern far from the neon glow of the city's lights. The place was so busy he could barely see the walls. Jaxon waded through a sea of modded-up drunkards until he found Sherae sitting at the bar. She was in her female form and wore a casual medium cut black dress with a small red jacket and matching red high heeled shoes that showed off her legs. Her blonde hair hung long and shaggy against her golden skin with bangs that stopped just past her thin yellow eyebrows. She could catch a blind man's attention. Several bar patrons approached her for her services. She politely informed them she was off the clock.

Jaxon had come her to thank her. To show her his appreciation for getting him to Murhaf when she had no reason to make that effort. For saving his life. It was mostly true. Her brilliant amber eyes met his and they sparked. She saw right through his dumb disguise and greeted him with an open-mouthed smile that wrinkled her eyes. Sherae gestured to the seat next to her and he sat. They shared a drink, this being his first ever. It was aqua blue, odorless, and had a bitter aftertaste that snuck up on him.

What they talked about wasn't important. Sherae caressed his new beard, pretending to like it. Her fingers dragged across his bald head, her fingertips emitting a dim glow when in contact with his skin. Jaxon wanted to ask her what that meant, but worried it might come off as an insult, or boring. She was an alien. Maybe it was just how her species was. The question was gone and all he could think about was the soft warmth of her touch. Her eyes went glassy and dilated. He worried he would fall into them. They exchanged words. She laughed at something funny he'd said and whispered in his ear. She took his hand and they left together.

Back at her bungalow, they went slow.

Sherae's smile never left her lips, which glowed with every kiss. Jaxon's nervousness didn't scare her. He'd only ever been with one other woman, and that hadn't even cracked his top one thousand fondest memories. His inexperience wasn't a problem for her. She was the professional. He let her lead.

They lost their clothes and made out on a small bed with fresh sheets that smelled vaguely of disinfectant and citrus. Sherae was a good kisser. She had to be. Their foreplay had gone on for longer than it should've before Jaxon had to call it quits. He wasn't rising to the occasion.

"I'm sorry," Jaxon said, trying to laugh it off and failing miserably.

"Don't be," she said. Sherae brushed strands of hair out of her face and held his gaze. "I'm in no hurry." She dragged her glowing fingertips across Jaxon's scars, noticing all the new ones he'd gotten over the past few weeks. She didn't ask how they got there.

"It's not you," Jaxon said.

"Is this your first time?" Sherae asked with a quizzical grin.

"No," Jaxon said with another forced laugh. *I really need to stop doing that*, he thought. It wasn't diffusing the crippling awkwardness. "I've been with girls before."

"I meant a girl like me," Sherae said.

"I didn't know there were girls like you," Jaxon said. "I just... it's always been hard for me. Bad choice of words. Let me rephrase. Letting myself be intimate with someone has never been... easy for me." Her hand started at the top of his head and moved down his face to his chest. Her entire palm glowed.

"Okay, what is that?" Jaxon asked.

"My kind..." Sherae said, then paused. "I can taste your emotions."

Jaxon bent his neck. "You mean like pheromones?"

Sherae's head bobbed side to side. "In a crude way, yes. It's like a drug. It can be intoxicating. I've never tasted anything like you before. I knew it when we first met, but I didn't think it would be this good. This potent. I wish I could bottle this and sell it." She pulled him in for a kiss and it was electric. She laid him down and found that his problem had stiffened.

What followed was a wet blur of hormones and emotion, both of them collapsing in a heated sweat. He enjoyed it, but not as much as she did. He would go unfulfilled, his thoughts scattered elsewhere. She stared up at him, sensing as much.

Sherae spread her arms and said, "Come here." Jaxon did as he was told. Sherae held him, her chin resting on his shoulder. Jaxon could feel her breasts on his chest, then past that, the beat of her heart. It hummed like a song. They listened to the rain pelting the metal awing outside of the window and, for the first time in a long time, Jaxon felt safe.

So it was quite the surprise, most especially to him, when the tears came. They poured out of him in a tide. He couldn't stop them. The pressure of the last few weeks, the betrayals, the deaths, the near-deaths, the violence. The memories that weren't his floating around inside his head like old ghosts. It was all too much and suffocating. He couldn't confide in anyone, not even those closest to him, out of fear that they would judge him or think less of him, or that they just wouldn't understand.

Sherae had seen his wound. She'd sensed it. Or maybe she just liked the taste of it. Her skin pulsed with its ethereal glow as she absorbed his emotions, taking his pain. Sharing it. Her tears dripped onto his shoulder and rolled down his back. She held him tight until she'd drain the grief out of him. Her glow dimmed and faded like a choked candle.

"I'm sorry," Jaxon said, his voice cracking. "This is so embarrassing."

"It's not," Sherae said in a tender, motherly sort of way. "It's normal. An orgasm isn't the only release some people need." Jaxon held her incandescent hand. She squeezed back.

They laid down beside each other, staring into the other's eyes. "Tell me about your job," Jaxon said. "Why do you do it?"

"I like working with people," Sherae said, that glazed look in her eyes that said she was still getting high off of him. "I like making them happy. In return I get to taste their pheromones. It's like candy." She shrugged. "And the money's good."

"So, it's not just sex?"

She giggled. "I have a regular who pays me to rate his cooking. A lot of my female clients just like having someone to talk to about their problems. This one woman, a real sweetheart, she pays me just to tell me about her kids."

Jaxon's gut knotted at the mention of children. "That sounds nice," he whispered. "A part of me was kind of hoping someday I'd be able to have a family of my own. Now that'll never happen."

Sherae blinked. "Why can't it?"

"The religion I joined. Turns out they secretly made me infertile. I can never have children."

Sherae shook her head and, with an upbeat smile, said, "Sure you can. You could have one right now. Tonight."

Her words confused, then stunned Jaxon. "You mean... with *you*?"

"No," she laughed. "With Murhaf. He can make one for you."

***

"I don't want a clone," Jaxon said.

He'd parted ways with Sherae, promising her that it wouldn't be their last meeting. He'd flown through the rain back to Murhaf's clinic, which didn't appear to be quite as shitty as he'd remembered. Jaxon had been brought to a section of the building that resembled an upscaled version of a mad scientist's laboratory. There were tall windowed cabinets filled with medicines and tanks filled with what Jaxon was really hoping weren't body parts. He regretted coming here with every passing second.

"I'm not trying to clone myself," Jaxon said.

Murhaf patted the air. "Oh no no," he said, a cigarette dangling from his lips. "It won't be a clone. DNA is complex, it holds more than enough genetic information that contains a wealth of dormant and recessive genes. I can rearrange those pieces and produce an entirely unique individual, just like a natural child."

Jaxon waved away the clouds of smoke hanging between them. "And it will be healthy? And able to have children of its own?"

"Absolutely," Murhaf said with a hearty smile. "I have a near perfect success rate. Never tried it with human DNA, but I don't see how that'd be an issue. You can design your baby right down to the chromosomes, though that would cost extra. Height, skin color, eye color, hair color. All the colors."

Jaxon stared at a strange machine that looked like a portable fishbowl with a life support system strapped to its base; an artificial womb filled with amniotic fluid. A blank embryo resembling a fleshy omelet floated inside, tethered to an umbilical artery.

"How long will it take to be born?" Jaxon asked.

Murhaf talked with his hands. "You can let it develop naturally or use growth stims to speed up the process. Full maturation could be as short as two months."

Jaxon coughed from the smoke. "Will the stims affect its lifespan?"

"Shouldn't," Murhaf said. "You'll need to administer an additional round of stims to slow down the growth process, but after that the child should live a normal lifespan for your species."

Jaxon stared at the artificial womb with such intensity he worried he might tune and break it. He imagined what the child would look like. What they'd be like. Then the fear set in. *This is a mistake. You are a wanted man. This is the worst condition to bring a child into this world. You are a fool for thinking this would work. Turn around and leave and never come back.*

"What kind of people do this?" Jaxon asked. "Is this crazy? Who pays to grow children in a lab?"

"Well, it's not a common operation," Murhaf said. "Given it's illegal." Jaxon's eyes widened. He hadn't realized he was adding another crime to his rap sheet.

"But it's usually people with dead kids," Murhaf went on. "Had a couple come see me about a year ago. Nice folks. Had a son. Died in some kind of traffic accident. They could have had another kid, but they didn't want a new kid. They wanted their kid. They kept some of his hair and baby teeth, which was more than enough for me to work with. So I gave them their boy back. But I think your real question is, do you really want to create a child given your recent... activities?"

Jaxon tensed. His mind scrambled to come up with a lie, then realized he was terrible at coming up with lies. "I didn't do any of the stuff they said I did," Jaxon blurted out. "I didn't kill anyone. No one was killed. The news service is full of shit."

Murhaf chuckled. "Tell me something I *don't* know." He breathed smoke. "The Protectorate, they're all liars and thieves. Their approved news services lie about independent worlds like ours all the time. Think we're all a basket of backwards idiots who sleep with our sisters. You should watch Iyana Gley's broadcasts. She's been reporting the truth about the Montanari coverage. But you're in their sights now. You're a wanted man. They'll be coming after you. Is that really the environment you want to raise a kid in?"

Jaxon couldn't rebut. This was a bad time to birth a child, but when had there ever been a good time? When would there ever be? Jaxon's handheld chimed, a connection request from Yoko. He accepted it.

"Hoo-mon, you don't owe me one anymore," Yoko's sugary voice piped through the device's speaker. "Now you owe me two. Meet me at the Blackout Cafe in Fancher Square. And try not to be seen. People are looking for you." She ended the connection. It was the perfect excuse Jaxon needed to stop himself from making a huge mistake that he could never take back...

He transferred the money to Murhaf's account.

"Very well," Murhaf said, then approached Jaxon with a hypospray. The four-eyed Taruc pressed the muzzle to Jaxon's arm. Blood kicked into the gun's hollow glass vial, filling it. It stung, but Jaxon didn't react to the pain. Murhaf inserted the vial of blood into a processor connected to the artificial womb and stabbed a few buttons. A program ran tests on the blood and spit out a full analytical readout.

"Everything looks good," Murhaf said. "So, do you want a boy or a girl?"

"Surprise me."

Murhaf plugged Jaxon's blood sample into a device that resequenced his DNA to make a wholly unique genetic profile. When the operation ran its course, the program waited for final confirmation before it began the insemination process.

Murhaf craned the keyboard so Jaxon could reach it. "Would you like to do the honors?"

Jaxon hesitated. There was still time to come to his senses...

He pressed the button.

The resequenced DNA sample shot into the blank embryo via the umbilical artery and immediately began changing. Becoming.

"Congratulations," Murhaf smiled. "You're a daddy."

***

Jaxon touched down at Fancher Square, a busy strip mall awash in virtual ads and housing various restaurants, boutiques, mod shops, and brothels.

The charge in both of his rocket boots dipped below forty percent. The added weight of the bulky artificial womb he'd been hauling didn't help. He wore the carriage on his back like a rucksack, the sloshing amniotic fluid inside the tank throwing off his center of balance whenever he banked.

Murhaf had given him a thirty second tutorial on how to operate the carriage. The life support system kept the chamber oxygenated and was powered by a high efficiency energy cell, with a backup cell on standby just in case the primary failed. Food and water were fed into an apparatus that would break down the contents into glucose, amino acids, and fats that would nourish the growing fetus via the umbilical artery. The carriage's casing was molded out of light weight medical grade cargonite, so it could probably take a bit of punishment without cracking the interior tank.

He would die before ever letting that happen.

Jaxon entered the Blackout Cafe and realized how literal its name was. The shop was a Faraday cage, completely shielded from electronic signals, cutting everyone inside off from the outside world. No neon. No overt uses of modern technology. Just walls, booths, and chairs.

At a booth, Yoko sat eating something purple that vaguely resembled grilled fish with a glass of ale. She caught sight of Jaxon, her eyes fixed on his bulky cargo as if it were a wild animal.

"There's a five-million cubit price on your head hoo-mon," Yoko said through chews, her unblinking eyes still locked on the artificial womb.

"That's a lot," Jaxon said. "Why aren't you collecting it?"

Yoko fake-pouted and swallowed. "Uthay offered me a full million to give you up, which means the real price is probably ten million."

"You didn't answer my question."

"When I have an answer I'll let you know," Yoko said, still trying to figure out what the carriage was. "But if anyone is going to collect your bounty it's going to be me— what is that?"

"It's a mobile maturation carriage," Jaxon said. He slid open the tank's viewing hatch to show Yoko the fleshy lump of cells growing inside.

Yoko's jaw hung open. "So whose baby did you steal?"

"I didn't steal anything. It's my baby. I had it made."

Yoko's eyes slitted. She sucked her teeth. "But... why?"

"Haven't you ever wanted a family?"

Yoko made a face like she'd tasted something sour. "That would mean having to put someone else's needs before my own. I'm far too self-centered for that, hoo-mon. Child rearing is very sacred to the Kish. If you aren't willing to sacrifice everything for your child then you simply don't have one."

"What about unplanned pregnancies?"

Yoko took a bite of her purple fish. "We don't have those," she said while chewing. "We can control our fertility cycle. Only wanted children are born."

"You mean, like, through marriage?"

Yoko groaned, the fish filling the inside of her cheeks chipmunk-style. "You make my brain hurt, hoo-mon. Marriages are extremely taboo in Kish culture. They're almost unheard of. If a woman wants a child she chooses from a list of potential donors and pays a male for his genetic material. Once the contract is finalized he will have no further contact with the buyer or the child."

Jaxon's face fell. "But what if a man wants a child?"

"The male vets potential surrogates and negotiates a weekly or monthly fee to lease a female's womb for the twenty-eight weeks it takes for a Kish fetus to mature. If the pregnancy takes longer he may be charged overage fees."

Jaxon's nose wrinkled. "Wait, pregnancy is viewed as a *rental*? Does that mean birth is considered an *eviction*?"

"Once the fetus is born and certified healthy," Yoko continued, ignoring his stupid question, "the female will have no further contact with the renter or the child."

"So... were you raised by your father or your mother?"

Yoko glared, her eyes saying *I don't want to talk about this.* "I just wanted to give you a heads up about Uthay. As a courtesy."

Flattered, Jaxon smiled, though he wasn't sure why. "I don't understand."

"I found a replacement for Betty's chassis. Beyond the catapult." Her inflection was dead serious.

Jaxon shrugged. "Okay. When do we leave?"

Yoko waited for him to figure out what she meant. He didn't. "That means you can't come with me, hoo-mon." She gestured to the carriage. "Especially not with *that* thing."

"Why can't I come with you?"

Her neck jerked in annoyance. "Have you ever been beyond the catapult, hoo-mon? It's a death trap. That entire stretch of galaxy is filled with nothing but killers, slavers and pirates. And that's if you're lucky."

"And you want to go there *alone*? What if something happens to you? What if you fall? Who's going to catch you?"

The corners of Yoko's mouth curled, seemingly against her will. Jaxon smiled in triumph. The amusement drained from Yoko's face, replaced with hardened cynicism. "You don't even know me, hoo-mon. You don't know what you're getting into."

"I know you can't do this alone. People are looking for me here. A secluded part of our galaxy sounds like the perfect place to lay low for a few weeks. I want to help you get Betty back. And besides, I owe you."

Yoko's dread receded. She wrestled with his logic verses her stubbornness, clearly making complex calculations behind those thick caterpillars of hers. The seconds stretched while they held each other's gaze. After a time, Yoko washed down her meal with a gulp of beer. She slammed the glass on the table, then said, "I have decided. I will be taking you on as crew. That means I am your captain now. You will do what I say, when I say it, how I say it."

"Sure thing, captain."

"You will also be my personal protection," Yoko said, as she dug Jaxon's crossglaive hilt from her shoulder sack and slid it across the table to him.

She did this because Uthay's goons had entered the cafe. Ten of them. Yoko had seen them enter, likely precipitating her decision to let him join her. The goons had cybernetic enhancements that made them look more machine than organic. They carried tasers and plasma daggers that glowed white with super-heated energy. There were a dozen civilians between him and them and the cafe was small and confined. Jaxon didn't want anyone to die. But they were ten strong, and he had a child to think about.

Jaxon stood from his booth, entering the narrow aisle separating the neighboring rows of booths. Five thugs in front of him and five more behind. All ten were huge, thickheaded and broad chested. They meant business.

The lead goon said, "We can do this quiet, or we can do this loud." His voice carried an electronic buzz.

Jaxon extended his crossglaive blade, the roar of its superheated edge acting as his reply. The lead goon jerked forward, much to his confusion. Jaxon was tuning. The plasma dagger wrenched out of the man's mechanical hand and into Jaxon's free hand, blade down. The crossglaive swung through the air and caught flesh. Fast footsteps came from behind him. He threw his dagger without even looking. It punched deep into another goon's chest, destroying one of the Tzipkan's two hearts. Jaxon didn't even know Tzipkans had two hearts a moment ago. He'd meant to aim for the man's arm.

Jaxon tuned the dagger back to his palm and reoriented himself when a linked memory flashed in his mind. Sabrene's memory. He was using her strategy. Her tactics. Sabrene's killer instincts were overwriting his judgment. Adrenaline wouldn't let him stop it. The time he'd taken to wrestle back control of his own mind allowed the goons to swarm him and he lost his crossglaive.

Panic and fear took control and he gave in. He let Sabrene's skills save him.

Jaxon fell into a kind of trance and all he could hear were the screams. Not the screams of Olen's settlers, but a brand-new remix.

The last goon standing kicked away Jaxon's dagger and the man wrapped his hands around the human's neck, hands which were thick as boxing gloves. Jaxon's vision blurred. He flirted with blacking out. Another linked memory floated to the surface and Jaxon cupped the fingers of his right hand, tuning. The goon's eye pulled itself out of its socket and into Jaxon's palm. While the man wailed, Jaxon grabbed a taser and put him down for good.

Ten maimed, but still living alien bodies lay on the floor among a scattering of severed limbs, the metallic stink of blood and burned metal wafting through the air. Jaxon gasped for air faster than his lungs could keep up. The restaurant patrons had evacuated at some point, except for Yoko.

"Good job hoo-mon," Yoko said as she picked the pockets of the goons writhed in too much pain to stop her. "It would have been easier if you had just killed them, though. Now they'll slowly bleed out. But I'm sure they didn't have families or a sick grandma or anything."

Fear and remorse shot through Jaxon's nerves like lightning. The taste of vomit bubbled in the back of his throat. All he could think about now was the safety of his child. He heard sirens through the walls. They were distant, but getting closer.

Jaxon spoke fast. "We need to leave."

"No shit," Yoko said.

***

"She's not ready," Cinzia said.

It'd been less than six hours since she'd begun repairing the

Saragos and already it was looking like a slightly newer ship. Jaxon stood near the loading ramp wearing the carriage on his back while Yoko haggled with the Kish mechanic.

"I can't stay here," Yoko said, her caterpillar eyebrows narrowed in a straight line. "I've got people after me. You see this blood on my suspenders? It's not mine, but it could have been. I would like to continue keeping my blood inside of my body. Can the ship fly?"

"Yes, but—"

"Then reimburse me for what you didn't fix so I can get out of here."

Cinzia frowned. "I didn't have time to get to the graviton regulator. It needs to be replaced," she said, drumming her fingers on her tablet.

"How long will the current one last? Minimum?"

"A few weeks, but—"

"I'll get it fixed by then," Yoko said. "I promise. But I'm leaving." Cinzia pursed her lips and exhaled through her nose. She tapped on her tablet and the hangar bay's roof opened up. The mechas still inside the *Saragos* filed out of the ship in formation.

"A lot of people go beyond the catapult," Cinzia said in a dire tone. "Many don't come back."

"That's because they weren't me," Yoko said. "I've done it once. I can do it again. Just you wait and see." She joined Jaxon on the loading ramp.

"And you're low on turret rounds," Cinzia added. "You don't want to be caught on the wrong side of the catapult without bullets. And Yoko, don't come back without her." Yoko waved Cinzia goodbye and the loading ramp ascended into the ship, its gears barely making a sound now.

In the cockpit, Yoko strapped on her gravity harness and ran preflight checks. Jaxon stopped off in the head to clean the dried blood from his skin and out of his beard. There wasn't time to change clothes.

By the time Jaxon secured the carriage and sat in the cockpit next to Yoko the ship was already breaking orbit and his gravity harness tugged at his shoulders and hips. The ship's gimbals adjusted so smoothly now that he barely noticed the transition.

"I was raised by my father," Yoko said, keeping her eyes on her screens. "Everything I am, all the skills I've learned, I owe to him. Not so much the drinking and the gambling though. He'd probably spank my ass for those. But he taught me how to survive. And even though I didn't always treat him with the respect he deserved, my father sacrificed his life to keep me safe."

"I can only hope that I can live up to his example," Jaxon said. She looked over at him, and they understood each other.

A beam of light shot out of the nose of the *Saragos* and pulled the ship into slipstream.

**

The Aurelio Nadekwe Jorstad Davault Graviton Gateway was the long-winded corporate name for what was colloquially known as the catapult. The giant monstrosity hung against the stars and resembled an asymmetrical ten-kilometer-long gun barrel; it split into three prongs with a massive spherical graviton reactor bolted to its ass.

After a brief layover at Kidwell Station, the *Saragos* arrived at a Protectorate security checkpoint. The ship was scanned by two Protectorate cruisers checking to see if the small freighter was hauling any high yield nuclear explosives that could be used to blow up the catapult. Apparently, someone had tried that at some point over the catapult's ninety-two-year operation history.

After the ship passed inspection, Jaxon helped cover the thirteen-thousand-cubit transit fee, which included a bribe to get the ship waved through the board-and-inspection checkpoint. The Protectorate didn't really care much about who was leaving their arm of the galaxy, only who was coming in. That would be a problem Jaxon would worry about later.

The *Saragos* queued in line with dozens of other ships, mostly cargo haulers, for an additional four hours. Jaxon cut his beard and spent this time attempting to draft a message to Akeema. Nothing he said sounded like anything other than desertion. He was leaving Akeema and Castor in the hands of the man who'd crippled them, but Martel had given his word. He was many things, but he wasn't a liar. Jaxon watched the video message he'd made six times before scheduling it to be delivered after he'd made the transit, like a coward. He left out the minor detail about the child he'd paid to have created, also like a coward.

The *Saragos* was given clearance to enter the catapult's acceleration arc along with sixteen other ships making the same journey; the bullets in the catapult's proverbial gun chamber. Each ship was instructed to turn over remote navigational control to the catapult's technicians to ensure a smooth transit.

Jaxon and Yoko met in the ship's gravcouch compartment, a room with reinforced radiation shielding that housed eight stasis chambers. They looked like metal sarcophagi and were commonly used in emergencies where a ship had lost its life support or the crew were stranded without communications. They were also pretty good at preventing the extreme g forces exerted by the catapult from turning fleshy beings like Jaxon and Yoko into lasagna with teeth.

"If you need to use the shitter this is your last chance," Yoko announced. "You don't want to enter stasis with waste in your guts, trust me."

Jaxon secured the carriage into one of the gravcouches. He kissed the casing before the couch's lid cycled shut. Yoko thumbed off her suspenders and lifted her shirt over her head, her clothes floating in a pile next to her. Jaxon didn't mean to stare. Her bra and panties didn't match, which perplexed him. Yoko's toes stood out; they were a much darker shade of gray than the rest of her skin. That puzzled him as well. A lot of things about her did. It made her more interesting.

Her chin rose and she noticed him watching. His eyes tracked up to meet hers and Jaxon froze, his brown skin hiding his blush. Her head tilted to the side in a curious sort of way. "I knew it," Yoko muttered.

"I, uh... I wasn't..." Jaxon stammered.

He didn't understand the sly smile tucked in the corner of her mouth. "You like what you see, huh hoo-mon?" Jaxon averted his gaze and her smirk became a grin. "Oh, don't pretend. You've been caught. No need to be ashamed. In my old neighborhood I was desired by many of the males... and even some of the females. You couldn't help it. I'm just too sexy." Jaxon's embarrassment continued and she giggled. "Well? Come on," she said. "We're going to have to see each other naked at some point, might as well get it over with. Let's see what you got."

Jaxon hesitated, but undressed. He made sure to keep his eyes above Yoko's neckline.

She had no such compunction. Yoko eyed him top to bottom and her smile faded, her face becoming ashen. Jaxon's mind jumped to her being disgusted by his nakedness, but it wasn't that. His scars. This was the first time she'd seen them. The scar tissue on his right side and back could pass for thick spider legs.

"Come here," she said, waving him over. Yoko handed him a cooling garment, a thin form-fitting body suit used to regulate the wearer's body temperature. "Put this on." He did. It reminded him of adult-sized onesie pajamas; it fit like a second skin. They helped each other zip up the suit's back.

Yoko fastened a medical monitor to his arm that made him think of a blood pressure machine. It paired with the cooling garment and would keep Jaxon asleep during the transit, then wake him when it was completed. Jaxon helped Yoko with her arm monitor.

"What happens if something goes wrong while we're under?" Jaxon asked.

"Then all our problems are over," Yoko said. "And my ghost will sue the Protectorate for damages."

Jaxon laughed.

He removed and stored his gravity harness. Floating in null g, he laid down in the gravcouch with Yoko's help. As the captain, it was her duty to secure her crew before herself. As much as she enjoyed playing the role of a selfish egotistical tyrant, now that Jaxon was part of her crew, her responsibility, he could see how she cared. Maybe not in the way she cared for Betty, but she took his welfare seriously. Yoko fastened a breathing mask over his face and the gravcouch's lid slid shut.

Her silver impish face was the last thing Jaxon saw before the gravcouch filled with oxygenated fluid and sedatives flooded his system. When he woke up, he'd be in the most dangerous part of the known galaxy, but until then, he would sleep.

The dreams came.
And with them, the screams.

Epilogue: Martel

He found Olen dead.

The revelation stabbed deep into Martel's heart, sharp as a prison yard shiv. She lay slumped over in her bed, one eye stuck open, the other half closed in an unsettling stare. A trail of dried blood leaked from her nose and the corner of her mouth. Her mangled emaciated body was cold as ice.

Martel had been preparing himself for this. He still wasn't ready. Tears fogged his vision. He closed Olen's eyes, wiped her nose and mouth. She looked asleep. Only the stillness of her broken chest betrayed her.

On the floor next to the bed, he found Akeema.

Her unconscious body twitched and spasmed as if she were a dying fish. Martel knew what had happened even before he'd reviewed the security footage and confirmed his suspicion. Olen had linked with her. A flash of anger heated Martel's skin. It was the betrayal. He wanted to grieve for his friend and mentor, but the rage overrode him. He aimed it at Akeema. Martel wanted to blame her for this, for forcing Olen into killing herself with the link.

But that wasn't the truth.

No one could have ever forced that woman to do anything she didn't want to do. If anything, she had talked Akeema into it. The security video confirmed as much. He saw the desire in the red woman's eyes. The lust for more power was what drove her, power she planned to use to kill him. He liked that about her. It was what made her so vulnerable to being manipulated.

Martel moved Akeema to a bed next to Castor and strapped her in place. She was comatose, but stable. He ran a quick scan. Her brain was a fireworks display of activity. She would likely come out of it soon, but there was no telling when. In his experience, the human mind tended to act a little funny after being meddled with by alien telepathy. Linking was, in a sense, a form of brain damage.

He believed Akeema would snap out of it. If Olen died before safely breaking off the link then, well, maybe she wouldn't.

Martel prepared Olen's body, wrapping her in a silk burial shroud. She wanted to be laid to rest on Zaspel next to her husband and son. He vowed to honor her request, but Martel wasn't ready to let her go. Not just yet.

He suspected there had to be some kind of plan at work here. Olen had set something in motion and she hadn't shared it with him. He thought he knew her so completely, that she'd held nothing back from him. Despite all he'd done for her, Olen hadn't trusted him with this. She'd managed to keep a part of herself hidden from him. It tasted like ashes in his mouth. He wondered if he'd ever known her at all.

Martel continued to have faith in the power of the album.

He'd been trying to revive the dead artifact ever since they arrived from Terezakis, hitting it with every variation of energy and radiation available to him. For almost two straight days he went with only a few hours of sleep and a dozen cups of coffee. He didn't even like coffee, but it never failed to keep him laser focused. It wasn't until Martel lifted the transmission blackout that things got even worse.

The *Jezebel* received a transmission from Jaxon. It was addressed to Akeema, but that wasn't going to stop him from seeing it even if her circumstances weren't so dire. Jaxon had chosen to go gallivanting off with his mouthy Kish pilot to the asshole end of the Milky Way Galaxy. Martel saw it for what it was. Desertion. He'd started drafting a response when the *Jezebel*'s sensors gave Martel the break he so desperately needed.

The album wasn't completely dead. It was emanating a low, almost undetectable signal pulse that his instruments weren't calibrated to detect, but the *Jezebel* could. Whoever, or whatever the album was trying to communicate with, it had received a reply.

Tracking the signal's origin wasn't easy. It was weak and scattered across lightyears. The process could take months, if not years to pinpoint. But he had a direction. A lead. He prepared the *Jezebel* for the journey. There would be no telling when he'd come back, so he had Akeema and Castor loaded onto the ship in medical pods. If there was another album out in the wild, he'd need their help tracking it down.

That only left Olen. He didn't want to leave her alone, and there wasn't time to take her body to Zaspel. Her grand funeral would have to wait. Martel prepped a stasis pod to act as her temporary casket. He stood over Olen's corpse as he held the album.

Something came over him, nagging at him. His grief gave way to intense rage and he began to tune, focusing an avalanche of furious anger onto the artifact. Nothing happened. He tuned harder. The album didn't seem to notice. Martel's energy drained and he stopped, breathing hard. A sharp pain raked his hand and he dropped the album on the floor.

There, the space around the charred black object began to blur. It vibrated, red veins of energy rippling through its surface. The album glowed hot and sunk into the floor, melting through it. In its place, a membrane had formed; growing and expanding like a cancer. The membrane prolapsed open and a series of slimy flesh-like roots pierced through, spreading out along the floor and walls like mold, wriggling and grabbing at whatever they could. Drawn to the commotion, one of Martel's mechas wandered into the path of the vines and they snaked their way inside the mecha's inner workings, destroying them from the inside out.

Martel sensed a presence from the membrane, and it sensed him in return.

He had seconds. Martel dashed for Olen's body as the vines multiplied and expanded outward, consuming the room. A pair of gray-red tentacles swung and stabbed at him. They were thick as an anaconda with barbed nubs along their length. Martel drew his crossglaive, slashing at the wiggling squid-like arms; they bulged and flexed like sentient muscles. His weapon wounded the creatures, burning their skin, but didn't slice through the monsters as they should have. They were resistant to energy weapons.

Martel cursed as more vines emerged from the opening in a coordinated attack, battering him and attempting to grab him. His crossglaive and tuning enhanced reflexes could only beat them back for so long.

Two of the tentacles coiled themselves around Olen's body and pulled her away into the membrane. Martel reached out with his tuning and grabbed her, stunting the action. One of the attacking tentacles jabbed his chest with the impact of a battering ram.

He stumbled backward into the wall before the expanding flesh vines could reach him. His hold on Olen was lost. Her corpse disappeared into the opening, the floor collapsing around it. Whatever this thing was, it had dug down through the building's floors, into the lower levels flooded by ocean. A tremor vibrated the entire structure as it began to collapse. The presence he sensed was getting stronger.

Martel ignored the pain rippling through his body and sprinted for the hangar. The tentacles chased him, coating the hallways and ceilings behind him. "Selassie!" he yelled into his handheld. "Prepare for emergency departure as soon as I'm inside!"

He stumbled and dropped the device. The tentacles crushed it. He crashed through a security door and burst into the hangar deck, diving onto the *Jezebel's* lowered boarding ramp. The ramp retracted before the monstrous octopus arms could invade the hangar. The ship's reactor ignited and pushed the *Jezebel* out of the hangar, the resulting exhaust plume obliterating everything behind it.

From a monitor, Martel watched the multiplying alien flesh-vines consume and demolish his base. They writhed beneath the dark waves, growing and expanding deeper into the planet like an infection and turning everything a vibrant shade of red. The violent waters churned and twirled on a massive scale, forming a gigantic whirlpool that could be mistaken for a sea of blood. It could be seen from orbit. Martel fired a pair of nuclear torpedoes into its heart. After the blinding flash and mushroom cloud died down, the eye-like vortex remained. If anything, it fed off the explosion, accelerating its takeover and consumption of the ocean planet.

Martel stared into the maelstrom of growing red vines and swirling tentacles of the blood red sea, and he felt it stare back into him. And it knew that he was afraid.

www.ingramcontent.com/pod-product-compliance
Lightning Source LLC
Chambersburg PA
CBHW011513240626
47154CB00010B/3016